TEDIUM TROOPERS

TEDIUM TROOPERS
PHANTASMAGORIA

Sunny Francis

PARTRIDGE
A Penguin Random House Company

To order additional copies of this book, contact
Partridge India
000 800 10062 62
orders.india@partridgepublishing.com

www.partridgepublishing.com/india

Acknowledgement

My sincere adulations to my God for everything;
my parents, who brought me up to stand up and deliver;
my wife and my daughter for being
my first reader and my critic;
The Acharya of Vidyakula, Mr Sidharthacharya,
IFS (Retd.), who continues to be the fountainhead
of my ever-springing Hippocrene;
my friend, Rohit Nayar for making the alphabets
fall obediently in place when his dexterous fingers
rhythmically danced on the keypad of his laptop,
and his wife Arti for her evening delicacies;
Very Rev. Dr Fr Jose Aikara CM, former
Chairman – ICSE, Delhi – for being with
me caring and motivating like my dad.
Rev. Dr Fr Baiju CM, Principal, De Paul College,
Mysore, for promoting the Author in me.
Mr Ramanamurthy for helping me with the cover pages.
Mr Marco Bale, for earnestly initiating the
fulfillment of my publishing journey;
Partridge Publishing Company;

Udayagiri, the Hill of the Rising Sun;
my fans for helping me to do, foes for forcing me
to undo and friends for fostering me to do;
my students, supporters, stakers and sympathizers;
Madhvi, for singing and sending those beautiful
audio files to enliven my twilight élan
and my readers who would make my literary Odyssey
ring like a wholesome chimer even on hostile terrains.

Dedication

To my teachers who taught me how to think clear and express my thoughts clearer.

ENVOI

My Dear Sunny,

What follows is really no foreword lest I be froward. It is mere something sent of little moment. As we are both aware of each other's captivation by the Bard of Avon he is popping up like Dickens' Charles' Head in Copperfield not only in conversation but in our manuscripts also. While I, naturally, enjoy your firstborn's infant cries I wonder if your love and rhythm means anything to barren readers.

Every Indian should be made aware of Darwin's Debauchery when he dealt with the Indian Puranas.

Also, I feel that the canonization of a world famous heretic, Che Guevara, is something that will live forever in all your readers' minds. Indeed you canonize all your fellow Keralites, like Namboodiripad and his Apostles. In fact you may well, perhaps, resurrect them. Those who do not appreciate Shakespeare may stigmatize your work, and would after a page or two of Che Guevara would find the stigma, holy and worshipful. After all, Bernard Shaw's Joan had anticipated her canonization centuries after she was burnt as a heretic!

I was delighted with the rescue of lovely Julia from death and gallant Rahul from lunacy and for not repeating the Bard's mistake of polishing off Ophelia and Prince Hamlet.

I do hope that your First-born will globally be a great success.

Yours ever,

V Siddharthacharry

1

The Abode!

4.30 am!

Jose Ivans held the Jerusalem Bible in his pious hands and knelt down at the Crucifix for the Angelus!

A habit since his childhood…!

His ancestors used to pray early in the morning. In fact, they said their Angelus punctually before 5 am.

Cecily Ivans, a content homemaker, used to follow her husband, Joseph Ivans, religiously after the Angelus on his routine morning visit to the farmhouse in the middle of a huge mango orchard, one mile away from *The Arcadia* - their ancestral home. Being a retired military Major General, Joseph Ivans was very particular about his daybreak stroll!

ADGP Francis Ivans and Headmistress Liz Ivans brought up their son Jose Ivans to be a well-disciplined young man!

'A disciplined civilian is better than a hundred thousand undisciplined soldiers!' His grandfather Joseph Ivans used to remind Jose Ivans whenever he petted his grandson!

Jose Ivans walked down his memory lane which lay like the winding country road under the pretty *Gulmohar* trees where spring used to prepare to meet summer!

The crimson pavement of the village used to haunt him since childhood, as it did when he became a man. It should always haunt him when he would grow old, "Or let me die! The Child is father of the Man!" His heart cried out as he successfully remembered the most striking line of Wordsworth.

The buzzing of his cell phone forcefully called Jose Ivans back to the present.

Janet Ivans was still sleeping.

'She joins me for prayers every morning at 5.' Ivans thought. 'It's only 4.30! Katherine must have already left for her workouts!'

Ivans called off revisiting his ancestral antiques as he was with the Holy Book in his hands. He opened it, bowing his head!

'1 Corinthians 13 ...!'

The cell phone beside him buzzed again. But Ivans' prided resolve overruled his impulse to read the SMS. He crossed his forehead and started reading from the Book.

The Giant Candle beside the Crucifix let out its steady golden glow as it usually did.

Verses 1-13...

Though I command languages both human and
*   angelic –*
If I speak without love,
I am no more than a gong booming or a cymbal
*   clashing.*
And though I have the power of prophecy,
To penetrate all mysteries and knowledge,
And though I have all the faith necessary to move
*   mountains*
If I am without love, I am nothing.
Though I should give away to the poor all that I possess
And even give up my body to be burnt
If I am without love, it will give me no good whatever.
Love is always patient and kind;
Love is never jealous;
Love is not boastful or conceited;
It is never rude and never seeks its own advantages;
It does not take offence or store up grievances.
Love does not rejoice at wrong doing,
But finds its joy in truth.
It is always ready to make allowances,
To trust, to hurt and to endure whatever comes...
As it is, these remain: faith, hope and love, the three
*   of them;*
And the greatest of them is LOVE.

Jose Ivans kissed the verse. He saw the prayerful candle throwing its light far... 'So shines a good deed in a naughty world', Ivans remembered The Bard of Avon thus musing in The Merchant of Venice.

'Tens of thousands of unfortunate and innocent citizens fall dead in the thoroughfares of militancy, war and terror every day.' Ivans thought.

'Iraq and Syria are torn apart…!

'There is no love anywhere there, anymore!

'They brutally persecute and prosecute the helpless humans aiming at the genocide of a particular religious sect through a modern Holocaust.'

His heart wept for the innocent victims in the Gaza Strip! Soon, his mind flashed back home.

The pictures of the two sisters hanging in Karta in Badau, UP after being molested, reflected on his inward mirror.

Vatican has urged humanity to fight such inhuman deeds through incessant prayers, petitions and penance by the faithful.

'Man has lost his faith', Ivans thought.

The cell phone buzzed again…

'Who might that be? It's not even 5 in the morning!' Ivans said to himself. 'Rose?'

He kept the Bible back to the velveteen shelf and locked it. Taking the handset he pressed the start-up key and touched the icon.

'3 texts: at 4.30, 4.31and 4.55...!'

With a lot of alacrity and anxiety he looked at the tiny screen.

He was right. It was Rose!

'Jo, read 1 Corinthians 13:1-13.'

He could not believe it.

'What's it? Extra Sensory Perception? What is that which connects both of us?

He typed a text back, 'Rose, I was reading the same and going to text to read it. Also, I will watch today's sunset with you on the beach.'

2

Jessica Rose parked her new wine red hatchback on her slot in the massive four wheeler parking yard, on the left of the huge gothic gate of Electronics India Private Limited.

On its right lay the endless stretch of two wheelers.

Swiping the card and going through the bio-metric cordialities, she looked at herself in the huge mirror fixed in front of the security check.

She was stunning!

The lavender saree neatly printed with small jasmine blooms lay pretty on her like a rich creeper on the idol of a Greek beauty neatly sculptured in alabaster. Her thick black hair rolled like a cascade vanishing in mid-air before touching the ground.

She loved herself that day...

Her 5'8", ideally measured, glorious form was the personal pride of Electronics India and the envy of its rivals. Her eyes were two stars; fingers fresh shoots, and feet lotus petals. Clean cut...!

'Great, Rose!' She said to herself. 'No one can ever say that you are the proud mother of a six year old son'.

She liked everything about herself that day, and the soft lavender her deodorant let out perfectly matched her saree!

'Thanks, Prem Khanna', she thought. 'This mirror is the only good thing you have done in this electronics desert'.

In fact, the idea of fixing the huge 20' x 10' wall mirror at the entrance of the security check was an idea of Prem Khanna, the CMD of Electronics India Pvt. Ltd., in order to enable each of the e-Indians see how one looked each day.

'The morning predicts the length of the day, Jo says'. She thought.

Jessica Rose appreciated the CMD's philosophy of self-check, though borrowed from someone, in the mirror by every single soul while standing in front of the huge body scanner at the security.

'Excuse me Madam!'

Jessica Rose felt slightly embarrassed as Krishnan Potti squeaked over her shoulders from behind.

In fact she had taken longer in front of the mirror and was lost in her thoughts.

She turned and smiled at Potti and quickly moved to her chamber.

'Potti is always like a court jester. Everybody likes him for his humour. The four-lane holy ash on his forehead will give everyone a false notion that he is a great devotee of Lord Shiva, the mighty Destroyer of the Holy Trinity of Hinduism', she thought, 'but, Potti behaves like Sir John Falstaff in The Merry Wives of Windsor.'

Jose Ivans and Jessica Rose called him Sir Falstaff jokingly and Potti liked it as he was a great fan of Ivans and Rose.

Rose knew that Ivans was in his chamber as his name board was glowing in the blue back light.

JOSE IVANS, MA, LLB, MBA
Vice President HR

It was a policy of the company that any name board operational will give out its blue back light. It had to be in off mode if the occupant was out or busy otherwise.

'Jo came early as usual', she thought.

Peeping through the split door, Rose officially greeted her boss.

'Good Morning, Sir'.

'Good Morning, Ms Rose'. Ivans greeted her back bringing a noble stroke of professionalism in his manful and dauntless voice!

'Electronics Indians are like that... Highly professional at work place', she mused.

Without exchanging anymore pleasantries, she left for her chamber.

'What happened to Rose?' Ivans thought to himself. 'She vanished so quickly, without thanking!'

He immediately got the answer to his query.

Prem Khanna passed by his door like a road roller.

He was the terror, anguish, fret and the end of many inspiring and aspiring trainees and even senior managers.

'Rose disappeared not without reason'. He smiled to himself. 'She wanted to avoid Mr Khanna!'

His table phone made a peculiar sound calling him back to the present.

He soon identified the voice over the phone.

Shiela Khanna, the Vice Chairperson and Joint MD of Electronics India Pvt. Ltd. and obviously the wife of Prem Khanna.

'Ivans, come to my chamber, soon...!' She urged.

Quickly grabbing the company diary and switchig off the nameboard, Ivans walked out of his room passing the glowing name board,

JESSICA ROSE, MA, MBA
Manager, HR.

3

Jose Ivans waited for the east wing elevator to come down, for a few seconds, enroute to Shiela Khanna's chamber on the 7th floor.

The high speed elevator soon took him to the 7th floor in seven seconds! Watchman Venkat was busy with supervising the routine cleaning of the *lounge*.

The lounge was a visual feast indeed!

Ivans liked all the motivational quotes displayed in the lounge. His Template Team had taken care of their display throughout the factory which sprawled over an area of one million square feet.

Jose Ivans and Jessica Rose, being personnel managers took a special care in enhancing the aesthetic and intellectual beauty of Electronics India Pvt. Ltd. Every e-Indian in the company bore a great regard for them for doing that.

Venkat with great respect wished Ivans, 'Good Morning, Sir!'

'Good Morning, Venkat!', Ivans greeted him back. 'How are you?'

'Fine Sir! But very sad to know that a seventeen year old was crucified in Syria by the terrorists. He was accused of taking pictures of those terrorists. It seems that they were upset with him. But I am upset with them, Sir.' Venkat expressed his displeasure.

'Not only you... the entire world is!' Ivans added.

'I wished I could...'

Before Ivans could finish, the sensor door parted.

'Every bit of this factory is on her finger tip!' Ivans thought. 'Probably, she might have been watching me on CCTV.'

'May I come in Ma'am.' He asked with all warmth and respect.

'Yes Ivans.' The reply was very cordial as usual.

He stepped in and the door closed behind.

Ivans felt that, he was transported to the palace of the queen of the Kingdom of Sheba. Of course, without a hairy hoof.

There was a buzz on his cell phone and simultaneously Shiela Khanna's phone also rang.

'Excuse me, Ivans. It's from Prem. Please be seated!'

She smiled through her eyes and picked the cell.

'OK Ma'am!' Sinking into the kingdom of softness of the sofa, Jose Ivans glanced at the SMS...

"Jo, don't commit anything for the evening to her. Finish all the reviews and meetings before 5 pm... Today's sunset is ours. It's beauty lies in the inward eye of the beholder! It doesn't turn crimson Ivans, it's our eyes. It turns red there, our sight is getting deceived. 'There is no art to know the mind's construnction in the face!' Then think about the universal mysteries."

Ivans' face bloomed lake a rose. Rose made him happy.

'Her texts are always laden with Shakespeare.' He thought.

His fingers flipped on the keyboard and there went an SMS at a pace of the lightning.

'Galatian 5:18'

> *...But if you are led by the Spirit, you are not under the Law!*

Ivans stared at Madam Shiela who was screaming at the CMD over the phone.

'Who told you to do that? That too in the evening?'

'It is the customary greeting between them.' Ivans thought. 'This is only the beginning. The pyrotechniques will slowly gain its altitude and by the evening, it will be brighter and sky high.'

This divine corporate mystery was only known to Jose Ivans and Jessica Rose.

Ivans looked at the statue of Neptune, taming a sea-horse, cast in bronze.

"The same statue I have come across in *My Last Duchess*." Ivans thought.

Madam Shiela's chamber was a unique blend of Greeko-Roman scuplture and Arabian upholstry. The small little niches on the tall and mighty walls were fretted with amazing and lively statuettes: Hercules with his shouldered club coming from his errand with the golden apples, Atlas with the sky on his mighty sinews, the little Cupid with his naughty arrows, Zeus on mount Olympus watching Olympics, Apollo with his lute, Venus' peacemaking with Juno and so on...

The wall painting had the richness of the Medieval and Modern masters like Angelo, Da Vinci, Van Gogh, Picasso, Braque, Le Fauconnier and Daly... 'The Gernica' and 'The Young Ladies of Avignon' were a visual surprise for Ivans as he was a great fan of Picasso and his cubism.

The Italian frescos on the ceiling was the perfect match of the already enriched Arabian rugs on the floor. One could hardly call it a an office room. Ivans always felt that he was in a museum or art gallery. The music played was soothing and the air was rife with a soft and inviting freshener. Ivans always loved the richness of Madam Shiela's chamber for its sensuous delight, if not for anything else.

Shiela Khanna enjoyed the role of the curator of the museum.

She was 51, but looked as if she were in her late thirties. She had no worries except for her beloved son and the bragging husband. Her only son, Rahul Khanna, had to be forcefully sent to rehabs six months a year: her eternal sorrow.

Ivans lost the count of the number of occasions when she wept before him for her son.

Prem Khanna took resort to alcohol and bragged eternally at home and office, thus forgot his child-sorrows if he had any!

Mr Khanna's only worry now was the company turnover. He never compromised on targets. One's annual target had been scooped up into half-yearly, quarterly and monthly. Firing employees was his hobby! Cruel man! He did not even have an idea of the painful affair of the company's personnel management. How the company reached its envious financial hieght. It was currently an 80,000 crore MNC. How many people's sweat and tears must have been used to fix each brick of that twenty storeyed buidling! Like the Great Wall of China, its bricks were placed on a paste of the blood of the workers!

Ivans was pulled out of his reflective world by Shiela Khanna's unusually high pitched screaming over the phone!

'You are a nasty old fool! How can you commit it in the evening? Didn't you know that I have to go for the show at the Metropolitan in the evening…? Christabel Marant is coming today. I'm the Chief Guest!' Madam Shiela boomed over the phone and snapped it.

Ivans knew Ms Marant...the funky French fashion designer.

'I am so sorry, Ivans… Prem is really silly at times.' She said.

'Always' Ivans thought. 'When is he not?'

'Ivans, anything to drink?'

'No Ma'am, it's okay.'

'Come on, feel free.'

Shiela Khanna pressed a button. Venkat showed up himself piously and respectfully.

'Two cups of tea… flavour…lemongrass.'

'Yes Ma'am.' Venkat disappeared.

'Ivans….!' Shiela Khanna resumed after reclining on her high-back Wilkhahn German Chair. She looked beautiful, aristocratic and delighted.

'Yes, Ma'am.' Replied Ivans.

'You have to be ready with all the files and be in the new conference hall by 9.55 am for the review. We will start it at 10.'

'Which are the main files, Ma'am? Attrition is very high! It's 44%.' Ivans was embarassed. 'Nowadays firing is more than hiring, Ma'am.'

'What was the department goal?' She asked with a smile.

'14%.' He answered.

'Okay! You be ready with the other files.' Shiela Khanna smiled again.

Ivans knew that she would defend him at the review as she was his Director.

'May I come in Ma'am?' Squeaked Venkat.

'Yes.' Her face became serious.

Venkat came in through the sensor door with the tea girl. She kept the Shangai tea kettle, with the impression of a red dragon on its stomach and the Italian porcelian cups on the side table and retired.

Venkat poured the hot tea into the cups. The aroma of the lemongrass filled in the room. Ivans knew that Shiela Khanna's eyes were on his face. He looked at her. Her eyes were wet.

When Venkat stepped out, Shiela Khanna spoke.

'Rahul went berserk last night. So violent that he broke his forehead with Prem's golf club. We got scared and at the end we had to……,' she sobbed, 'we had to….. fire the tranquilizer three times….and then….. then, he fell.'

Crystal drops rolled down her rosy cheeks and her motherly bosom heaved as if it would break.

'Ivans…. I…. am the most unfortunate mother and wife in the world…!' She could not hold back her sorrows.

'Excuse me Ivans, we will meet at 9.55.'

She got up and pushed the door of the anti-chamber. When the door closed, Ivans woke up from his trance and walked out. He heard the sensor door close behind him.

'Celebrities chase disasters though life gives them every reason to celebrate it.' Ivans thought. 'It is because they are chased by a sense of emptiness with its vice-like grip in their heavy abundance!Painful alloofness, amidst multitudinal fan following or unchartered listlessness when adorned in the glitz and glamour of worldliness, is their ardent companion.'

He remembered reading something similar to it somewhere, while the elevator was dropping its height faster and faster.

4

'The beauty of sunset is in the mind of the beholder, Rose!'

Ivans whispered over her shoulders, holding the entire mystery of the evening phenomenon in his eyes.

The beach was slowly getting evacuated.

'The sun never sets, Jo; he never rests nor reddens, nor does he dim out! It's our sight that does it all! He ever burns...only burns. He doesn't know anything else...shouldn't know! Our mind is wrapped up in mystery...mystery everywhere and in everything.' Rose said as she could read his mind.

There was a sea-change in the sea. The mother of the fisher-folk: she now laughed as she caressed the shingles with her soft hands. All were hurrying and scurrying homeward.

Rose and Ivans sat at the foot of the statue of Mary the Immaculate.

'Jo.'

'Yes Rose?'

'Tell me the legend of the Church on the Hilltop. You had once promised it.'

'There is a great mystery in the Idol.' Ivans said. 'When the Portuguese settlers in the 18th century reached 5 nautical miles away from this seascape, they were caught in a storm and about to be drowned. They prayed for their life to the Mother. Presently, there was an Oracle heard from the depth of the sky that they should sail shoreward. As they were sailing, the demoniac storm metamorphosed to a divine spirit which safely took them to the shore. On reaching the shore they saw a silver casket lying there, and opening it Padre Florencio saw Mary the Immaculate resting in it: so beautiful and almost breathing life. He took the idol of the Mother in his hands and carried her to the hilltop and sheltered her in a cavern on the cliff. The entire crew decided to settle here itself. Padre Florencio initiated the construction of a small Church on the hilltop and the idol was venerated and erected in the Church. Ever since, Mary the Immaculate has become the guardian of all the sailors who passed by this landscape. The huge guardian statue of Mary the Immaculate was erected on the shore where the casket was found, during the post independent era and special rituals and prayers have been held on the shore on the first Friday of every month.'

'Rose...!' Ivans called her, coming back to the shore from the world of legends and gods.

'Yes my Jo.' Her heart heaved.

Ivans knew that words were getting choked in her throat. She was trying to tell him something very grave.

The tides were getting stronger and the dusk slowly receiving the night.

'Now...it will be the reign of the dark for some time and then the day will break. Light will prevail; it will rule the world for a few hours and then the night will settle once again! Just like the game being played between life and death!' Ivans said to her like a good teacher.

'But, some domains of the world where certain people live will always be wrapped up in the dark.' She said swaddling herself in her saree like a nun.

Her voice resonated a deeper note of philosophy.

'Rose... are you not scared?'

'Of what Jo, whom?'

'Of the dark, the sea, the tides, the winds, your haunting memories, yourself and me?' Ivans said.

'No, never...!'

'Why?'

'I am with my Guardian Angel. His name is Jose Ivans! He will protect me from all the evil. My *91:11*!'

Ivans looked into her eyes as if in a dream and saw another sea rumbling in the depth. He watched the crimson disc going down into the abysmal depth of her eyes...there...he saw himself, Janet, Juan and Rose Ivans playing on a moon-blanched shore.

'Jo, why didn't you take me into your life? Do you know how much I longed for that? Even now, my heart bleeds when I recall how I stood with the wedding card neatly printed, tucked in my arms:

Jose Ivans
Weds
Katherine Samuels!

'Why did you do that, Ivans...why?'

The sea in her eyes was now roaring with a flood.

'I...didn't know that you...!' Ivans could not complete.

He knew that her sobs were corresponding with the pulsation of his heart...and empathy was the vital unifying force of their inner selves.

Silence was no more biting them with its razor sharp teeth. It rather pushed them gently into the sunless bottom of their past.

On returning from an incredible voyage through their past, Ivans called her. 'Rose...!'

'Tell me Jo.'

'Silence can effortlessly sail across the ocean of love and cast two hearts on its two opposite shores... and it can once again bring both on the same shore to throw them again to different unknown territories if they are not still eloquent...!' Ivans said.

She knew exactly what he was speaking.

A Venetian Gondola was gliding back from the direction of the offshore oilrig, to the quay with its last solitary passenger. The undulating tides tossed it into the sky and from the shore the vessel looked as if it were hanging in the mid-air against the purple evening canvass!

'Pathetic fallacy!' Rose sighed. 'Embarrassment... everywhere...embarrassment! It is getting solidified..! Grief is plenty... Glee is sparse!'

'Yes Rose, you are right.' Ivans agreed. 'God has never measured virtues in barrels...but in coffee spoons...that's why vices walk the ramp everywhere...they are always in the majority ruling the poor virtues who in minority are destined to wait for His Second Coming for salvation!'

'No Jo...! No...! There is no question of the Christ coming again, instead, He will reincarnate like Jose Ivans.'

'Come on Rose, the Immaculate will be embarrassed at our ranting.'

They got up and shifted their seats to a higher dune nearby.

The evening breeze shook the lush black tresses of Rose which brushed his face leaving the shampooed fragrance in his nostrils. He got enticed and burnt for at least a touch... but he would not...!

'I am Jose Ivans. The erstwhile hero of thousands of youngsters at the college. The most adorable daddy of Janet and the role model of Juan. I should not bring shame to their brows...though Rose might be vulnerable at this moment; she is legally and ritualistically still the wife of Martin, that devil.'

Ivans blew the perfumed desire out of his nostrils very hard and drew a lungful of nauseating sea scent to douse the fire burning within.

When it was brought under control, he resumed normally.

'Rose, why did you say that the Christ...?'

'Jo, I know what you felt... I also felt the warmth!'

'By the way, why are you doubtful about His Second Coming?' Ivans switched the focus.

Rose accepted his mind changing game gracefully.

'My dear Jose Ivans, two thousand years ago, we clinically gave him a cross. The cruellest act! Worse than a gibbet to finish him off like a criminal. If He comes again, He knows that we are waiting for him with deadlier missiles, chemical and biological weapons. The Father in Heaven will never send His Son again to us. He knows His folly should never be repeated. He may send the Holy Ghost, instead, to swoop down and annihilate the man gods and devils to save his own people.'

'Ha, ha, ha!' Ivans laughed just to agree to what she said.

'A very intelligent and reflective brain indeed.' Ivans proudly thought.

The passing beams of the twilight after sunset is like the distant memories flashing on the reflector of one's hapless mind; they leave the indifference of a soulless detachment in the mundane hearts of the viewers. They make one think about the void that precipitates in the house of a dead when the last visitor also bids his adieu to the dispossessed.

'Jo...' Rose called him unusually with a haunting pull and intimacy in her voice.

'Yes my Rose.' He answered looking at a solitary star blinking for nobody.

'Will you marry me?'

Ivans jerked up as if caught in a storm.

'W…h…a...t!' Ivans gasped.

'I asked you, will you marry me?' Her voice was clearer and stronger this time.

'But... Martin?' He mumbled.

'Jo, I am ready to snap this knot, if you are ready. He is a devil and sex maniac. He needs only my body. His pastime is only that. I am tired of my life, Jo... I am tired...your Rose is tired... Jo... I would have killed myself yesterday but for Juan and you...!'

She wept hiding her face in her palm. Ivans held her hands lest she should fall. He drew her tearful cheeks towards his and wiped her tears.

Just then the Church bell chimed on the hilltop for Vespers. They looked at the little Church on the top. The evening flames from the poor fishers' huts had already started burning. Those yellow tongues adorned the hillside with the golden spots of real life.

'Their existence is a potent reminder of the existence of the Creator.' Ivans mused. 'Their faith is unshakable.'

Ivans and Rose rose to join old Joppe in prayers as he struck a match stick and burnt the giant candle before the statue of Mary the Immaculate of the shore.

They prayed earnestly for the first time for their union.

A few strangers also joined them soon for the Vespers. All strangers! But, they were united by one God; one faith.

'What might be the faith of each one of them...?' Ivans thought to himself.

All of them faithfully stood there; folding their hands, closing their eyes and bowing their head.

'The faith of the devotees is the faith of the God; their colour is His colour; their power is His power...! All faiths are one...! All Gods are faithful...! But..., not all men!' Ivans thought looking at the air of piety that held its mighty sway over those devotees. 'Faith brings strangers together... The same faith rips their hearts... And keeps them perpetually divided and isolated... It leads them shelterless and miserable and make them go in search of new gods as the Bard of Avon rightly mused,

...misery acquaints a man with strange bedfellows!'

Ivans' cell phone shivered in his pocket. He pulled it out and decoded the screen.

Katherine's text...!

'Are you still in office or with that slut? Going for the show... Jan is with Clara... She was crying... I slapped her quiet.'

Ivans hurriedly flipped the phone back to home screen and hid it from Rose.

'Did she see the text?' he felt ashamed of himself as his eyes accidently fell on Katherine's name on his wedding ring which always made his finger pain and itch.

He grew more miserable.

'Katherine and Clara are the two sides of the same coin. Both are unrelenting and ruthless. One is the mistress, the other is the maid. Katherine's selfishness will match up with that of Clara's devilishness.' Ivans thought to himself.

His heart wept for Janet...!

He had to go...

Rose, reading a feel of urgency in his face, said, 'Jo, I know you have to reach home soon. Let's call it a day. See you tomorrow. Katherine is going to the Metropolitan, isn't she? The Marant show is on... I saw a flash on the TV. Is Janet with Clara? Hurry up or else she will hurt the child.'

Ivans was thoroughly relieved... It seemed that she didn't see the text.

His own self bowed before Rose.

'What an intelligent and noble lady she is.' He thought.

His heart thirsted to declare...

'Rose... I am ready... Snap the knot and come into my embrace...!'

He stretched out his arms and stood there in the dusk before her for a moment.

'What is this Jo? Come, let's go. Janet is alone.'

Struggling to hide his embarrassment in the evening gloom, Ivans grinned at her.

Boarding his Havana, they heard the Church bell chime once again at the end of the Vespers. The singing of the choir overflowed across *Fisher's Valley* which was instantly joined by the fisher folk from their huts: an age-old practice!

The recessional hymn would be sung by all the natives of the valley together with bowed heads, closed eyes and folded hands wherever they were. At one point of the singing, thousands of tongues and hearts will be one in unison...!

Ivans and Rose joined the chorus with old Joppe singing:

Nearer my God to Thee... Nearer to Thee...!

5

'Therefore, life is a feast..., celebrate it!' shouted Prem Khanna.

Prem Khanna - the terror, anguish, fret and the end of many aspiring scientists and engineers of Electronics India – was at the podium of The Patriarch, the only seven star hotel of the City. The quarterly review had made him over-excited. It showed a growth of 30% in the turnover. All the departments were firing through all the cylinders as per the annual plan.

'Win..., go on winning...that's the aim...that should be the aim...that was the aim! Therefore, celebrate it...!'

'Bulls make him laugh and bears make him scream!' Ivans thought.

Prem Khanna's de-motivational talk was highly egoistic and boastful. It went on as if it would not end. The Executive Dinner was the centre of attraction of everyone.

It was 8.55 pm. The buffet was ready in the dining hall. The cocktail aroma of multi-cuisine delicacies started to slowly drift out of the exquisitely lighted dining hall to the tension-packed conference hall.

It was irresistible.

Prem Khanna was not in a hurry to conclude. It seemed that his nose got stuffed as he exhibited his strong immunity to the aroma. More than 90% of the two thousand executives must have heard the same old story of his own struggle to overcome all the teething problems of the company when he started it 28 years ago. He had a very small capital of Rs.10,000/- on hand and that was his paternal share...

Prem Khanna looked at the audience over the tortoise frame of his pair of spectacles which was slipping down to the tip of his parrot nose. Almost four thousand eyes were staring at him listening to his bravados on the stage, but two were kept closed. They were that of Shiela Khanna.

'His bragging knows no bounds.' Shiela Khanna thought.

It was her dowry and jewellery together that fetched him Rs.5,00,000/- to begin the company 28 years ago.

'The beggar had not even one rupee on him to begin the business and now the liar boasting of his paternal 10,000.' She thought.

Therefore, she kept her eyes closed and wished her ears also were shut. She did not want to hear the shameless scandal again from the *upstart crow beautified with her own feathers.*

On the other hand, Prem Khanna wished her eyes were closed forever, for she was the only one who knew that he was a terrible liar.

Thus, Madam Shiela took a firm decision to keep her eyes and ears shut whenever Prem Khanna stood before a mike.

Looking at the threatening and frightening spectacles before him, through his pair of spectacles, the CMD pushed his glasses up with his diamond ringed right index.

He continued like a modern Hitler.

'Today, *my* company is like a slow moving passenger flight in a very clear sky. That is not healthy. Electronics India Pvt. Ltd. should be like a fighter bomber...with a greater precision and speed! *My* aim for the next five years is and should be the only motivating factor in *your* life.

'From 80,000 crore, the turnover in the next five financial years should be one million crore.'

Four thousand eyes closed in fear and shock and two eyes opened to look at the joker.

Only Shiela Khanna knew how she struggled to keep the company alive, growing and steady.

'The fool knows only to sit in his office and swagger! He doesn't even consult with anyone before making such a public announcement! Idiot! The COO, the bugger, has manipulated the entire speech to win his heart.' Madam Shiela gnashed her teeth.

Prem Khanna was known for making such shocking and unrealistic statements. He resumed like a winner after winning a Grand Slam Championship.

'One million crore will also be a small amount then. *I* will be spending 50% of our profit on CSR instead of 20%. *My* company's Corporate Social Responsibilities are received by the poor wholeheartedly. The poor and the needy should be held close to *my* company. *You* must all learn how to serve those people and wipe their tears.'

'Rose, aren't you aware of Stella's termination?' Ivans looked at Rose and asked her softly. 'She was fired yesterday. The COO, Mr Jayaprakash Sawant, had a crush on her and she never yielded. She was reported falling short of the unrealistic targets set by Mr Sawant. Prem Khanna asked her to quit her job immediately. It was 8.30 pm yesterday. Her company car was confiscated and I was asked to complete all the formalities before 9 pm. She pleaded for mercy. She is a widow with two small daughters...and now Prem Khanna's heart throbs for the poor and the needy. Great Corporate Social Responsibilities...!'

Rose looked into Ivans eyes. Their eyes were red in the chandelier glow as they were angry and upset.

"Mark you this, Ivans!

> *The devil can cite Scripture for his purpose.*
> *An evil soul producing holy witness is like a villain*
>   *with a smiling cheek,*
> *A goodly apple rotten at the heart...*
> *Oh, what a goodly outside falsehood hath!"*

Jessica Rose stopped woefully!

The Merchant of Venice! Jose Ivans looked at her proudly. She used to timely and profusely quote either from the Bible or from Shakespeare, which both of them mastered at their Masters. That was one similitude of many between them.

Ivans' cell phone quivered in his pocket. Tilting his body to the other side, he pulled out his phone from the inner pocket of his blazer and unlocked the screen.

'Going to sleep...! Hope you will come before midnight.'

Ivans sighed as if he had just rope-traversed the Niagara Falls.

'One night, without fight!' Ivans thought.

'Katherine?' Rose asked.

'Yes.' Ivans sighed again.

'Angry?'

'Always.'

Rose stopped her queries as she knew that she would hurt him further.

Ivans kept his phone back and looked at the audience.

'Therefore, life is a feast...celebrate it...'

Prem Khanna was in a mood to damage his vocal chords. He started screaming at the top of his voice.

No one moved from their seats. All were quite. The repercussion of the announcement of the one million crore hung like the Sword of Damocles over all their heads. They knew it very well. The top management would start persecuting and pressurising their subordinates to hit their target. Thus, the poor operators would not go home even at night. How could they go without meeting their daily targets?

The young engineers were bubbling with enthusiasm when Ivans and Rose recruited them to the company. All their zeal died out even before their induction. The trainer devils would literally kill the youngsters by torturing them day in and day out. Everything would be in the name of training.

Two days ago, Ms Dhriti, a young brave heart slapped Col. Somshekhar, Senior Vice President, BD and broke her service bond throwing Rs3,00,000, for the training session being so torturous.

'Attrition being 44% and with inventory worth 6000 crore, how will you reach your target in five years, dear Prem Khanna?' Ivans asked a little louder.

Potti and Rose looked at Ivans wondering what happened to him.

Jose Ivans continued, 'Silence is the loyalty of a revolutionary! It is like a time bomb! It will blast when time is ripe! People in the hall will prefer dying of cardiac arrest as they are forced to hold even the heartbeats because they are afraid that the watchdogs of aristocracy will misinterpret even those beats as louder and therefore anti-Khanna.'

Potti looked at the stage with the meekness of an innocent lamb as if he was not involved in any of Ivans' deliberations.

'There are a few in India who can afford to have even a football ground inside their houses, and there are millions who don't have even a house. This is India! *Saare Jahaan Se Achcha Hindustan Hamara.*' Prem Khanna's speaking got transformed to preaching.

'Therefore, life is a feast….celebrate it….' Potti said before Prem Khanna could say it.

'Rose, can you hire a gun from someone? If I don't kill this Potti, the CMD will kill all of us.' Ivans whispered.

'When will he stop his ranting, Ivans?' Rose could not hold back her impatience.

'In half an hour', Ivans replied.

'No….he will stop in another 5 minutes.' Potti said in a calculative tone.

'How do you know?' Ivans asked.

'He started braying at 8.15 pm and now it is 9.45 pm! Generally, a diabetic patient cannot hold the down-rush in his bladder on the pelvic floor this long. He will stop just now. Look at the grin on his face!'

Rose smiled at both of them as all the three looked at the stage.

"Till now, you all slept more than 5 hours and wasted your precious time. From today onwards *your* slogan is…. *Work is Worship*. If Work is worshiped, you will never feel sleepy. Don't ever forget your TARGET. Therefore, life is a feast…. celebrate it…Here I stop! Good Night!" the CMD croaked.

'I am sure it has started leaking.' Potti said victoriously.

Prem Khanna, pressing and holding his front box with both his hands, rolled out of the stage hurriedly and disappeared into urinal.

'Potti the prophet! He can even predict when one can get the nature calls.' Ivans said.

'For 15 minutes, no menace from Mr Khanna!' Potti declared!

Ivans laughed and Rose joined him with her beautiful smile.

All of them got up and moved quickly to the dining hall of The Patriarch.

Their sigh of relief pushed open the door of the conference hall….!!!

6

The cell phone trembled in Ivans' pocket. He pulled it out and pressed the receiving key.

'Where are you, Jo?' Rose inquired.

'Near the second food booth! Where are you?'

'Near the wall aquarium! Don't waste time. I've already picked your food and am at the table. Come soon'.

In fact, Ivans was with Shiela Khanna as she was giving him a few instructions. Jessica Rose went alone to the booth and collected food for both of them.

Ivans moved quickly through the lines and reached where Rose was.

The Australian Golden Pearl Arowana was sailing like a submarine in the giant aquarium. It was a visual feast. A few executives were standing close by and admiring its sail.

All of them wished Ivans as he passed by…!

Ivans spotted Rose waiting for him. In the violet light, she looked like Hera, the most beautiful Greek goddess – perhaps more beautiful than Aphrodite!

His eyes bloomed with joy and pride.

They knew they were more than colleagues or friends….!

'Welcome, Prince Ivans!' she whispered and waited for him to sit.

While sitting, at a glance, Ivans watched the silent e-Indians drinking and dining like living shadows! The dominant feel in them was fear. The crisscross of the multi coloured beams of the electric bulbs drew unfamiliar and queer designs on the executives.

The fearless spoons, forks and goblets were making a commotion everywhere, but not the e-Indians. The cutlery knew how to be brave, though controlled by the fearful hands.

The deadly tedium was suddenly broken when the live band snapped it with the evergreen number of Andy William's 'Where do I begin…?'

At the end of the song, through the reluctant executive applause, they heard a shrill shouting…

'Therefore, life is a feast…, celebrate it…!'

Potti was shouting at the top of his voice, spinning unpredictably as a weathercock did on a cottage roof.

'He really celebrates his life.' Ivans said.

'I feel jealous of him. He can do it even when cumbered with all his work pressure.' Rose replied.

'Some are born to laugh and make others laugh, while others are to weep and make others also weep.' Ivans sighed.

'There are two more kinds Ivans,' Rose resumed. 'People who weep but make others laugh, and who laugh, but make others weep!'

Ivans did not want to carry on the conversation in that mood. He feared it catching a philosophical vein.

'If drinks don't loosen up the pressure chambers of one's tormented brain, then why do they drink? Their fear simply gets multiplied; liquor breeds fear; Mr Khanna breeds fear!' Rose had already started to enjoy the philosophical ride.

'Is this CMD's celebration of life? Is it what he wants?' asked Ivans.

'Yes, this is also a kind of celebration, perhaps the best!'

This time the reply was not from Rose. It was from Potti. He swayed from side to side with a goblet half with his favourite cocktail,

'Liquor is the key that opens the locks of human conscience. But, our locks are so rusted that we cannot open them with plain keys. So, I prefer multiple keys – cocktail.' Krishnan Potti was so emotional that his voice broke when he spoke. 'Each of the e-Indians is a continent – unexplored; unknown to each other...so near...yet so far...! Therefore life is a feast..., celebrate it...!'

The dining shadows turned their heads to look at Potti as he was unusually louder. Potti moved away unsteadily with his empty goblet and waded his way to the bar tender for another large peg.

The fellowship counter was still overcrowded.

The Arowana was still navigating the shady kingdoms of the mini ocean.

Rose looked at Ivans. He was following the route of the Arowana voyage.

'His eyes are big and eloquent!' Rose thought. 'He is the most handsome chap I have ever met.' Rose told herself in a state of stupor.

Ivans was the only one who gave her a sense of security. She forgot all her personal griefs.

'So near...yet so far...!' Rose thought.

The band was going to play another popular tune.

Ivans looked at the violet light which was falling on the white wall like the divine trickle from a half frozen holy fountain. The glance of Jessica Rose was now on the ice cubes in the glass of her cold coffee. She had brought it for both of them. She knew that Ivans liked cold coffee so dearly.

She knew everything about him.

'Jessica Rose', Ivans thought, 'another unknown continent for others, but not for me. Every woman is a dark continent: the more you explore, the less you know!' Ivans looked at her... he saw two big violet drops dripping from her lotus eyes and falling into her cold coffee!

The ice cubes in her glass were now thawing faster than normal, absorbing the heat of the tears.

'You know... Jo! Martin is a very good husband now! He doesn't hit me on my face of late. Instead...' she shook like a wounded lamb caught in the claw of a hungry lion...!

'Instead...?' Ivans asked curiously.

'Instead..., he is so happy and contented in digging his cigar butt into my abs...whenever he makes love...he has nicknamed it *love-tattooing*. I hate him..., Ivans, I hate that devil!'

'The moron is using an oxymoron – *love-tattooing*!' Ivans boiled within with an uncanny rage. 'An act of the cruellest fashion of a heartless passion! *The unkindest cut of all* as Mark Antony wept in Caesar!'

Rose quickly picked up the cold coffee and blew it colder and gulped a mouthful.

'Sheer instance of the Dissociation of Sensibility', Ivans remembered *Hamlet and his problems!*

'Poor Rose...she had even forgotten that the coffee was cold!' Ivans thought.

'Rose, in that case, Katherine and I have not been burdening each other for the past five years. We live the life of two celibates after she had gone to her father's home to deliver my angel Janet...she accused me of being responsible for her fallen breasts due to perfunctory feeding. Janet was quite unnecessary and accidental according to Katherine. No such misadventures she would bear any more. She is the member of more than four health clubs now. Each club is concentrating on shaping every part of her body: one for limbs, one for abs, one for bust, one for face and so on...! She spends minimum Rs.75, 000/- a month on her beautification! How much do you, dear?' Ivans asked.

She gave him a sullen look.

'I breastfed Juan for four years. My child is my delight in my life Jo...other than you,' Rose whispered. 'I'll do anything for both of you, Ivans...even lay down my life! Martin curses me for being a mother... Juan and I are his liabilities! He slapped Juan for insisting on getting a teddy bear on his birthday last time. For him, birthdays are harbingers of death! Thus, one should be mournful on that day!'

'My goodness!' Ivans exclaimed. 'Janet has already asked me to buy a gift for Juan's next birthday. Last time what you gave her was also a teddy bear which she still hugs and sleeps.'

'You know Ivans, Juan and I have already planned something very special on both of your birthdays this year.'

Ivans looked at his wrist watch which Rose had gifted to him on his 34th birthday last year. It was Swiss-made and very pretty for his handsome wrist...so snug and shy!

His eyes fell on her pretty hand adorned by a diamond watch that he gifted on her birthday.

'How closely we are knit!' Ivans pondered. 'In the preamble of our relationship love, self-denial, compassion, empathy and adulation are the guiding principles!'

Ivans lifted Rose from the cistern of tears where she had already started gauging its unfathomable depth.

'Rose...!' he called her tenderly.

'Sorry Jo!' she sobbed, 'I don't believe anyone else.'

'I know Rose... I do understand...! You used never to shed more than one drop from your eyes...but today!'

She tried to reply something but words got stuck in her throat. She struggled to breathe normally.

Rose toiled to steady herself and once again tried to speak.

'Look at me Rose.' Ivans interrupted her effort and said. 'Look into my eyes! They are two mirrors held for you to look in and cry, as you told me the other day when I was sharing my smouldering distress with you.'

She buried her face in her palms and wept bitterly.

Ivans did not know how to comfort her. The hitherto loud band dropped the height of its pitch and it would stop soon.

'What would you do to help Rose, Ivans?' Ivans helplessly asked himself.

The band again softened down its pitch.

'Jo, do you know?' Rose said. 'He, Martin is a cheat. He cheated my papa and took me away into a world of perennial sorrows.'

'Really?' Ivans asked and looked at her curiously.

'Yes, Jo! Papa had suffered heavily from the global meltdown and the market value of his stocks had massively crashed. Unfortunately for us, my marriage was fixed at that time with Dr Terrence Thomas, a renowned cardiologist at St Lucia.'

'Then?'

'Then... Papa borrowed Rs 15 lakh from one Mr Louise for the marriage and the entire money was spent on my jewellery, costumes and the party. That fatal night of our marriage... Terrence and I went to the third floor of his new house, for our bedroom was on that floor. He was speaking to me in the balcony leaning on the railing. Soon...!'

Rose struggled to breathe.

'Soon...! The railing collapsed and the entire frame went down with Terrence. He fell to the ground with a sharp iron rod piercing through his heart. He died before we could do anything... On the way to the hospital he left me for his eternal abode.' Rose wept bitterly.

Ivans wished he could hold her hand and tell her... 'Rose... my dear I'm there for you...!'

The band was about to cease!

A few more warm drops fell into the goblet and some of them shattered on the table for nobody.

'The next day, Papa took me home after the funeral: never to go back. After a few weeks Mr Louise came and demanded his money back. Papa wept before him and begged for... more time, but he would not go away. I took off all my jewellery worth Rs.10 lakhs and gave it to Papa. But, Rs.5 lakhs had still to be raised. Papa folded his hands before Louise and pleaded for relaxation. Louise had to recover the money at the earliest as he had borrowed the money from another one.

'Two days later, Louise came back home with a man. He had an occult exterior and hungry look. Louise introduced him to Papa as the person who lent Rs15 lakhs to him. He fixed my price as Rs15 lakhs and took me away from my Papa. I came to know that my Papa collapsed that evening and left the world for Mummy. The man who bought me is Martin, Juan's father.'

Rose emptied the glass and looked at the chandelier hanging over the heads of the musicians. The band was embarking on a new number.

'Therefore, life is a feast...celebrate it...!'

The loud hollering of Potti went off like a gunshot just behind Ivans!

Jessica Rose and Jose Ivans were jerked back to the dining hall. Ivans sighed...the biggest sigh ever.

The band started another number:

In the arms of the Angel fly away from here...

'Come on Mr Jose Ivans and Mrs Rose Ivans...!' Potti brought them out of the deadlock.

Both of them got the shock of their life. Though Potti got kicked and slipped his tongue, both of them sort of enjoyed the way he saluted Rose.

'Look at this, you wowsers...what is this?' Potti asked them pointing at the goblet in his hand. 'This is alcoholic *Aqua Regia*...not a mix of the real H_2SO_4 and HNO_3, but, the *Sexy Alligator*, my best cocktail friend.

"Harry Croswell has vulgarly defined cocktail as '*bittered sling*'" Potti continued. 'It renders the heart stout and bold and fuddles the head! It makes one democratic and secular. Having swallowed a glass of it one is ready to swallow anything else! Ha... Ha... Ha, ha...! Therefore, life is a feast...celebrate it...! You young abstainers...just begin with *Korobela*... Okay...! Now, I am going to have *Sex on the Beach*...!'

Potti shocked everyone with his last four words. Only the bartender and a few sponges understood that it was a strong cocktail.

'Therefore, life is a feast...celebrate it...!'

Potti's distant voice was softer.

The nasal drone of the COO, Mr Jayaprakash Sawant was heard, being amplified, in the hall...! He was speaking from the personal suite of the CMD.

'Thank you ladies and gentlemen.'

The drunken faces of the Board Directors and their cronies flashed on the big screen in the dining hall.

'From tomorrow onwards, ours will be a new generation company. Work... work... work... and make money and profit, and live a happy life at the end.' The COO paused.

'Who wants to celebrate at the end of one's life man?' Potti shouted. 'I am with our CMD. Therefore, life is a feast..., celebrate it...!'

'Thank you, Potti...you are showing that you know how to celebrate it. All the best!' The COO retorted and vanished from the screen to escape Potti's further outrageous vocabulary.

'Ladies and gentlemen, the last number of the day!' The MC announced, not in a hurry...but the executives slowly started moving out of the hall.

The band played the nostalgic Elvis Presley number:

Are you lonesome tonight...?

Jose Ivans and Jessica Rose listened to the number and watched the lonesome Arowana sailing aimlessly. They took the last sip of their cold coffee and silently walked to the car park.

'Sorry Jo... I spoiled your evening...! Sorry..., I shouldn't have wept...!'

Ivans kept his fingers on her lips and said in muted tones, 'Good night Rose Ivans...see you tomorrow. Sweet dreams...! Therefore, life is a feast...celebrate it...!'

Though tongue-tied, Jessica Rose spoke through her eloquent eyes... 'Thank you my Jo...my everything...!'

She sat on the car like a fairy and took it out with utmost dexterity...while driving, Rose was so light hearted in the car that she could not help singing John Denver's *Country Roads, take me home*...the car glided along the floodlit highway like a fairy sloop...

Ivans was leaning over and helping Krishnan Potti with the seat belt of his car as he could not locate the socket of the buckle. Ivans' cell phone vibrated in his pocket...

'Good night Sir... Therefore, life is a feast..., celebrate it...!' Potti squeaked indistinctly with all the heaviness of an overdose.

'Good night!' Ivans waved at Potti, praying for his safety.

He took his phone from the blazer pocket and saw the missed call of Rose.

Dialling back, he sat on his BMW 7 series Havana. The wheeled-palace rolled out of the mighty gates of The Patriarch.

'Jo, do you remember the send-off we, the Minors, gave you, the Majors, on the eve of your leaving the college...?' Rose asked passionately. 'We sang together...'*Country Roads, take me home...!*'

'Yes my Rose!' He remembered the evening.

Rose had already started singing the song in her exceptional singing voice.

Jose Ivans joined her on the chorus over the phone...

There was the pleasing pain of a pause... Rose shouted... 'Jo, sing the next stanza please!'

Ivans' mastery and flair in singing was in fact envied by everybody in the college.

He took off...full throated... vocal barriers untrammelled ... heavenly voice flowed out! Years of self-imposed ban on singing had done nothing to his voice...

Both of them wiped a nostalgic drop from their eyes simultaneously and picked up the chorus together...

Ivans resumed knowing that the songs sounded highly autobiographical...

Rose picked up the right vein and sang:

Jose Ivans and Jessica Rose became one soul and one heart in the chorus...

They went back to their beloved Alma Mater along the country roads...! They saw their lonesome classrooms...! Soon, they were full of caring classmates...affectionate and enlightened professors...! Beyond the winding corridors... they felt the enticing cool breeze, seductive evening shades of the tall trees...the irresistible Globe Theatre built for the Bard and the alluring green of the playground...

They forgot their cares at the workplace, the revised targets, the stress and strain of the job...the CMD and the COO, Katherine and Martin...the insult and the assault...the denial and the upheaval...!

At the centre of all this musical fantasy they saw two little cherubs – Janet and Juan lulled by the tender arms of the all-consoling Morpheus...the god of sleep and dreams!

They drove so light hearted and unruffled after a long... long...time. Bound together by the Potti magic...they remembered what he said, 'Rose Ivans'!

7

'On 24th November, 1859, the world heard of the biggest theft! It was bitter in taste, rooted in foundation, stronger in fabric and heretic in religious fraternity, for the name of the thief was allegedly Charles Darwin.'

Ivans and Rose looked at the speaker who stood on the podium of The Orator, the 2000 seater International Convention Centre of The Emperor - the latest born among the star hotels of the City. The Emperor was located in the quiet and tranquil suburb of the City and was a favourite haunt of the western tourists especially for its sylvan ambience and serene environs...the first choice of most of the visiting country heads if they happened to visit that province.

The speaker winked at Ivans and Rose after dropping the bombshell. Krishnan Potti was presenting his paper in the Annual World Conference of *Phantasmagoria* – an International Organization of starry eyed idealists, inventors and innovators.

Phantasmagoria had units all over the world. Its roots were very prominent at National, State, District and Province level of each member country. It also very efficiently coordinated its activities even among schools to promote budding trailblazers at their tender age.

The organization was universally popular and globally known as *Phantasmagoria*. Potti was the Indian delegate selected for the conference in which he had to present a paper which should be so crazy and unique that it should keep the audience spellbound throughout the scheduled twenty minutes.

The moderator would count the *Ayes* and the *Nays* on the monitor, cast by the attendees, and would show the animated signboard *GET LOST* on the big screen, if the number of the *Nays* was more than 50% of the members in attendance at any stage of the presentation.

The theses presented in the conference were selected at country levels. The best three from each country would be evaluated at continent level and finally from each continent the best three papers would be selected to be presented at the Annual International Conference. The best three of those eighteen would be awarded: USD 3 million, 2 million and 1 million for the first three places respectively.

Ivans and Rose could attend the conference only because of the Potti aura as his thesis was the best from India. Being the best Phantasmagorist, Potti could admit two guest nominees to the conference. The second best Phantasmagorist could send one nominee and the third one none.

The tinted compact fluorescent lamps flooded The Orator in multi-hues giving it an enchanted air of *Phantasmagoria*.

The crowd was in full attendance with Phantasmagorists and their nominees from 150 odd countries.

Krishnan Potti looked at the audience as a magician did. There was a paper-drop silence in the hall. They had even failed to breathe for a moment as they had never ever heard such a beginning from any idealists ever before.

'My dear co-Phantasmagorists, it was on 24th November, 1859, *On the Origin of Species by Means of Natural Selection or the Preservation of Favoured Races in the Struggle of Life (The Origin of Species)* was first published by Charles Robert Darwin. It shook the foundations of all the religions, especially Christianity which preaches the wondrous works of God, the Omnipotent Creator! The Origin of Species challenged and mocked at the Book of Genesis, one of the most beautiful pieces of literature which proclaimed the existence of God and the creation of Universe in Christian terms.

'Darwin roared with pride and probity that the Book of Genesis was nothing but a hoax: a humorous and malicious deception. However,150 years have passed and not even a cell has evolved. Now, they say that Neanderthals are not the forefathers of Homo-Sapiens but they were contemporaries.

'Primates diverged from other mammals about 85 million years ago. The family of Hominidae evolved from Hylobatitae (Gibbon) family 20 million years ago, and about 14 million years ago, Orangutans evolved from the Hominidae family. Bipedalism – practice of walking on two legs - started 14 million years ago though some of us, even now, don't know how to.

A guffaw was let loose in the hall.

'The present Homo-Sapiens took almost 200,000 years to evolve and reach the current stature. The Theory of Evolution advocates that life first originated in water. Years later life was transferred to the land through amphibians and then reptiles, quadrupeds, then tripeds and finally bipeds.

'Friends', Potti resumed like a victorious invader. 'Joseph Dalton Hooker, the Botanist-friend of Darwin the Hypocrite, travelled extensively in the Himalayas prior to the publication of The Origin of Species. Edward Blyth, the Zoologist who was in Calcutta for 21 years had already started sending letters to Darwin since 1855 and Horace Hayman Wilson translated Vishnu Purana to English from Sanskrit in 1840. Blyth worked as a curator in the Museum of the Royal Asiatic Society rooted in Calcutta and H H Wilson himself was its Director.

'Now, you might be wondering why I relate these names and stuff to Darwin for proving my point that Darwin is the greatest copycat in the world. Those three names mentioned above and many more have been communicating with Charles Darwin and he happened to hear about the ten incarnations of Lord Vishnu through the four Yugas – the Ages. These ten incarnations are beautifully described in Vishnu Purana as *DASHAVATARS*– the ten incarnations.

'My Humble effort is to save Christianity with the help of Hinduism for all of them preach the same: peace! After all, why do we hate each other? Don't we know that there is Ram in *RAM*zan and Ali in Deew*ALI*?'

Applause was unimaginably loud.

'The first Yuga, Krita or Satya Yuga, witnessed the first four avatars of Lord Vishnu. The second Yuga, Treta Yuga, witnessed the next three avatars of The Lord. The third Yuga, Dwapara Yuga, witnessed the next two avatars and the last Yuga, Kali Yuga, witnessed the last avatar. Its ratio is 4:3:2:1 counting from Krita and 1:2:3:4 counting from Kali. The number of avatars and the number of years of the Yugas are also laid in the same ratio. Krita or Satya spread over 1,728,000 years, Treta 1,296,000 years, Dwapara 864,000 years and Kali spreads over 432,000 years.

'The ten avatars were taken by Lord Vishnu for He is the Preserver of the Holy Trinity – Brahma the Creator, Vishnu the Preserver and Shiva the Destroyer. As Hinduism is the oldest religious faith in the world, *the concept of the Holy Trinity was given to the world by India.'*

Potti looked at the audience. They appeared as if they had taken *Aqua Regia*, the strongest cocktail mix of Potti. Not an eye winked! But, Potti winked at Ivans and Rose and gave the audience a grin and resumed.

'Dear Phantasmagorists, Vishnu Purana explains the Theory of Evolution in better, wiser and clearer terms than the great Charles Robert Darwin. Life evolves through ten stages in Vishnu Purana.'

The number of *Ayes* was steadily increasing and *Nays* decreasing on the screen. It never dropped below 75%.

'Life first appeared in water according to Vishnu Purana. Darwin also agreed with it. Matsya, the fish, was the first avatar. Darwin said life first appeared in water as a unicellular amoeba. The second avatar of Vishnu was Kurma, the turtle. Darwin accepted the concept of amphibian life. The evolution started from water and climbed on to the land. The third avatar of Vishnu was Varaha, the pig, which got rid of its amphibian reptile status to a fully quadruped terrestrial status. The Origin of Species blindly supports the same idea. The fourth avatar of Vishnu was Narasimha, the half man and half lion, showed the evolution of animals to Homo-Sapiens.'

Ivans looked at Rose. They could not believe what they heard. No one had ever heard anything crazier than that. Potti was in a war like mood.

'Doesn't he know that he is going to be the immediate cause of the third world war' Ivans whispered to Rose.

The *Ayes* on the monitor touched 90!

'Man was not fully evolved from animals when Lord Vishnu took his fifth avatar as Vamana, the giant – a crude ogre.' Potti resumed. 'The sixth avatar of Lord Vishnu was that of Parashurama, the cruel axe-man who brutally hacked all the warriors and even his mother. He was not intellectually evolved, though physically a full man. Lord Vishnu came to this world through his seventh avatar, Rama, the complete man and most revered God. He was the finest soul in the world. All the physical, mental, spiritual and emotional properties blended perfectly in him. He was later known as

Shri Rama of Ayodhya. The most interesting factor is the silence of the great Darwin after the evolution of Homo-Sapiens. He was not sure as to what would be the next evolved shape of human beings.'

The *Ayes* were rising!

'Vishnu Purana says that man will intellectually evolve to be a more practical entity like Balram, the plougher – the eighth avatar of Lord Vishnu. He would move further and become the embodiment of purely tactical, strategical and practical mindedness in the ninth avatar of Lord Vishnu in Krishna, the intellectual and practical blend of divinity.'

Rose observed almost all the delegates drying their juice glass in one gulp and even without wiping their lips staring at Krishnan Potti, who apparently failed to evolve from Narasimha at least in his appearance. He neither was tactical nor strategical, but always humorous, though named after Lord Krishna.

'And the last one is Kalki, the deadly trooper of tedium and repetitive cruelty and exploitation of the weak and the poor.' Potti continued. 'Darwin failed to foresee that man will eventually lose is humaneness and embrace animosity, and thus, will start evolving back to animals. The intellectual evolution will lead us to a total apocalyptic catastrophe at the end of the Kali Yuga – the present age – which will last for approximately another 427 thousand years more. It had already started in 3102 BCE.

'Darwin's calculations and discoveries are chiefly based on the information he received from the Vishnu Purana through his trusted English disciples namely, Hooker, Blyth and Wilson. They deftly hijacked the Theory of Incarnation from The Holy Book and regularly supplied stolen stuff to Charles Robert Darwin who presented the same theory in the name of The Theory of Evolution. This was the biggest 'stainless steal' and the most blatant lie in the history of mankind. The lie Darwin told was that his observations and collections on the islands of Galapagos contributed to the inception of his Theory of Evolution by Natural Selection. In fact, he had already formulated The Theory soon after hearing about The Theory of Vishnu-incarnations from his friends in India. Even Wallace was kept in darkness and was made to believe what Darwin told the world! *Alas!*'

The big screen now showed only *Ayes* and no *Nays*: 100% *Ayes!*

Krishnan Potti was simply unstoppable.

'Srimad Bhagavatam describes that evil and decadence will reach their zenith in Kali Yuga. Righteousness, truthfulness, cleanliness, pity, life expectancy, physical and mental efficacy will all diminish day by day. Wealth alone will be considered as a sign of man's good birth, behaviour and acceptance. There will be a big chasm between the rich and the poor. The poor will lead a life more miserable than that of the caged animals. Law and justice will tarry for the beck and call of the rich. Men and women will live together only for pleasure. Love will be stifled to death at every nook and cranny of the world.

'Success in business will depend only on deceit. Manliness and womanliness will be judged according to one's expertise in sex. People will change. All will be forced to change one's own religious faith. The one who cleverly juggles his or her work will be considered as scholars. Dress will make men and women; wealth will fetch virtue; hypocrisy will be accepted as the order, and marriage will be reduced to mere legal contracts. Beauty will be skin-deep; temples will be deserted; audacity will be accepted as truth; charity will be preached only for one's own name and fame: not practiced; youngsters will never respect the elders, and parents will be treated as mere facilitators.

'The earth will be full of gangsters and scamsters; corruption will be let loose everywhere; struck by famine and drought people will eat each other and drink their blood; farmers will kill themselves having been mortgaged their possessions; anxiety and disease will rule over the world and they will be assisted by natural calamities like storms, tremors and floods. Children will disown their parents but not their property. Gender selections and foeticides will be rampant; vulgarity in life and language will be in fashion; family, society and country will be divided within themselves.

'Countries will rise against countries; stronger siblings will sell out the weaker ones; men and women will be engaged in flesh trade and they will drug themselves for momentary joys; ignorance will be bliss and knowledge pain; man gods and woman goddesses will mount on high seats of religions and preach on debauchery and materialism; men, women and animals will be abandoned or killed after being used;

cities will be ruled by thieves and goondas guided by atheists and dirty politicians, and together, they will eat up the simple citizens incapable of understanding this evolution. Humans will be tired of this terrible and *tedious* state of mental, physical spiritual and emotional decay!

'Then, Kalki, the barbaric *Tedium Trooper* will appear on horseback and scatter all the cruel and the unjust wielding his mighty sword by reaping their dirty heads. Thus, Kali Yuga will see the end of injustice in the world and the next Maha Yuga will start with Krita where Dharma, the Bull will rule standing on all the four legs, where Perfection and Truthfulness will prevail; then Treta where the bull will rule on three legs and truthfulness decline from 100% to 75% resulting in the dawning of Dwapara where the bull will be seen on two legs and the measure of goodness will dip further to a 50% low.

'Finally, Kali Yuga will arrive again and the bull will stand on one leg and rule the world in that miserable and wretched posture and truthfulness will fall headlong to 25% and then plunge to 0% where Kali the relentless *Tedium Trooper* will appear again. The ratio of 4:3:2:1 is repeated with utmost precision. This will mark the end of another cycle and next Maha Yuga will start...! This cycle will be repeated for 1000 times to make one Kalpa which is just one day for Brahma, the Creator!

'*Darwin miserably failed to predict this evolution* and the Theory of *Survival of the Fittest* may be applicable in this context. That was another theft.

'Let's all chant the name of the Supreme God to escape all those horrible occurrences predicted in the Vishnu Purana. Read the Indian Puranas and be more educated and enlightened. Proclaim to the world that you have found it in India, the land of Ayur Veda and Yoga.

'India is a land of unsung heroes! The first physician of the world Charaka and first surgeon of the world Sushruta lived in India in 8th century BCE and 6th century BCE respectively. Rishi Kanad proposed the First, Second and Third Laws of Motion in 6th century BCE through his Vaisheshika Sutra. Newton copied it in 1686 AD in The Principia. The Vedas, the Shastras and Sutras had defined the String Theory, the Super String Theory, Quantum Mechanics, Aero Dynamics, Astronomy, Astrology, Mathematics, Medicine and so on in clear terms. Pythagoras and Archimedes were clever enough to lift their theories from the Vedas. Lagadha –13th century BCE, Apurthamba – 6th century BCE, Aryabhata – 5th century BCE, Bhaskara 1 –7th century BCE and Bhaskara 2–12th century AD were the greatest Mathematicians ever lived on earth.

'Later, Jagadish Chandra Bose of Calcutta presented radio to the world in 1895 which was done by Marconi only a few months later. The test tube baby concept was first told to the world by Dr Subhash Mukhopadhyay of India and not by Dr Robert G Edwards of England. The prediction of inventing devices like gramophone, electric bulb, motion picture and so on could be seen in the Vedas. No one has an idea of, even, who Shiva Ayyadurai is! He is the one who invented the modern e-mail. Had he been an American or a European, he would have been hailed as greater than the founder of Microsoft.

'Darwin could have escaped this shame, had he told the world that the source of his discovery was Vishnu Purana. The Theory of Evolution is not even a small grain of sand on the seashore of Indian Puranas.

'Darwin Debauchery could not refute The Book of Genesis! Christians need not panic!

'Long live *Phantasmagoria*! Thank you and good night!'

Krishnan Potti closed his laptop, removed his specs and switched off the mike as he was the last speaker for the evening.

No one could hear anything as the ovation was deafening. The august congregation pushed their way to him for a selfie, a snap or at least a smile; or a hello or a handshake; or a glance or a glimpse...!

Potti came straight to Ivans and Rose. Ivans hugged him and Rose shook hands with him.

Soon...! The announcement broke through the commotion... 'The best speaker of the conference is... India's Krishnan Potti. The award consists of USD 3 million and a platinum citation of the same worth.'

The second and third places went to a German and a Brazilian respectively, and an Indonesian received a consolation prize.

While driving back home, Ivans and Rose were speaking about the headlines which would hit the media, the next morning.

Phantasmagoria Shocker for Darwin Debauchery
Or
Indian Cure for Darwin Virus
Or
Oriental Anti-Virus for Occidental Virus
Or
Indian Unearths Darwinian Fraud

'Whatever it is…it is going to rock the world and shake the foundation of many a scientific contention on the creation, the evolution and the destruction of life on earth.' Ivans said.

On dropping Jessica Rose back home, Jose Ivans noticed the dim yellow light in a room of her house.

'The devil might be reading the Bible! He does it every time before he attacks me. Tonight will be longer…!' Rose sobbed reclining on the co-driver's seat.

Ivans crossed her forehead and said The Lord's Prayer…

Our Father, who art in Heaven,
Hallowed be Thy name.
Thy kingdom come…

Ivans crossed her forehead again and said, 'Rose, our Good Lord will surely deliver you from the evil Martin. Go…the Heavenly Father has seen your tears and heard our prayers!'

They felt proud of each other for their deep faith in The Lord.

He crossed her forehead for a third time and Rose with her eyes in fearful piety opened the door of the car and stepped out. Her cheeks shone brighter, in the yellow stream of moonlight, as they were damp. In a vain attempt she tried to smile as she said...

'Good night! My Jo...'

'Good night! My Rose...', he promptly replied.

Ivans watched her beautiful heaving gait while she walked, though unwillingly, towards her house. Rose turned back after closing the picket fence gate and looked at Ivans. He waved at her.

Rose opened the front door of the house with the spare key which she used to keep in her handbag, and disappeared for a while. She turned on the light in her bedroom on the first floor facing the street. His 7 series Havana was ready to glide into the unusually blue blanched *full moon*.

The entire spectacle reminded him of a scene in *Dover Beach – the honeymoon poem of Mathew Arnold,*

Come to the window, sweet is the night air!

Ivans thought that the time was ripe for the Nishagandhi to bloom on land and the blue lotus in water.

Rose appeared at the window as if she had heard Arnold's Poem, being chanted by Ivans, in telepathy...!

He watched her exquisite silhouette through the blinds, which she parted and waved at him.

'An epitome of beauty!'

He felt a sudden surge of passion within. Even a simple touch would have made the unseen buds of human flesh bloom and spill its honey at that moment.

He was going through an emotional short circuit somewhere in his ever reliable metabolism which was instantly repaired and rectified by the gentleman in Jose Ivans.

His Havana glided like a swan just to enter the stream of the turbid ebb and flow of human misery – the only faithful friend of man on this perilous and unknown shore of life.

The moon was full...the earth was rejoicing in the beauty of the moon. She alone knew the torturous moments she was going through...!

'Poor Moon, you might be sweltering and weeping now as the Sun who so brutally exercises his burning desires on you...! You suffer everything quietly lest you should shiver and suffer at night in the dreadful track of lonely nights...! Therefore, happily bear the irrevocable solar violence...at least...you can get rid of your loathsome lunar loneliness in the cruel company of the Sun. As Jessica Rose does!' Ivans soliloquised.

Ivans was not in a hurry to reach home. He drove slowly with the Full Moon on his face. He was driving his Havana down his memory lane...he soon reached Udayagiri, the village where he was born.

His vehicle moved along the country road, under the pretty *Gulmohar* trees...! The Crimson pavement was still the same. His grandpa Joseph Ivans and grandma Cicely Ivans used to walk along the same pavement at the break of the day. At the end of the road-strip there stood a country house... the Kadachirakkunnel House of Iyppachan and Annamma! Though Iyppachan was not handsome, he was hardworking and genuine. Annamma was god fearing and stunningly beautiful: an *Othello* and *Desdemona* combination with the only exception of having no *Iago* in the village.

Udayagiri was an immaculate countryside with an industrious and innocent folk...!

The Moon was steadily climbing!

8

Full Moon!

Punctually, Iyppachan's balls started climbing upwards, and Annamma started reading the Holy Scripture!

All the villagers came outdoor hearing the heart-rending cries of Iyppachan and Annamma's screaming of the Holy Verses.

They all knew that Iyppachan's balls would start climbing only on full moon nights and it would be definitely after 10 pm. When the torsion begins, Iyppachan would hold his bag of worms with both the hands and start rolling on the cot lengthwise uttering terrible cries as if he would die in a few minutes. Their sons, Denis and Toms would have already escaped to *The Arcadia* for asylum and slept long ago expecting a nightmarish culmination of this tragicomedy. The daredevils of the village would march towards Kadachirakkunnel House to witness this high drama on the full moon nights.

In the middle of all this anarchy, the only soul peacefully resting would be Annamma who would be reading from the Holy Book in a sing-song tone. The particular scripture she would read during that fateful night would be The Book of the Psalms.

Ivans had the glorious visuals of Annamma reading the scripture, in the candle light, kneeling on the veranda of Kadachirakkunnel House. The floor of the house was plastered with a thick paste of cow dung and powdered coal which would be allowed to dry in order to give the floor a natural cooling effect.

The golden form of Annamma, kneeling on the veranda in the candle light, revisited Ivans.

Her headgear was of silk with golden border and her chatta - the country top and mundu - the dhoti were speck-less and snow-white. They were traditional for the Christian women in Kerala. Her face was like that of Desdemona and limbs seemed as if they were cut in white marble. She was strong in the construction of body and mind. The villagers rushed to the front yard of the Kadachirakkunnel House and crowded there on full moon nights mainly to see Annamma and not to sympathise with Iyppachan. No electric bulb would burn in the village as electricity was unknown to them. The only sources of light for the villagers would be kerosene lamps and candles. A lantern would be burning in the bedroom for assisting Iyppachan to roll properly on the cot without falling down from it.

Ivans remembered the night when he witnessed this ceremony for the last time. It was the previous of his first day away from his ancestral home, *The Arcadia*. The next day, he would enter another face of his student life. He would be sent to Ooty to join Good Shepherd International Residential School – GSIRS, the best residential school in India run by the most celebrated and revered educationists of the era.

That very night, while Iyppachan was rolling, Annamma was reading Psalm 139. When Jose Ivans joined the crowd with his grandparents, Annamma read verses 11 and 12:

> *If I say, 'surely the darkness shall cover me,*
> *The light around me become night',*
> *Even the darkness is not dark to you;*
> *The night is as bright as the day,*
> *For darkness is as light to you.*
> *For it was you who formed my inward parts;*
> *You knit me together in my mother's womb.*
> *I praise you, for I am fearfully and wonderfully made!*

Seeing the Ivans, Annamma hushed up her scripture recital and with respectful decorum looked into the bedroom. The crowd had already split into two and cut a way for Joseph and Cecily as they walked and entered the bedroom accompanied by the little Ivans. There, they saw Iyppachan wriggling like a worm in a frying pan holding his balls with both his hands. He was wearing only a *lungi* – the loin cloth.

Annamma resumed her scripture reading more religiously as Iyppachan screamed at the top of his voice, 'Joseph Sir... *ente unda*...! Both are missing. They have just escaped to my stomach...!'

Jose Ivans could not help laughing for in Malayalam language, *ente unda* means *my balls*. Cecily Ivans, stepped out of the room as usual and sat on the tripod behind Annamma.

'Ah...one is here, I got him...,' Iyppachan located a small lump of flesh below his ribs and would not let it go out of his grip.

'Take him to the Mission Hospital now, if they are not in the bag.' Kunjappan Chettan, the owner of *CHE*, the village teashop expressed his concern from the crowd.

'Yeah, before they re-appear behind his ear studs, they should be located and their ascent should be blocked. Then, they should be slowly rubbed down to the bag as the nurses of the Mission Hospital usually do.' Barber Neelandan commented from the dark.

'As it occurs only on full moons, I suspect it be the work of demons!' Mathai Chettan, an elderly neighbour, said. 'His gestures resemble that of the possessed!'

'Then, call the village sorcerer and get consecrated talismans to tie on Iyppachan's waist and wrists.' Broker Thommy squeaked with enthusiasm.

Joseph Ivans ordered them to be quiet.

'Grandpa and grandma are never tensed and so is Annamma. All of them know how to keep their cool.' Jose Ivans thought.

Annamma now entered Psalm 140 and Iyppachan must have completed 1000 rolls.

At a glance, Annamma saw the only wicked soul in the village, Andrews, who would go after every woman and would always be unsuccessful in his lustful nightly errands. This nature had earned him a nick name *Kozhi* Andrews, as *Kozhi* meant a village cock who would go after every hen of the village.

Seeing *Kozhi* Andrews in the crowd, Annamma shouted verses 1 and 2 from Psalm 140:

> *Deliver me, O Lord, from evildoers;*
> *Protect me from those who are violent,*
> *Who plan evil things in their minds...!*
> *And stir up wars continuously...!*

Hearing this, Andrews vanished into the dark shades of the mango trees never to return that night.

Annamma mellowed down her voice and with a sigh resumed the chanting of verses 4 and 5:

> *Guard me, O Lord, from the hands of the wicked...*
> *Protect me from the violent who have planned my*
>   *downfall...*
> *The arrogant have hidden a trap for me,*
> *And with cords they have spread a net...!*

At this point, Iyppachan screamed, '*Ayyo...ente unda...* Joseph Sir...*ente unda...*!'

All in the assembly laughed...and soon they stopped laughing as they saw two embers burning in place of Annamma's eyes. One look from her was enough to control the entire village. Her golden face was now red with anger which made her more beautiful.

Joseph Ivans understood what Iyppachan wanted.

Philip, the faithful driver of the Ivans brought the Jeep, the only automobile of Udayagiri. In a minute, Iyppachan was shifted to the floor of the Jeep where he lay on a bed with his left hand on is bag and the right on the lump, which he had discovered up among the ribs. The Jeep flew out of the front yard of Kadachirakkunnel House and shot like a bullet to the Mission Hospital.

As the crowd depleted, Annamma closed the Bible, picked up her trusted sickle, blew out the candles, closed the door, lowered the lantern flame on the veranda and went with Cecily Ivans to *The Arcadia* to sleep beside her children.

The Jeep moved like ghost driven on the winding country road.

Iyppachan was driven to the Mission Hospital in half an hour. Joseph Ivans and Jose Ivans sat in front with Philip who was an expert driver. Philip was with Joseph Ivans in the Army. The Major General took his trusted driver Philip along with him on retirement. Philip took pre-mature retirement and followed his master to Udayagiri. Philip and his family lived in the farmhouse of *The Arcadia*. He was more a custodian than a driver.

At the hospital, room no. 18 was kept ready for Iyppachan as it was full moon. The young nurses Lily and Daisy were helped by Philip and Barber Neelandan to shift Iyppachan to the room where he started grunting like a wild boar. His eyes were still bulging and body was sweating profusely.

Sister Daisy presently injected the stock medicine into Iyppachan's right bum as his hands were busy and stiff holding the balls. Sister Lily gave him two tablets, one red and the other blue. They changed his dress to white hospital clothes.

Now, Iyppachan seemed to be happy and relaxed as he was with his beloved nurses. The beautiful Lily and Daisy requested them to leave the room and spoke something only to Joseph Ivans. He came out of the room shortly and all of them left for Udayagiri by midnight.

In the meantime, both Lily and Daisy were busy with Iyppachan, exactly locating his lost *undas* which would eventually be rubbed down to the bag by daybreak. Iyppachan would doze off happily and peacefully in the hands of Lily and Daisy after knowing the fact that he had not lost his *undas* instead they were well positioned, intact and be ready for the next Full Moon.

Back in the village of Udayagiri, all the families would be earnestly praying for Iyppachan and special offering would be made during their parish feast at St Mary's Church or on their annual visit to the Arangam Mahadeva Temple for keeping all the villagers safe from the haunting of *Aana*

Marutha, the blood sucking evil spirit locally known for her lusty quest and erotic pranks as Iyppachan was undergoing.

On reaching *The Arcadia*, they saw light in Cecily Ivans' room. Francis Ivans and Liz Ivans had already slept as he had to go to Ooty the next day morning. Both Cecily and Annamma were engaged in serious conversation. When they saw the high beam of the Jeep, both of them came out to the front yard of *The Arcadia*. Leaving the Major General and his grandson at home, Philip drove the Jeep to the interior of the village to drop Barber Neelandan and a few others. On their way to Neelandan's house, *Kozhi* Andrews was spotted right in the middle of the road in the high beam of the vehicle. As the Jeep approached him, the *Kozhi* jumped into the field and vanished into the thicket.

Seeing Annamma, Joseph Ivans scolded her in a mild tone, 'Annamma, this time you were really harsh and ruthless. There is swelling and can be a small rupture too.'

'What else could I do, Sir?' she was apologetic. 'He was drunk and forcefully insisting too.'

'She did what anybody would do...!' Cecily Ivans supported.

'Hmmmm...!' Joseph Ivans walked into his room leaving his pipe in the ashtray in parlour and his cane on the stand.

Jose and Cecily quietly followed him and Annamma retired to the penthouse to sleep beside Denis and Toms.

The moon was still full and shining. The young Ivans lay beside his grandparents; the lights were off, but the moon streamed into the room through the velvet drapes. He could not sleep as he would be leaving his grandparents the very next day to study at Good Shepherd. He would miss everyone thoroughly. His father Francis Ivans had already come home to take him to Ooty. Jose Ivans quietly listened to what his grandparents were speaking, though he did not quite comprehend what they were speaking.

'Why don't you tell Annamma to stop this cruel joke, Cecily?' Joseph Ivans sounded seriously.

'What else could she do? She is on her full cycle!' Cecily Ivans whispered. 'This time, the shot was unusually harder, she told me!'

Jose Ivans slowly entered his slumber land as he did not understand anything about the *cycle and the shot*.

The mystery over the cycle and the shot remained in little Ivans' mind as an enigma which was not unravelled until he attended a session on human reproductive system in Biology in his 9th grade.

There is a monthly cycle in women which is called menstruation and it is the periodic discharge from the inner lining of the uterus at intervals of about one lunar month from puberty to the menopause.

Later, while attending human psychology and sexology in men, Ivans understood in a subtler manner that men have their cycles too. The twenty eight day lunar cycle will make all the living organisms wax and vane. It will also have a strong impact on all men's sex drive. The entire lunar cycle of twenty eight days can be divided into four quarters consisting seven days or a week. During these days, the moon moves from one sign to the other namely the Fire Sign, the Earth Sign, the Air Sign and the Water Sign. Fire makes men more animal like, Earth instils a sense of care and maturity, Air is for intellect and Water is for lust. Therefore, during the new moon, men are more internally focussed as the moon vanes and the carnal drive will strike its lowest key. During the full moon men desire to be seen, expressed and embraced. Passion will rise and drive will peak.

Jose Ivans eventually realized the relation between the cycle and the shot. During full moons, Iyppachan would take a bottle or two of the strong country punch from the village toddy shop and with his soaked brain he would move along the lonely village road. Mounted on his wild horse for a ride, he would approach Annamma at great pace. But, Annamma would already be peddling on her cycle on all the full moons which would drive Iyppachan wilder. The velocity of Annamma's cycle could never be matched up with Iyppachan's wild horse.

On his failure in making Annamma mount on his horse from her cycle, Iyppachan would shift himself from the wild horse to a pink elephant. He would now start venerating all her heavenly forefathers and even her grandchildren yet to be born with words carefully chosen from his filthiest stock.

In this process, he would try to ceremoniously remember all those wonderfully reproachable epithets that he had learnt during his short visit to the village school as a student which alone helped him to discontinue his otherwise dull school life in sixth grade. Iyppachan's abusive song could be otherwise described as his *Full Moon Litany*.

He would begin the *Litany* with the veneration of the Late Mr Anthony, Annamma's beloved grandfather describing him as a poisonous snake, and then he would come down to her poor grandmother – the Late Mrs Theresa Anthony. Iyppachan's censorious and ranting pitch would slowly become louder and louder and that would be a sign for Dennis and Toms to quietly escape from Kadachirakkunnel House to *The Arcadia*. If they got late, they would be witnessing the most unpleasant spectacle in their life.

As the *Full Moon Litany* progressed, Iyppachan would be effortlessly jumping from one branch of Annamma's family tree to the other counting its twigs, leaves, shoots, stems, blooms, fruits and so on. Annamma would still be respectfully silent as this was the only time she would get to remember all those members of her clan, dead and alive. Iyppachan had very specially and cleverly coined adjectives for Annamma and her parents. He would first venerate her father who had died without giving him the promised dowry of Rupees Two Thousand fully. According to him, Annamma's father, the Late Mr Alexander had to give him Rupees Fifty more when he died. In fact, Kadachirakkunnel House stood in the two hectare plot worth Rupees Twenty Lakh which Mr Alexander bequeathed to his daughter.

Then, there would be the veneration of her ailing mother who used to stay with Annamma's younger brother in the faraway district of Calicut.

Iyppachan's typical feminine vocals would shout, 'Your mother, Rosamma Alexander...the slut...!'

At this point, Iyppachan would whine like a mongrel as though it were getting castrated.

The sharp shooter in Annamma would precisely land an ominous crotch shot on Iyppachan's centre of gravity with her right knee. Annamma could never stand his *Full Moon Litany* venerating her most beloved mother as a slut.

Iyppachan would start rolling on the cot screaming and holding his bag while searching for his lost *undas* and Annamma would take the Bible!

This was a relation between the cycle and the shot which his grandparents talked about on that full moon night.

Jose Ivans laughed...the heartiest laugh he had ever had since his childhood.

His Havana was still gliding with the full moon overhead.

9

Jose Ivans woke up as the constable on beat knocked on his Havana's window with his lathi. He could not presently sensitize himself to the location as he was dreaming. The constable blew his whistle and gestured his order to him to leave the place as it was already deserted. He saw something like the statue of Mary the Immaculate standing before him. Slowly, he realized that he was on the beach.

'This sea is like his mother, she will receive everything... never rejects anything.'

The frost on the windshield had already hampered his visibility and he turned on the de-icer of his car and slowly things were clear to him. The Church light from the hill top was still glowing. Ivans looked at his Havana clock: 4.30 am.

As he looked on, a flame was abruptly lit in the valley. The fisher folk would soon wake up from their sleep and light up their lives with those small little flames of hope: though small, yet very bright...!

Through the thin film of a cordial mist Ivans watched the valley getting adorned with more and more golden spots with every single passing minute.

'In ten minutes, the entire valley will be overflowing with the amber blaze from those poor huts.' Ivans thought.

At 4.45 am, the Church bell chimed every sleeping soul back to life.

At the 5 o'clock bell they would all join the Church choir to sing before the commencement of the Angelus of the Church Breviary.

'What a great faith!' Ivans marvelled at the fisher-folk's unshakeable trust in the existence and rule of the mighty heavens over the earth.

'Life is really a celebration for them every second!' Ivans thought. 'They celebrate every possible way. They work hard, earn only a little, spend everything on food and medicine, live a few years and then fall to rise. Still, they will never fail to smile, to laugh, to share, to care, to pray and to celebrate their life throughout.'

The Church bell chimed...5.00 am.

Its peal resounded throughout the valley chasing the still dandling evil spirits back to their yawning graves.

The fisher-folk, which was yet to learn *how to catch men,* sang: *It's well, it's well with my soul...!*

The mournful hymn of Horatio Spafford!

Jose Ivans lowered his head and rested it on the velvet wrapped steering wheel of his Havana and closing his eyes joined the poor fishers in the singing of the hymn unto Him...

The beat policeman was furiously impatient with Ivans as he hit on the car window more harshly and gestured for his sudden departure.

Ivans suddenly thought about his daughter Janet and he sat uprightly on his seat. Soon, his 7 series darted along the long stretch of the highway towards *The Abode*.

Behind him in the valley, the hymn was still overflowing... it reminded him of the heart of a father who loved his daughters.

It was his own heart!

10

Jose Ivans almost gate-crashed, and in flew his Havana. Its wheels burned and smoked as it squealed to a halt in the porch of *The Abode*. Durwan Ashok rushed to the porch to see what happened to his master, but before that Ivans had already reached his bedroom.

There lay his little angel...his beloved daughter Janet. He sat beside her and glanced at her...! Her breathing was not gentle and rhythmic.

It was still dark outside. The LED shine in the room was soft, but bright. It was clear that she had not slept with Katherine and must have insisted on seeing him before she slept. Ruts of tears were distinctly visible on her rosy cheeks, and some of those drops were still seen crystallized on them.

Leaning forward, he gently kissed on her forehead and whispered in her ears...

'My Jan... Daddy loves you so...much...! Pardon me for not keeping my promise that every day I would sleep beside you.'

He sensed two little soft arms hugging him tight. He heard an angelic voice whispering in his ears... 'Daddy...!'

'Where were you?' Janet sobbed. 'You know, Mama slapped me four times when I kept on asking for you and when I started crying, she pushed me out of her bed. I fell down on the floor. Then, Clara Mom came and dragged me out of Mama's bedroom and pushed me into your room.'

Ivans held his little daughter close to his heart and kissed her again.

'I cried for you, Daddy... I tried to call you, but the line was dead! Where were you Daddy...? Don't leave me alone, my Daddy...please... I'm afraid of Mama and Clara Mom...! They'll kill me, Daddy!'

Janet started weeping loudly hugging Ivans.

Keeping his fingers on the little lips, Ivans glanced at the land-phone... Its wire was pulled out of the socket.

'Katherine is a clever player...she has started playing again wisely.' Ivans mused.

'Daddy will never go anywhere, leaving you alone again, my Jan...!'

'Never?'

'Never...!'

'If you go...your Jan will cry and cry and she will die... Okay?'

'My Jan, my everything... Daddy will not go anywhere without you...!'

He kissed his daughter again. A drop of tear fell into her jet black tresses and a second tumbled down upon her face.

He carried little Janet to the bathtub and splashed some warm water on her face. Using the face wash, she cleaned her face first and both of them brushed their teeth and performed the primary ablutions.

In five minutes, Jose Ivans and Janet Ivans were ready for the Angelus. Kneeling before the Crucifix, Janet lighted the huge candle. Crossing his forehead, Ivans opened the Holy Book. Janet, covering her head, closed her eyes in prayer and crossed her forehead.

Her most beloved Daddy started reading Psalm 121 from the Jerusalem Bible:

> *I lift up my eyes to the mountains;*
> *Where is my help to come from?*

Janet joined her Daddy as the child prodigy knew the Psalm by-heart! The candle flame steadied itself as they chanted the verses.

> *My help comes from Yahweh*
> *Who made heaven and earth.*
>
> *May He save your foot from stumbling;*
> *May He, your guardian, not fall asleep!*

You see — He neither sleeps nor slumbers,
The guardian of Israel!

Yahweh is your guardian, your shade,
Yahweh at right hand.
By day the sun will not strike you,
Nor the moon by night.

Yahweh guards you from all harm
Yahweh guards your life,
Yahweh guards your comings and goings,
Henceforth and forever and ever.

'Amen!'

Ivans kissed the verse and closed the Holy Book.

Janet and her Daddy spent a few minutes in silent prayers.

On rising, the little one blew the candle out and punctually kissed her Daddy...

'Good Morning, Daddy!'

'Good Morning, my Jan!' Ivans hugged his Jan.

Both of them walked away straight to the royal kitchen of *The Abode* and made a cup of coffee for Ivans and a cup of warm health drink for Janet.

They sat at the revolving table in the mini dining hall and took their drinks with honeyed doughnuts from Finland.

Janet finished her drink and snacks and went to the study with her Daddy's permission.

It was 7am.

Durwan Ashok brought the newspapers to Ivans. He took the Times of India in his hands and went to the library.

Ivans glanced at the front page headline in red letters.

Phantasmagoria
Indian wins USD 3 Million at the World Conference

At that moment, Ivans heard the soft roar of an engine near the porch.

He saw Dr Solomon Samuels come out of his Benz with Tiger the Bulldog.

Tiger was his most trusted companion since his wife's sad demise three years ago.

Mrs Rebecca Samuels died a painful death at 55 as she fell a hapless prey to breast cancer.

She was alone the source of love and warmth in the entire Mamalassery family.

Katherine was her only daughter. But, she inherited all her viciousness directly from her father. Dr Solomon Samuels was popularly known as *Dr Evil* among the patients and his colleagues for his cruel and cut-throat nature.

Dr Samuels used to never allow his lady patients, who were in the family way, to deliver normally. He would ruthlessly cut them open to take out the babies. In a way, the patients also liked it as they could entirely get rid of the long and painful process of childbirth and its aftermath. According to Dr Samuels, he only helped his clients, who were so worried and anxious of losing their beauty and shape, to finish the entire ceremony of nativity within half an hour on the OT table. As a result, the young mothers were happy, Dr Samuel was happier but the unfortunate parents and husbands of those beauty queens were terribly upset as Dr Evil would scheme out an appalling drain of their common purse.

By and by Dr Evil became one of the most influential and richest surgeons in the City. Name, fame, ego, power and pride became his confidants. The ferocious Tiger became as devilish as his master from the systematic training of his master.

Katherine came to Ivans' life through his mother Liz Ivans. Liz and Rebecca were childhood friends, and both of them loved each other very much as though they were sisters. When Liz Ivans was the Headmistress of All Saints English Medium School in the City, Rebecca Samuels was an English Teacher in the same school!

When both the mothers devised a marriage between their children, no one protested, although Katherine was the mirror image of her father. She was ill-famed for being headstrong, egoistic and cruel too. She used to brutally hit her house maids by making reasons.

Liz Ivans was guilt-ridden seeing her beloved son suffer from the tyrannical sway of her daughter-in-law.

She had once sobbed hugging her son, 'Pardon me Jo...! It's Mama's fault...! Irrevocable! Mama cannot redress it... pardon me, my son. Mama has sinned against you...! When Rebecca asked me, I couldn't deny...!'

Liz Ivans cried...the warmth of her hug was doubled as her tears seeped through his thick hair. He looked up only to see those ruddy drops, which were not tears but his Mama's remorse, repentance and regret...oozed out as if blood...red red blood...!

His mother's face resembled that of Mother Mary's when she watched her son drip His precious blood on the cross. But, her son was dead and then risen. Here, Liz Ivans' son was still on the cross; that too, still breathing and not dead... therefore, no resurrection...!

Ivans remembered the glorious spectacle of a comet whizzing past the western horizon on that day as his beloved Mama and Dadda kissed him and Janet goodbye and left them for Francis Ivans' office.

Katherine had already left for her morning workout even without uttering a word to them. The parents of Jose Ivans used to pay occasional visits to *The Abode* during weekends. Janet would never let her grandpa go so easily.

She would rest herself on his broad chest and play with his fancied moustache. She used to like grooming her grandpa's moustache to various styles: from a handlebar to the trucker and so on with her baby comb.

Whenever her grandparents left her after their visit, they used to give Janet a bunch of Thousand Rupee Notes which would often count even twenty to twenty-five at times. It would straight away go to a joint account of Jose Ivans and Janet Ivans.

That Monday, Francis Ivans had to leave in a hurry as he had to attend an emergency meeting in his office. His boss himself had called him over and asked him to reach his office in half an hour.

Liz Ivans insisted that she would also go with her husband as there was a medical appointment for her in City Hospital. The daring young driver Madan braved the early mist of 6 am and off flew the black Range Rover as if it had wings!

Upon this, Janet went to her study and Ivans to the audio-visual theatre. The AV of *The Abode* itself was a visual treat. It was a fifty seater theatre with all the modern amenities. The acoustics were done by technicians from Madrid, whom Jose Ivans had met during one of his visits to Spain. The work of the famous Teatro Real de Madrid was done by them.

Switching on the TV, he sat back on the sofa. Roshni, the maid brought three cups of hot coffee, but had to take two back.

Flipping through the channels, Jose Ivans saw Asianet
breaking news in red letters.

Jose Ivans stopped the rollover there for a while. The news
was beyond anything he could bear. He broke down and
fell into the sofa dropping the cup from his hands. Janet
and Roshni ran into the theatre as they heard the cup fall
and break.

The news was still breaking on the TV.

ADGP Francis Ivans and Wife die at a Road Accident.
Police look into the possibility of a sabotage.
His driver has been rushed to the City Hospital.

No one knew what to do! The entire world of *The Abode*
came down to a standstill. Durwan Ashok rushed to the
theatre and besprinkled his master's face with ice-water.
Even Clara dialled Katherine from the land-line and her
phone was either engaged or not reachable. She might have
been talking to someone who had failed to attend that day's
training session as she was only keen about her trimming
down.

Jose Ivans somehow reached the hospital and the bodies
were in the morgue lying well-guarded. He saw a crowd in
uniform and could not remember and connect the events
coherently. He wept bitterly hugging Janet tightly.

Later, Katherine came to the hospital. Ivans wept seeing her
and tried to speak..., 'Kathy... Mama and Dadda...!'

'Okay... Okay...! Behave yourself Jo.' Katherine retorted curtly. 'Six months back I also lost my mother...then, I didn't see such a great passion in you...! Clara, take Jan and go home.' She ordered!

Katherine plucked Janet away from Ivans' hug.

'I want to see my grandpa...my grandma...please... Daddy... I won't go with Clara Mom. I won't go...tell Mama not to take me away...' Janet screamed.

Ivans heard Janet's scream like a distant melancholy song as he was in a trauma.

He saw, as if in a dream, the nursing assistants roll away both his beloved parents clad in spotless white.

The entire arena was cordoned off by the personnel.

The bodies were shifted to the police headquarters after post mortem and there they lay in state.

Then, the funeral procession left for Udayagiri. The entire village mournfully and prayerfully gathered there to pay the last rites to their beloved Francis Sir and Lizy Teacher. His Dadda and Mama were put to their rest in the cemetery of St Mary's Church, close by Joseph Ivans and Cicely Ivans.

Very many cold hands held Ivans' hands for a moment or two and tongues manifold said something in muted tones.

Jose Ivans was on a transcendental shore of desolation where he could only hear the mournful melody of the departed souls. It was the pandemonium of the mythical purgatory. His eyes searched for familiar features...faces...but none!

He could see only strange faces with fiery eyes, parched lips, bloody tongues and puckered foreheads. Numerous tongues of Infernal Blaze licked those curves on their foreheads straight: soul mending...!

He stood near the well of the razing fire which humans dread most, while alive.

Suddenly, Jose Ivans saw a ring of celestial fire: at the centre of which his Dadda and Mama journeying towards Heaven accompanied by the mighty angels.

They passed by the Purgatory and their son. Jose Ivans shouted and waved at them.

They looked at him with vacant eyes. They did not wave, nor did they smile.

Jose Ivans experienced an uncanny feel of being orphaned and dispossessed for the first time.

> *When beggars die, there are no comets seen;*
> *The heavens themselves blaze forth the death of Princes!*

Jose Ivans remembered *Julius Caesar* standing and shouting outside the Purgatory parapets.

'Death the Reveller celebrates after severing even the very taproot of my family tree!' Ivans whispered to himself, 'Janet is the only root attached to me now. O, Heavenly Father... keep your exceedingly sublime Thwarting Angels away from my Jan...please...!' he pleaded glancing at the glorious Sacred Heart of the Christ that hung on the library wall.

Through his blurred vision, he saw two apparitions standing near the door!

11

Jose Ivans sprang out of the sofa seeing the apparitions at the door.

'Mr Jose Ivans,' one of the apparitions shouted. 'Do you think that my daughter should still be your wife?'

The voice of the apparition was that of Dr Evil.

'No...!' Ivans wanted to answer but voice got stuck in the throat as his mouth was dry.

'Kathy told me that you always come home late.' Dr Evil threw another question. 'Is it right?'

Ivans did not venture to answer.

'I've heard that you've been roaming with one Ms Jessica Rose on the beach near the Fishers' Creek late at night. Is it true?'

No answer.

'You've been spotted together by my people on the beach regularly. Therefore, I've decided to take my daughter with me to my house. She is taking Janet also along with her.'

The last sentence scorched Ivans like a leaf by a flash of lightning.

'No...my angel...my Janet...!' Ivans painfully exclaimed.

Ivans screamed as if he saw a nightmare and wiped those brimful drops from his eyes to see Dr Samuels and Katherine standing at the door.

He shivered and was out of breath seeing both the apparitions clearly at the door.

Dr Evil resumed...

'When I got my daughter married to you, she was the most beautiful girl in the City. In the first year itself you forced her to be a mother against her will. She wanted to take up *modelling*; you tried to spoil her career. If she bore your seed, she would get disfigured, you thought! And thus, she would remain with you forever as a slave. My daughter started hating you at that very moment...you are a sadist.'

Jose Ivans did not really understand what Dr Evil told him. That was not there even in his most distant dreams.

'You forced Kathy to breastfeed your daughter which would further make her dream-entry to *modelling* all the more difficult. Somehow, my daughter managed to restore some of her lost physical properties through hard workouts. Then you emerged with another proposal. You needed a second child to give the first one a company.'

Ivans tasted a nauseating flavour of bitter irony and acidic sarcasm in the voice of Dr Evil.

'My daughter,' Dr Evil proceeded, 'got the shock of her life from your crazy idea. If I allow her to live with you anymore, it will be suicidal. Therefore, I have decided to take my daughter with me now itself, without any further delay. She has already signed a contract with Christabel Marant and is starting *modelling* next week at *Lakmé!* She is ready to break the contract with you! Soon…!'

'But, Papa…!' Ivans tried to speak.

'Who's your Papa? Don't call me *Papa* anymore! Kathy told me how you abused me only for teaching her how to be independent!'

'Okay….! Now, let *Kathy* speak…', Ivans retorted gathering all his battered manliness, 'Can you go Kathy, leaving all of us back here?' Ivans asked.

'*Yes, I can.* Jan and Clara are coming with me. I can't stay here anymore. You're cruel and selfish. You can live with that slut, Jessica Rose after we're gone!' Katherine screamed.

'*Katherine….!*' Jose Ivans raised his voice.

'Don't howl, Mr Ivans!' Dr Evil shouted, 'my tiger has better barking skills….! Come sweetie…..pick up your bags. Clara, help Kathy!'

Dr Evil grabbed Janet's little hand and tried to pull her who was standing at the entrance of the library crying and watching this entire melodramatic episode with bated breath.

'Daddy….! I won't go…. Daddy….!' Janet cried out trying to get herself released from the *evil grip.*

As Janet tried to escape from Dr Evil, she bit his hand.

'Bitch….!' Dr Evil pushed Janet very hard and she fell on the ground.

Janet cried so loud.

The entire household rushed to the library to know what happened to their little angel.

On this, Katherine slapped Janet and pulled her out of the room.

Jose Ivans sprang up like a tiger towards the door, but before he could do anything, Katherine latched the mighty library doors from outside and shouted at the inmates to get dispersed.

Katherine moved towards her car dragging Janet, and sat inside her Aston Martin. Dr Samuels' driver Johnson loaded their luggage in the Benz.

Both Dr Evil and his dog sat in the car.

The cars flew out of the gates of *The Abode*.

Janet Ivans' heart-rending sobs could be heard in and around *The Abode* for a long time.

Ivans sat on the sofa…..*orphaned and dispossessed*!

His royal pedigree was the only disgusting cause of his wretched inaction!

Jose Ivans did not go to Electronics India that day.

For the first time in his life, he felt a war like agitation and miserable loneliness protesting somewhere in his heart. The acclaimed cool of his inner-self started getting warmed up…..! His razor-edged reasoning had already launched a series of fresh attacks at his already tormented conscience.

'Why was I so resigned when Janet was forced out of her paternal asylum? Where were my manly nerves when Dr Samuels and Katherine tried me in their savage and lopsided court of justice? How helpless I was when they unleashed their ugly and unjust allegations? I had never even touched or looked at Rose with anything not permitted by the society! All were cooked up by the devoted daughter and attested by her passionate father.'

Ivans' heart sympathetically revolted against his Mama and Mrs Rebecca.

'Poor souls….! They must be feeling ashamed of their defeated skills of match-making. Women like Katherine should never be allowed to enter the sacred institution of marriage…..! There should be solid legislative amendments and guidelines for people who intend to be in the wedlock.

'All should be psychologically processed and medical fitness certificates should be procured from psychiatrists on their mental health. There should be expert and detailed report on the stability and integrity of one's sociability, behavioural patterns and connectivity with people. If one could not pass the psycho-metric eligibility test for coupling, the government should not allow one to get married.

'Katherine and Martin would have been the best match! Rose, Juan, Janet and I would make the best family in the world.'

A volcano was fuming in Ivans' tormented brain…it could erupt anytime.

He sat on the sofa staring at the deep blue vintage Bible, dwelling in a leather coated luxury in the shelf.

Getting up, Ivans slowly grabbed it. After latching the door from inside, Ivans sank into the sofa.

Stretching himself on the sofa, he looked at the ceiling of the library and his eyes caught a lizard clinging onto it. Its chirping made him remember a verse from the **Proverbs – 30:28…**

> *Lizards, which thou canst catch in thy hand,*
> *Yet they frequent the palaces of kings!*

'How confident a little lizard is whom man can hold even in their brutal hands! Yet, how confidently and surely she enters even the royal chambers of the kings' mighty palaces! Men are cowards...they can destroy anything.' Ivans thought.

'Destruction in any form is the earliest reaction of a loser, but not even the last resort of a winner!' Ivans wished he could cry out.

He really cried...! Hot blood flowed out of his inconsolable eyes. He hugged the Bible tightly and closed his eyes...!

Ivans did not want to sleep, but sleep wished to visit him in his couch. She laid her soft hands on the desolate forehead of the poor child, like his loving Mama. He was presently with Liz Ivans. They were now on an off-day evening stroll on the winding country road of Shanthipuram in the village of Udayagiri which would eventually lead them to *CHE,* the country tea shop!

12

Shanthipuram...!

Jose Ivans saw the red August branches of his beloved *Gulmohar Tree* under which the floral carpet seemed waiting for him for a roll. The little Ivans lay on the road and started rolling and thus receiving a red carpeted welcome from his companion tree.

'Jo...don't soil your trousers.....get up my darling, please...!' Liz Ivans used to fondly scold him for lying on the road filled with the crimson petals of *Gulmohar* blooms.

'No, Mama.....please.... I love my *Gulmohar*....! She sheds those blooms knowing that I am coming. See Mama.... see.....she loves you too Mama!' He used to tell his mama looking at the *Gulmohar* branches dropping the petals upon both of them. The fresh breeze now would push a few more upon them.

'Jo, stop this nonsense....! Get up and come....we are late.... it's getting dark!'

Jose Ivans would get up and follow Liz like an obedient pet.

When they passed by the villagers, pacing down the country road, they would bow down in salutation to their beloved Lizy Teacher in respect and smile at the little one in love.

The lady teachers in Kerala, *God's Own Country,* are called *Teachers* and gents are addressed as *Sirs.*

The villagers were going to *CHE*, the country tea cum grocery shop of Shanthipuram. The shop was owned by Kunjappan Chettan, the last word on revolution: Marxism, Leninism and Communism. But, no one knew about the real *Che* more than Barber Neelandan did. *CHE* was active only two times a day: the morning session and the evening session. The former would be held from 6.30 am to 10 am and the latter from 5 pm to 9.30 pm.

Kunjappan Chettan's tea was a delight to country tongues. The morning session would be catering only dosa and chutney – the fermented pancake and coconut and roasted red chilly ground chutney.

All the heads of the families of Shanthipuram would religiously assemble at *CHE* in the morning and the evening of everyday. One cup of *CHE* tea cost 10 paise and two dosas 40 paise: chutney was free of any cost. Thus, 50 paise, equal to half a Rupee, would give any customer a sumptuous breakfast.

Kunjappan Chettan had put up a board at *CHE*, '*Innu Rokkam, Naale Kadam*' which meant *Cash Today, Credit Tomorrow,* as he firmly believed in the famous adage *Tomorrow Never Comes.*

However, Kunjappan Chettan was not very strict about collecting ready cash *only* from his trusted customers. All the names of the elderly male members of all the families in the village could be found in Kunjappan Chettan's Book of Credit. Even the village officer used to refer to Kunjappan Chettan's Book of Credit, in case he wanted some information or clarifications as to whether a new villager had come or an old one gone from the village. The accuracy of the data in the book was trusted even by the government officials. Kunjappan Chettan could correctly say if a new baby was born in a family or any one left the village to rest in peace. He would collect the credit from everyone on a monthly basis without fail and all would abide by his instructions.

Kunjappan Chettan was an iconic character of Shanthipuram which means the *City of Peace*, though no one knew how that village got that name. But, peace definitely prevailed everywhere in the village. Shanthipuram lay 1 ½ km away from Udayagiri. All the villages of the Province were connected to Udayagiri through a network of winding country roads. All knew all at Udayagiri. All its inhabitants had migrated from Travancore, the central districts of Kerala a few decades ago. When they came to that village, it was collectively called *Pattappara*. The land was blanketed by thick forests and was infested by wild animals.

Quickly, the immigrants cleared some ground, pitched a tent, fenced the area and there came up many an enclosure in that manner. They had to fight only with the wild animals, poisonous snakes, malaria, chicken pox, and rarely small pox but not with human beings. They could survive all this as everything was pure there: clear sky, new earth, fresh brooks, wild honey and new life. Everything was churned out of purity and unity. They loved each other irrespective of their name, caste, colour, wealth or ism. Even when they quarrelled, it was purely done. They stood up sincerely for their rights and sincerely loved each other once again soon after the dispute was settled. It is said that no one could hate anyone for long at Udayagiri – The Mount of the Rising Sun. Kerala was once a conglomeration of innumerable villages of that sort!

Shanthipuram...the City of Peace was such a village connected to Udayagiri – the mini township. Shanthipuram was not polluted even by a bicycle. The only disturbance was the occasional evening visit of the patrolling Police Jeep which would steadily climb the winding country road to reach *CHE*. The constables would alight at *CHE* and enjoy the evening delicacies of Kunjappan Chettan: *Tea and Parippu Vada – the deeply fried Dhal Vada*. According to Kunjappan Chettan, his *Parrippu Vada* was world famous, though it was circulated only in Shanthipuram!

Head constable Kuttan Pillai and constable Mathukkutty would, then, ask some routine questions to the people who would be present at *CHE* in the evening. They were very kind and friendly with the people of Udayagiri. But, they always remembered not to give the cost of the evening tea and Kunjappan Chettan never forgot to ink their names on a separate page of his Book of Credit after they had gone: only for his satisfaction which would also be viewed and reviewed by him and his wife daily, at night before sleeping.

After the departure of the Police Jeep the crowd in attendance at *CHE* would go back to their respective seats to resume their evening rummy. It was stopped only for a while when they heard the steady engine of the Police Jeep climbing the hill. Broker Thommy would soon recover the cards which they had hidden under the banana leaves, and Thadathippara Avaran would happily strip his *lungi* by himself to be spread on the mud baked floor for laying the cards, before anybody ventured for plucking it from Avaran's waist, as he was the only one who regularly wore under-wears. All of them were great lovers of freedom! They abhorred slavery in any form and wanted liberty everywhere!

The morning schedule at *CHE* was very uniquely planned. As Kunjappan Chettan was busy in blending tea for his esteemed customers, over his furnace, Barber Neelandan was entrusted with the Herculean task of reading the Malayalam newspapers loudly and clearly to the curious audience. The only two newspapers they subscribed were Malayala Manorama and Deshabhimani – the Patriot. Though Manorama was superior and technically perfect, Deshabhimani was not loved less by all the people as they had the revolutionary fire burning in them.

CHE!

The name of the tea cum grocery shop itself showed the glow of revolution. It was Barber Neelandan who named it after Che Guevara, the wild flame of revolution which was blown out in the Amazon Basin of Bolivia in the latter half 1960s. It was in *la Higuera*, the fig tree, of *la Vallegrande*, the big valley, of the Bolivian Andes precisely in 1967.

It was the pride, privilege and passion of Barber Neelandan to read all the news items from both the papers without fail. Being a communist, he would read only the headlines and few selected columns from Manorama as it was hailed as a right-wing paper. He would start reading Manorama at 7 am and finish it by 7.30 am. His loud drone reminded the listeners of some retired old ballet singer suffering from acute asthma. However, no one dared defy his recitation skills as others had their own limitations like stage-fright, illiteracy, farm-work, short-long-sights, marketing agro-products and so on.

Fortunately, Neelandan did not have any of these. Gradually, he became famous as *Akashvani* – the Hindi name of All India Radio – which was used by the younger generation as a weapon to tease him. When they call him *Akashvani*, he would become furious and would take out all his choicest obscenities to abuse the entire kith and kin as Iyppachan used at Annamma on full moon nights. Neelandan's tongue was the most dreaded weapon in the locality. But, if he was not tickled, he would remain very gentle, affectionate and helpful too.

While reading Deshabhimani, Neelandan would deliver every column with great punch, passion and punctuation. He would not forget even to take out his inborn declamatory talents while reading articles on AKG – the greatest communist India has ever seen. AKG's dauntless war heroics for the rights of the poor sections of Kerala had become legends and were scripted and featured even in many a ballad, drama and film.

Neelandan would take approximately 2 hours to finish Deshabhimani. By 9.30am all his devoted listeners would rise, thank Neelandan and Kunjappan Chettan and leave either for their farms or homes with a pledge that they would reassemble at *CHE* at 5 pm.

Kunjappan Chettan would soon close the bamboo doors of *CHE* and slowly climb the hillock to reach his house on the top and rest there by reading the other news items which Neelandan had left in Manorama or listening to the real *Akashvani*. At 1 pm, Orotha Chedathy, his wife, would serve him with lunch and then he would sleep till 4 pm. Orotha, the local version of Rosa, all his five children and the villagers loved him dearly for he was a communist every inch. However, he loved all the Congressmen as his brothers. He believed that *Political Harmony should be Kerala's Facebook as Communal Harmony was*!

At 4.45 pm the hollering of Barber Neelandan from *CHE* would wake up Kunjappan Chettan. Washing his face and limbs and drying them on the hem of his *mundu* he would slowly climb down the slope to *CHE*. Within five minutes the bamboo doors of *CHE* would be opened and the furnace would blaze from firewood. Neelandan would lay two stools, taken from *CHE,* outside at a corner and open his cloth-bag. He would then spread out his cutting and shaving paraphernalia: shaving knife, brush, soap, a pair of scissors, comb and a broken piece of mirror. His trusted customers were aged above forty years as youngsters preferred to go to Udayagiri where a new hair cutting salon was opened with a revolving chair, a front and a rear full mirror, a trimmer and a sprinkler.

The new salon was only a deception point according to Neelandan and all the populace of the village, where the young barber Suresh had neither dexterous hands nor an artistic brain. Neelandan had both.

'The youngsters are fooled by that swindler!' Neelandan said to his old customers who used to sit on the other stool laid before him. They were obliged to agree with him as he would make such bitter statement, on their own children for going to Suresh, only when his knife slid down their throat clearing the last bit of the shaving foam from their larynx. They had to agree with him...!

Most of the citizens of Shanthipuram were devout communists, and all of them, above forty years, had been made to confess their love and allegiance to communism by Neelandan while getting their beards done. If his customer was a Congress loyalist, Neelandan would ask him when his knife reached the throat,

'All the Congress leaders are corrupt nowadays, aren't they?'

The poor customer would reply obediently and piously, 'Yes, yes...!'

'You are going to cast your vote to our candidate in the next elections, aren't you?' Neelandan now would press his knife harder against the customer's throat.

'Yes...*definitely!*' The Congress loyalist would agree with Neelandan assuredly.

All at *CHE* would be laughing loudly at this. But, Neelandan would be very serious, so be his unfortunate customer.

In the meantime, Kunjappan Chettan would have ignited a discussion of that day's newspaper reports, or anything of global importance, 'President Nixon's resignation due to Watergate scandal; the Indo-Pak war of 1971 and the birth of Bangladesh; slow growth of Indian economy; the necessity of communism in Saudi Arabia, Nicaragua and so on.'

On this, Neelandan would start with the legacy of Che Guevara and his speech in the UN general assembly on 11th December, 1964 and the like.

Once, Kadachirakkunnel Iyppachan introduced a new topic of the latest addition of the youngest born to the Genus of Parotta...the Kerala Parotta.

Broker Thommy, described how he happened to eat that Kerala Parotta at a Thaliparamba restaurant when he went for a wedding ceremony which he himself had brokered. The Parotta was fluffy and soft, round in shape and rolled in layers. His hyperbolic narration made all drop their jaws as he told that he undid the layers of the spiral disc and stretched them to see the length of one Parotta. It was something between 20 to 30 metres.

'Liar...!' shouted Naanu Ashan – the village school master.

'Yes, liar...!' Everybody shouted confirming the school master's outburst.

Upon this, Thommy had to compromise on the length of the Parotta. He was forced to reduce a few metres. Finally, they all fixed it something around 10 metres. They did not want to spoil the enthusiasm of Thommy.

'If that's so...', Neelandan shouted, 'this Parotta is a revolution! Long live Parotta...! Long live Broker Thommy!'

'Yeah...!' all agreed. 'Long live Broker Thommy and his long Parotta!'

'If we stretch all the Parottas of Kerala and join them, they will be longer than the railway tracks of the entire state!' Neelandan mocked at Thommy's extraordinary efforts in immortalizing the Kerala Parotta, while putting the lather on the thick beard of Karankal Thankan.

'It will go even beyond Madras!' Thabathippara Avaran expressed his loyalty towards Barber Neelandan.

At this, Broker Thommy lost his temper. He could not stand the shame of being mocked at publicly.

Kadachirakkunnel Iyppachan started laughing at Broker Thommy shaking his head hysterically as an epileptic patient.

'You support the Barber...? I know why...tomorrow is full moon. The Barber will come to help you to search your lost *undas* at night. Keep both your *undas* with him now itself before they are lost!' Broker Thommy shouted at Iyppachan.

Barber Neelandan, hearing this got on to his toes. He left Karankal Thankan's beard half done and charged at the Broker. Thankan would not allow Neelandan to leave him without the full shave of his beard. He tried to stop the Barber by holding his *Lungi*. As the pull was very hard it came off from his waist and Thankan stood there with Neelandan's *Lungi* in his hands. Neelandan was left only with his vest.

When Neelandan charged at Broker Thommy, the spectators of the *Twilight Audience* broke into a delirious howling. They started hooting, shouting, whistling and clapping. Neelandan was well positioned like a wild cat, snarling and spitting at the Broker. The Barber barbarously wielded his shaving knife and sprang at the Broker. Neelandan's urination-kit was now fully visible from his back and it swung like a malfunctioning pendulum of an ancient wall clock between his skinny legs. All the attendees of the *Twilight Audience* cheered and jeered at both the combatants profusely and impartially. Neelandan, flying through the air, tried to catch hold of Thommy. As the Broker successfully dodged the Barber, Neelandan fell right on his stomach. The aborted attempt made him all the more furious.

At this, Thankan with a lump of lather on his face and with the *Lungi* of Neelandan in his hand, tried to clothe Neelandan from his back. Neelandan's unexpected back kick on his chest made Thankan fly back as seen in a film stunt and he honestly fell on the road, with a thump, on his rumps, and sincerely uttered a hell like yell.

At *CHE*, things were getting more hilarious in the evening sun.

Broker Thommy broke through the lines of the spectators to escape from Neelandan and jumped out of *CHE*, and somehow precisely landed on the stomach of Thankan who was lying on the road supine with the shaving lather on his face and *lungi* in his hand. Thankan, already hurt on the rumps, started wriggling on the road like an earthworm when put in concentrated saline water.

The Broker, smelling a rat everywhere, took to his heels through the bushes in the vicinity and vanished never to return to *CHE* for a few weeks.

Neelandan snatched his *Lungi* from a struggling Thankan and wrapped his waist quickly with it, and tried to follow Broker Thommy's lightning sprint track, but gave it up as the Broker was faster and surer on the jungly routes than the Barber.

'Don't think that you have won…..! One day I will get you and that day I will break your lunch box.' Neelandan screamed at Thommy.

The Broker might not have heard it clearly as he was still sprinting for his life along the bushy tracks.

The *Twilight Audience* at *CHE* watched the thicket being shaken by Thommy for a while and admired and wondered at his speedy flight.

'Take Thankan to the Mission Hospital!' suggested Thadathippara Avaran.

'Who will go with him?' Naanu Ashan asked.

'Why, Iyppachan and Neelandan should go with him!' Kunjappan Chettan gave his ruling.

The village ambulance, an easy chair, was soon brought by Avaran. The school master was kind enough to wash the lather from Thankan's unshaven part of beard which made him look funnier than before.

Altogether, six people lifted Thankan and shouldered him on his way to Udayagiri.

All the students going back home on foot from the primary school of Udayagiri looked at Tankan's half beard and no one would hold back their laughing instinct, even his own children.

Philip was, luckily for Thankan's bearers, driving his Jeep to Alakode to pick up Joseph Ivans who was returning home from Hyderabad, after a visit to his colleague when he was in the Army.

They lowered the village ambulance and shifted Thankan to the Jeep. Driver Philip drove the Army Willys M606 (ej3b) straight to the Mission Hospital.

Iyppachan and Neelandan who were nominated to escort Thankan by Kunjappan Chettan sat beside their victim in Willys. Kunjappan Chettan knew that Iyppachan was well known to the medical staff of the Mission Hospital, especially to Daisy and Lily, for his full moon visits to them.

Punctually, Barber Neelandan reached the Mission Hospital the very next day, for Iyppachan's admission, with his knife and shaved off Thankan's half beard free of cost.

13

That day, when Liz Ivans and her son reached *CHE* after enjoying the floral tribute from the little Ivans' endeared *Gulmohar*, Barber Neelandan was standing in the middle of the *Twilight Audience* and telling another Che Guevara legend of his Congo expedition. He also told them how Che Guevara's face resembled the Christ, when he was laid on the manger-like concrete slab on the laundry house of Vallegrande Hospital on 10th October, 1967.

John Berger, the English Art Critic, later observed that Che's visage looked like the Lamentation over the Death of The Christ-painting in Milan by Andrea Mantegna.

'Tell about his death, Neelandan', Broker Thommy demanded.

Now, the Barber and the Broker had become thick friends once again during the Panchayat, the local governing body, election and worked together for the Communist Party and won all the seats for the party in the Panchayat. At Udayagiri, as told before, people could not be at loggerheads with each other for long.

'No...!' Neelandan said. 'I request Joseph Sir to tell us the entire story of Che as I saw him read Che's biography at *The Arcadia*.

Major General Joseph Ivans got up from his seat and stood in the middle the *Twilight Audience* and started the story of Che Guevara.

Seeing his grandfather at *CHE*, Jose Ivans went to him climbing the slope from the road. Driver Philip drove the Army Willys down the country road to drop Liz Ivans at *The Arcadia*.

Neelandan was in high spirits and fully charged as the little Ivans joined the *Twilight Audience* and sat beside General Ivans. *Generation Gap* was yet to be invented!

'Che Guevara was born on 14th June, 1928 in Santa Fe, Argentina.' The General told with a beaming face. 'His childhood was not very colourful and promising. Still, he managed to become a medical doctor in 1953. His Alma Mater was the University of Buenos Aires. Then, Che visited the Guatemala jail secretly, the most dreaded centre of American capitalist tyranny. There he learnt more about the necessity of *Revolution*, sharpened his revolutionary edge and perfected his vision of a liberated and unified Latin America.'

Kunjappan Chettan lighted a *Dineshbeedi*, so did Thadathippara Avaran!

'In 1955, Che arrived at Mexico, found a job and started working as a medical doctor at the Hospital Central of Mexico City. In June he met Raul Castro and on July 18th Fidel reached the Mexican capital.' The General continued. 'The meeting of the three was like the meeting of three mighty waters at Cape Comerine.'

The *Twilight Audience* at *CHE* dropped their jaws. Neelandan looked at the General, sipping the evening tea.

'Fidel Castro later commented, *When I first met him, Che was already an educated revolutionary, and we knew what we were going to do!* Che already joined M-26-7, *the 26th of July Movement of Fidel and Raul.* The name commemorates the revolutionary attack on the Santiago de Cuba Army barracks on 26th July, 1953.' Joseph Ivans took the *Twilight Audience* along the crossroads of Revolution. 'On July 24th, 1955, all the three were arrested for their alleged revolutionary activities and were later released upon the request of Lazaro Cardenas, the former President of Mexico. They still managed to keep the true communist flame burning in their emotional furnace with their ambitious bellows.' Joseph Ivans was really an intellectual giant. The 6'1" General was telling the story of el Che Guevara as if he was enacting *The Passion of the Christ.*

'On 25th November, 1956, the Revolutionary Trinity with 79 comrades, left for Cuba at the dead of the night. The leaking old yacht Granma, progressed her journey on river Tuxpan of Mexico. It took seven long days for them to reach Los Cayos. Their arrival was already noticed by CIA and got hunted. The group had to split. On 5th December, Che got ambushed and seriously wounded in his neck. Actually, a box of bullets that hung on Che's chest stopped one bullet of his enemy from a machine gun and got reflected to his neck. This was the most difficult situation in his life. The conflict between the doctor in his heart and the revolutionary in his blood started grappling with each other. This time, it was a fierce dual. Sitting wounded in the bitter-sweet Cuban field of sugarcane, Che had to take a decision: Doctor or Revolutionary!

'The CIA was closing in... Che was heavily loaded! On his back there lay a huge bag of medications and his chest the heavy box of bullets. He could hear a gun battle between the CIA and his fellow guerrillas. At this, Che unloaded the medications and throwing the bag among the sugarcanes, ran to the warfront hugging the bullet crate on his chest. The Doctor in him was thoroughly defeated by the revolutionary in him.' Joseph Ivans paused.

The *Twilight Audience* was totally engrossed in the legendary story of Che Guevara.

'On 16th December, 1958, Che's troop blew up the bridge over River Falcon thereby they could snap all the connections between Havana and the other cities. The media flashed the news that Ernesto Che Guevara had died in a military ambush...!' The clever story teller in Joseph Ivans stopped there as if the story ended there.

The *Twilight Audience* showed their utter disappointment by shaking their heads vigorously and clicking their tongues objectionably.

'But...!' Joseph Ivans brought delight to Twilight by resuming the story. The audience was delighted to know that the story would continue.

'But...! Radio Rebelde confirmed that Che was alive and he captured all the remaining soldiers of the combined forces of the CIA and dictator Batista of Cuba.

'On December 21st, Che met Fidel at a coffee plantation and together they attacked the barracks of La Plata and tasted their first victory. It was Che's guerrilla warfare that brought them success. Seeing his valour and brain, Fidel appointed Che the Commander of the Revolutionary Army. Fidel, Che and Raul were dearly loved by the natives. They supported them in their freedom quest. The following months were very crucial. Che led the rebel Army with great planning and precise execution of the same. Che's Army unit never tasted defeat. Fidel's diplomacy and Che's mettle started working wonders with great chemistry. Fidel promoted Che to the leadership of the Revolutionary Army. Thus, Che became the Commander-in-Chief of the guerrilla force and the undisputed leader of all M-26-7 units.

'By the daybreak of the New Year day of 1959, the Cuban dictator Fulgencio Batista fled after looting Cuba. Batista had taken 3 billion USD along with him. This is approximately 2 Lakh crore of Indian Rupees now. The very next day, Friday, 2nd January, Che entered Havana to take the final control of the capital. Fidel took six more days to arrive Havana. Both the Castro brothers reached the capital on Thursday, 8th January, 1959. Che handed over the entire control to Fidel, thus, proving that he was a loyal comrade.'

There was a long ovation from the *Twilight Audience* for revolutionary Che's loyalty.

'The next day, Fidel took over as the President of Cuba. Fidel's dream was fulfilled, but, Che's not. He wanted to chase his dream...a dream which was later proclaimed by Martin Luther King of America...a dream to liberate the world from poverty, exploitation, imperialism, racism and tyranny.'

'But, how did Che die?' Avaran asked curiously.

The evening rummy was suspended for the day. He was so happy as his *Lungi* would not be plucked that day.

The attendance of the audience in the twilight was full that evening.

'Che, soon left for a world tour.' Joseph Ivans sounded commanding in the story telling techniques. 'Though he was second in command in Cuban government after Fidel Castro, Che did not enjoy the new white collar aura of the Cuban freedom. He knew that the cake of Cuban freedom was not even half baked. Che felt like a fish out of water among the Cubans. He eventually visited countries like the UAE, Egypt, Thailand, Japan, Indonesia, Pakistan and even India.'

'Wow...!' there was a sensational outburst among the *Twilight Audience at CHE.*

'Yes...', the General resumed, 'I was among the security personnel of VK Krishna Menon, the then Defence Minister. I could see him very close and I even shook hands with him.'

At this, Neelandan suddenly knelt down and grabbing the General's right hand, he kissed it. His eyes were full with tears of an inexplicable emotional outburst.

'He met Prime Minister Nehru!' Joseph Ivans emphatically proceeded, 'and, even a few villagers were met by Che who hugged and garlanded Che. Later, Che wrote in his diary, *Nehru received us with an amiable familiarity of a Patriarchal Grandfather.* Che was only 31 years old at that time and Nehru was 70. It was in 1959. On 10th July, Che visited Calcutta and left for East Pakistan. While Che was in Delhi, journalist KP Bhanumathy interviewed him for *Akashvani*.'

Barber Neelandan looked at everybody to ensure that the General was not targeting him.

'Ms Bhanumathy later commented, *If we ignore his military uniform, heavy boots and Monte Carlo Cigar, his simplicity and politeness was like that of a Holy Priest.* The most famous line in the Che interview was, *The struggle for freedom begins from the hunger of the people.*'

Kunjappan Chettan eyes were shining with an unusual glow for being a proud communist. Neelandan and Broker Thommy wiped their tears and listened to the General with the curiosity of two military trainees listening to their commander.

'In Cuba', Joseph Ivans continued, 'Che was given a number of portfolios like the Industrial Minister and the Chairman of the National Bank. However, Che was not happy with being a bureaucrat, nor was he keen in any designation. His vision was not only liberating Cubans, but first the entire Latin Americans and then the entire population which was oppressed by the capitalists anywhere in the world.

'In April 1965, Che along with 100 guerrilla fighters from Cuba reached Congo with a mission to liberate it from the tyranny of the Imperialist forces which had overthrown the socialist independence hero and Congo's first democratically elected Prime Minister Patrice Lumumba.'

Kunjappan Chettan served free special tea, vadas and *Dinesh beedis* to the *Twilight Audience* to show his joy over Che's gritty rebellion in liberating the Slaves of Imperialism throughout the world. That day no names would enter his Book of Credit.

'The Congolese rebel leader Laurent Kabila's support to Che was not enough to liberate Congo from the capitalists. They only wanted to taste victory without fight and bloodshed. After six months, Che ended his revolutionary mission in Congo by sending the Cuban guerrillas back.'

The *Twilight Audience* at *CHE* was sad. They shook their heads in disappointment.

'Then…where did Che go, grandpa?' asked the little Ivans, 'Cuba?'

'No, Jo…', said the grandfather. 'While in Congo, Che had written a farewell letter to Fidel Castro in Havana which should only be revealed to the public if he got killed in Congo. But, Fidel had already made it to the public. Che had written in that letter that he was snapping all his connections with Cuba for the sake of revolution and liberation of the world from Imperialism. Being a man of great self-respect, Che would not go back!'

People at *CHE* expressed their disbelief by blinking at the General.

'Could Fidel do that…?' Neelandan was angry. 'Why?'

'Yes, Fidel did that, he had to do that!' Major General Ivans sounded double sure. 'There was an element of fear somewhere in the heart of the Castro brothers. They feared that they would lose their popularity and the love of their kindred to an Argentinean, the Doctor who loved guns and bullets more than his stethoscope.'

'Then…?' the *Twilight Audience* chorused.

'Then, as a result of that, Che had to spend the next six months in Dar es Salaam and Prague, and there he prepared himself for Bolivia. As he was doing that, he secretly travelled back to Cuba and paid a short visit to Fidel.'

'Why? He shouldn't have!' Broker Thommy shouted.

'Yes, he shouldn't have.' Naanu Ashan agreed.

'That was Che!' the General proudly said. 'He would never keep any grudge or bitterness in heart for long. Also, he met his wife secretly and wrote his last letter to all his five children to be read to them upon his death. He concluded the letter thus:

> ....*Above all, always be capable of feeling deeply*
> *Any injustice committed against anyone, anywhere in*
> *the world.*
> *This is the most beautiful quality in a Revolutionary.*

'Giving his last hug to his wife, Aleida Guevara March, Che left Cuba for Bolivia. Before leaving for Bolivia, he altered his exterior by shaving off his iconic beard and trimming the long beautiful Guevara hair somewhat shorter to dye it grey to give him the look of the middle aged Uruguayan businessman, Adolfo Mena Gonzales. Earlier, Che was Ramon Benitez in Congo.'

'Smart boy, Che!' Certified by Kadachirakkunnel Iyppachan.

'Yeah, very smart...!' Thadathippara Avaran co-attested.

'Prrrrrrrrrr.............t!'

Broker Thommy opened up his renowned alimentary canal fully balancing his body on his right buttock. Then, he *back*-bugled in agreement. The Broker was well known throughout Udayagiri for his long, trumpet like, wind-breaking.

The *Twilight Audience* laughed and dropped their stomach, holding their nose with one hand, and fanned the sickening foul fragrance away with their shawls and some with their hands.

General Ivans gave a terrible stare to the Broker and there Thommy sat like a scared tortoise.

'Thommy...!' Kunjappan Chettan's ruling came, 'That was really unnecessary and untimely.'

'Sorry.....! I apologise. I will be careful next time.' Broker Thommy stammered.

A huge blob of spittle flew like a shooting star with a trailing end over the *Twilight Audience* from the pan stuffed mouth of Thundi Chacko and fell on the road. And it unfortunately missed Karankal Thankan's nose. Had it not missed his nose, it would have been another fight similar to the *Barber-Broker* fight.

Anyway, they lost out a golden opportunity!

The General paused for a few seconds to get the house in order and to make sure that they were seriously involved in the story. He resumed.

'On 3rd November, 1966, Ernesto Che Guevara secretly arrived at La Paz, Bolivia.'

'Oh, no!' Neelandan expressed his disappointment by shaking his head as if he sensed something ominous was going to happen.

The *Twilight Audience* sat quietly casting their looks at the masculine face the General which was glowing in the amber of the furnace flame and the twilight at *CHE*.

'Che had already prepared the Bolivian soil for the grand reception of the seeds of revolution. His men and his guide Tania, an East German born Argentinean girl had already done their revolutionary homework in Bolivia. But, unfortunately the Bolivian Communist Party, which had requested Che's help to liberate their mother country from Imperialism, betrayed him. He had to face a similar criticality many times in his life and that had made the revolutionary in him stronger. Che now approached the patriotic peasants for their support but they also refused to help him as the Bolivian Government had already begun a very effective propaganda campaign that emphasised on the internationality of the revolutionaries. In fact, they were a group comprised of people from many different countries like Cuba, Argentina, Peru, African Congo, East Germany and so on. There were some Bolivian rebels too in the guerrilla troop.

'Despite the rejection, Che mustered his well-trained guerrilla force comprising 50 men and started their liberation operations as ELN - National Liberation Army of Bolivia. They were well equipped too. Under the able leadership of Che, they scored a number of victories against the clueless Bolivian Army regulars.

'The first half of 1967 brought good luck to Che and his comrades. They won several skirmishes against the native troop in the Spring and Summer of the year. The government became panicky as Che's guerrillas routed all the military efforts of Bolivian soldiers. At this juncture, the government sought the help of the US. The opportunistic CIA presently sent a battalion of American soldiers to fight their most dreaded enemy, Che. Also, they would train the stranded hapless Bolivian Army to learn at least how to retreat without being shot from behind by the guerrillas of Che. The CIA joined their hands with the Bolivian Army in ground operations too against Che.'

General Ivans again paused for a moment and glanced at his grandson. He was more engrossed than the usual *Twilight Audience*. No one moved an inch. All the eyes were on the face of the General...not a leaf quivered, nor did a bird chirp in the bushes. Most of the listeners were now squatting with their elbows supported on their knees. Not an eye would wink nor would they close their mouth...all the jaws were dropped.

Enjoying his current Aesopian Aura, General Ivans asked, 'Where did I stop?'

'The CIA joined hands with the Bolivian Army against Che', chorused the *Twilight Audience*.

'Thus, the Bolivian 2nd Ranger Battalion, trained by the CIA Green Berets and the CIA personnel started their *Operation Che Guevara!* After a month's rigorous search there broke out a skirmish between a squad of Che's Guerrillas and the detachment of the Rangers on the banks of the Masicuri River. Che's column, numbered 22, started returning northwards in search of a safer area.

'After two weeks of a hazardous and exhausting Odyssey through the bleak mountain ranges of the Andes, the column of Che halted in the village of Alto Seco. They were malnutritioned, starved, thirsty, barefooted and had only six blankets for 22 men. There, in the village school, Che appealed to the local people for support, in a public meeting, to liberate Bolivia. Almost at the same time, a local informer betrayed their presence to the nearby garrison of Vallegrande. Sensing the danger, Che's super brain ordered his comrades to quickly evacuate the place. With the Army in their tail, the guerrilla vanguard was ambushed near La Higuera on 26th September. Three of them were shot dead. And now only 19 remained. Out of that one was fatally wounded and another seriously ill. On 28th September, the joint Army captured two deserters from Che's column. One of them was a cook of the troop. They were reduced to 17.'

At *CHE*, the *Twilight Audience* had forgotten even to draw their breath. Neelandan was now kneeling before the General as all others bit their nails wrecking their nerves. It seemed that the air was now explosive. The entire scene at *CHE* would have looked like a modern *Sermon on the Mount* for any distant onlooker. But, the content of *this* sermon was of a different colour.

'As the cook was captured and executed by the Rangers, Che and his loyal comrades had to starve almost every day. In addition to this, Che's childhood friend, Asthma, started revisiting him frequently. He became very weak and the mosquito bites gave him painful swellings on his body.'

It seemed that the *Twilight Audience* had swallowed up their tongues to the abysmal depths of their stomachs.

'In the first week of October, Che and his impoverished comrades took shelter in the dreadful Yuro Ravine of the Andes near La Higuera. On 7ᵗʰ October, an informant apprised the Bolivian Rangers of the location of Che's encampment. On Sunday, 8ᵗʰ October, they encircled the entire area with a battalion of 1800 troopers against only 17 weaklings of Che's poor army. Still, a dreadful battle broke out between the stranded 17 and the ill-disposed 1800. Che and his companions fought bravely with the Rangers and the hell-hounds of the CIA, to escape from the Ravine. Willy, Che's Bolivian comrade, was leading the centre group of Che to cover the already sick and terribly exhausted Che. They tried to break out of the CIA-Rangers cordon. Willy was just at the point of clearing the steep wall of the Ravine when Che, following Willy at a small distance, got suddenly shot in his leg and fell.'

'Oh... Che...why did you get shot?' the *Twilight Audience* lamented.

'Willy could have escaped, but he would not. He remembered how Che had covered him and his comrades on several occasions when they were about to be killed by the enemies. Che had great love and respect for the Christ and he always believed in **John 15:13...**

No one can have greater love than to lay down his own life for his brothers!

'Willy turned around and sprinted back down the cliff where Che lay wounded. He suddenly carried Che on his shoulders out of the direct line of firing. Che, though he was injured and lying on Willy's shoulders, fired his rifle at the Ranger who was pointing his gun at Willy, thereby blew up the head of the Ranger to pieces.

'Willy brought the bleeding Che to a small covert where, he thought, he would hide Che and go to the warfront. However, they were soon spotted and surrounded by another group of Rangers who opened fire at them. Che and Willy, shot back at them till one bullet knocked off Che's endeared beret and another incapacitated his trusted M-2 Carbine. Willy placed himself between the Rangers and Che and moved his comrade out of the fire again. Covering Che, Willy exchanged fire with their enemies, but as they got exposed, Willy was almost instantly struck down by a shell shower from the machine guns of the Rangers. Willy fell on Che still covering him.'

Joseph Ivans saw all the Twilight eyes overflowing with the passionate drops of helplessness which made the famed General's mettle also melt. He also broke down.

'At this', the General resumed after clearing his throat and wiping his eyes, 'a few Rangers rushed towards them demanding their surrender. Willy, though wounded, seeing them approaching Che with their guns shouted, *This is Commandante Guevara. Show him respect.* Che slowly got up with the usual smile on his face. In spite of those sufferings, Che was cool. The Rangers were afraid and hesitated to come near him. They did not know how to approach him.

Knowing this, he lifted both his hands and offered him to be bound and taken.'

At *CHE*, the *Twilight Audience* was enshrouded in gloom and bitterness. No one uttered anything, but looked down with disappointment and distress.

'By 4 pm, they left the canyon for the nearby village. Che was carried by four Bolivians. He was stretched out on a blanket while the wounded Willy and El Chino were forced to walk all the 7 kilometres. Che, Willy and El Chino were taken, tied up and beaten up brutally. The cruel Rangers brought them to the village of La Higuera by 7 pm, where they got them locked up in separate rooms. For, it was said, there was no person more feared by the CIA than Che as he had the capacity and charisma necessary to direct a struggle against any form of repression of the traditional hierarchies in power. The village school where they were locked up had 2 classrooms and 1 office room. It stood on a small hill which lies at an approximate height of 2000 meters above sea-level. Che was held in the middle room.

'The soldiers of the Bolivian Army were forced by the watchdogs of Imperialism to hit Che everywhere on his body. He would receive every blow with a stony look at his persecutors. Che could at the same time, hear the terrible cries of already dying Willy and El Chino from the flanks when beaten up and hit with the rifle butts on being questioned. But, Che would never utter a word. He would only look at the broken walls of the room with a broken heart through his glassy glance on receiving the brutal blows with the butts after removing the recoil-pad.'

The *Twilight Audience* at *CHE* was now weeping. All of them sat down on the mud baked ground with their tear torn eyes still cast on General Ivans. His language and the story had attained the perfect blend of a sublime style which would keep even the most unproductive audience engaged and engrossed.

'The CIA would not allow anyone to enter the lockups, nor would they provide any food or drink to those noble revolutionaries. No sound was heard from the rooms of his comrades by Che. *They are either dead or unconscious,* Che thought. Che's right leg was severely wounded and one bullet had even scooped the entire flesh of its calf. It is said that Che at a time told one of the Bolivian soldiers, *I am thirsty!* None of them would give him even some bitter beer to quench Che's thirst who had even forgotten when he had had his *Last Supper*. Without his beret, in his long beard and thick matted hair, he resembled *Jesus of Nazareth*.

'*Was Che The Lord's Second Coming?*' Major General Joseph Ivans paused and took a long breath.

'Yes,' Broker Thommy shouted, and all others nodded in agreement.

'Che was in confinement with Willy and El Chino in rooms on either side: *a symbolic representation of Mount Calvary.*

'Throughout that night, the CIA and the Rangers were drinking and dancing around a fire celebrating Che's captivity. They thought that revolution would die along with Che. They even discussed who would keep which of his beloved personal belongings as mementos after his death.

'Felix Rodrigues, the CIA commander of Che-search-party, insisted that he wanted only Che's Rolex watch as a souvenir; another demanded his pipe for his memory; a third one was interested in his diary-memoir. A Bolivian had already grabbed his legendary beret and another, his beloved M-2 Carbine from the Yuro Ravine itself. As many of them wanted Che's renowned olive green uniform, it is said that they decided to throw dice for it.

'The repetition of a page from *The Calvary Chronicles* – enacted 2000 years ago!'

No one at *CHE* said anything: their tormented souls would not generate any response except for an awe-inspired glance at General Ivans' face.

'Dr Ernesto Che Guevara did not have anything else other than those poor effects left with him to boast of. Che was lying all this while in the dark classroom on the ground. His limbs were bleeding and tied up. Just then, a legion of Bolivian red ants invaded Che through the dark night. The smell of fresh blood could not be resisted by those dreadful little monsters. The attack was so painful that Che wanted to cry out. They bit his wounds and spewed their acid on the ruddy mouths of the cuts, which burned the raw flesh of Che. But, Che would not cry...! *I am Che Guevara... I cannot cry and should not.* He groaned through his teeth biting his wrists which were tied up. Che closed his eyes and shut his mouth to protect them and resist the fiery acid attack of those Bolivian dragons.'

The *Twilight Audience* looked like mourners of their brother who has just breathed his last before their eyes.

'There lay the greatest revolutionary-philanthropist of the world, after the Christ, in a dark classroom of the village school of La Higuera. He longed for sleep that had left him ever since he embraced Marxism.'

The *Twilight Audience* had already mounted the portrait of Che in their hearts somewhere close to the portrait of their Lord Jesus. Che had already attained immortality before his death. Even Neelandan and his Hindu brothers present there accepted Che as another saviour of the oppressed of the world. None of them present there would take their bleeding eyes from General Ivans' face.

'It was 3 o'clock in the morning. Revolutionary Che lay there unable to resist even the bite of an insect. The pathetic plight of the greatest revolutionary made him open his eyes. Che started mumbling something which was not very clear. He was drunk with pain; so drunk that the Bolivian dragon and the Ranger-shells could no more cut through his benumbed senses. Hunger and thirst lulled him with their softest hands and took him to the land of the benevolent slumber.

'Che tried mumbling something in pain.

'Suddenly, Che felt a stream of tender light filling in the room through the roof-rents which was accompanied by a celestial melody floating in the air and flowing slowly down towards him. Che opened his eyes in sleep and raised them to look about him.

'He saw the winding pavements and the foggy daybreaks, the sunny mornings, the warm rooms and the crimson evenings of an Argentinean village, Alta Gracia. Che went into a small house where he saw his father Ernesto and mother Celia engaged unusually in a cordial debate on their children's future. His Mama took him to the Parish Church and there they knelt before the altar and the Crucifix above it suddenly started bleeding through the real stigmata. Young Che ran out of the Church frightened, and watched the natives playing chess on the lush green of the Pampas where his first school, Colegio San Martin, stood. He saw the stream Chicamtoltina flowing busily down to Rio de Anisacate with a romantic warble as usual.

'Che came down from Alta Gracia to his Cordoba Dean Funes College for his graduation. He joined his friends for a rugby match on the banks of Rio Primero. Then, Che went to Buenos Aires to his grandmother where he joined the University for Medicine. Che continued his quest of experiencing the life of the poor through his *world famous tour*. In the process, he motor-biked and hitchhiked with his intimate friend Alberto Granado; went to Chile and with a burning heart watched the deplorable plight of the miners of Chuquicamata copper mine; sharpened his revolutionary intent and formulated his ideas of unconditional war against human exploitation while stopping at the historic *Machu Picchu*. At Machu Picchu, Che planned his future revolution after watching the destroyed Inca Civilization.

'Che wept for the lepers at San Pablo, on the other side of the Peruvian Amazon. He remembered experiencing the love of lepers. He saw the nuns and the doctors who worked for the lepers as a part of the ritualistic life; not their service. River Amazon stretched between the lepers and their comforters like a hungry anaconda. The comforters stayed on the other bank as they obviously feared the dreadful malady more than the trial of the *Last Judgement.*

'Che remembered himself diving into the flooded river from the doctor's quarters at a rainy night and swimming across it defying the mighty waves, the aquatic carnivores and his childhood friend Asthma. On reaching the other side after crossing 4 km of the Amazon width, he was received by the hapless leper victims with shouts of joy and warmth. There, Che did not even hesitate holding the decomposed, distorted and decayed limbs of the lepers who were abandoned even by Death. *Even Death had serious inhibitions as to when to claim the lepers of San Pablo: so disgusting, sickening and nasty were their physical and living conditions,* said Dr Hugo Pesce – the militant doctor at Lima to Che and his friend earlier. Dr Pesce, also a leading leprosy researcher and Marxist, was instrumental for Che to read Marx for the first time in his life. Thus, Che discovered that there was a flame of revolution burning in him: an emphatic and empathetic flame for the poor and the oppressed.

'The Amazon strip between the lepers and their so-called comforters lay as a symbol between the haves and the have-nots: the gulf between the rich and the poor. The nuns and the doctors would not go near the lepers without gloves, mask and the other medical attires. Against the advice of even Granado, Che would go to them always without a glove and the other medical guards. He would sit with them; wash their open sores; remove the puddles of pus; medicate them and bandage them. After that he would feed them with his beautiful smile on his Christ like face which would force the lepers to see their *Saviour* in him. At times, Che would even sleep beside them in the leper shacks. He could not see sufferings of humans in any form.'

'Yes, that's true!' Kunjappan Chettan sent out his consent.

'Now, Che and Granado had to move from San Pablo. It was too difficult for Che to break his *Samaritan Bond* with the lepers. They even raised a small fund for Che donating all their poor savings, to reward Che's incomparable spirit of Christ and charity. Throughout the previous night of their departure, the lepers sang and danced for Che and his friend and gifted Mambo Tango – the raft for them to leave for Leticia. One of the singers had no eyes. He shouted at the end of each song, *I sing for my Jesus, I can see Him sitting before me!* The accordionist's right hand had no fingers: all of them had decayed and fallen off! He tied some sticks to his wrist and played the instrument for Che. Che wept for them and hugged all of them without any fear of getting infected. They then started down-stream, before the daybreak, on the flood of Amazon, with another flood in their eyes, and reached Leticia.

'On reaching back Buenos Aires via Columbia and Venezuela, Che was totally transformed to be a Good Samaritan! The philanthrope in Che experienced the biggest emotional vacuum in his life ever and thus a trouble ridden Che decided to pursue his medical degree with a recharged passion. In 1953, Che was ordained Doctor Ernesto Guevara.

'Dr Guevara reached Guatemala on the eve of the Christmas in 1953, travelling through Chile, Bolivia, Peru, Ecuador, Columbia, Costa Rica and Nicaragua. It was in Guatemala where Dr Ernesto Guevara was given *Che,* the nickname. In Guatemala, Che witnessed the cruelest and the darkest face of Imperialism: he was made to witness the heartless exploitation of the helpless Mayan population by the United Fruit Company run by the US. The liberal Jacobo Arbenz government was overthrown in 1954 by the CIA supported military junta and for supporting the Mayans, Che entered in the CIA hit-list and thus, had to take asylum in the Argentine Embassy. It was there, Che got committed ideologically to Marx.

'Refusing repatriation, Che reached Mexico and there met Raul and Fidel. He witnessed their journey to Cuba, their struggle to liberate Cuba and his triumphant entry into the City of Havana in 1959.

'He went to Congo and finally to Prague!

'Che then met Hilda Gadea, back in Havana, his first wife and Hilda his first daughter. They still adored him for what he was. He, then, visited his second wife Aleida Guevara March and their four children: Aleida, Camilo, Celia and Ernesto. All waved their hands at him and were happy for him.

'Che soon left for La Paz, leaving all the bureaucratic comforts, to fight for the natives and liberate the entire Latin America thus to form the Unites States of South America. On reaching La Paz, Che did not get the support from the natives. He looked at the first guerrilla encampment at Naeahuazu Gorges and being betrayed by the locals, he moved towards Rio Grande and crossed it in search of a safer place. He received news that, Tania and 7 others were caught and brutally killed. Finally he remembered reaching the Yuro Ravine and the last battle and being taken. El Chino, Che and Willy were only three of the many brave red stars of revolution. They would bleed till the last drop for the sake of the poor and the oppressed: violently passionate and empathetic.

'Suddenly, Che felt the presence of another person in the La Higuera lockup. It was none of the Rangers. He opened his eyes to see a glorious form in the middle of a beam of soft light. It was the most fantastic and fabulous spectacle Che had ever seen in his 39 years of life. It was the most striking manifestation of divinity.

'The figure turned its face towards Che. He was frightened and shocked. The figure had an identical face that of Che. The face was brighter than lightning and the robe brighter than snow.

'*El Cristo...!* Che whispered and closed his eyes in fear and disbelief. When Che opened his eyes, he saw Jesus sitting beside him and fear gripped him firmly for the first time in his life.

'*Che...!* Jesus called him. His voice was both the manliest and the sweetest Che had ever heard. It resounded like a thunder in his ears. Che's eyes overflowed with joy and *hope.*

'*Cristo, mi Cristo...!* Che cried.

'*My Che, my child, don't weep...!* Jesus said and he raised his right hand and placed it on Che's stress-ripped forehead.

'It was the softest and coolest touch Che had ever known. He saw the Saviour's Holy Wounds in His palm, still fresh and bleeding.

'*Por qué mi has abandonado?* Che wept.

'*I haven't, Che!* Jesus said with a sea of compassion in his eyes. No human can ever measure its depth.

'*I was always with you, Che; but, you couldn't see me as you were blindfolded. I was waiting for you to call me. I came to you the very moment you called me. It was 3 in the morning when you mumbled….. Cristo….mi Cristo, and I was here. I unbound you from the fetters and taking you on my shoulders we set out on a short journey in which I showed you the path you walked along.*

'*Por qué hiciste eso mi Cristo?* Che whispered.

'*I did that because I wanted to show the way you had trodden all these 39 years. It is crimson with human blood that you have shed along with your comrades. Unpardonable, Che...! It's totally unacceptable to my heavenly Father...!* Jesus said.

'Che could not utter anything. He was full of guilt and remorse.

'*Why did you throw your stethoscope and pick up a gun, Che?* Jesus said.

'*There was no other way in front of me, my Lord. The world was infested with injustice and wickedness; exploitation and villainy; hypocrisy and nepotism; hatred and bias! What else could have I done, my Lord?* Che retorted. The revolutionary in him suddenly woke up.

'*But, you shouldn't have taken arms in your arms!* Jesus said.

'*My Lord, if you can pardon me, let me tell you something?*

'*Yes, my son!*

'*Lord,* Che said. *I remember an episode where you also lost your cool and chased those vendors out of the Church with your whip. Even, you couldn't bear with those unjust manipulators and their injustice. Then, what about this mortal, purely of blood and flesh?*

'Jesus smiled! Che could see the Heavenly peace in His face and feel the honeyed air of His speech. It was infinitely cooler than the breeze of the Alta Gracian Pampas.

'*Yes my son, but I didn't take anyone's life, nor did I hurt anyone. I was acting as my Father ordered me to do so. Under whose order did you massacre those innocent people in Cuba, my son?*

'Che was tongue-tied. There was no answer to that query in his revolutionary kitty.

'*Don't hesitate, my son. I know what you are thinking. You were going to tell me that you killed those innocent people under the order of your conscience.* Jesus mind-read Che.

'Che felt ashamed and embarrassed. *My Lord, I killed them because no peaceful means would work out in solving the problem. In Turkey, France, China, Russia and in Cuba, tens of thousands of innocent people were butchered by the Imperialistic dictators! I had no other way before me than the bloody path.*

'*Che, it's not mandatory that you should be like those blood thirsty power mongers. Greatness is not in facing the tyrants with tyranny but with love and compassion.*

'*Would it have worked out my Lord?*

'*Yes, my Che, haven't you heard of Buddha, Muhammad, Gandhi, Mandela, Cesar Chewas, Lincoln and Martin Luther of America? They had won the struggle with a heart to struggle, showing love and compassion resulting in non-violence. Non-violence is a weapon more powerful than all your guns and grenades and tanks and bombs. It would shake the very foundation of tyranny and oppression and any form of abuse. Explosives may destroy a few concrete towers and take few more innocent lives but love will cause no damage. It can conquer the malicious hearts that promote evil, hatred, terrorism and blood-bath. Though love cannot control the deadly weapons, it can control the hand which holds them.*'

The *Twilight Audience* at *CHE* even forgot that they had their families waiting for them to return for their evening prayers and dinner. They would not go.

Joseph Ivans was reliving the life of two greatest revolutionaries in the world.

'Che, raised his eyes to see Jesus in the middle of a halo. The light was still soft and soothing. He could feel the presence of so many celestial beings whom mortals called Angels. However, Che was still lying in darkness. His gaze was clogged by the brilliance of the Lord's face.

'*But, I was just following Marx, mi Cristo. I am a communist.* Che said timidly.

'*Who was Marx and what is communism?* The Lord said.

Marx was a humanitarian and communism is radical socialism. Che tried to explain.

'*True! But, Marx was a true campaigner of what I have taught the world; and communism is nothing but a compilation of my teachings. Marx was never against me or religion; he was against the practitioners of evil in religion like opium eaters of the society. I have chastised them more harshly and compared them to a brood of viper and whitewashed tombs. Basically, all the Christians are Communists and Communists are Christians. Both are selfless, guiltless and fearless. There should be true Communists in the world. They are the custodians of goodness and apostles of peace: the true Communists are those who are the comrades of labourers and who are heavily* laden with worries. I know that anyone who lives in comfort shall necessarily be cold-hearted, self-centred and naturally unwelcoming; and thus morally disgusting, spiritually half-baked and emotionally vacant!

'Ernesto Che Guevara opened his eyes now fully for the first time. He looked at the Saviour of the world with a pair of astonished eyes.

'*Tell me about a greater communist than I am and show me a sterner revolutionary than this Christ!* Jesus said pointing at his own chest.

'Che lowered his eyes in shame.

'*Mi Señor, mi Dios.*

'*But, my resolve was always ushered by pure love and compassion.*

'Che dropped his eyes in total submission.

'*You forgot or rather did not want to put your sword back into its sheath; for all they who draw it shall perish by the same.* Jesus said with the self-same divine smile on His face.

'*Lo Siento, mi Jesus!* Che cried like a child.

'*Since you feel sorry, the Heavens are happy….my Father has heard you calling me and your redemption will not be delayed.* Jesus said.

'*Garcias, mi Seňor!* Che wept hiding his face in the palms of his tied up hands. *Now, will your Lordship allow me to visit my family for the last time to tell them that I have met you?*

'*But, it is too late for you Che. I will tell my Angels to do that.* The Lord said. *My Father has sent me to you only for one reason. When we walked your life again, we halted at San Pablo for a longer period of time. Do you know, why?*

'*Por ello, mi Dios?*

'*Because, you were serving me when you served those hapless lepers. You relived the life of the Good Samaritan which is almost extinct in this world. You were full of love and compassion: more Christian than those ritualistic nuns who lived on the other side of Amazon for fear of the malady. That is the only reason my Father sent me here to you, to this place which has the name of La Higuera – the fig tree whom I cursed one day for not giving any yield to anyone. You have been brought here by Satan and he has thrown you to your enemies and abandoned you. But, my Father will not forsake you and, thus, I am here with you now.*

'*What should I do now, my Jesus?* A crestfallen Che asked The Lord.

'*You wait here. My Father will soon send my Helper to you from Heaven: The Holy Ghost! He will come and command you what to do. I can assure you of one thing that the world will chant your name since today for being a friend of the poor and the oppressed. All those who tortured you here would pay heavily for that.*

'El Salvador kissed Che's forehead. Closing his eyes in Holy fear, Che heard the Angel sing, *Hallelujah!*

'Eso es suficiente para mi, mi Seňor! My Lord, that's enough for me!

'Che kept weeping by closing his eyes and folding his hands before The Saviour. The light dimmed out, the Angels vanished and The Saviour was seen nowhere.

'The greatest revolutionary's retribution was now complete!'

14

The *Twilight Audience at CHE*, now demanded a break. They wanted to sit quiet for some time and weep alone for Dr Ernesto Che Guevara who voluntarily chose to be a revolutionary and thus, embrace death willingly.

At *CHE*, time was creeping like a snail. They did not know how long they sat wrapped up in silence. After a while, Kunjappan Chettan broke the silence.

'We are all blessed to have heard of Che, the Second Christ who was second only to the Christ!'

The little Ivans looking at the face of everybody could not hold his tears back. Major General Joseph Ivans laid his hands on his grandson's tender shoulders and consoled him.

'Take the child back home, please sir.' Naanu Ashan suggested. 'It seems that he's overwhelmed by Che's suffering and remorse. This story is not for children.'

'No, I won't go. I want to hear it fully.' Jose Ivans insisted.

'Okay, we will go home together.' Joseph Ivans maintained.

'After the retribution, what happened?' Parayankuzhiyil Joy inquired.

'After that, Che experienced a divine peace in him. He felt as if icicles were hanging inside his tormented heart. A heavy weight was lifted from his already warped conscience.

'He opened his eyes to see his Saviour for one last time; but nobody was there before him to see, except for the yawning darkness.

'As Che was still wondering at the awe-inspiring spectacle, suddenly a flash of lightning lit up the entire village of La Higuera which was accompanied by a deafening peal of thunder. It was 5 in the morning. The Rangers, sleeping after being drunk, screamed like devils and ran down the hill ripping a thick spread of darkness. Still shrieking and running as if evil spirits being chased by a sorcerer, the steaming Rangers bumped into the wayside trees and boulders of huge rocks and rolled down the hill.

'Back in the school building a splendid celestial occurrence was being staged. It was terrific in nature and superlative in its kind. Through the rents of its roof there descended a multitude of blazing tongues of fire and settled on Che, who lay on the floor vacant and drained out. The roar of the tongues was like a rumble of a tremor and the blast of a violent storm. The villagers of La Higuera ran out of their huts to save themselves from an earthquake, but what they saw on the hilltop was something more shocking and frightening. The school building, where Che and his comrades were confined to, was on a celestial fire. They later said that they even saw divine apparitions guarding the school building with blazing blades. There followed a cloudburst which was held only on the hilltop, and then the spectacle vanished.'

The *Twilight Audience* sat there not knowing what to say.

'After the shower, Che slept peacefully.' The story teller resumed. 'No Bolivian dragons were there to disturb him anymore.

'Mother Sleep visited him on his lowly couch for the first time since he left Havana.

'Che was woken up by the drone of a flying machine. It was 7 in the morning. A few military personnel flew in from Santa Cruz with a warrant of the Bolivian President, General Rene Barrientos, that Che should be executed with immediate effect.'

'Oh...! No...,' Barber Neelandan and Broker Thommy shouted in negation.

'But, who would perform such a heinous act?' The General soliloquised.

'None... None would do that...' all of the *Twilight Audience* chorused.

'None of the local soldiers who ran down the hill early in the morning would come back to the village school for fear of life.' Joseph Ivans reiterated.

'The sun clock ticked on. It was 8.30 am. Che expected somebody from the force to come to him. He saw through a slit in the door a few strange soldiers passing by his room. Upon shouting one of them hesitantly approached his room. Che saw that the soldier's face was tormented by terrible war fatigue and fear.

'I want to meet the school teacher for a minute! Che shouted.

'The soldier disappeared without any utterance. At 9 am, Che's door was pushed open by four armed soldiers and from the side there appeared a young lady of 22 years: Julia Cortez, the school teacher. She was as frightened as a rabbit.

'Don't be afraid, come in! I respect teachers...for they are enlightened and most respected by revolutionaries! Che said it with a placid shade of respect on his face.

'Ms Cortez came in.

'I am sorry...there isn't anything here for you to sit! Che said.

'In fact, it's I who's to be sorry. This is my school and there isn't anything for you to sit. Throughout the night you might have been....! She mumbled with fear and embarrassment.

'It's okay, Madam! I wanted to see you to tell you about the pathetic condition of this school, your students and the teachers. It's anti-pedagogical! It should change...the world should change. The bureaucrats and the rich are basking in luxury and comfort. They are rolling on Rolls-Royce and Benz cars. It's common everywhere in the world. They are very few however

they decide the fate of the majority – the poor and the needy. They attain this by instilling fear and exercising force on them. It's possible to change this sickening plight of the unprivileged if the teachers of the world can give the children of the exploited a maternal nudge thereby kindling a little flame of an intellectual revolution. It shall one day burn down the entire vault of the pride and the prejudice of the boastful aristocracy! That's all Madam. Goodbye!

'Julia Cortez could not face the fiery eyes of the greatest revolutionary among humans. His gaze was overwhelming, piercing and tranquil. His face reminded her of *El Salvador*! She left the room ashamed, embarrassed, tongue-tied and terrified. Che's short speech sounded almost like *Christ's Sermon on the Mount* to her ears. *The world should change. The teachers should ignite the students for a better tomorrow. The flame that Che just kindled in me should be kept alive forever.* Ms Cortez thought to herself and left him excited and content.'

At *CHE* everyone took a deep long breath, but did not speak anything.

'A few minutes later, Che heard a loud ruckus from outside his lockup. It was on *who would take Che's life*. No one was ready!

'Lt. Peres, who was about to carry out the execution, even refused to enter the school building. Seeing all this, Che smiled from his room. Peres forced Sergeant Huanca, one of the Rangers, to shoot Che down. At this, Huanca picked up his rifle and walked steadily. But, he went straight to

Willy's lockup and opened the door. Willy was lying on the mud floor with his limbs bound. The sleeplessness of the entire night hung on his eyelids. Huanca rifle-butted Willy at which he opened his eyes fully, and managed to squat on the ground with a groan.

'*You are going to be killed!* Huanca grinned at Willy.

'*Do it, you traitor...*, Willy shouted.

'Upon this, Huanca's rifle reported several times.

'*I am happy to die next to Che!* Willy shouted and then fell on his face with his knees firmly rooted on the ground.

Joseph Ivans watched the *Twilight Audience* wiping their eyes.

'Che hearing Willy's shout, felt proud of his friend and knew that his own life was not a waste. Murderer Huanca came out of Willy's lockup and walked straight. All decided that he was going to kill Che. However, crossing Che's room, he went to El Chino's room where the Peruvian revolutionary received his murderer with the famed scorn on his face.

'*If your toy has anymore pellets, don't waste my time,* before Huanca could say anything, El Chino demanded. *Willy is waiting for me above. Make it fast!* He shouted pointing at the sky.

'The Sergeant was shocked. He had never seen such brave-hearts ever before. Though his hands shivered on the trigger, yet his rifle spat out fire. El Chino fell on the ground shouting *I don't regret dying as Che is still alive!*

'Huanca, the killer came out exhausted and sweating. He felt guilty and dejected. He sat on a boulder, outside the school building, with his rifle still fuming.

'Che hopefully looked at the door of his room for his murderer to come, but no one came. He remembered the heavenly occurrence of the morning. The tongues of fire must have descended on Willy and El Chino too.

'There were unwarranted persuasion, plea and even pressure on the soldiers in order to motivate someone to kill Che, but no one would go into his room. Finally, Mario Terran, a 31 year old Bolivian Ranger, who was notoriously alcoholic, volunteered and came forward for the assassination. His reason was nothing but Che's guerrillas had killed, in an encounter, three of his fellow soldiers who also had their first name *Mario*.

'Suddenly, the door of Che's cell was pushed open and then there appeared Felix Rodriguez, the Cuban turned CIA chief of *Operation Che Guevara* squad. He told Che, with great respect and regret, that he was going to be killed shortly.

'Che appeared to be astonishingly calm.

'*What do you think about your immortality after death?* Rodriguez asked.

'*I am not thinking about my immortality, instead, I am thinking about the immortality of Revolution!* Che replied.

'Rodriguez hugged Che and took his leave.

'After a few minutes, Mario Terran entered the room with his rifle in one hand and a beer bottle in the other. He was heavily drunk. If Che wanted, he could easily overpower Terran though his limbs were tied up. But, Che would not do that. He looked at Terran peacefully, standing on the floor.

'*I know why you have come. Do it!* Che said.

'*Kneel down!* Terran's tongue was loose and not clear.

'*Better to die standing than live on knees!* Che shouted.

'*Kneel down!* Terran screamed.

'*Cool down, point well and shoot! Man can be destroyed; not defeated!* Che said reminiscing his friend Hemingway.

'At this, Terran pointed his rifle at Che and put his finger on its trigger. Terran hesitated...with his hands shivering and body sweating.

'Terran contemplated...!

'Seeing Terran's reluctance, Che thundered...

'*Shoot me you coward! You are killing only a man called Che Guevara. Not Revolution...! S...h...o...o...t...!*

'Upon this Terran opened fire as if in a dream, hitting Che in the legs and the hands.

'*Long live Revolution...!* Che shouted and fell writhing in pain.

'Oh...! What a fall, my comrades...!' General Ivans looked at the *Twilight Audience*.

They had neither a reply to give nor tears to shed.

All of them sat there as if they had lost someone so dear in their family. Who would console them? The General held his grandson close to him and resumed.

'Che dug his teeth deeper into his wrist, lest he should cry!

'Terran then fired several times. Receiving each bullet, Che whispered, *mi Señor, mi Dios.* The final shot went through Che's throat ripping his pharynx.'

No one of the *Twilight Audience* at *CHE* uttered anything nor did they look at each other. All of them left the tea shop pregnant with multiple questions. They went away as if leaving a Churchyard after the funeral of the most beloved member of their family.

They heard the steady roar of the military Willys climbing the hill towards *CHE*. Philip was coming to pick the General and his grandson.

It was midnight!

15

Jose Ivans woke up from a trance hearing the big bang on the door of the library. He was still lying supine on the sofa with the Bible hugged tight to his heart.

He could not, for an instant, call himself back to his surroundings as he was in Udayagiri for long. The Che Guevara hangover still lingered in the library.

The emotional precipitation of the unusual reverie still settled on his eyelids.

The lizard was nowhere to be spotted.

Suddenly, Jose Ivans remembered the bizarre incident that befell his family that morning: Katherine's rift and her retreat; Dr Solomon Samuels' advocacy for his daughter. Janet's pathetic looks and childhood distress flashed on his mind.

'Poor child...my Jan...!'

Ivans jumped out of the sofa. He kept the Bible on the table and gasped.

'What was that bang that woke me up?' he wondered wiping the big drops of sweat from his brows with his right hand.

Once again there were a series of loud eruptions of hammering on the door.

Jose Ivans looked at the huge clock hanging on the wall: 5 pm! Eight hours of resignation from this inflicted world of disillusionment…..!

The solitary cabin of his inner-self had been occupied by a few pure guileless souls for eight hours. He enjoyed the company of his Mama and Grandpa along with the innocent country folk at *CHE*: a self-imposed exile of eight glorious hours!

The commotion outside the room made him open the door with a sort of solid disdain on his face and alacrity in his heart.

Jose Ivans saw an unexpected crowd in front of him. There stood Madam Shiela, Krishnan Potti, Venkat, James and Durwan Ashok. Behind them stood Rose carrying Janet with Juan standing beside her.

'What happened to you, Ivans?' Madam Shiela said with love and authority in her voice. 'We have been trying to trace you out the entire day. But, you were traceless!'

'Ma'am, I….!' he did not know what to speak. How could they understand his disposition?

'No, don't try to explain anything in your HR terminology.' Madam Shiela said in her jovial way without shedding the gravity of the situation.

'The entire Electronics India was trying to get you connected, Sir', Krishnan Potti said in an official tone.

'Why didn't you receive our calls, Jo?' Rose could not hold back her eagerness. 'Where is your phone? It was ringing, but no response!'

'We called you many times.' Madam Shiela said. 'As there was no response, I tried to connect Katherine. There was no response from her too. At the end, I spoke to Ashok over the landline and thus we came to know all by three in the evening, that… you were at home. I went to Katherine, collected Janet and came here.'

Jose Ivans opened his mobile screen lock to see, to his surprise, hundreds of missed calls from several company heads as well as colleagues. He cast down his eyes in embarrassment and shame.

'Daddy,' Janet sobbed in Rose's hands, 'I also called you many times!'

He snatched his daughter from Rose and kissed on her bruised cheeks which were blue with slap-marks. Though Janet kept weeping, yet she felt safe and snug in her Daddy's arms.

'Mama slapped me with both her hands...here and here!' Janet pointed at her cheeks and broke down.

Ivans was clueless as to how he would console her.

He hugged her again and kissed on her lush black tresses.

Janet hid her little face in his heart and wept.

'Don't cry my Jan, my dearest child.' Ivans gasped in grief and agony.

'Excuse me!' Ivans stepped out of the library.

Rose took Janet from Ivans clasp and made her lie on her maternal bosom.

They went to Janet's room with Juan.

Potti walked with Ivans to the parlour following Shiela Khanna.

She sat on the grand Chesterfield Sofa.

'Everything is royal about *The Abode*, but it was never a home. A house is made up of mere bricks whereas a home is made up of pure hearts.' Ivans thought. 'It could never be a home.'

Venkat and James went out with Ashok for a stroll in the garden.

Potti sat on the window couch and looked at the beautifully displayed orchids in the garden. It stretched endlessly from everywhere to everywhere around *The Abode*!

Madam Shiela Khanna instructed Ivans to sit facing her as he was reluctant to sit before her.

Taking his seat, Ivans looked at her with his woebegone eyes.

He could hear a billowy clamour raising somewhere deeper in her heart. Her dark eyes were like two dark windows that opened to a sea of sorrows.

Ivans looked outside through the window. He saw a solitary evening bird flying eastward. 'Poor bird!' he thought. 'It's either lost its way or expelled from the flock. However, it should still fly till the wings carry it; till its lively body grows heavier for those beautifully stretched out wings; till it can defy the law of gravity; till it falls to the kindly earth. Mother Earth is the mother of all mothers, all forgiving and all consuming. The bird is not afraid of anything: the weak trees and their twigs, inclement weather, prowling carnivores or the attack from its own kindred, because it doesn't believe in anything else but only on its own wings.'

'Ivans, I know what you are thinking about.' Shiela Khanna said.

Ivans gave her a melancholy look on returning from his *Never Never-land*.

'Life is to be lived, Ivans.' Madam Shiela added. 'If we don't live our life, it's just like a candle unlit, kept in the darkness. Living life is like a lit candle. It will burn and diminish slowly giving light to those who grope by thus fulfilling its purpose.'

'If so, my life is lit at both the ends, Madam.' Ivans said looking at the western horizon. 'It's wastefully burning out at a quick pace towards nothingness.'

'Whatever it is,' Potti added. 'It's a beautiful thing! If a candle is lit at both the ends, it's prettier, brighter and more useful, though less usable.'

'Though shorter and painful', added Madam Shiela with a smile.

'Look at the shooting stars, Madam', Potti philosophised. 'Though it's shorter than even a candle, it lights up the entire horizon, adorns the sky and enlightens the vision of fools like me.'

Ivans gave Potti a strange look and a cold smile. He looked out at the late blooms of chrysanthemums near the fish pond: a symbol of the purity of intentions.

'What's this, Jo? Go and get ready... Jan and Juan want to go to beach now.' Rose said, in respectful authority, approaching them.

She carried a tray in her beautiful hands and was followed by two cute cherubs – the baby angels – Jan and Juan.

'How many times I had dreamed of a family like this', Ivans thought, 'a happy one! Only a woman can be a homemaker; not a man. She can be a home breaker too; not a man. That's where Katherine succeeded. Is the entry of Rose to the parlour a symbolic preview of what is going to be later?'

Rose covered the teapoy tastefully with tea and biscuits. The aroma of lemongrass floated in the air when she poured out the steaming green tea into the exquisite cups of Chinese porcelain. She offered the first cup to Shiela Khanna, and then served Potti and Ivans last.

Another symbolic representation of sweet homemaking!

Venkat and James had already been served in the garden by Durwan Ashok.

'Very good!' Shiela Khanna appreciated Rose.

'What is good, Madam, the evening green tea or evening bay-watch?' Potti said in his witty tone.

'Both', Shiela Khanna said sipping from the cup, 'a visit to the beach in the evening is as refreshing as this tea.'

'You're right', Potti said, 'but there is something better than both of this.'

'What's that?' Madam Shiela grew curious.

'Her effort is! I do appreciate Rose for her natural instincts and her presence of mind as an event manager.' Potti was unusually full of seriousness and those who expected a witty answer were more surprised at his wisdom.

'That's what that makes Rose a brilliant star in the galaxy of Electronics India!' Shiela Khanna said proudly.

Rose kept mum. She sat on the side sofa and smiled at Ivans. He looked into her eyes and tried to give her back the same.

Janet grabbed Ivans' wrist with both her hands and pulled him coaxingly.

'Daddy, get ready please', Janet said, 'Juan and I want to watch today's sunset together.'

Ivans got out of the sofa with an apologetic gesture of asking permission from Shiela Khanna. Rose also rose from her seat. They looked at each other astonished at their timing.

They remembered a daybreak SMS that Ivans had once sent to Rose.

'That's right...! Get ready and go fast before the sun goes down!' Shiela Khanna also got up taking the last sip of the tea and wiping her lips with a tissue.

She walked to the little angels and kissed on their cheeks. She noticed the bruises on the little cheeks of Jan. The mother in her heart pounded within in a revolt. Shiela Khanna walked out of the parlour quietly but gracefully.

Krishnan Potti shook hands with Ivans, waved to Rose, hugged the little ones and followed Madam Shiela Khanna. He was to inaugurate another *Phantasmagoria Club* in the City library.

The western sky was unusually pink that day.

16

The beach was lonely!

Janet and Juan flew out of the car just like two morphini-butterflies. Janet was in blue frock and Juan in blue jeans and t-shirt.

Parking his 7 series Havana, Ivans came out. Rose also emerged out of the car from the co-driver's seat after leaving her sandals in the car. Her elegant and beautiful rose Georgette saree, embroidered with the golden white flowers and a rich maroon border lay hugging her gorgeous build.

All of them liked walking bare-footed on the pebble-strewn shore.

The ideal vital statistics of Rose made her most enviable for women and adorable for men. The quick breeze shook her thick curls with a romantic breath which made her more attractive. Rose wrapped herself with the long trailing pallu of her saree and followed Ivans to the sea giving a deep obeisance to him.

Janet and Juan were already in the sea. They ran into the flood when the waves receded and ran back when the waves rushed to touch their soft feet. It seemed that the sea was also playing with them like a small child.

'The sea is another mystery, like the heart of the woman. No one has ever seen the infinite wealth of her coral islands, pearls and oyster beds lying submerged in her: the most incomprehensible facet of the multi-dimensionality of the universe.' Ivans thought.

The evening sun was hanging on the west: almost touching the horizon. It looked like a huge disc of fire: so big and imposing; scary and mystical.

'Jan and Juan, stop playing for a while. Come….let's sit near Mother Mary's grotto and watch the sunset.' Ivans said.

'Come fast….' Rose said.

The kids stopped playing and ran towards them. Rose walked with Ivans holding the little hand of Janet. Juan ran and held Ivans' hand. He carried him in his arms and walked towards the grotto.

All of the foursome felt very happy as they sat on the sand dune near the Guardian Statue of Mary the Immaculate.

Ivans looked very fresh and cheerful with Rose and the children. He was in a cream t-shirt and black jeans. The Swiss watch that Rose gifted to him on his birthday glowed on his wrist in the evening sun. Its gold chain girdled his wrist with a pendant halo. His masculine face, broad shoulders, virile brows, big and expressive eyes and thick black hair with a golden blush gave him a chivalrous demeanour.

His tall and robust build gave him the look of a Greek hero at the War of Troy. His voice was deep and sweet. And his movement was quick and graceful. There was a rhythm in everything that Ivans did. When he moved, the passersby stood and stared at him in admiration and appreciation.

Jose Ivans was the most complete man Jessica Rose had ever known.

'Wow...! It looks like a big red saucer!' Juan exclaimed.

'Yeah' Janet agreed.

'It will soon disappear and go down. Jo, take a snap of the setting of the sun.' Rose said. 'I mean...a selfie.'

Ivans took a selfie in which Rose and he were sitting side by side flanked by the children: Janet sat near Ivans and Juan near Rose. The snap was a visual delight. All the four looked so vibrant and elegant with the evening glow in the frame.

Now, the sun was half sunk.

The beacon of the oilrig started flashing with a dull red beam.

'Where is he going every day, uncle?' Juan said looking at the sun.

It was still going down.

'Madam Charlotte said that the sun doesn't go anywhere.' Janet said. 'It's because of the spinning of the earth.'

'Your Madam is right.' Rose said smiling at Janet.

'But..., there are different myths about it in different Mythologies.' Ivans said.

'What's the difference between myth and mythology, Daddy?' Janet said.

'Auntie will explain it better!' Ivans said with a smile.

'Auntie...please... Auntie!' Janet pleaded.

'Okay... okay, dear Jan.' Rose consented. 'But, watch the sunset first.'

All the four curiously looked at the sun going down the sea. It slowly sank to the bottomless depth. They watched its rosy upper tip vanish, leaving the crimson shades on the western horizon. The Venetian Gondolas appeared in the horizon like white swans sailing towards the shore.

'Now... Auntie...please...the myth and the mythology.' Janet said prayerfully.

'Well...myth is a traditional story like a folklore often told with supernatural elements in it, whereas mythology is the collection of such myths.' Rose said.

Rose realized that children did not understand it fully. She remembered what Jose Ivans taught her at the workshop – On Being a Good Communicator. *A Good Communicator knows the Audience.*

So, Rose explained it through simplified illustrations.

'A myth is a story taken from great books like the Ramayana or the Mahabharata. Those Holy Books make the Indian Mythology. There are different mythologies like Greek, Roman, Egyptian, Chinese and so on.'

'Mom, tell us the myth of sunset please.' Juan said.

'Uncle is a better story teller: *Living to Tell the Tale*!' Rose smiled at Ivans.

Her complimentary phrase reminded him of the autobiography of *Gabo*.

'Juan, do you know where the sun has gone?' Ivans said.

'No, Uncle...'

'He has gone to *Hades*, the Underworld, to light it up!' Ivans said.

'Really...?' Janet became involved.

'Yeah, really...!' Rose complimented Ivans.

'While we sleep at night, the Spirits in the Underworld are awake, and some privileged ones will even be permitted to pay a visit to their living kindred on earth.' Ivans said.

'What are kindred, Uncle?' Juan grew more inquisitive.

'Not *what...*, *who...*who're kindred...', Rose corrected Juan.

'Kindred are blood relatives!' Ivans said. 'However, they have to return to *Hades* before the daybreak next day, or else they will be trapped here on earth. While moving from the Underworld to the earth, the Spirits see their way in the sunlight. Sun will be burning there at that time and here we will be in darkness.

'Now, look straight beyond the horizon over the rig!' Ivans pointed beyond the sunset zone.

'Don't you see clouds over there?' Ivans said.

'Yes, we do.' The little ones chorused.

'They are the perfumed smoke rising from the altars of their temples. They will be worshipping their Gods like Zeus and Pluto as it is morning there now; the sun had just risen there.' Ivans said.

The younger ones dropped their jaws. It reminded Jose Ivans of sitting at *CHE* before his grandfather.

Rose smiled through her eyes at Ivans.

'There are a group of islands lying beyond *Hades*', Ivans continued. 'They are called the Happy Isles, Elysium – *The Isles of the Blessed*. Entry to the Happy Isles is strictly restricted. Everyone who is dead cannot get admitted to Elysium. This privilege is given only to a few who have challenged death, fought with Him violently and then surrendered with a smile on their faces: the real brave-hearts. The fearless who die as martyrs will get an easy and quick entry to *The Isles of the Blessed*.'

'Can we go there?' Juan said.

'Yes...!' Ivans replied.

'Be fearless, straight and defy death. You can go there!' Rose added.

'Who are the people already reached there, Daddy?' Janet said.

'Why, Achilles, Caesar, The Apostles, Che and so on.' Ivans said.

'Who were they?' Janet said.

'Achilles was the Greek hero of Trojan War, Caesar the Roman General, The Apostles of Jesus and Che Guevara the greatest revolutionary after the Christ.' Ivans said.

'Where will you go, Uncle?' Juan said.

Ivans gave an embarrassed smile at Rose. She gave back the same.

'Sure...the Happy Isles.' Janet said proudly. 'My Daddy will go only there.'

Rose looked at Ivans and smiled at him with a childish pout.

Ivans held Janet close to himself and kissed on her cheeks.

Janet squeezed herself to curl into his hug like a kitten and softly rubbed her bruised cheeks against his palms. Ivans looked at the slap marks on her tender cheeks and sighed.

'But, Uncle, how will we know whether one reached the Happy Isles?' Juan was more eager.

'If you come here on the same evening after the death of your kindred and look beyond the sunset zone after the sundown, you can see a new bright star shining in its new horizon. That's the soul of the departed flaming, smiling and cheering at you after reaching there. All those brave hearts will look like flames there. Then, we will sense that it rains over the Happy Isles. It's not the earthly rain that we experience here. It's a shower of nectar, the holy drink of the gods which makes them immortal. In nectar the soul will be washed pure before giving it the rank of a flame.' Ivans paused.

'Daddy, where are my Grandpa and Grandma now? Can we see them now?' Janet curiously said lying in Ivans lap.

At this, Ivans raised his right hand and pointed at western sky.

'Can't you see those two bright stars near those scaly red clouds?' He said.

'Yes Daddy.'

'You, Juan?'

'Yes Uncle.'

'They are Jan's Grandpa and Grandma.' Ivans took a long breath.

'Daddy, will you take me also, when you go there?' Janet said. 'I want to set Grandpa's moustache.'

'No, Daddy will go first and wait there for you to come there. I will book your room beside your Grandpa, Grandma and me.' Ivans said with a loud splutter of laughter.

Rose cradled Juan on her lap and put her head on Ivans' mighty shoulders: the most fulfilling moments in their life so far.

The last gondola also anchored at the quay as the twilight dimmed out.

'The sea will soon start bemoaning in a million tongues!' Ivans mused.

A few tourists who alighted ashore walked past the foursome.

A Spanish lady smiled at them and gave both the kids a balloon apiece and said, 'Buena noches!'

The kids looked at Ivans.

'Good Evening!' Ivans replied.

The tourists bowed and proceeded to the grotto.

Janet and Juan ran to the shore with the balloons and started to fly them in the evening breeze. The breeze was very gentle. They held on to the thread and the breeze was now gathering momentum.

Janet's thread got snapped in the game and the balloon fell into the flood.

As Janet started getting worried, Juan gave his balloon to her and ran into the sea to retrieve the balloon which slowly drifted out into the depth.

Sensing a danger, Ivans ran out into the sea and carried Juan on his shoulders after picking the balloon from the sea.

Ivans, carrying Juan, reminded Rose of *Christopher,* the one who carries Child Christ on his shoulders and crossed the flooded river during that night.

Rose also came running towards them carrying Janet in her hands. All of them got wet. Rose left Janet on the shore and wrung water from her clothes by bending forward. In this process, she bared her rosy feet and her plump shapely calves.

Suddenly two local teens brushed past Rose by throwing their smutty comments at her. In the heat of the moment, Juan, released himself from Ivans grip and shot a stone at the juvenile delinquents.

One of them got hit right on his head.

Before they could do anything, Juan showered a few more stones on them from the nearby gravel-dune. The teens had to take to their heels as Ivans also charged at them roaring like a lion. Juan and Ivans ran after the eve-teasers, accompanied by Janet. Together, they chased them out of sight.

Rose stood on the shore looking at the episode with a proud heart. She realized that she was a blessed mother. Juan was only six years old: so brave and so protective! Her breast which fed him throbbed out of pride and joy. Her motherhood had already started its celebrations. Her life was not a waste after all, so was of Ivans.

Night had fallen!

The beacon light from the tower of the oilrig was now flickering more prominently with a glorious red beam.

Old Joppe lighted the giant candle before Mary the Immaculate in the grotto.

He started the Vespers.

He was soon joined by a few strange tourists.

Ivans and Rose took the kids to the grotto for the Holy Rosary of Mother Mary.

As it was a Friday, Joppe started the *First Sorrowful Mystery, The Agony in the Garden*!

After 1 *Our Father*...and 10 *Hail Mary*...there was a miraculous experience for all the prayerful there!

Janet Ivans, the four and a half year old child prodigy led the entire Rosary and the Vespers. She said all the Mysteries with utmost precision, piety and passion. This made all happy and proud of Janet. Ivans, Rose and Juan watched their beloved Jan praying, filled with the Holy Ghost!

After the 5th Mystery, Old Joppe said the concluding prayer.

All rushed to Jan and petted her. Some shook hands with her, some tried to touch her and the Spanish lady who gave the balloon came forward and hugged her.

The Church bell chimed, from the hilltop, marking the end of the Vespers.

Presently, the Church choir started to sing the recessional hymn...

The old rugged cross...!

The entire *Fisher's Valley*, illuminated in the golden spots of flames, resounded the hymn. Every hut on the hillside was praising the wonders of The Lord. They got a good catch that day; their bread winners were brought back home safe. The mighty waves of the sea tossed their vessels only to cast them ashore, though there were moments of perils off the shore. Their children ate their fill and were happy.

'Their life is a real feast and they know how to celebrate it.' Ivans reiterated in his musings. 'They are the blessed ones who never bother about their tomorrows, as The Lord is with them.'

When the happy foursome boarded the 7-series, the choir was singing the most inspiring stanzas of *The Old Rugged Cross*.

All the four together sang it full throated and the Havana wheels rolled out of the beach to the highway.

Though Old Joppe had blown out the giant candle at the grotto, the two bright stars of the Happy Isles were still shining upon the Havana, beyond the flickering beacon of the oilrig.

17

Shiela Khanna always held herself gracefully in an effort to safeguard her royal aura in the society. The adorable woman and the sharp business acumen in her formed a deadly combination that earned her global fame as the most powerful businesswoman of the continent. Almost all the global publications like Forbes and Fortune featured hers as Asia's most sought after face of the Industry.

However, Shiela Khanna was seldom appreciated as a good wife nor was she considered as a successful mother by Prem Khanna.

Shiela Khanna could never stand Mr Khanna's foolhardiness in decision-making.

He was seldom tactical, never strategic and always impractical in business ethics. He would always be rash with their clients and harsh with their workforce.

Terminating business contracts and his employees was one of his sports other than golf.

It was Madam Shiela who held the entire empire of Electronics India without breaking in spite of Mr Khanna's relentless effort to get the company dismantled through his thoughtless actions.

Mr Khanna desperately tried his hand at anything and everything to prove that he was the Numero Uno of the company but, all his attempts resulted in utter disappointment and great loss!

On the other hand, Madam Shiela was blessed with the Midas Touch! Whatever she had undertaken, reiterated Electronics India's invincibility as the premier electronics manufacturers in the sub-continent. It was possible for her as the entire workforce of the company was with her round the clock.

The efficient team-HR of the company, under the exceptionally talented Jose Ivans, knew exactly what they were doing. They had their clear departmental goals and those goals were defined as *HR-SMART* Goals: *High-Rated, Sustainable, Multi-skilling, Altruistic, Revisable, Trendy* Goals. All the rival companies envied the HR policy of Electronics India Pvt. Ltd. It was the only non-unionized company of the country in its stature.

Jose Ivans and his team were always alert of any unrest and proactive in their approach. *CAPA, Corrective Action and Preventive Action*, was its major fortress and was religiously followed.

Prem Khanna would also try to topple the applecart of Madam Shiela in his own way. He would ruthlessly shout at anyone in the company at any time anywhere. He would terminate employees by making reasons. A poor production executive was once terminated with immediate effect for overtaking his Lamborghini on a Maruti-800 on a holiday in the City. It even led to a big furore among the dejected executive colleagues of the terminated. The agitation was cleverly foiled by the team HR under the able leadership of Ivans. In fact, the poor executive was speeding in the City in search of an anti-venom as his pregnant wife was picked by a snake and was fighting for life in City Hospital.

In another incident a fresh graduate trainee was slapped by Mr Khanna as she cut across his way while he was on rounds. No one should move while he was on his *unprofitable* rounds. It was cast in stone that everything should come to a standstill while he moved on the aisles of the company like a road-roller. The trainee's mother came with her friends and relatives to unleash an attack against the CMD, but Madam Shiela sent Ivans and Rose to douse the fire. They got them somehow pacified and sent back.

Prem Khanna was not like this earlier. After marriage, he had to at least act that he was good as his lovely wife became the most beloved of all the stakeholders of the company.

Then, there came Mr Jayaprakash Sawant to the company. His entry was against the wish of Madam Shiela. In fact, Mr Khanna wanted to bridle Madam Shiela and her team and prove that he could run the company even without Madam Shiela and the HR.

The COO, Mr Jayaprakash Sawant, also known as JPS, started to envenom the CMD's vein. Slowly, Prem Khanna got more detached from his staff. All of them were sincere to him and respected him as he was the husband of their beloved Madam. With the arrival of the COO, the entire staff of the company started detesting the CMD.

JPS even succeeded in turning Mr Khanna against his wife and their only son, Rahul Khanna. Prem Khanna eventually made it a habit to hit Rahul at night.

One day, Prem Khanna even belted Rahul for no reason. Rahul was accused of bunking his classes during his final semester of BBA and smoking cigarettes. Those allegations were baselessly floored by the COO. Rahul was the best student of his college and was admired by everyone for his sterilized character.

It happened that Rahul had gone with his teachers and classmates to attend the funeral of his Professor's father who passed away after a prolonged illness. As the college bus was overcrowded, Rahul and his friend drove the latter's car to the Churchyard, for which Rahul had taken prior permission from his mother.

JPS, chanced to see Rahul with his friend in the City and reported the same to Prem Khanna adding his own flair and flavour to the story. He reported to Mr Khanna that Rahul was spotted smoking on a car with his girlfriends.

That night, the poor boy was belted brutally by Prem Khanna. The boy knelt down before his father and cried for mercy folding his hands. But, his father was overdosed, and the devil would not stop. Rahul was hit till he fainted.

Madam Shiela Khanna was not at home that time as she had gone to City Hospital to visit Ms Madhavi Madhukar, the Company Counsellor, as she was recovering from a mild attack of jaundice. It was Anarkali, the kitchen girl who informed Madam Shiela immediately about Prem Khanna's domestic violence, over phone.

James, Madam Shiela's driver, drove her Rolls Royce black Phantom as if it were a warplane. He was even ready to jump many a signal and take any unfamiliar cuts to drive a 7 km stretch of highway as fast as possible. He parked the car in the porch of *Dream Mansions* within 5 minutes from the take-off.

Off went Shiela Khanna, without waiting for any customary courtesies from her servants, straight to Rahul's royal suite – Crystal Mansion – on the seventh floor. The high speed elevator took only seven seconds to reach the spot.

Storming out of the elevator, she rushed to Rahul's chamber which was a majestic *Glass Case* where he lay unconscious and bleeding. Mr Khanna was just coming out of the room self-content after playing his parental role in the most responsible way according to the expression on his countenance.

Shiela Khanna could figure out what might have happened.

'Why did you do this, Prem?' She shouted. The mother in her started a mutiny against the devil.

At this, he wielded the belt at her and she was struck! The buckle of the belt fell right on her back. Shiela wriggled with pain like a worm. She saw Prem Khanna brandishing the belt again like a gladiator. Before he could land it, with the agility of an acrobat, Shiela caught hold of the belt and pulling herself close to him she gave him a tight slap...!

It was not expected by both of them. It somehow happened! Prem Khanna fell flat on the marble. His massive and shapeless body lay knocked out like a Sumo fighter on the marble slab.

It all happened in a few seconds. James and Anarkali could not watch the show as they came late. They missed out it by a whisker: a narrow shave of Prem Khanna from the status of a fallen and defamed Titan.

Thus, Shiela Khanna was crowned as the undisputed ruler of Electronics India Pvt. Ltd. and Dream Mansions. Thereafter, Prem Khanna would never move an inch beyond her say.

James and the other gentlemen-in-waiting of Dream Mansions carried Rahul to St Lucia Medical College in the City. His head was cut open at many spots and bleeding heavily.

As for Prem Khanna, he was left lying on the floor unattended to regain his lost senses by himself.

At St Lucia, press reporters were clamouring for news about Rahul Khanna, the only heir to the Khannas' legacy. They demanded detailed information about Rahul's condition or at least a medical bulletin. But, Dr Jouhra Begum, the Chief of the Medical Staff, would not allow anything to get sneaked out. No information could be obtained by anybody from the hospital without her permission. Dr Begum was the most famous surgeon in the City, and also a thick friend of Shiela Khanna. The media had to keep quiet as they were clueless of Rahul's whereabouts, nor were they audacious enough to report any hearsay, without solid proofs, as the entire Law and Order was at Madam Shiela's beck and call.

Rahul stayed in the hospital for three weeks. That was the most peaceful time he spent ever since he went to college... no disturbance from his father. Angels, clad in pure white and smile-adorned always served him without rest.

Prem Khanna never visited Rahul in the hospital. It was partly because of his ego and partly his timidity and fearful apprehension of being interrogated and exposed. He did not know what Madam Shiela did to preserve the goodwill of the family and the organization. She had reviewed the entire episode with Dr Jouhra Begum and Dr Dona Sandra IPS, the spirited City Police Commissioner. Madam Shiela had immediately sent her personal attorney to the state capital to meet the Chief Minister and the Home Minister for she always believed in the age old maxim: prevention is better than cure.

However, that incident was a turning point in Rahul's life. The youthful cheer and zest of Rahul vanished from his person. His big and eloquent eyes lost their brilliance; his broad and lusty shoulders surrendered their robustness to timidity and his high and gutsy head dropped its height. His spunky and handsome face turned sinister in its looks with the deep and long buckle-cut above his right brow: his father's gift!

Rahul dropped out of his college and very seldom came out of the *Glass Case* of his *Crystal Mansion*: a self-imposed house arrest.

Madam Shiela Khanna tried her best to get her beloved son's real life back, but to no avail. Rahul Khanna was in the grip of a terrible depression. He stopped talking to all, except Freddy his room boy. Freddy efficiently and stealthily trafficked tranquilizers to Rahul. He started with cigarettes and through weeds to cocaine and to brown sugar.

Rahul got confined to narcosis by himself.

Freddy was the only one who had access to the *Glass Case*. All their actions were performed so furtively that no one could realize the gravity of their offence.

Once, Anarkali got almost killed for entering his room for cleaning toilets. She was hit with a golf club so hard that she had to be admitted to St Lucia for a severe head injury. Madam Shiela's abiding persona got everything hushed up without a police case.

The narcotic affair between Rahul and Freddy surfaced when Freddy could not provide the routine dose to Rahul for a week as the room boy was arrested for his alleged role in a street brawl among the petty drug peddlers of the City on the beach. Freddy was not in attendance at *Dream Mansions* for six long days.

The first day, Rahul was anxious at Freddy's absence. The entire day he was thinking about the boy and his safety. He could not sleep the whole night nor could he eat anything.

This was reported to Madam Shiela by Anarkali.

Madam Shiela herself went to Rahul's chamber to know the reason of his restlessness.

The sight was shocking for the Mother!

Rahul's eyes were blood red and he was wild. He had a high body temperature. She called Dr Begum over the phone and managed to get a few tabs.

Giving strict instructions to the inmates regarding Rahul's care she left.

That day Rahul slept peacefully.

The next day, Madam Shiela had to leave for Delhi for an International Business Conference.

Prem Khanna never cared for Rahul. He was busy with his golf, friends and clubs; and celebrating his life with alcohol.

The same day Rahul got long bouts of convulsions...he fell on the ground with a shiver; thick foam and fluid flowed out of his mouth. No one dared enter his room. Anarkali tried to push the door open at one time but failed as it was locked from within. The inmates could still see everything through the gap in the thick drapery hanging inside the *Glass Case*.

Anarkali dialled Madam Shiela's number; not reachable!

No one tried Prem Khanna's number as they were either afraid or did not want him to be there. All did hate him to the core.

Luckily for *Dream Mansions*, Rahul sat up after a while, and all the inmates, watching him, withdrew themselves to their own chores. However, the night was very spooky for all of them. All the glamour and grandeur of a peaceful life at Dream Mansions, dreamed by Shiela Khanna and her son once, was reduced to merely nightmarish and uproarious. The inmates could hear the terrible cry of Rahul while violently searching for something and breaking the priceless antiques, tastefully displayed on the showcases of the glass walls of his chamber.

An air of despondency hung around his dispirited and sunken eyes.

At the height of violence Rahul nail-scooped the flesh out of his thighs and cheeks by digging them deep!

Withdrawal symptoms!!!

When Shiela Khanna arrived in the morning, she was totally disheartened. Rahul was lying on the floor in a spill of blood and puke: his hair matted and clothes torn. They were sticky with the thick and stinky fluid. Several gashes were made on his stomach and wrists with the jagged edges of the broken glass pieces.

'Rahul...my son! What's this...? My God...!' the mother broke down and wept over her unconscious child. Her resilient instinct immediately urged her to react. Suddenly, she gave him a wash and put fresh clothes on him. She shifted him to St Lucia. Dr Jouhra Begum quickly put him on the ventilator and intensive care was given to save the life of the crown prince of Electronics India – the techno-giant of the sub-continent.

Rahul's blood group was A –ve and there was no stock in the blood bank. Madam Shiela had to be pricked for that.

Life at *Dream Mansion* was never peaceful ever since that incident.

Rahul spent most of his time in his *Glass Case* having been lost in his narcotic dreams. He seldom came out. As Freddy was still in jail, Anarkali pushed some food for him through a small slit at the bottom of the door. They were all afraid to go to the 7th floor.

The inmates did not know what to do with Rahul. They started leaving the house for fear of death: one end the father and the other end the son! One is a villain and the other is a victim!

Rahul very seldom went out of *Dream Mansions*! If he did, it was only in search of dope-holes and to eventually befriend the dope peddlers of the City.

Madam Shiela could not sit at home round the clock and play the *Guardian Angel* of her son. However, she worked hard and wanted to be at home whenever she was in the country. She even delegated her duties to the other Directors so as to free herself for attending to Rahul. The files were brought home for checking and important meetings and reviews were held at *Dream Mansions'* conference halls. It allowed Prem Khanna and Jayaprakash Sawant to regain their lost grounds to Shiela Khanna's brigade.

Jose Ivans and Jessica Rose carried all the important messages to their Madam on an hourly basis. They tried and succeeded to minimize the damage to a great extent but, the CMD and COO caused terrible disturbances in the company. Firing, sacking and infighting became synonymous with Electronics India.

Shiela Khanna had to come back to the organization and act immediately to put an end to the Khanna-Sawant run of tyranny. The company was on the verge of an employee strike and dirty politicians had already sharpened their saws for breakthroughs.

The Iron Lady of Electronics India did come back...

Madam Shiela Khanna immediately straightened all the curves in the organization. Her CEMS MIM from IIM-Calcutta and the Doctoral Degree from Harvard Business

School had come really handy. She busted the CMD-COO syndicate using the *3H Combination: Head, Heart and Hand Magical Combination.*

Electronics India's corporate wellness was restored to the utter disappointment of its business rivals and the dirty politicians.

Shiela, Ivans, Rose – *SIR* – became a unique formula of success. They had together conquered many a steepy peak and stuck their victory flag on its crest.

People called this phase as the Emergency Period of Electronics India Pvt. Ltd. During this quell, Shiela Khanna had to declare a series of sanctions: economic, ethic, behavioural, social and so on for deterring any form of abuse in the organization. Madam Shiela had kept everything and everybody under her absolute control unlike Mrs Indira Gandhi. Mrs Gandhi failed because of the waywardness of her subordinates. On several occasions, the COO had to be called to her office and warned for his vested personal interests in the company legacy and its women employees.

JPS was made to mellow down, or at least show that he did.

Shiela Khanna had her own confidants posted everywhere in the organization to watch out for the COO and his coterie.

There was even a bated version of talk among her rivals that the Government of India practiced a form of Crony Capitalism favouring Shiela Khanna.

All this did not dawn to her on a fine morning when she woke up after long sound sleep. For this, she had to sacrifice almost everything else in her life.

She had to send Rahul to a remote rehab centre, in consultation with Dr Ali Masood, the father of Dr Jouhra Begum. The head of the centre Dr Michael George was a batch-mate of Dr Ali at Christ Church, Oxford. Rahul stayed at the rehab for 14 long months. He limped back to his normal. According to Dr George, Rahul had been bailed out of the Capital Punishment through a miraculous escape. He had to forgo his education for keeping himself alive.

Shiela Khanna withdrew herself from the membership of all the social and cultural NGOs and entered her own world: a world of astute calculations, smart speculations and brave decisions. She stopped movie, music and meat and thus became a pure vegetarian in every sense. She smiled only when it was obligatory and spoke when it was required. She abandoned all her craze of grand and costly jewellery and attire and wore only the varied shades of white cotton *salwar kameezes*. It gave her a nobler and richer aura and a total acceptance everywhere. This was the time when Shiela Khanna got detached from all the luxuries of her *personal life*. She started feeling the air of a widowed life and turned more saintly every day.

The professionally oriented *SIR,* the formidable trinity, admirably ran several projects under the CSR of the company and thus *SIR* brought happiness back to the homes of all the e-Indians: the poor and the needy that were destined to stay in direful living conditions.

Shiela Khanna became the byword of selfless service, love and compassion. She started celebrating her womanhood with a difference, giving a new definition to success and contentment. No one knew that there still burnt quite a few more embers in the grate of that womanly hearth, except for Jose Ivans and Jessica Rose.

18

Good Hope!

The Global Centre for Detoxification and Rehabilitation Programmes of *Dr Michael George!*

The sprawling 500 hectare precincts of *Good Hope* lay, far flung from the City, in the lap of nature. However, the landscape was stained by a meandering rivulet *–Red Viper.* The stream with its bloody flush glided, through a mysterious glen, past the evergreen tropical woods at its own pace and will and thus disappeared through a narrow glen beyond the Raven Cliff into a dark cistern.

No one did ever dare to go near the glen even in broad daylight for the cistern at its end into which the *Red Viper* fell and disappeared. It was guarded by predatory ravens from a cliff all the time.

The cistern used to let out terrible sounds like impure and crooked souls being tormented and cleansed at the bottom.

Even the herdsmen of the locale would not let their cattle graze on the lushy meadows – *Haunting Meadows* – near the glen for they believed that the place was haunted by demons. Thus, the glen came to be known as the *Canyon of*

Hellhounds. The glen divided the *Haunting Meadows* into two halves: one part was an infinite stretch of grass whereas the other side in the west finally tapered off and disappeared into a dense pine forest.

It was believed that the spirits who lived on the *Haunting Meadows* would lure the unwanted and unfortunate humans with their irresistible and haunting melodies, as the *sirens* did, and lead them to the bank of the mysterious *Red Viper* and then to the end of the *Canyon of Hellhounds.* The spirits would place them on the tip of the slab, proceeding from a huge boulder, which overlooked the precipice of the cistern. Thus, the entranced mortals would spring by themselves into the bottomless cistern which was believed to be infested with dreadful snakes, greedy alligators, giant violet tarantulas, blood thirsty and sword-edged rocks, creepy creepers and even carnivorous flora. It was also believed that a dragon used to frequent the area as it was his inherited domains on earth.

It was about 3 decades ago in the summer of 1980 the young and entrepreneurial Dr Michael George came to the *Haunting Meadows.* There was a Post Graduate Medical Degree from Christ Church, Oxford with him to boost his resolve and boast about the academia of his Alma Mater. Being the only heir to a traditionally well-off Christian family, Dr Michael George bought the 500 hectare plot. However, it was against the will of his parents. The hardness of his resolve and the softness of the parental love negotiated there and then compromised.

On the *Haunting Meadows* Dr Michael George planted his dreams.

Slowly, *Good Hope* took good shape and there came up huge blocks of structured buildings with offices, a cathedral, detention cells, living quarters, counselling wings, winding and never ending corridors, shopping malls, gyms, refectories, *mini-Bodleian-libraries, Sheldonian* theatres, subterranean vaults, gardens and an Oxford-size *Tom Quad* with the fountain, *Mercury.* The seven tonne bell – *Great Tom* – on the *Tom Tower* would have surprised even a tourist coming after visiting all the Seven Wonders of the World.

The midnight peal of the *Good Hope Great Tom* added more eeriness to the locale, tearing the blanketed peace of the slumbering demons on their wintry beds: their wakeup call!

Dr Michael George had also not forgotten to construct a huge rampart like compound wall with bastion, and a few more specially encrypted vaults and dungeons underground. The vaults were used to keep addicted VVIPs with a high profile bio-data and of secret nature, while the dungeons were used to keep the most dreadful, violent and criminal like clients in isolation from among the junkies who were brought for detoxification of any kind.

However, *Good Hope* stood on the dream like *Haunting Meadows* on the bank of the *Canyon of Hellhounds* as a symbol of hope, love and redemption. It had become a trusted centre of rebirth for many who had lost their normal life in the corridors of narco-delirium. The victims who took asylum in *Good Hope* belonged to various luminous strata of the society. They were brought there for having been seriously addicted to drugs, weeds, alcohol, food, music, sleep, sex, love, gambling and even religion and God.

There were rooms at *Good Hope* suitable for all the addicts according to the nature of addictions and the subsequent behaviour. Some of those were very cordial and mild and they were given cosy open rooms even without doors. Some rooms had doors but no locks; certain rooms were with doors and locks but never locked; some were like prison cells with rugged iron bars and rough floors and strong walls, which were darkly lit; some were like strong rooms of RBI mints – very solid and well-guarded!

Good Hope had some of the best medical brains of the world with Dr Michael George round the clock and they were all well-equipped to deal with any calamitous incidents or state of affair of that sort. The entire staff of *Good Hope* knew how to keep their heads on their shoulders whatever situations cropped up.

The centre was well appreciated for its initiatives in conducting *OJTs – On Job Training* and *PD – People Development*.

The HR head of *Good Hope* was Dr Mohan Prakash: a batch-mate of Jose Ivans at Stanford. Dr Prakash joined Stanford Business School after doing his MBBS at AIIMS, New Delhi.

Dr Michael George had realized that Medicine and HR would have been a unique combination for the successful run of *Good Hope*. Thus, Dr Mohan Prakash shifted to India from the US. However, his two daughters stayed back with their mother Alice, a US born Indian, for their education.

Dr Prakash revolutionized the entire scenario of doctor-patient relation at the centre. As a result, doctors came out of their luxury suites and walked along with the patients as their kin. The burning compassion in their eyes and cooling love in hearts did the magic. Slowly, whoever enrolled came back to life with a good hope to live a very normal and social life.

Social stigma against the sufferers receded from the fundamentalist-heart of the society.

However, the pre-de-addiction period of each patient at *Good Hope* was far from being a cakewalk. Sometimes they had to be kept in quarantine as they were dangerously violent. Some of them used to attack the doctors with whatever they could grab from their vicinity. The dreadful screams of the frenzied addicts at night used to stir the entire brood of the house, in sleep. The bewailing of the invalids of the centre would often be countered by the nocturnal vulpine-bemoaning of the hellhounds from the Canyon. If *Great Tom* pealed at the same hour one would feel that the Purgatory gateway was somewhere near.

Some of the sick were kept isolated in primitive encampments lest they should assault themselves to death. They were *thanatomaniacs* – obsessed with death. A few of them had to be locked up disrobed or else they would strangle themselves to death. Very few had to be kept in fetters as they hurt themselves by hitting their heads on the stone walls or digging their nails into their own eye sockets.

The most dangerous and critical cases were of the *heroinomaniacs* and *necromaniacs*. They would go to any extent to get their routine dose.

Inmates addicted to heroin used to develop dilated pupils and parched lips. They would pop out their tongues with thick drool dripping and panting like a mad dog.

Necromaniacs were more dangerous than *thanatomaniacs*; they were driven by multiple complexes. Necros would be obsessed with killing females to sleep with them. They hated people being alive while sleeping with.

Pre-de-addiction programmes for *theomaniacs* and *sitomaniacs* were very interesting.

Theomaniacs would relate everything to God and religion. They would also see God in everything: prostrate to every single thing, go around or touch them in ascetic melancholy and holy fear. They would believe that their pious gesture would venerate even the inanimate marble slabs on their way, and thus would roll on them unwilling to stamp them with feet. The *theomaniacs* in their cells would affirm that their up-kept legs gave them infinite and uninterrupted freedom to cut the rotten cheese at godforsaken nights. Their boisterous tooting would give a comic whirl to the gathering midnight tension of the *Haunting Meadows*.

Sitomaniacs would very seldom lose their temper. They would be very happy and cordial if they got to gluttonously bite something. They would roll on the meadows like a road roller eating anything with abnormal craze. Dr Michael George himself was surprised to see addicts eating 50 to 60 *Triple Decker BLT Sandwiches* and drinking 30 bowls of *lobster bisque* per day.

Melomaniacs were a visual delight. They would get their earpieces plucked deep into their ear canals and play the mp4 or the ps4 turning the volume controller for the maximum output. They would be springing on the *Haunting Meadows* like grasshoppers making their spectators laugh their head off.

Dr Michael George and his team gave up the primitive strategies and the worn out tools of their pre-de-addiction programme like humiliation, torture and scare to confess the truth about the nature their doping and so on. *Good Hope* had its own indigenously developed de-addiction tools to be used at its different stages.

The de-addiction programme at *Good Hope* would commence once the victims gave their consent. They had to willfully undergo the therapeutics, counseling, medication, meditation and so on. Administration of downers, tranquilizers and pacifiers should be bravely endured and encountered. Then the real brutes would emerge out from their hideouts: the withdrawal symptoms! Withdrawals would start striking both physically and emotionally. This would be a very sensitive stage. Even death would happen if the staff of *Good Hope* were not alert.

The 3 pillars of the de-addiction period that worked wonders at *Good Hope* were the *3 Ds – Devotion, Diligence and Dedication* from both the parties – the doctors and the dopers.

The dopers used to suffer from seizures like heart attacks, strokes, agitations, convulsions, fever, insomnia, palpitation, sweating, delirium, tremors, trauma and so on at this stage. However, *Good Hope* survived all those testing times and stood taller than any other Centre known for detoxification, in and around.

Dr Michael George's unshakable faith in The Lord took the ship forward despite the deck being hurricane-hit.

The post-de-addiction was comparatively easier for the doctors as well as the dopers. The divine grace of every human would be experienced at this stage: the once fresh needle points would then be dry, the cuts and ruts on body be healed and the heartbeats normal.

The end of a tight-rope traversing!

Dr Michael George and his *Good Hope* presently shot to fame: nationally and internationally. He stood as the Archangel of Hope and *Good Hope* his fortress to protect the ill-fated preys from further invasions of the vicious narco-evils.

Awards, accolades, medals and recognitions started parading on the *Haunting Meadows* of *Good Hope*. Almost all the renowned narco-experts and analysts around the world befriended Dr Michael George and happily accepted his invitation to present papers at *Good Hope* Medical Conferences, or to be a part of his Medical Team.

Dr George thought whatever he did was for the good of mankind! However, he did not know that he was also creating deadly enemies against him. The philanthropic and Herculean tasks of Dr Michael George to bring the unfortunate narco-freaks back to the mainstream of life sounded alarm bells in the underworld. The drug barons, runners, dealers and peddlers, living an affluent life in perfect harmony were terribly disturbed.

The sub-continental coronary arteries of trade and culture which were once used for exchanging oxygenated life blood were now seized by the Afghan militants and their outfits. They used the channels like the old Silk Route to flow opiated killer blood: the real smoky narco-corridors.

Dr Michael George and *Good Hope* volunteers were successful in blocking this smoking blood flow through India thereby disrupting and shattering the winged dreams of the drug barons to pump the intoxicants to Sri Lanka and Maldives through the Indian artery. RAW – the Indian intelligence agency had warned the state about a possible terror attack on *Good Hope* or its crew; collectively or individually.

The police was on red alert and ready to foil any eventuality in this regard. The report of the RAW was always kept confidential. No one knew about it except for Dr Michael George.

19

Dr Julia and her crew had the quickest means of communication that were available in the world. Her Personal Assistant Ms Pooja Chhabra and Itinerary Manager Mr Shabbir Imran kept her posted on everything at *Good Hope*. They were the smartest among her young brigade. They had the fastest fingers on the keyboard and the smartest brains on thoughts to match up with that of Dr Julia. Information would be flashing on her iPad every second about *Good Hope* life wherever she was.

Dr Michael George and Dr Mohan Prakash personally executed and quietly celebrated every personal joy and professional triumph of young Julia. She romped around everywhere in *Good Hope* chirping through the crispy and medicated air of its confinements.

After the successful completion of her Medical Degree at Christ Church, Dr Julia took over as *Good Hope's* Director of Medical Operations. At Christ Church she was a rank holder Gold Medallist throughout.

Julia was the only omniscient entity of *Good Hope*... admissions, discharges, entries, exits, sessions, conferences, income, expenditure, interviews, transport, security, mess, PD, PRO, recruitment, retention, anything and everything.

Dr Julia received perhaps the best mentoring available in the world for her mentor was Dr Mohan Prakash from Stanford. Soon, Dr Julia's became a household name more often chanted than that of Dr Michael George. Though only 25 years old, she knew how to blow the lid off any broil before it was fully cooked: always proactive.

When Shiela Khanna brought Rahul to *Good Hope* for the first time, Julia was attending an International Conclave of a very serious nature at Geneva. Her iPad alerted her and Rahul's picture along with a detailed life history flashed on her screen:

Name	*: Mr Rahul Khanna*
Gender	*: Male*
Age	*: 26 years*
Father	*: Mr Prem Khanna*
Mother	*: Dr Shiela Khanna*
Nationality	*: Indian*
Patient Chronicle	*: Mr Rahul is a high profile client willing to seek rehab help at Good Hope. He is the only successor to a multi-million worth electronics giant – Electronics India Pvt. Ltd. Mr Rahul...*

'He is genuine!' She thought.

Dr Julia flicked her iPad back to the conclave slide after giving permission for the patient's admission to *Good Hope* by pressing the green button.

After seeing off Shiela Khanna, Dr Michael George and Dr Mohan Prakash stood at a marble slab near *Mercury* on *Tom Quad*. They watched Madam Shiela's AugustaWestland disappear among the evening clouds of the western sky.

It was 7 pm.

'Sarah loved both of us so dearly.' Dr Michael George said to his HR Manager. 'It is impossible for us to take the fact in that she is not with us.'

Dr Mohan Prakash looked at the marble slab: the most revered spot at *Good Hope*. Dr Michael George and Dr Mohan Prakash were standing at the tomb of Madam Sarah Michael George.

'What had really happened to her, Sir?' Dr Prakash showed his loyalty to the family.

'CLL!' Dr George replied.

'My God!' Dr Prakash expressed his shock.

'Yes….! Chronic Lymphocytic Leukemia!' Dr George sighed.

'Diagnosis?'

'It was very late!' Sarah used to get sore-throat and ulcers in her mouth. Later she suffered from pneumonia. She was taken to the Christian Medical College, Vellore. She had already lost her appetite, grew pale and got swollen glands. At the CMC they subjected her to a series of tests like Lumbar Puncture and Bone Marrow Aspirations and Biopsy. There they confirmed CLL in Sarah.' Dr Michael George got choked and struggled for breath.

Dr Prakash could not respond presently. Quietly, he stood in front of the neatly cut and inscribed black marble slab near the fountain *Mercury*: her ever springing intimate friend!

Madam Sarah Michael George
Blossomed: 25.12.1960
Withered: 25.12.2005

Here rests the sweetest flower; care-trodden,
To wake at the bugle of Angelic Cord'n;
To meet with her Lord; to beg for His pard'n,
And to bloom 'gain in His Heav'nly Garden!

'The *Epitaph* is in *Iambic Pentameter* and beautifully composed!' Dr Prakash said.

'Yes, my Dean Dr Charles Brown at Christ Church composed it in memory of Sarah!' Dr Michael George remembered his professor at Oxford.

'Madam Sarah's treatment?' Dr Prakash asked.

'Everything on the globe! Chemo, Radiation, even stem cell transplantation! Hungarian Physicist Alexander Ferenczi's Beet Juice Therapy was also tried. But Sarah left for the Eternal Abode for her last sleep on the Christmas day: her birthday!' Dr George wiped a tear or two from his fretted and furrowed cheeks. 'Thus, Julia and I were left alone in this wretched world without her.' He paused again.

'Sarah was the most beautiful lady I had ever met.' Dr George carried on as if he was in a trance. 'She was the eldest daughter of Lord Mathews a very powerful landlord of Travancore. He was knighted by the King of England for his bravados during the British rule in India. He was so brave that the Armed Forces of England had to retreat from Travancore before they could conquer it.

'Our marriage was the biggest carnival of the province and my dowry was a Rolls-Royce, Rs 1 million and 100 acres of cultivable lands 40 years ago. The marriage was soon after my Christ Church saga. It was during the spring of the year and we stayed at my ancestral home, for a short period, in our hometown. Sarah was as happy as a fawn: always springing and shining in brilliance and the perfect beauty. She was in fact more beautiful than Julia.'

Dr Mohan Prakash remembered the portrait of Madam Sarah niched below the Sacred Heart in the vestibule of *Good Hope*. She looked like Homeric Eos, the goddess of Dawn: so bright, vibrant and pretty.

He looked intensely at Dr Michael George.

'When Autumn set in, I bought the *Haunting Meadows* from a Gowda landlord of Mysore and we moved to the *Haunting Meadows* before winter came. Mr Krishnappa Gowda was so loving and helpful, as any *Kannadiga* is, that I could withstand all the parental troubles from my ancestral home. My parents showed great displeasure and dissent at my move and even told me to live here alone. My mother would not send Sarah with me to the eerie domains of the *Haunting Meadows*.

'It was the parental love and support of Mr Gowda that helped me to construct the foundation storey of *Good Hope*.

'The weird folklores regarding the strange life on this place were well known to the folk of my town. They even told my parents that the young girls living on the *Haunting Meadows* would never bear children. Being a progressive young man, I didn't believe in any of these scuttlebutts. Thus, defying all the oppositions and outcries of all concerned, we started living here happily and peacefully. In the 2nd year of our life here, Mr Gowda passed away after suffering from a cardiac arrest. I lost a father like figure in his unexpected and untimely death.' Dr George paused again as he was busy in his recollection.

'But, those were superstitions, weren't they?' Dr Prakash said in an excited tone, 'Julia was born!'

Dr George smiled at himself and continued.

'Sarah couldn't carry a child for long though the medical world certified that we had no flaws. It was also said that no one could ever become a parent if one fell into the vicious aura of the meadows haunted by non-human entities. Sarah used to get horrific, evil looking visions and see figures incredibly distorted to look at. Every time we used to feel like we were followed by black fogs and lurking shadows.

Both of us wore Holy Rosaries around our necks blessed by the Bishop of our Diocese which would keep us out of the demonic realms.'

'Most incredible...!' Dr Mohan Prakash exclaimed.

'Yes, most incredible!' Dr George gasped trying to recollect more from the past. 'Every second in the meadows was a painful experience for us. No one was ready to work here, at *Good Hope*. I had already started the construction of the first storey with the help of the labourers hired from Tamil Nadu and Andhra Pradesh. The chief architect Mr Jacob Wren from London had already left the place after successfully designing *Good Hope!* He was so frightened at the terrible apparitions he used to see and the frightful cries he used to hear from the vicinity.

'Most of the labourers would leave the place the very next day of their arrival as the night was so full of spooky experiences. Every brick that the masons laid the previous day would be seen pushed off its place, the next morning.

'Nothing worked out! Sarah would not go anywhere leaving me alone. I had forced her to go to her parents and stay with them for a while. She told me that she would not leave me here even though she would get killed: either live together or die together. That was my Sarah!' Dr George sobbed.

Dr Prakash searched for words to comfort him but...!

'Five long Winters and short Summers passed by. One Winter evening of the sixth year, there came a Friar. He had dark bright eyes and long white hair. His flossy beard flew in the air like a fine sheaf of silk. He was the most renowned demonologist, and revered too: the one and only Rev. Dr Fr Henry Narimann. Fr Narimann was said to be conducting his paranormal operations in collaboration with the famous Warren School of Occultism, Connecticut.'

Dr Prakash got more and more involved with every detail from Dr George.

'As I have already mentioned, Fr Henry Narimann was the most dreaded ghost hunter in the world. The moment he stepped on the meadows, there were tremors and quakes everywhere. It seemed that the entire frame of *Good Hope* would collapse. Trees fell, storms were unleashed, owls hooted, bats and ravens took off and they flew around the Raven Cliff.

'Fr Narimann was very strong and dauntless. He held out his silver Crucifix in his hands which shone in the dark by itself with its flashes of azure. All the legions of the paranormal entities screamed and aired a series of attack against Fr Narimann; but the priest would not move. He told me to gather everybody and everything on the *Haunting Meadows* and then drew a triangle with us inside. We should not go out of the triangle which was bound by a potent spell.'

Dr Prakash forgot to breathe a moment.

'Holding out the Crucifix in his left hand and the Holy Sprinkler filled with Blessed Water in his right hand, Fr Henry Narimann went out into the *Canyon of Hellhounds* through which the *Red Viper* slithers. His white cassock glowed blinding bright in the flashes of lightning, and a cyclone was gathering in the pine forests on the other side of the glen. Fr Narimann suddenly rose and flew through the air and landed on the other side of the *Red Viper* which turned blood red and rushed down into the cistern panting and bloodthirsty.

'Lightning and thunder scaled up their frequency and power as the Friar started his witch-hunting. We were still watching the high drama standing inside the triangle, awe-stricken! We heard an uproar as if it were from Hell. He was shouting, *You, wicked slaves of Lucifer...! I am going to punish you for haunting this place and plaguing my people!* At this, the demons screamed and pleaded with the priest, *No... No... don't punish us...we will abandon this place forever...! Have mercy on us!* Their voice sounded like the roar of a broken dam. *No, I am going to cleave these pine trunks and I will drive you into them and confine you to the entrails of them forever!* At this, a few of those lesser demons ran and jumped into the cistern and escaped.

'Fr Henry Narimann reminded me of *Jesus at Gadarenes* and *Prospero of The Tempest*. He flashed the Crucifix at those pine trees. At once they were all cleft, and at another flash, billions of blue rays were shot at those legions of fiends from the Crucifix. Every one of those evil ones was hit by the Holy shafts of light charging, driving and bulldozing them into the burrows of the cleft pine trunks. Fr Narimann immediately sprayed the Holy Water on the trees to give them their normal guise. The trees became wholesome and normal with the spirits confined to them. As they were spellbound they couldn't move out. The demons were monstrously weeping, screaming, roaring and protesting. But, they couldn't defy the power of Fr Narimann.

'Slowly, everything died out. Then, Fr Narimann came back to *Good Hope* and delivered all of us from the spell.

'It was a new moon day; and was also a Friday. The diabolic powers of ghosts would be peeking on such days. However, Fr Henry Narimann was more powerful than their collective strength. We requested him to stay with us a few more days, but he left before the daybreak as he had to deliver a lecture on *Telekinesis* and *Clairvoyance* in Pune. No one knew how he came here and who told him about *Good Hope*.'

'When did all this happen?' Dr Prakash said as he was greatly relieved.

'Three decades ago.' Dr George answered. 'Even now on new moon Fridays you must have heard the bemoaning of the spirits from the entrails of those pine trees from the other side of the *Canyon of Hellhounds*. Some of our young and enthusiastic boys, who still work with us, wanted to prove that all these fuss and hassles were merely bogus and baseless.

'When I was at Stockholm attending a conference five of our boys crossed the *Red Viper* on a Friday after lunch, with their saws and axes. Wearing a scorn on their haughty chins they walked straight into the pine woods. There, they quickly started sawing a solitary pine. To their utter shock the tree along with the other pines started to swing and swirl as if they were caught in a whirlpool. They started protesting by screaming at the boys and scolding them as the demons cannot stand iron in any form. As the boys used a power-saw, the pine fell within seconds. Hearing the screaming of the souls the boys ran helter-skelter. The liberated demons chased the boys grunting like wild boars. They even heard the name of Fr Henry Narimann being revengefully called out from the depth of the tree trunks. One of the boys even fainted as the spectacle was so scary...! There gushed pure blood from the butt of the tree and its trunk which they felled. The tree started gasping as if it was dying. Its branches were throbbing and struggling for breath. The trunk transformed to be of pure raw flesh reeking and smoking and behaving as if it was beheaded by a butcher.

'*We will avenge, we will avenge; be sure...beware...!* The boys heard a Satanic chorus swearing on Hell.

'Then the tree became quiet! A flash of lightning and a burst of thunder followed. The boys somehow escaped carrying the fainted and took asylum in the Cathedral. They stayed there in prayers till I came back.'

'Good Heavens!' Dr Mohan Prakash managed to swallow some air and looked seriously at the prophet-like face of Dr Michael George.

'Sarah and I, slowly but steadily, started building our *Good Hope*. We conveniently tried to forget all those nightmarish experiences of those years forlorn. I know that you are now more interested to know about Julia.' Dr George paused a while and glanced at Dr Prakash.

Presently, *Great Tom* struck the midnight hour to augment the creepiness of the story.

'It was the 5th year after the veneration of *Good Hope* by Fr Narimann.' Dr George resumed after a deep breath. 'What I am going to tell you now can be described as the most interesting of our otherwise chequered life. It was the spring of the year. Everything about *Good Hope* became beautiful as Sarah conceived and was in the family way.

'All the de-addiction programmes were comparatively easier and turned out to be more successful. *Good Hope* got its ISO and other International Accreditations needed for an organization of its colour. We started to take up programmes funded by the UNESCO and the WHO. Money started flowing from every quarter; every season and for every reason.

'Seasons revolved.

'It was a beautiful Autumn Sunday. Sarah and I were sitting on the sun-lounger at *Mercury* enjoying the evening tea and feeding the fish in the pond. My valet Jimmy rushed from the North Gate suddenly and panted before me. It seemed to us that he had seen some apparitions again on the *Meadows*.

'*Sir*', he puffed!

'*What's the matter, Jimmy*? I said.

'*Sir, a lady has been pushed out of a taxi at the North Gate. She's unconscious!* Jimmy was in a shock.

'*Then, where is the Taxi? Who is with her?* I said rising from the lounger.

'*The Taxi sped away, Sir. Though we tried to trace it, we couldn't. The driver was masked and the taxi didn't have a plate!*

'Sarah also got up. We ran towards the North Gate leaving our evening tea at *Mercury*. At the gate, the sentinels had surrounded the lady, but were waiting for my orders. We broke through the personnel and reached her.

'There lay a young lady: pallid and drained. She showed no signs of life in her. She was bleeding through the gashes on her elbows and head. She was in a night-coat and lying on her side; folded into a coil. I checked her pulse: very weak and sometimes vacant. I saw needle points on her forearms.

'*Addicted!*' Sarah said looking at my face. She knelt down to help me in stretching the lady straight. We made her lie supine, and Sarah presently whispered into my ears that the lady was with child.

'*Bring the stretcher, quick...!* Sarah shouted, before I did. The lady was immediately taken to one of our subterranean ICUs as her identity was unknown and arrival was surreptitious.

'As you know, admissions to subterranean territory are strictly restricted. We allowed only Jacqueline, the staff nurse to come with us to the vaulted ICU. Jacqueline was my cousin and was a master of *Cryptography*. All the confidential records of *Good Hope* had been converted to codes through encryption by Jacqueline, which could be decoded only by both of us at that time.

'As her breathing had to be supported, we gave her oxygen. I cleaned and dressed her wounds; they were not deep. Though the lady was still unconscious, I noticed that her pulse slowly picking. Sarah sat beside her through the evening with the Holy Rosary in her hand.

'Everything seemed normal for the moment. I went out of the ICU just to chat with Dr Ali Masood in the City: my batch mate at Christ Church. The BSNL, the then DoT, was kind enough to provide us with their service 25 years ago. Thanks to Mr Sadashiv Mishra, the MD of DoT and my great supporter from Delhi.

'As we were talking over the phone, Sarah shouted and frantically gestured to call me into the ICU. Sensing a danger, I told Dr Ali to start immediately from the City to *Good Hope*.

'Entering the ICU, I saw the lady lying in a puddle of thick black blood, still bleeding profusely. Sarah was panic-stricken. Jacqueline tested her blood. It was A +ve. I instructed Jacqueline to give her my blood as it was very critical. She sank into a deep coma. Sarah's prayer and our effort kept her alive for one hour for Dr Ali reached *Good Hope* in one hour. His ambulance stood at the South Gate and wheezed heavily like a dying patient. It had run a stretch of 60 miles in an hour: an incredible feat as the road was not vehicle friendly those days.

'Dr Ali and two of his medical staff rushed to the ICU pulling all their medical equipment out of the ambulance. They were smart enough to set up a provisional OT in another vault adjacent to the ICU. Dr Ali, after completing all the necessary formalities quickly, shifted the lady to the OT. I stood near him while Sarah sat outside and said her Rosary. Dr Ali asked me to be mentally prepared for anything. The next hour was a crucial hour of anxiety and uncertainty. Dr Ali's hands were very sure about what he was doing. He told me to get ready with two incubators.

'*Twins; premature; hardly 8 months; girls!* Dr Ali said. I ran out to break it to Sarah.

'What I saw almost made me faint. Sarah was lying on the floor unconscious in blood. I didn't know what happened, what to do, where to run and whom to attend. I carried Sarah in my arms to the ICU and Jacqueline was instructed to be with her. She put Sarah on drips.

'I ran back to the OT only to see Dr Ali enshrouding the lady in white.

'*I am sorry Michael; I tried hard, but...!* He said with a deep regret. He uncovered the face of the unfortunate mother of the two: lying peacefully, without any worry, with closed eyes and a divine smile on her face...!

'*Gone forever! She has left for a world where no needle-points can disturb her anymore.* Dr Ali said.

'*Yes, Ali…, yes!* I whispered pulling the shroud back to cover her face. *She left no trace back: no name, no address, nothing, Ali.*

'At that moment one of Dr Ali's staff rushed into the OT.

'*Sir, the second one has just stopped breathing…it seems…please help us!* She was breathless.

'We rushed to the cell where the babies lay in the incubators.

'*Shift the baby to the morgue with the Mother.* Dr Ali said after his investigations. The first born also seemed to be dying. It lay almost still in the incubator.

'I soon remembered my Sarah. Dr Ali and I ran into the ICU. The bloody spectacle in the ICU broke our hearts. Dr Ali gave Sarah all the possible medical assistance to recover and save the baby in her womb. Things appeared to be limping back to normal. Dr Ali and his team left for the City by three in the morning.

'The next day evening, my maternal uncle, Fr Amos came here and we laid both the mother and the baby to rest in the *Primrose Garden* behind the Cathedral.

'But, Sarah, Dr Ali and I had noticed the two letters – *MG* embossed on a golden pendant attached to a chain which was held in the right hand of the lady tightly. Before casketing her, I released the pendant from her cold clasp and removing the chain from her neck gave it to Jacqueline to be handed over to Sarah. It's still in Sarah's cupboard.

'On the following day, by 4 am, Jacqueline took Sarah and the other baby in our ambulance to Dr Ali's hospital in the City. I stayed back. In Dr Ali's hospital, Sarah suffered a tragic miscarriage. However, the other baby lived.

They came back to *Good Hope* only after 2 long years. They had stayed with my parents during the period.

'Thus, Julia, my daughter was born...!'

Dr Michael George slowly walked towards his East Gate Apartment leaving Dr Mohan Prakash near Madam Sarah's lovely tomb surrounded by flowery rose plants. He looked at his watch, it was 2 am.

Dr Mohan Prakash walked back to his quarters at the West Gate, passing by Dr Julia's office.

'*Mysterious! Incredible!* But, who's *this MG?*' The world knows only one MG: *The Mahatma*!'

While walking back, the two mysterious letters *MG* came bouncing and they started booming in his head.

20

Rahul Khanna sat in one of the underground detention vaults of *Good Hope* for an individual post-de-addiction counselling session specially designed for him. He had regained his youthful cheer and zest. The brilliance of his eloquent eyes came back to him, his big and lusty shoulders were robust again and his gusty head was held high over the shoulders once more. Though Rahul's spunky handsome face started shining, his great father's gift was still there above his right brow: the deep buckle-cut.

Rahul's abiding personality was able to bloom delightful blossoms in the hearts of his onlookers. Rahul was sitting opposite to Dr Mohan Prakash and Dr Julia with the other counselling staff. She felt unusually happy and upbeat seeing Rahul's bright face. Rahul admired the sublime nature of the young doctor. Her fairy features could not be readily ignored by even an ascetic in *Spartan Penance*!

'A divine creation!' Rahul thought.

Throughout the session, Julia and Rahul were exchanging their looks; bartering their smiles, sharing their warmth and fusing their hearts! *Love at first sight!*

'Love is a peculiar thing!' Julia thought. 'It brings skies down to earth, straightens the crooked, levels the mountains, hoists the lowly, moistens the parched, deletes the boundaries and rewrites history. What an amazing mood love brings!'

Rahul was very positive and full of determination to say *No to Drugs.* He really felt ashamed of his past deeds, especially in front of Julia.

Dr Arvind, an intern at *Good Hope,* brought *The Gita* for Rahul to take his Anti-drug Consumption Oath. The oath was traditionally taken in the Cathedral: a rich Sacrament of good hope at *Good Hope!*

After the post-de-addiction counselling, every patient had to take the oath touching their respective Holy Book before leaving the centre. It would keep the person emotionally bound to *Good Hope* and keep the person off narcotics and its by-products. Almost all of them would live a happy life thereafter; but, a few would be brought back – addicted more seriously than before as the society was more worried about them in criticizing and would not spare them unless they got fully destroyed.

During the oath taking ceremony of Rahul, they heard the faint drone of a chopper landing on the air-strip which lay stretched like a huge black monster, taking a nap, beyond the *Primrose Garden*. Shiela Khanna had landed to take Rahul back to a new life in *Dream Mansions*.

The oath taking ceremony was highly religious and ritualistic. The person would be given a wine-red gown and a purple graduation cap to wear. The adherent would hold a lighted candle in his left hand and keep his right hand on the Holy Book. Then, the oath would be administered by Dr Michael George to be intoned by the pass-out. The oath was called the *Oath of Good Hope*.

Rahul stood in his ceremonial dress and took the oath:

> I, Rahul Khanna, hereby solemnly pledge
> That I would abstain from the shameful act
> Of using any performance enhancers,
> To regulate, improve or hamper
> The natural powers within myself,
> Thereby I would attempt to inspire my friends and foes
> To live a drug free life for the benefit
> And progress of my country
> And mankind as a whole!

After the oath, the *Good Choir* chanted the globally renowned hymn *Pass it on...!*

As Rahul joined them after changing his ceremonial robes, the entire team proceeded to congratulate him on his speedy recovery. Then all of them moved to the parlour. Shiela Khanna was so excited that she got her son back after 14 long months. The mother hugged the son and kissed on his cheek to mark her joys. The entire crew of *Good Hope* was so excited to see Shiela Khanna, the most powerful businesswoman of Asia. They stood in the parlour for a while and Shiela Khanna walked towards the doctors with her folded hands to thank them. She bowed down before Dr

Michael George with her eyes overflowing: a reflection of her inner-self. What she felt was known only to her.

Dr Julia was meeting Madam Shiela for the first time. Her grace was amplified as she was clad in her pure white suit. The young doctor soon fell to Madam Shiela's grace and became her die-hard fan.

'A rare combination of richness, goodness and simplicity!' Dr Julia thought.

Madam Shiela and Dr Julia started admiring each other from the very moment they met.

Dr George introduced his team to Madam Shiela.

'This is Dr Mohan Prakash, the HR head of *Good Hope*.' He said.

'Oh yes, we have met when I came to drop Rahul the first time.' Madam Shiela asserted. 'As both of us were busy, we couldn't make a formal introduction to each other. *Good Morning, Doctor*!'

'Good Morning Ma'am. Your son is back to life. Congratulations!' Dr Mohan said.

'You're from Stanford, aren't you?'

'Yes Ma'am….but how….?'

'Mr Ivans has told me everything about you.'

'Really? Thank you Ma'am.' Dr Prakash said humbly. 'He was my batch-mate, the best of all of us!'

'Yes, he is! He holds us all together.' Shiela Khanna said.

'Your best catch....!' Dr Prakash smiled.

'Sure!' Shiela Khanna said to Dr Prakash.

'Perhaps the best HR Manager in the world!'

Shiela Khanna nodded and attested wholeheartedly and looked at Dr Julia.

'This is Dr Julia, the Director of *Good Hope* Medical Operations and my daughter.' Dr George introduced Dr Julia proudly to Madam Shiela Khanna.

'Good Morning Ma'am!' Dr Julia wished Madam Shiela exchanging customary pleasantries: hugs and kisses.

Tea was served with snacks and dry fruits. Madam Shiela was greatly impressed by the branding strategy of *Good Hope*. The grand medieval-like monogram of *Good Hope* was embossed on every article used in *Good Hope*: envelopes, letter heads, furniture, cutlery, curtains, napkins and wrappers, electronic and electric gadgets and so on. The hedges on the *Haunting Meadows* were also trimmed and pruned to read *Good Hope* which was imposing at a bird's eye view.

'The branding is done mainly for three reasons!' Dr George explained after reading Madam Shiela's mind. 'First, it will instill a sense of belongingness in the inmates; second, to check thefts and third, of course, the branding itself!'

All laughed at the second reason. Though humorous, it was a very reasonable reason.

Shiela Khanna incidentally noticed Rahul and Julia nourishing a likeable chemistry between them. Their eyes were always locked and their silence was eloquent enough to tell a mother what they meant. The mother started seeing sense in her own life.

'It's worth living it.' She thought.

While taking leave, they exchanged their business cards and goodies among them.

Dr George was given a Harry Winston of pure white gold. Dr Mohan Prakash was gifted a platinum Cross and having brought nothing for Dr Julia, Madam Shiela removed the platinum Cartier La Dona from her wrist and tied it on the young lady's wrist. The watch was the highest bid at the Geneva Auction and the bidder was Madam Shiela Khanna.

On boarding the chopper, Rahul glanced at Julia which seemed to be asking her, 'Will you be there to hold me?'

The lotus eyes replied, 'Yes I will!'

They had not spoken anything orally, but everything was very clearly communicated.

While flying back to the terrace of *Dream Mansion*, the mother looked at her son. She noticed the receding dark melancholy shades of his face. She grabbed his hands and ran her palm on the trailing needle points on his forearms. The son devotionally looked at his mom. His innocent smile dimpled his face.

He took the goodbye card of *Good Hope* in his hands and after reading its wordings silently, he handed the card out to his mom. The mother took the card from him and read:

> *Faith makes everything strong;*
> *Love makes everything easy;*
> *Hope makes everything possible!*
>
> > *-TEAM Good Hope*

'Mom,' he said.

'Yes, my child?'

'I'm afraid I'll will get you offended, if I...!'

'Why this formality... Rahul...?' She said. 'I know that you want to tell me about your new Julian Hope at *Good Hope*! Yes...?'

She laughed heartily hugging him.

There bloomed awe and wonder in Rahul's big eyes!

'How... Mom... You...?' he asked her holding her shoulders and trying to hide his embarrassment.

'Don't be embarrassed. I *am* your mom.'

'Mom...you are, but something more than that...you are my everything...my mom, dad, brother, sister...friend and everything...! I don't trust anyone else in this world...! Only you Mom...only you...!' Rahul wept on his mother's bosom.

There he offloaded all the cumbersome worldly vices which tormented him till date.

A mother's bosom is an emotional junkyard: a place for her children to dump their numerous, nameless and ignorant emotional bundles!

'Don't worry, when time comes, I will talk to Dr George and Julia.' She said.

Rahul hid the blush on his face in the tenderness of his mother's heart.

Back at *Good Hope,* Julia stood there for a while watching the chopper going out of her sight. Dr Michael George and Dr Mohan Prakash walked back to *Tom Quad* from the air strip. While walking, they slowed down for Julia to catch up with them. They smiled at each other as both of them were on the same page reading Julia's open book.

Julia joined them quietly; very unusual about her! She was silent...the spring on her heels was worn, and the chirping on her lips was gone!

Dr George cleared his throat!

Julia smiled...a sad smile!

> *She never told her love*
> *But let concealment like a worm i' the bud,*
> *Feed on her damask cheek, she pin'd in thought,*
> *And with a green and yellow melancholy*
> *She sat like Patience on a monument*
> *Smiling at grief!*

Dr Prakash shouted and burst out with laughter.

'Uncle...!' Julia whined.

> *Love looks not with the eyes, but with the mind,*
> *And therefore is winged Cupid painted blind!*

Dr George sing-songed!

'Et tu, Elders? Then fall, toddlers!' Julia doubled up and quickly disappeared through the parlour.

'By the way, how you and Shakespeare...?' Dr George wondered.

'*Twelfth Night* was directed by Jose Ivans at Stanford and I played Duke Orsino of Illyria. And you and Shakespeare?' Dr Prakash was curious.

'Christ Church! Weekend tryst with the Bard at The Globe!' Dr George mused as if he was revisiting his London days.

'I think the little one is infected!' Dr Prakash said.

'No, it's not mere infection, nor infatuation!' Dr George said seriously. 'It's love...pure love! She is thoroughly smitten!'

'Anything in your mind?'

'Too early to respond. Let's wait for the right time.' Dr George said with a sigh looking at the portrait of his beloved Sarah. She was smiling at him from the niche under the Sacred Heart of the parlour.

While shaking hands with him, Dr Prakash looked into his eyes. *They were wet!*

Dr Mohan Prakash stood alone in the vestibule watching the Iron Man of *Good Hope*, Padma Visbhushan Dr Michael George getting out of sight, double-bent and care-crunched!

He turned about and raised his eyes at Madam Sarah Michael George. The garden-fresh smile on her face was fading and her dazzling eyes were brimming.

However, the divine glow on the steady brows of the Saviour above would never fail, nor fade!

21

'Daddy...!' Janet shouted. 'Mama... Uncle Potti is also there!' Janet came running to Ivans.

She was holding out the English daily in her hand.

Ivans let out a sigh of relief and took the paper in his hands.

He was surprised to see Katherine on the front page of the paper. She was seen among the glitz and glamour of the *Christabel Marant Lakmé Fashion Show.*

'She looked as beautiful as the Keatsian Siren: *La Belle Dame Sans Merci*!' Ivans thought.

The photo showed Katherine ramp walking in a gorgeous moonlight suit with pearls shining on her ear studs and necklace. The smile looked enchanting in the converging beams of the rainbow lights at The Metropolitan.

'Madam Shiela used to go for the show every year.' Ivans thought. 'The show was being held yearly by the NGO, *The Khanna Foundation*. It used to crusade drug-abuse and human trafficking in India and abroad under the able leadership of Madam Shiela Khanna.'

Ivans read the footnote:

Katherine Samuels ramp-walks in Christabel Marant's Oriental Suit at the India–Walks–in–Style Lakmé Fashion Show, which was held at The Metropolitan under the aegis of The Khanna Foundation – an International Organization that fights against Narcotic Consumption and Human Rights Violation. Ms Katherine is the only daughter of the renowned Surgeon of The City, Dr Solomon Samuels; and she is unanimously elected as the Star of the Show and will represent India in the World Fashion Week of the Fall at Paris, next week.

Ivans' heart got cut and blood clots hung on the walls of his inner self. Katherine *Samuels!* 'How soon my name is deleted! *Daughter of the renowned Surgeon of The City!*' Ivans thought. 'She has snapped the relationship between Janet and me! *La Belle Dame Sans Merci!*

'How can she do that? She is not only a wife, but also a mother. Any privileged woman can deliver a child, but a blessed one alone can become a mother. Giving birth alone doesn't make her a mother!'

Ivans looked at Janet. Her eyes were also wet.

'Poor child...half orphaned before five years of age!'

He curled his arms around Jan and glanced at the daily. Krishnan Potti was smartly standing on the podium of the Orator, The International Convention Centre of The

Emperor and inaugurating 50 *Phantasmagoria* clubs together formed at different organizations consisting of schools, colleges, clubs, companies, social media and so on. Potti's name shot to fame instantly after the paper presentation at The Emperor on Darwin's bluff on The Origin of Species at the Annual World Conference of *Phantasmagoria*.

'In spite of his busy public life, Potti never failed in his professional life.' Ivans thought.

'Daddy... Auntie...!' Janet pointed at Madam Shiela's face in Katherine's photograph. She was royally seated in the front row and was watching the Kat-walk.

'Jan!' Ivans called.

'Yes, Daddy!' Janet replied.

'Jan, my child, I wanted to know how you reached back home that day, when Mama carried you away from me?' Ivans asked. 'How did Shiela Auntie reach you?'

'Daddy..., that day, I kept crying after leaving you. I wanted to see you and to come back to you. Mama slapped me several times for crying and Grandpa shouted at me and Clara Mom pushed me into the TV room. There, I called you over the land-line Daddy, but you didn't receive. I lay on the sofa and looked at the bulletin desk. There, I saw the journal of The Khanna Foundation with Shiela Auntie's photo. Taking Auntie's number from the journal, I called her and cried. Auntie told me to stop crying and be happy. After sometime, Mama came in. She boxed my ear and scolded me for calling Auntie. Clara Mom had overheard me.

'*Cleverer than her Dad, so crooked! Who is Shiela? Your Granny?* Mama slapped me again and pushed me down from the sofa. I cried and cried and slept on the floor.

'Then I woke up hearing the honking of a car! It was Auntie's car. She shouted at Mama and asked where I was. Mama opened the door and Auntie saw me lying on the floor. Auntie came in and picked me in her arms and hugged me tight. Auntie kissed me here, Daddy!' Janet said touching her forehead.

'Then?' Ivans asked.

'Then Auntie asked Mama, *Are you a mother?* Then Grandpa came out and tried to stop Auntie from taking me out. She shouted at him also and asked him to shut up and get lost. Grandpa soon disappeared from there and was never seen again.

'Then Clara Mom came there and tried to stop Auntie. Upon that, Auntie just gave her a tight slap and screamed, *Stop me if you can. I know you, but you don't know me well!* Coming out of the house, Auntie warned Mama, *Don't disturb Jan and Ivans anymore and don't think that your money will always win.* Auntie's heart was beating fast, I knew, and her eyes were burning like fire. She took me to her car and ordered Uncle James to take the car to *The Abode.* When we came out, I saw Rose Auntie and Juan sitting in Uncle Potti's car and they waved and smiled at me.

I also smiled and stopped crying. I lay on Shiela Auntie's lap and slept. When I opened my eyes, I was here.'

Janet lay coiled in the warmth of her Daddy's heart and smiled.

Ivans' heart heaved with gratitude and admiration for Madam Shiela.

'Okay, honey...now get ready for your school.' Ivans said kissing her and he got up.

'Yes, Daddy..., come early. Today is Juan's birthday.'

'Yes Jan, I know... July 18th...where is the teddy bear?'

'It's in the cupboard, Daddy!'

'Is it wrapped and labelled?'

'Yes, Daddy, Roshni Auntie has already done it.' Janet chirped and moved out to her chamber to get ready for school.

'Wait...' Ivans said. 'Wish him and go!'

She came running back to him. Ivans dialled Rose.

Rose picked up the phone.

'Happy birthday, Auntie... Where is Juan?' Janet shouted with joy.

'Thank you...! Please wait Jan.' Rose replied.

Ivans turned on the loudspeaker of his cell phone.

They heard Rose call Juan, and he came running and took the phone.

'Hello!' Juan responded.

Both Ivans and Janet sang together:

Happy birthday to you, dear Juan…

Juan laughed and hoorayed!

'Thank you Jan….! Thank you Uncle!'

'You are welcome. See you in the evening.' Janet and Ivans chorused.

Rose was also ringing with joy.

'Done!' She cheered.

'Bye.' Ivans said and dropped the line.

Ivan presently guessed that Martin was not there. Both of them sounded like a chime in the wind….so free and so fearless.

Ivans got ready for office and joined by Janet at the breakfast table: traditionally covered with grand Anglo-American dishes. There were eggs with sides, hash browns, potatoes, fruits, pancakes, muffins, cookies, apple wood, smoked bacon strips, chicken apple sausage, patties, steak medallions, mushrooms, chicken stew, green rich tea and south Indian dosa chutney and sambaar.

This was a regular practice at *The Abode* done in memory of Francis Ivans and Liz Ivans as they had liked to see their dining table covered in a similar fashion.

Roshini and her crew efficiently and religiously performed it with a global flavour.

Ivans ate dosa with chutney, and sausage. While he enjoyed his green tea, Janet ate bread and butter and drank her favourite strawberry milk shake.

Seeing Janet off to school, Ivans came to his office room to check the e-mails.

The cell phone quivered on his pocket. On the screen he saw an SMS from Rose,

Jeremiah 1:5…Jose Ivans opened the Vintage Bible in the library and read.

> *Before I formed you in the womb I knew you;*
> *Before you came to birth I consecrated you;*
> *I appointed you as Prophet of the Nations!*

'Thank you Rose! ***Mathew 22:21-22!***' Ivans texted back.

22

While parking the hatchback on her space, Jessica Rose noticed Havana of Jose Ivans at her right.

'Jo has come to his office as usual: 30 minutes before time. This is what that makes Jose Ivans so special.' She proudly thought.

Leaving the sunglasses in the car, Rose came out with her bag to be greeted by all who came across. Her statuesque and classic looks were held auspicious for the entire Electronics India fraternity except for the CMD and the COO. Prem Khanna and Jayaprakash Sawant hated her for two reasons: primarily for being the confidante of Shiela Khanna and then for being very close to the mighty Jose Ivans.

Rose looked exceptionally pretty that day as the broad black hem of her rich wine chiffon saree was embroidered with closely knit orchids of rich cream shades. The soft aqua deo gave her a fairy flavour of a heavenly breeze and her gaits were unusually admirable that day when she moved.

It was her son's birthday!

The smile on her face reminded everybody of her name: Rose!

Her fairness was not only external, but everyone knew that it was springing from a fairly fair heart.

Swiping the card and subjecting herself to security check, she looked at herself in the giant mirror. She loved herself more that day!

'Jo's name board is not glowing. He is not in his chamber.' She thought.

On reaching her office, she saw the tastefully arranged sweet packets freshly come from the company confectionary. She had placed the order for them the previous day itself.

Rose pressed the calling bell. Ms Lakshmi appeared.

'Good morning, Ma'am!' Lakshmi said.

'Good morning, Lakshmi! Kindly distribute these sweets to all in HR and Admin. Also, these to the Managers, of all disciplines.'

Rose gave those special packets, wrapped up in papers with roses impressed on them, to Lakshmi and sat down to look at her mobile as the alert was flashing.

Rose saw the text of Ivans:

Mathew 21:21-22

She flipped through the mobile e-Bible and came on the page where the verses were displayed. She read:

Truly I say unto you,
If you have faith and do not doubt...,
Even if you say to this mountain,
'Be lifted up and thrown into the sea',
It will happen!
And all the things you ask in prayer,
Having faith, you shall receive!

Rose closed her eyes in a silent prayer: her work in the office began in that fashion every day.

Leaning on her chair she received a call from Madam Shiela.

'Good morning, Ma'am!' Rose wished.

'Good morning, Rose! I saw you on the screen.' Shiela Khanna replied. 'Please come to my chamber, urgent!' She dropped the line.

'Madam is unique.' Rose told herself. 'Very effective, though always non-formal.'

Rose did respect Shiela Khanna for that.

'Working with Ma'am is a delight.' She thought.

Rose took her pen and the company diary and quickly walked to the east wing elevator. The lift shot up like a rocket and halted at the 7th floor in seven seconds.

The purity, cleanliness and morning freshness of Electronics India were felt everywhere in the air. The soft and sweet freshener gave the ambience a divine feel. Rose always loved Madam Shiela's blend of aesthetics and kinaesthetics with her business ethics.

The sensor door opened before Rose and she stepped in.

Madam Shiela Khanna welcomed her with her usual beautiful smile.

Ivans was also seated in a chair facing Madam Shiela.

'Good morning, Rose!' Shiela Khanna said.

'Good morning, Ma'am!' Rose replied. 'Good morning, Sir!' Rose never quit her official tone.

'Good morning, Rose!' Ivans greeted her back.

'Please take your seat.' Shiela Khanna said.

'Thank you, Ma'am. Just for you.' Rose presented the sweets to Shiela Khanna and took her seat.

'Juan's birthday!'

'Great! How old is Juan now?'

'Six years, Ma'am!'

'Wow! Give him my greetings too!'

'Sure Ma'am. Thank you!'

Shiela Khanna pulled out the cute case of a pair of Zoobug baby sunglasses and handed them out to Rose.

'Give it to him. He can wear them on the beach.'

She pulled out another case and gave it to Ivans for Janet.

After sharing those sweet moments among them, Madam Shiela became serious.

'Now, something very serious in my life!' Shiela Khanna sat up leaning forward.

Rose and Ivans looked at her as two primary kids did at their Headmistress, but, with every word that she spoke, they got promoted to the upper grades in seriousness. They grew every second in mood and mien: involved and pulled up.

'Parenthood is a lifelong sacrifice! That may be the reason why people...!' She paused and then resumed after looking at them. 'I mean, some people think that parenthood is a mere waste in life. They run after fame and money.' She paused again.

She did not mention Katherine's name intentionally for fear of spoiling the warmth among them.

'As you rejoice now in Jan and Juan and their strokes of genius, I also had a child to celebrate: my Rahul! His amazing feats were my delight, every second during his school days.

By and by, everything dipped and nosedived into rehabs and de-addiction centres, and I was struggling to build Electronics India, you know. In the institutional landscape I had to keep the soil intact lest it should erode. The struggle was *Do or Die*! When both of you joined to reinforce me with more effective and fresh strategic artillery, my arsenal became stronger. Your never ending supply of smart and judicious arms and ammunitions made the exhausted weaponry of my professional rivals blunt.' Shiela Khanna stopped to look at her audience and saw that they were matured enough to make the best sense out of the metaphor.

'Now, the time has come for the coronation ceremony of the Prince. Rahul will take over the baton from me soon. But before that we have to defang the CMD and the COO. Their unholy union is still active and effective to harm us.' Shiela Khanna was surprisingly dominating and assertive in her speech.

'Venkat eavesdropped on both of them yesterday and brought the most shocking conspiracy of the duo till date.' Ivans and Rose looked at Shiela Khanna curiously.

'JPS is brainwashing and pressurising Prem to accept Ms Rekha Sawant as the daughter-in-law of the Khanna's...! Impossible!' Shiela Khanna sounded like a hard rock when hit with a hammer. Her firmness was absolute.

'I won't allow it as long as I can breathe.' She was calm now.

Ivans and Rose knew what she meant. They had witnessed the same calmness in her before the execution of any of her master plans since they came in. She would never let the plan of the COO happen.

They looked at each other and nodded in agreement.

'Rekha is very haughty and headless too: pampered and spoilt.' Shiela Khanna resumed. 'She often gets very strong bouts of epileptic seizures. She grew furiously choleric at a public function recently, and threw her glass of whiskey at her mother's face.'

'My Goodness!' Ivans exclaimed.

'When was it, Ma'am?' Rose said.

'Last Sunday, at the engagement of Dr Malhotra's daughter. Mrs Geeta was in tears. Poor mother, I know her heart!' Shiela Khanna said. 'JPS later consoled himself by telling that it was quite normal in this generation!'

'Great father!' Rose mused.

'Now, JPS has swayed Mr Khanna in favour of him, and Venkat told me that they are planning to visit *Dream Mansions* tomorrow for the formal proposal. Prem has already fallen into the vicious clutches of *Mr COO*!'

'Don't worry Ma'am, we will foil his crooked plans.' Ivans said.

That was enough to console Shiela Khanna.

'Ivans is a *man of words*. He will do what he says.' Shiela Khanna thought.

'How, Ivans?'

'Simple, Ma'am!' Ivans said. 'We will shift Rahul to *Good Hope* today itself.'

'Great...!' Shiela Khanna sprang like a lamb beside its mother sheep. 'That's the most practical way.'

'Today itself, I will fly him to *Good Hope*. Let him stay there for a while. Mr Khanna will be leaving for Vienna day after tomorrow.' Shiela Khanna said.

'And will be back, only after three weeks.' Rose said.

'You're right.' Ivans said. 'When they come tomorrow, you will be staying with Rose at *The Abode*.' Ivans said to Shiela Khanna. 'But, that's only a temporary solution, Ma'am. We need to chalk out something permanent. Mr Sawant eyes only at the wealth of the Khannas. If he succeeds, he will soon oust the Khannas from the helm and then we all know what he will do.'

'Yes, you're right!' Rose said. 'Where is the solution? We should think bigger...!'

'The solution is, Rahul's marriage.' Ivans said. 'With another suitable girl!'

'Immediately...!' Rose said.

'Absolutely...!' Shiela Khanna said with joy and pride.

Team *SIR* was once again at work!

'I am proud of both of you for your thought processing. Now, we are on the same page of a glorious thriller.' Shiela Khanna said.

'Where's the girl?' Rose said.

'There's a girl!' Ivans smiled.

'Here's is the girl!' Shiela Khanna said.

She pressed the button and there came the picture of a dazzling face on the big screen.

'Flip and watch.' Shiela Khanna handed the remote out to Rose.

'Beautiful...wow...amazing...so pretty!' Rose sounded very excited. 'Who is she?'

'The Princess of *Good Hope*!' Ivans said.

'How... you know?' Rose said.

'That's Ivans.' Shiela Khanna said admiring Ivans' intelligence.

'Sure, I appreciate it.' Rose said proudly.

'She is the daughter of the legendary dope crusader Dr Michael George of *Good Hope*.' Shiela Khanna said.

'She is Dr Julia Michael George, the Director of Medical Operations at *Good Hope*.' Ivans said. 'A very capable girl with an exceptional professional acumen! Dr Mohan Prakash has told me.'

'A young lady of great personal integrity too.' Shiela Khanna said with a sense of possessiveness.

'But...how will it be possible?' Rose sounded sceptical.

She looked at the exquisite feminine characteristics of the young lady admiring her.

'It's possible only if they publicly pledge their love between them.' Ivans said. 'Summarily, Mr Khanna and Mr Sawant should be officially informed.'

'Both of you are driving it home; but we don't have much time to sit here till the cows come home.' Madam Shiela showed urgency. 'As far as Rahul and Julia are concerned, they are committed to each other. Their bond is deep and mature.'

Ivans and Rose sat back relieved, but looked askance at the door.

'Don't worry.' Madam Shiela said. 'Venkat is at the door. Even the CMD cannot enter my cabin without permission.'

Shiela Khanna spoke it putting a dagger in her voice.

'That's great!' Ivans praised her for being precautious.

'Madam is a great planner and a clever executer as well.' Rose thought.

'Last night, Dr George spoke to me over the phone. Julia has already spoken her heart out to him, and Rahul to me!' Shiela Khanna said with a winning smile. 'The quirkiest thing about them is that they haven't spoken anything about it to each other. Also, they don't know that the other has spoken about it to their parent.'

'Very rare and strange!' Ivans said.

'Just like us!' Rose thought.

Ivans and Rose had never confided that they loved each other. But, they knew it.

Shiela Khanna whimsically smiled at them.

'Very interesting!' Rose said. 'In normal cases the boys and girls will tell their parents about it only after they have fixed their marriage.'

'No, Rose,' Shiela Khanna said picking a humorous vein. 'They would go with an invitation card to their parents and cordially request them to be there for the wedding! That's the fashion.'

'Those youngsters are well educated.' Ivans said. 'Some better educated ones will keep it as a great secret till the delivery of the first baby. Can you tell why, Rose?'

'Yes, I can. Because, midwives are almost extinct and, if any alive, they are costlier than even orthopaedists and cardiologists. Parents are always complimentary products and therefore, free of cost.'

All of them laughed and took out their tension.

'Okay! When should I speak to Mr Khanna?' Madam Shiela said.

'What are you going to speak, Madam?' Ivans said.

'I am going to speak to Mr Khanna that he shouldn't disturb Rahul as he is coming to normal. Marriage is at present far away from him.' Madam Shiela said.

'That's right.' Rose said.

'Then, send Rahul today itself to *Good Hope*.' Ivans said.

'I request both of you to go with him. You can also see Julia and Dr George. Of course, your friend Dr Mohan too.' Madam Shiela said.

'But, then, you will be staying alone at *The Abode*. Is it Okay?' Ivans said.

'That's alright.' Madam Shiela said.

'I wish I could go.' Rose said hesitantly. 'But, today is Juan's birthday.'

'What to do?' Shiela Khanna said.

'I have an idea Madam.' Ivans said spontaneously. 'As Martin is out of station…gone to some godforsaken place… even God doesn't know where, we will take Juan and Jan also along with us to *Good Hope* and celebrate his birthday there if Ma'am can have a word with Dr George. Also, your chopper is a 7 seater.'

'Done!' Madam Shiela could not hide her joy. 'I will do it right now. I will stay back at *The Abode* and we will keep the CMD and the COO under surveillance.'

'Also, our company travel policy forbids Ma'am travelling with both of us together.' Ivans said gathering information from the HR manual.

'When is the take off?' Rose showed her excitement!

'2 pm.' Madam Shiela said.

'Rose, you leave at 11 and pick up the kids from school and go home.' Ivans said. 'I'll come and pick all of you up from your house at 12.30. From there, we will reach *Dream Mansions* latest by 1.45 pm. Thus, the take-off can be at 2.00. Okay Ma'am?'

'Okay, excellent!' Madam Shiela could not help appreciating their effort.

They broke for the execution of their plans with immediate effect.

At 2 pm, Madam Shiela's chopper took off from the terrace of *Dream Mansions* with her rapid action force. Standing on the terrace, Shiela Khanna watched her *Skylark*, AugustaWestland *en route* to *Good Hope.*

23

The aerial view of *Good Hope* through the chopper windows was really fascinating. *Tom Quad* was the main attraction. The chequered block of red roofed white buildings having the flag posts stuck on their foreheads were lovely and alluring. A thick pine forest was *Good Hope's* natural fortification.

It was really enormous!

The *Haunting Meadows* were rich and lush and the *Red Viper* looked like a large red snake sleeping idly in the *Canyon of Hellhounds* among the trees. The airstrip looked like a black monster basking in the corner of a sanctuary. As the machine dropped its height, things appeared clearer and more natural.

There was a crowd standing near the air strip beyond the *Primrose Garden*. Some of them were holding placards, banners and welcome boards. They showed *Welcoming the Kindred Home!* and *Happy Birthday to Juan!*.

Skylark landed at 2.15 pm in *Good Hope*.

Holding teddy bears and wearing sunglasses, Jan and Juan came out of the copter.

Ivans was received by Dr Prakash. They hugged each other and exchanged the Stanford warmth.

Rose was greeted by Julia with a hug. The love and joy of Dr George was very conspicuous while embracing Rahul. The buckle cut on his face was almost removed through surgery and a slight make up would hide it fully.

Rahul looked terrific and his flawless build was able enough to capture the regard of pretty damsels of any rank arousing their curiosity.

Julia looked at Rahul and their eyes celebrated the presence of each other. She cast her eyes down accepting his lordship. Rahul introduced his crew to the hosts and Dr Prakash described Ivans as the best Human Resource expert in the world.

'This is my buddy, Jose Ivans, the best HR pro in the world.' Dr Prakash shouted with pride.

'No..., this is my Daddy.' Jan's comment drew laughter from all.

Julia took Jan in her hand and kissed her on cheek.

Ivans introduced Rose to everybody.

'This is Ms Jessica Rose, Senior HR Manager of Electronics India.'

'No..., she is my Mummy!' Juan said like a measure for measure, which brought both the parties even closer with a hearty laughter.

'Children are great ice-breakers.' Ivans thought. 'Their goodness leisurely cuts through even the hardest mental barriers of adulthood!'

'Hello, Rose! I am Dr Mohan Prakash. This is Dr Michael George and this is...'

'Dr Julia Michael George.' Rose said interrupting Dr Prakash.

'Oh! How come you know her?' Dr George grew curious.

'Madam Shiela has shown us her snaps.' Rose confirmed.

'Your Daddy?' Janet said to Julia pointing at Dr George.

'Yes, my Daddy.'

'He looks like Fr Faustino, our Parish Priest.' Janet said.

'Jan, he is your Grandpa.' Ivans said.

'No...my Grandpa is ADGP Francis Ivans. He is not here with us. He left for the *Happy Isles*.' Janet said seriously. 'This is Julia Auntie's Daddy.'

'Okay, Jan. Accepted!' Ivans conceded defeat.

Dr George laughed a hearty laugh and hugged Jan.

Then they strolled down to the Refectory cutting across *Tom Quad*. Team *Good Hope* had set everything ready for the cake cutting ceremony. Six candles, six balloons, six giant chocolate bars, six small mounts of toffees and a huge six storeyed lip-smoking black forest cake.

The *Good Hope* crew had dexterously displayed multi-coloured balloons, confetti, ribbons, banners and also placards wishing *Happy Birthday to Juan!*.

Juan had never experienced anything like that ever before, nor had they expected such stunning cordiality and pleasantries.

All his previous birthdays had been disappointment and forgettable too as Martin used to scold Rose because he did not believe in birthdays. Martin had even slapped Rose on her face once and literally threw Juan to the living room sofa for they had insisted on celebrating his birthday.

Good Hope choir sang Happy Birthday to him as Juan blew out the candles and cut the cake with Rose. Cameras flashed, balloons blasted and hands clapped and all sang the song with the choir. The most memorable and cherishable birthday of Juan's so far.

After tea, the-small-foursome: Rahul, Julia, Janet and Juan went out into the garden. The children ran everywhere as if they were in the Paradise.

In the meantime, the-big-foursome: Dr George, Dr Prakash, Ivans and Rose walked towards the apartment of Dr George at the East Gate.

Everything at *Good Hope* was a wonder for the visitors. What attracted Ivans and Rose was the planning and the pristine ambience of the centre. There was music everywhere: even in the chirping of the birds and the rustling of the leaves in the breeze.

'Ariel's Island!' Rose said to Ivans.

'Prospero's Island!' Ivans added.

'I hear a fairy singing somewhere...so enchanting!' Rose said.

Dr George and Dr Prakash walked ahead of them in silence. Rose and Ivans followed them.

They reached the East Gate passing by beautiful gardens, ever-springing fountains, swishing fish ponds, sparkling duck ponds, orchestrating aviaries and squeaking rabbit warrens.

'I wish we had stayed here for a while.' Rose said.

'Let Rahul and Julia walk down the aisle, first!' Ivans said.

On reaching the Conference Hall of the East Gate apartments, the-big-foursome sat engaged in a serious discussion. Ivans told them everything in detail: the legacy of Madam Shiela, the incompetence of Prem Khanna, the cunningness of JPS and the suffering of poor Rahul. He also told them what Madam Shiela expected of Dr George.

'Madam Shiela wants the kids to be together.' Ivans said. 'She loves Julia so much and admires both of you for your dedication and intelligence.'

'Mr Sawant and his relatives are going to *Dream Mansions* tomorrow to see Rahul, and officially talk to Madam Shiela.' Rose said.

'Let Rahul be here for a few days. *Good Hope* is the only hope of the hopeless.' Ivans said. 'Madam Shiela can fight with the entire clan of the Sawants if her son is safe!'

'Tell her not to worry about her son.' Dr George said. 'He is my son too. Julia has already spoken everything to me and I could see her heart. It's red!'

Ivans felt reassured and Rose let out a sigh of relief.

After their discussion, Jose Ivans video-conferenced with Madam Shiela and kept her posted about their discussions and decisions.

The graceful picture of the abiding Business Baroness in pure white suit flashed on the giant screen of the Conference Hall.

'Hi everybody!' Shiela Khanna greeted them.

'Hi Shiela!' Dr George greeted her back.

'Good evening Ma'am!' Others chorused.

'How are you all?' Shiela Khanna said. 'Where are the kids?'

'Fantastic, Shiela! The kids are in the garden.' Dr George said. 'How are you?'

'Superb, Doctor!' She said. 'They are coming home tomorrow. I am going to *The Abode* at night.'

'I was telling Rose and Ivans to tell you not to worry. Rahul is my son too.' Dr George said.

'Thank you very much, Doctor. I am relieved and obliged.' Madam Shiela said.

'Be assured Ma'am.' Dr Prakash said. 'We are with you.'

'Thanks to you, all.' They saw Madam Shiela wiping her eyes.

'Please keep Rahul with you for a few days, Doctor, till everything gets settled here.' She said. 'Things are very grim here.'

'Done...! Shiela, done...! Don't worry. We will take care of him.' Dr George said.

'Ma'am, we are starting now itself to be with you. Is it okay?' Ivans said.

'Okay, Ivans. If your mission is accomplished, you can start now itself.'

'Done, Ma'am. We will hold a few more discussions and board by 7 pm.' Ivans said.

'Very good.' Shiela Khanna appreciated their effort.

'Rose...' Shiela Khanna called her.

'Yes, Ma'am.'

'How is my daughter?'

'Matchless, Ma'am!'

'Thank you. Tell Rahul to take care of her.' Shiela Khanna said.

'Yes, Ma'am.' Rose said.

'If it's convenient, kindly visit *Dream Mansions* next Sunday.' Shiela Khanna said.

'Okay. We'll let you know.' Dr George said.

'Goodbye, Doctor!'

'Goodbye, Shiela! God bless you!' Dr George wished her back.

They watched the beautiful face of Madam Shiela Khanna vanish from the giant screen.

Dr George was so happy as Rahul was coming into the life of Julia.

'The multiple counselling sessions and psychometric tests conducted on him had proved that he was a simple selfless loving and gullible boy with great IQ and EQ. He would be upset only when his most beloved ones are disturbed. He would love Julia more than I loved Sarah.' Dr George thought.

They held very serious discussions about the alliance.

Dr George was astonished at Jose Ivans' planning and vision. He had never seen a perfect man as Ivans was.

'I am a novice before his professionalism and planning.' Dr George thought.

Rose was also complimenting Ivans in his thought processing with timely interventions and interpretations.

Dr George was really impressed.

'No wonder in Electronics India's rapid and enviable progress. The magical combination of Shiela, Ivans and Rose is unique.' Dr George thought.

'Where are the kids?' Dr George said.

'In the garden.' Dr Prakash replied.

Coming out into the garden, they saw Rahul and Julia sitting under the creamy-white flower canopy of Julia's *Champaka* tree. The amber rays of the evening sun set the spot on fire and they appeared like two *Gandharvas*! They were enjoying the warmth of their love under the tree.

An evening breeze gently pushed its starry flowers upon the young lovers as if the tree had preserved all of them for that auspicious moment. An embalmed fragrance floated through the fresh air of the evening.

Jose Ivans remembered his beloved *Gulmohar* who also used to push her blooms upon him in Udayagiri.

Janet and Juan came running and shouting how they won their school games over each other and how they were planning their stay overnight at *Good Hope*.

The shouts of the children cast Rahul and Julia back on the shores of this petulant sea of life once again from the cosy shores of a blissful sea of love and contentment.

'O, darling, we are flying back today itself.' Ivans said to Janet.

'What?' She expressed her shock.

'Why, Mama?' Juan said with great displeasure.

'Shiela Auntie wants all of us to be back today itself. We'll come back soon to stay here for a few days, won't we, Uncle?' Rose said to Dr George.

'Yea, you will. We are planning your Christmas at *Good Hope*.' Dr George said to them.

They reluctantly consented to go back; partially because Shiela Auntie asked their parents to return and partially because they would return to *Good Hope* for Christmas.

Slowly, Rahul and Julia joined the group. Both of them were masked in the rosy amorous veils.

The last phase of the dusk threw the residues of its evening glow on their youthful blush adding more hues to their divine grace.

Two swans moved eastward in the sky as if they were in a leisure-flight.

'They've no pain and anguish of petty human thoughts nor do they want anything.' Rose thought.

Dr George also noticed the birds and marvelled at them.

All in the crowd were exchanging several decorous pleasantries. Julia's *Champaka* stood lonely after the blessed lovers left the place. The Tree had preserved many fortunate blooms to anoint Rahul and Julia. It swayed in the breeze, apparently happy with its mistress.

Dr George remembered his Sarah who had planted it, had brought it up along with Julia. Sarah used to sit with him beneath it every day as the end approached her.

'Well done, my darling!' Dr George conveyed his congratulatory remarks to the tree by means of their own extra sensory perception. 'I am proud of you!'

'Thank you, Dad!' The tree shed a few more blossoms in response.

'Soon, Julia will also go leaving me alone, but, you will not.' He thought to himself.

The tree agreed with him showering another bestowal of blooms.

The night had already fallen and the breeze picked momentum.

'Sir, let's board before it's too late.' Ivans said to Dr George.

'Yeah.' Dr George replied as though he was in pain of leaving his own kin.

The boys had already loaded their AugustaWestland with a cargo of goodies, confectionaries and toffees.

Jose Ivans, Jessica Rose, Janet and Juan bade goodbyes to *Good Hope* and embarked on the return trip.

The chopper quivered and snarled like a huge wild cat and with a sudden jolt it gained vertical height and soon went out of *Good Hope*. The inmates of the wonder world stood beneath waving and smiling. The kids were shouting *Thank you Uncle and Auntie.*

'Julia and Rahul are made for each other, everyway.' Rose and Ivans thought.

'Married life is a duo-trapeze-act. Both the artists will be playing the roles of a flyer and a catcher in turns. The success of the act solely depends on the timing. In absence of a perfect understanding between them, the flyer will fall to death as there are no nets and harnessing used here except for the trust, passion and support between the flyer and the catcher. Once off the board, a player can return to the board only on two occasions during the course: on the successful completion of the act or being hurt and disabled by a careless or a wily partner.' Ivans thought.

The *Skylark* had already started scaling the infinity of the starry blue!

24

The Lady of Fortune kept turning her wheel with so much of enthusiasm as ever. Nature shared her spoils equally among all the four seasons. The wild Summer sinews matured themselves to be christened the Autumn. Its sweet burdens of mellowness soon fell down to slumber, and lay on the frozen bed of the punishing Winter, only to be bugled back to the grandeur of the Spring and to breathe the freshness of life, lungful.

The vernal glory of the proud nature was hung on the boughs of each plant.

The mortal celebrated each of their gains and mourned their pains. Janet and Juan celebrated their Christmas at *Good Hope* as they were promised. Jose Ivans and Jessica Rose grew mightier in the company with the blessings and support of Shiela Khanna. Electronics India Pvt. Ltd. became stronger and more dependable in business: its turnover in the third quarter of the FY was raised to 140,000 crore from 80,000 crore.

Katherine Samuels was declared the Modelling Icon of India by IMTA and never climbed down from cloud nine. She became the *Prima Dona* and the face of all the International trendy shows. She also featured the front pages of all the leading magazines in Vogue and Style.

Krishnan Potti was highly successful in blending his professional priorities with personal obligations. Potti was the long and the short of the Company exports and the most wanted celebrity of the *Phantasmagoria* organization in the country. He had eventually inaugurated the 1000th *Phantasmagoria Club* in the City before the Spring set in.

Prem Khanna and Jayaprakash Sawant clung onto each other against their common enemies: SIR. The COO's plot of making Rekha, his daughter, the Khannas' daughter-in-law received big jolts and got many times miscarried by the collective-SIR-intelligentsia.

Though Mr Sawant conceded defeat on several occasions, the deadly secretion of his venomous greed and foiled intent was kept ready in bitterest corner of his heart for the invincible Triumvirate of the Electronics India. The haughty and clever Rekha Sawant vowed to remain a spinster till she could become the old lady of the crown prince of Electronics India.

Only a wolf would whelp another wolf; not a sheep.

Rahul and Julia spent the most beautiful time of their life, mostly at *Good Hope*: a holy, steadfast and lifelong intimacy. They never declared their love for each other publicly, but they knew that they held each other very close to their heart. They were celebrating their love every moment they lived.

Love untold is better experienced than told!

Dr George knew why the *Champaka* overburdened her branches that year with those creamy white blooms. It was for Julia and Rahul. There was a rhythm in everything at *Good Hope.* Everything bounced back to normal.

'Nothing was normal here ever since my Sarah was gone.' Dr George said to Dr Prakash.

Now life was taking a big turn...! It was taking a new route: a route to the City of Joy and Peace. Julia brought Rahul back to the track of education and the heat of examination. He stayed at *Good Hope* under the pretext of de-addiction and prepared for his finals. He got admitted to Calcutta St Xavier's, and was flown back and forth during his exams. All eagerly awaited the results. Then, Dr Prakash would go and get him enrolled in Stanford for his PG Programme.

Dr George vigorously resumed his anti-drug campaign throughout the Indian sub-continent, also in Africa and America, which certainly blew the sugarcane juice of all the drug runners off the sniffing corridors.

All of them fought vigorously against social evils and traditional wear and tear of the unfortunate mortals. They were the *Tedium Troopers!*

The Lady of Fortune waited for none. Her invincible hands continued turning the invisible Wheel. As for Rose life was more meaningful and peaceful to live. She lived for the other 3 Js: Jose, Janet and Juan. She realized the rooting of a new seedling of love growing in her heart, and enjoyed its green sprouts emerging after drinking enough from the warmth of her self.

'It would soon be a big tree to carry the fruit of our love.' She thought.

She did not know where Martin was, nor did she ever want to know. He hardly ever came home. He dropped in only once in eight months.

'When he came last, it was *Deewali*!' She thought.

Rose and Juan had illuminated the entire house with *Diyas* – the earthen oil pots with a wick of light in each of them. After bursting a few crackers Juan had gone to sleep.

Rose was reading Gabo's *The Autumn of the Patriarch:* an exceptional word painting! 'He really lived for telling tales.' Rose thought.

She was totally engrossed in reading. The entire neighbourhood was involved in bursting crackers. For them life was a feast and thus they celebrated it.

The noise of the outside world gradually sank into a fate of absolute nothingness as Rose was taken aback at *the fight of the Patriarch with the cows in the palace.*

After a while she was rung back to her real senses by the long toll of the calling bell.

It came to her ripping through the incessant blasts of the crackers outside. She looked at the wall clock. 11.45 pm.

Rose marked the page and rose. After closing the book she walked to the door. The bell was still clanking. There were *Diyas* burning everywhere. Anxiously, she looked out through the peephole.

Martin...!

She started to sweat like Death and stood there wan and vacant.

Now, he had started banging and then kicking on the door and also kept the bell-switch clicked.

'Open the door..., you bitch...! Open..., sleeping like a pig...!'

His tongue was loose and speech was lewd.

As he went louder and louder with the bell, the neighbours opened their doors and came out to join their children who were bursting the crackers. All of them had gathered at the door of Rose.

They showed their impatience by shouting at him.

A brawl was brewing outside.

As Martin was on the verge of hitting their immediate neighbour, Adbul Khader, a retired School Master and righteous man; there came a shrill and piercing shout like a command.

'No...! Stop...! Don't touch him...!'

Rose stood at the door like Nemesis, the goddess of revenge. Her eyes shone like two flames, ready to burn the devil down.

The scream brought everything to a sudden halt.

After a while, Martin unsteadily trudged into the house.

The neighbours slowly dispersed...tongue-tied!

Rose closed the door and turned around to look at the devil sitting on the sofa in the living room. He grinned at her with his opium stained teeth.

His eyes were red. He had matted white hair, bushy brows and stubbled face.

He smelled liquor when he spoke through the pulpy froth of his spirited mouth.

The stink of sweat was spreading in the room from his soiled body and clothes.

Juxtaposed with Rose!

He took a cigar from the pocket of his tattered shirt and biting it lit a matchstick.

Thick white rolls of smoke started filling in the room.

Rose stood there holding her breath as her lungs retaliated and refused to breathe.

Her inner-self had already started to revolt.

As the puffs burned the cigar smaller in size, Martin looked at Rose and beckoned her over both with his head and hand together.

She did not move. She would not. She should not...

He greedily looked at her glorious form with his x-ray eyes.

He rose and balanced himself on his feet.

Rose knew what he was up to. She wanted to run away and escape from the brute, but her legs were cast in lead. They would not obey her heart.

Martin wobbled like a moonwalker and slowly moved towards her.

He would soon quell her routine resistance and relish on her prided boons, which would not be offered to the rogue anymore.

His cigar butt glowed like coal. The fire would not die until the devil dug the burning butt into her abs: the love-tattooing.

The very thought of it made her heart skip a beat or two. She had to do something: something very unusual to escape from him.

Martin came closer to her, still wobbling, and stood before her. The whiff of his sweat and the alcoholic stink of his breath made her feel like puking.

Rose felt losing her senses which made her very sick.

At that moment, she could not hold anymore.

She threw a mouthful of puke on his face.

'You bloody bitch...!' He shouted and slapped hard on her face.

Rose looked up at the reeling Crucifix hanging on the wall. It faded out of her sight as she swooned from fright and shock!

When she woke up at the daybreak, Juan was sitting beside her and crying. Everything in the room was messed up and her clothes and hair had the stink of alcohol. Her burning abs told her what the devil had done before he left.

She wept bitterly hugging Juan tight and looked up again to see the blurred letters on the board hanging beside the Crucifix: *God has a purpose for your pain, a reason for your struggle and a reward for your courage*!

Deep down in her heart, she could hear the tearful lamentations of her broken self: 'I am sorry Jo, I couldn't stop the devil. If love is my religion and my body is its holy Abode, you're the only God enshrined in my heart – the sanctum sanctorum! I'm sorry, forgive me, my Jo!'

Ever since, she desperately awaited Martin to come home, for Ivans had clearly instructed Rose as to what to do next time, if the devil came!

Jose Ivans and Janet Ivans lived a calm and committed life. Their relation grew consequential and thus ideal. The Daddy and his Darling became the most trusted friends ever. Katherine Samuels was remembered by *The Abode* only when she ramp-walked on TV or in newspapers. The very sight of Katherine in the media made Janet's blood curdle. It could make her look like an autumn leaf: pale and sickly.

When Ivans business-toured, Janet was well protected by Rose and Madam Shiela.

Janet grew very confident and religious. The Catechism classes on Sundays drew her closer to her faith. She slowly became dauntless and her thoughts attained a logical height compared to her age group. Juan was her best friend who equalled her in wit and witticism.

SIR worked together to bring out the first ever complete HR Policy Manual of the Company which was hailed as the Magna Carta of Electronics India Pvt. Ltd. It made Prem Khanna and Jayaprakash Sawant the deadliest enemies of SIR.

Firing became illegal unless sanctioned by at least two of the DCC – Discipline Core Committee – of the company which consisted of Prem Khanna, Shiela Khanna and Jose Ivans.

The HR manual laid down the Guiding Principles of the functional and the structural domains of the company. SIR stood invulnerable and their bond became unassailable!

Ivans took up writing as his pastime and produced some quality write-ups which were published by the leading periodicals. The Times of India Sunday supplement brought out one of his sonnets which was widely read and appreciated for its musical quality, structural perfection and unique theme.

'Daddy...! Your photo...!' Janet rushed to Ivans one morning with the Times of India.

Ivans was framing the concluding couplet of another sonnet in Iambic Pentameter sitting in the library.

He raised his eyes and looked at the morning freshness on Janet's face. The soft room freshener perfumed his sensitive nose. It was divine.

Janet spread the daily on his desk.

'Wow!' he exclaimed.

There was his picture in the paper along with his sonnet under the title:

Snow-white Liars!

- Jose Ivans

When Spring brought her glimpse of glorious glows,
And woodlands still lay in their icy sway;
I saw you, at dawn, pace your dewy way,
Calling those birches from their wintry doze!

The grass did gaily bear your tender feet;
My Gulmoh'r had spread her rug for your state!
You really look'd like the Immaculate,
As the Church choir sang in tune with the beat!

When a wretch'd candle lit up your face
Kneeling at the Virgin, why did you cry?
For Her own Son, with Ichor yet to dry,
Smould'ring tears hung on Her maternal gaze!

Christ is born, through ages, from blessed wombs;
We too are born to give Him cross and tombs!

Ivans could not hold his joy and excitement. He held Janet so close to his heart and kissed her. Janet kissed her Daddy back and looked into his eyes. They were wet. Of course, she could not read the ebb and flow of life rising and falling in them.

'Why are you crying, Daddy? Your Jan didn't do anything.' She said wiping his tears.

'I didn't cry honey! It's joy...pure joy! Nothing else.' He said.

The cell phone shivered in his pocket: unknown number!

Ivans hesitated and received the call.

'Good morning, Ivans!' the voice was so familiar.

'Good morning...but...?' Ivans tried to figure it out.

'Ivans, this is Prof. Muhammad.' The voice confirmed the identity – his English Professor at SN, Kannur.

'Oh Sir...! My God...!' Ivans screamed out of joy and pride. He jumped out of his seat with respect.

'I'm sorry, I couldn't link it...!' Ivans said this with deep regret.

'It's been so long since we spoke...! *Five years have past...!*' The Professor said.

'*Five summers, with the length of five long winters.*' Ivans said.

'*And again I hear your voice.*'

'*As if rolling from a mountain spring.*'

'*With a soft inland murmur.*' Prof. Muhammad shouted with joy.

Prof. Muhammad had taught him *Wordsworth's Tintern Abbey* in his Masters at Shree Narayana College, Kannur.

The best teacher had spoken to his best student exactly five years ago.

'My child!' The Prof. said. 'Yes, Sir!' Ivans replied as if in a dream.

'I've just read your sonnet in the newspaper. Beautiful! Simply amazing! It's classy and classic too.' The Prof. went on. 'Keep writing and I will ensure that they are published.'

'Thank you, Sir...and I will.' Ivans said.

'Your sonnet is traditional and stands matched up with that of the Masters!' The Professor exclaimed.

'Thank you, Sir!' Ivans said. 'How are you, Sir?'

'I am alright but for some senile concerns. Thanks Ivans.' Prof. Muhammad said. 'Now I hang the wire and will call you later. All the best and goodbye, my son!'

'Goodbye, Sir!' Ivans was still in a trance.

It was unbelievable that his most beloved teacher had called him over and appreciated him.

Even the most celebrated scribblers of the day would not get such an appreciation from Prof. Muhammad, though they would die for it.

Janet was still sitting on his parental lap and enjoying the warmth of his pounding heart. Ivans' cell phone alerted an SMS. It flashed:

Isaiah 11:2! *Congrats for the Snow-White Liars! You were busy.*

Janet brought the Bible, opened the *Book of Isaiah* and read:

> *The Spirit of the Lord shall rest upon him,*
> *The Spirit of wisdom and understanding,*
> *The Spirit of counsel and might,*
> *The Spirit of knowledge, and the fear of the Lord!*

Closing the Bible, Janet smiled and looked at the wall clock.

'Daddy, school bus will come in 10 minutes.' She ran out of his hug to get ready.

Ivans smiled and with a sign of relief and contentment went back to the world of *The Bard of Avon*!

25

When March came marching, everybody was in a euphoria at Electronics India Pvt. Ltd., except for Prem Khanna and Jayaprakash Sawant. The financial year brought a great profit to the organization. The SIR became stronger and more sought after in the firm. The position of JPS became more vulnerable and he knew that he had already lost much of his ground from under his feet.

Attrition fell to 2% from 44% and Inventory was reduced to its half – 3000 crore. The turnover touched a new height as expected.

Prem Khanna kept himself circumspect and alert as he feared SIR and their popularity in the company ever since the implementation of the HR Policy Manual.

SIR became a cult within the org and worshipped by all except for the duo and a few like Col. Somsekhar.

They were also struck by the Global Insecurity Syndrome – GIS.

'Subsequent to the creation of man, people on hot seats have been plagued by an uncanny feel of being insecure. It had first struck the heavenly Lucifer, the Archangel. Since then the world has witnessed some of the cruellest episodes of exterminating the potential rivals of the men-in-sway using the luxury of their money, muscle and mandate. It is true everywhere: family, factory or faith. Its mutability and sanctity could never be catechized, as it's futile.' Jose Ivans thought while booking the podium of The Patriarch online for the Annual Executive Dinner of Electronics India Pvt. Ltd. on 23rd April.

23rd April! Holy Saturday! The day before Easter, the Resurrection of the Saviour. The birthday of the Bard!

CMD Prem Khanna will stand on the podium of The Patriarch and deliver his customary Annual Complimentary Speech to the invited guests, clients and the executives of the company on that day.

'The Annual Dinner of the year will be full of pleasant surprises!' Ivans thought.

The turnover of the company in the previous FY would be made known to the public and the magical number for the next FY would be unveiled by Madam Shiela after Mr Khanna's complimentary address.

'It is also celebrated as the Blue-ribbon day of Electronics India. Departments and exceptional e-Indians will be awarded Gold Medals by Madam Shiela Khanna for their performances. The biggest surprise will be Rahul Khanna's coronation as one of the Directors of Electronics India.' Ivans mused.

Prem Khanna was at first not ready to bring Rahul on the board, but Madam Shiela's toughness and famed resolve showed Prem Khanna his place and he had to yield.

'But, bombshells will blast in the horizons of The Patriarch when Madam Shiela's final announcement erupts like a volcano. Many a castle in the air will be levelled on the spot. Mr Sawant's heart would be broken into pieces as his wicked plans will be bulldozed and burnt forever. The Patriarch, engulfed by an emotional inferno, will be reeling under the ruthless invasion of Madam Shiela on the diabolic Prem Khanna, wily Jayaprakash Sawant and a few of their leech-like vassals.' Jose Ivans could not help smiling.

'Anything can happen!' He said to himself. 'We should be well prepared for anything. The next is Easter!'

Ivans went to sleep after saying *The Lord's Prayer*! It was 11.30 pm. Janet was with him like a Barbie Doll on the silken bed.

While kissing her goodnight, he realized that Janet looked exactly like his grandmother, Cecily Ivans: so beautiful!

'Thanks to the Good Lord! Not like Katherine.' He took a deep breath.

Smiling to himself, Ivans lay down to be lulled by the muses, and soon was carried away into the world of fantasy where there is no turbulence; only pacifying tranquillity.

Half way, up the pearl-strewn pavement of his pleasure gardens, Ivans thought:

'Life is a frequent commute between one's own fairyland and this trouble-torn planet. A hapless man desperately endeavours to shift himself to the happy shores of his dreamland whenever he is about to drown in the perilous sea of sorrows of this world, and does mostly succeed in saving his life, in a Herculean Effort. He then casts himself back on these temporal shores once it is declared safe here. It recurs very many times, in a quick sequence, before it is time for the final go! Which is real, and which is not?'

Almost hitting his slumber-land, Ivans heard his cell phone quiver.

'Good night, Ms Incognito!' Ivans whispered as he was entering the kingdom of Morpheus, the god of dreams. 'I will see your mail tomorrow!'

When Ivans rose in the morning, it was 4 and drizzling outside. While drying his hair after a hot water shower, he remembered that his mobile had alerted him about an e-mail almost close to midnight.

He woke Janet up. As she was busy getting ready for the Angelus, Ivans flipped through the e-mails. He looked at the mail posted to him at midnight.

The phrasing of the mail shook him up thoroughly and he experienced a mental tremor within himself. To his utter disbelief, the salutation of the mail was very intimate.

'Dear Jo,

I even don't know if this mail ever deserves your attention and time. I do confirm and confess that I had sinned against God and you! If you still hold even an ounce of your old divine patience with me in your precious heart, I humbly beg you to pardon me once and come home with Jan. I want to see both of you together, Jo! Please do it before it is too late. I still remember that conversation between Death and Life which you told me when I fought with you. *Death asked Life, 'Why does everyone love you and hate me?' Life replied, 'Because I am a beautiful lie and you are a painful truth!'*

'I love both of you Jo, a lot...! Now, I know how much both of you mean to me!

Yours apologetically,
Katherine.'

Ivans' heart grew heavier. After closing his laptop, he took the Bible and opened the Holy Book.

Isaiah 52:12

> *Yahweh marches at your head,*
> *And the God of Israel is your rearguard!*

He could not proceed as his heart was at breaking point. It would soon crash into a thousand crimson pieces.

Is Katherine aiming at an unconditional compromise?
If so, is it good for the family and the society?
Will it give Janet a blissful life in future?
Well, should I be ready for the shameful sacrifice?
I'll then be portrayed as crafty for others to chastise.
Janet has chosen Rose and Juan, never is it a vanity,
As her beloved kinsfolk, contrary to her own nature!
I cannot betray them for the whole Paradise!

Why should I dole out, for my defence, this pretext?
Those three are guiltless, the world does know!
It is my terrible state of passive indecisiveness
That makes this issue more pathetic in this context!
Katherine's sudden going kept me over-vexed;
I do regret, now, for not acting quickly to vow
My delight in Rose, thereby, Katherine's earnestness
Towards Jan and me, couldn't have been much flexed!

But, this mail is utterly shocking for any creation
Known to Katherine's complexion! She's in stress!
Unless she is in distress, I swear, she won't thus solicit!
Though I hear her plea, I fear Dr Evil's contention!
We are really caught on the horns of Dispensation!
The interpreters' statutes won't escort us to impress
The watchdogs of marriage, for an easy exit!
I cannot ask even Rose for a conclusion on convention!

'In the name of the Father, the Son and the Holy Spirit...'
Janet started the Angelus.

'Amen!' Ivans startled and replied.

He was cast back on the shore of this temporal world after his wrecked mental navigation.

The sublime smartness of his soliloquy did not comfort him. Though reminded of his golden student life, and his rhetoric skills, the content of the soliloquy inflicted him like an unknown malady.

'A reading from the **Book of Psalms: Psalm 23**.' Janet proceeded:

> *Yahweh is my shepherd, I shall not want.*

As both of them knew it by heart, they chanted it with a lot of precision and devotion.

> *In grassy meadows he lets me lie*
> *By tranquil streams he leads me to restore my spirit*
> *He guides me in paths of saving justice as befits his name.*
>
> *Even were I to walk in a ravine as dark as death*
> *I should fear no danger, for you are at my sight.*
> *Your staff and your crook are there to soothe me.*
>
> *You prepare a table for me under the eyes of my enemies*
> *You anoint my head with oil; my cup brims over*
> *Kindness and faithful love pursue me every day of my life.*
> *I make my home in the house of Yahweh for all time*
> *to come.*

'Amen!' Both said together. Janet smiled at him through eyes and kissed him Good Morning!

'How happy these children are! Jan has already forgotten Katherine, and does not even ask for her Mama. I wish I could be born again as my Mama's *Jo*. How joyful those days were!' Ivans thought to himself.

'Life is like a sportive calf having been fed to his fill from his mother's udder. He grows everyday proportionate to the joy of his master, whereas, his master dreams a day ahead when he will take his clueless victim to the abattoir. So is Fate! She brings us up to be finally sent to her bloody altar to appease the angry Synod of a fretful Pantheon.' He thought and looked outside the window only to see the drizzling getting intensified.

Jose Ivans was lost in the labyrinth of indecisiveness. He did not have anyone to share the impasse he was in; nor was there anyone to show him a way out.

That day Ivans himself dropped Janet at her school and drove straight to *Dream Mansions*. Madam Shiela was waiting for him as she knew it.

'Good morning, Ma'am!' Ivans greeted her.

'Good morning!' She smiled and led him to The Crux –mini-conference hall.

Ivans opened the mail box and pushed the iPad to her.

She read the mail with the alacrity of a baby, watching a shooting star.

After reading the mail, she looked at Ivans. She was disturbed and perplexed.

'What should I do, Ma'am?' Ivans expressed his helplessness. 'What can you read between the lines?'

'Ivans', Madam Shiela spoke clearly and emphatically. 'Don't take a hasty decision. Neither commit nor deny. Wait for a day or two. If it's genuine, we will get the sequel of this mail soon. If there's none, sleep over it.'

'Alright, Ma'am.' Ivans felt relaxed. 'Should Rose know about this?'

'I was going to tell you', said Shiela Khanna. 'Let Rose not know anything till the sequel comes. She will break down, Ivans...! She has no one else...nor does she trust anyone else...!'

'I won't betray her trust, Ma'am!' Ivans said.

'Ivans.' Madam Shiela said.

'Yes, Ma'am!'

'The Podium of The Patriarch?'

'Done, Ma'am.' Ivans said. 'I did it last night.'

'Very good! See you in the office.' Madam Shiela said.

'Done, Ma'am. Goodbye!' Ivans said.

He drove relaxed to Electronics India!

26

Jose Ivans was well before time in Electronics India Pvt. Ltd. Parking his Havana he walked to his chamber through security check. The giant mirror reflected his glorious image admired by the fellow e-Indians. All smiled wishing him *Good Morning.*

'Who knows that a volcano is fuming in their Vice-President's heart?' Jose Ivans thought while wishing his colleagues back.

That was a normal day. Ivans and Rose spent time in their respective chambers getting ready for the Annual Executive Dinner. Occasionally they got calls from Madam Shiela asking for a clarification.

In the afternoon, Rose and Ivans sat in his office for giving the final touch to the Dinner Agenda. Both of them pooled their ideas and complimented each other giving the finishing strokes to the Compendium of the Event.

In the evening, the SIR sat together in Madam's chamber for finalization and approval of the Compendium. All were happy as the work was done.

Rose left the office by 5 pm as she wanted to go to the City Mall for shopping with Jan and Juan.

Ivans stayed back to finish a few more files.

It was his dream to declare Electronics India paper free by the end of the current FY.

While working on the system the mail alert flashed on his mobile and the iPad.

The most unexpected had happened!

Ivans read:

'Dear Jo,

Forgive us for what we have done!

We have been taught by Heavens what life is all about! These days are terribly long and cruel. If you are the same Jo who knows only how to love, you'll come! I know that you *shall*.

Awaiting you and Janet,

Prayerfully,

Your Papa,

Solomon Samuels.'

Ivans sat there for a while as if cut in rock. He could not even believe that Dr Evil could write such a mail to him.

He remembered Dr Samuels scornfully shouting at him:

'Who's your Papa? Don't call me Papa anymore.'

Ivans immediately forwarded the mail to Madam Shiela's personal e-mail ID and leant back in his chair.

'Truth is bitter and painful too.' Ivans thought. 'Dr Evil dropped such a mail, so entreating and pathetically poising himself. I am in deep trouble. When God pushes me thus to the edge of difficulty two things can happen: either He will send His Angels to hold me when I fall, or give me wings to fly towards His mighty Heavens!'

'Now, the sequel has come!' Ivans jumped out of his chair, sweating.

His cell phone called him back to his senses.

'Yes, Ma'am.' He responded.

'Come.'

'Yes, Ma'am.'

Sitting on the chair in Madam Shiela's office, Ivans knew that he was sweating between his brows.

'There are two issues to be sorted out.' Madam Shiela said.

Ivans looked at Madam Shiela. His eyes were blank.

'Listen carefully.' Madam Shiela said.

'Yes, Ma'am.'

'First and foremost is the bond between you and Rose. I know that's very strong; both of you dream of a life together soon. It started in your college days. Cruel fate scripted the first scene of your romance without any compassion for either of you. However, there was a twist. Here, you met again and I was made a facilitator. I am on your side. As Katherine chose her own way and distanced herself from your family, you can surely push the papers for the Dispensation of your marriage immediately.'

'Yes, Ma'am.' Ivans said placing faith in her. 'But, I will be the first in my family to act in that fashion.'

'So what?' Madam Shiela was assertive. 'Do you want to be the first one to commit suicide in the family? Or, the first murderer?'

Ivans swallowed his tongue and gazed at her.

'The second thing', she resumed, 'it's about the mail. There might be something either tricky or critical from Katherine's end. It may also be an attempt to compromise, or a trap, or a claim on Jan, or to entrust something, or even to ask you to sign the papers for divorce...or anything else! Whatever... you are going. Don't worry. I will take care of your safe going and coming. But, before going tell the entire story to Rose. Show her the mails. Both of you should be on the same page. Go to Katherine tomorrow with Jan. You can go after our preview of 23rd April.' Madam Shiela spoke like a Lady Judge.

'Yes, Ma'am.' Ivans accepted it wholeheartedly.

Rose and Ivans stood on the beach watching the pleasure boats sailing beyond the oilrig with the foreign tourists. Jose Ivans opened the iPad and pushed it towards Rose.

Ivans saw pearly beads of sweat hanging on her beautiful nose. She was tense. After reading both the mails, she gave Ivans a bleak smile.

'It's the medicated bandage of a smouldering heart.' Ivans thought.

'Why don't you speak anything, Rose?' Ivans said closing the iPad and keeping it on the backseat of the car.

'Nothing, Jo.' She said with a sigh looking at the sea. 'I am happy that you're meeting her. You have to go with Jan and I also want an end to this state of indecision. At least we will come to know what's what. Hope everything will be well tomorrow. The end justifies the means.'

Jose Ivans moved close to Jessica Rose. She stood leaning against the back door of the car and looked at the oilrig, across the sea. A brinish breeze tried to blow their hearts cold. The crashing tides tried to sync with her cracking tone through a beautifully composed pathetic fallacy!

'The tides and Rose have the same voice: broken and jarred.' Ivans thought. 'Both are sad, deep, equivocal and thus unintelligible.'

He wanted to put his hand on her shoulder and fondle her curls. He thirsted to tell her looking into her deep deep eyes, 'Rose, Ivans is ever yours...!'

But, his hands would not move and tongue would not click... he was nobody to her...officially, socially and religiously they should be strangers...not even known to each other.

The breeze whiffed brushing her thick tresses which hung like a dark cascade vanishing quickly in the mid-air after rolling a few miles down from an upright mountain peak, through a deep valley between two beautiful hills.

Her eyes took the whole evening grandeur of the sunset into them and shone bright and full with an eloquent calmness. He felt that they were pleading with him not to leave her alone.

'Rose..., my love...my everything!' He called her with love and compassion.

'Jo..., my life...my all!' She wept forcing her face into the warmth of his heart.

For the first time, Rose knew that his heart tolled for her. It was shouting her name.

Ivans felt her heart was beating the rhythm of his own heart.

When the sky came down to the earth and met her somewhere in the distant region of an unknown horizon, his Rose and her Ivans knew that their hearts were merging at one point, to be one forever.

Just then the Church bell rang from the hilltop for the Vespers. A blessing from above! Old Joppe lighted the giant candle at the grotto. A small band of believers gathered there to pray.

Rose and Ivans stood near his Havana and watched *Fisher's Valley* getting chequered with the golden spots of flames in the overwhelming darkness: an amazing evening spectacle! The Venetian Gondolas had already returned to the quay of the *Fishers' Creek* and anchored for the day.

'Their faith is another wonder of the world for me!' Ivans thought. 'Life is not qualified by the wealth of the world; nor by the brand of vehicles; size and luxury of the living mansions and overflowing depositories but one's faith in his own ideologies: only faith, nothing else!'

'I believe in you, Jo, for I know you! But, Katherine...!' Rose said.

'You don't worry, Rose.' Ivans said. 'Tomorrow is the Judgement Day in my life. Trust in The Lord!'

'I do trust in Him..., my Jo, *my Jack*!' Rose said sounding like the wholesome chime of the distant Church bell, from the hilltop, which floated in *Fisher's Valley* marking the close of the Vespers. The closing hymn was soon carried to their ready ears and upbeat hearts!

Nearer, my God, to Thee, Nearer to Thee!

As Jose Ivans drove his Havana out of the creaking shores to *The Abode, Fisher's Valley* was resonating with the profound hymn like the rumble of a deadly tremor!

'*The skies are painted with unnumber'd sparks* as Caesar spoke in the play!' Ivans thought.

Both of them joined the chorus of the hymn as usual.

27

As Ivans' Havana drew nearer The Palace, Janet was busy with her latest PS version. She looked fairylike in her maroon frock with cream top. The rosy hair-band was a coronet on her thick glossy hair. Ivans slowed down his car at the huge feudal gate of The Palace.

Janet raised her oracular eyes from her PS and saw the wraithlike gate open. Sensing the surroundings she soon started to scream as if she were under a demonic possession. She threw the PS and wriggled like a worm caught in the beak of a crow.

'No...! Please take me back... Daddy... No...she will kill me... Daddy...please... Take me to Juan!' Janet started sweating profusely like a lamb roasted over a hellfire.

She folded her hands before her Daddy and begged him not to take her into that house haunted by Dr Evil.

Ivans parked his car and placed Janet onto his lap and held her tightly on his paternal bosom.

'My Jan, don't cry.' He said.

'No, Daddy, please take me away from here.' Janet pleaded.

'No one will do you any harm. I'm here to take care of you.' Ivans assured her. 'Don't worry honey, my Jan..., don't worry!'

Though Ivans held her so tightly, she tried to escape from his clasp. She was violently shivering and her heart frantically pounding.

In that mix-up Janet rose on Ivan's lap and fell on the steering wheel flat with her back pressing on the horn. It got jammed. The horn tore apart the eerie stillness of the bleak afternoon. The blast gave Janet another unexpected shock; slowly she stopped struggling and became quiet. Ivans lifted her from the steering wheel and laid her on his lap. When the horn was released, stillness returned.

The traumatic shock had pushed Janet virtually into a state of coma.

Jose Ivans kept sitting in the car, holding his unconscious daughter in hands, not knowing what to do. He looked at her face. He could not see her. She seemed lying submerged in the depth of a pool of tears.

Once again Ivans felt he was gripped by his notorious domestic inaction. He blinked his eyes for a clearer sight. But, clarity was far away.

He was surprised that no one came out of the house even after all this fiasco: neither Katherine nor any Samuels. This was not the kind of reception he anticipated.

He had expected both of them at the front gate itself.

Ivans finally emerged out of the vehicle holding Janet in his arms.

> *Lend me a looking glass!*
> *If that her breath will mist or stain the stone,*
> *Why then, she lives!*

Ivans cried out like King Lear staggering with his senseless Cordelia!

He stood there in the porch sweating and not knowing what to do. Even the dreadful Tiger of Dr Evil did not let out a growl!

After a while, Ivans heard a click at the huge front door. The planks opened like a monster's mouth before swallowing its prey! The dismal lull of a necropolis pervaded the air in that gothic structure of senseless bricks.

Clara appeared to him at the door. She looked tasteless and sluggish. Her vacant eyes did not convey anything to him.

'But, can Clara be that simple? She looked like a fresh widow: white saree and plain forehead; no ornaments and not even slippers. Have I come to the right place?' Ivans asked himself.

Clara's nails were unpolished, hair unkempt and brows bushy!

'Very strange!' He thought.

She looked somewhere in her fifties: a genuine look.

Ivans went up the steps and toddled through the huge parlour and the conference hall.

Clara was walking before him as his mute guide.

From the conference hall she entered the corridor, eastbound, which led him to the Royal Suite of The Palace. It was the last word in luxury, where Ivans and Katherine had stayed after their wedding.

It was indeed in the master bedroom of that suite that Katherine and Ivans had celebrated the consummation of their love.

The room was impeccably designed in opulent shades. Its colour-blend was irresistible and blissfully erupting.

It was there where Katherine had conceived Janet.

Memories started parading on Jose Ivans' already riddled heart.

Clara stopped at the door of the Royal Suite. She struck the clapper. It sounded like a cloister bell. Ivans waited there with Janet lying senseless in his arms. Sweat still hung around on her pretty face, but her breathing was almost rhythmic.

The mighty wooden panels of the door moved and parted from the clasp of each other.

The red carpeted floor of the Royal Suite brought fresh stalks of memories to Ivans. He relived a few of them: the first of everything with Katherine nostalgically flocked around him.

Suddenly, Dr Evil stood at the door.

He looked pallid: someone brutally assaulted by fate and stripped off the perennial scorn on his face.

'Very unnatural and surprising!' Ivans wondered. 'Impossible!'

Seeing Ivans carrying Janet, Dr Evil stepped aside for him to enter.

Ivans walked in...

The interior of the suite was realigned. Earlier, the king-size bed of the master bedroom was placed in the middle of the wooden floor. Now, it was pushed to the farthest end from the entrance. The low beams of the flameless LED pillar candles, stuck at the head wall of the bed, would have paint-brushed a visual feast to the onlookers and embarked them on a different mind-set.

The purple strawberry scented wax of the candles filled the room with a pleasant mood. The rich amber lamps fixed at the corners were glowing with a sorrowful flicker.

'All are newly installed!' Ivans thought.

He was partially blinded as he entered the dimly lit room from the brightness of the day outside.

It was 3 pm.

His eyes were looking for Katherine.

'Where is Katherine?' he wanted to ask Dr Samuels.

Ivans couched Janet gently on a Croissant Sofa and turned towards the anti-chamber.

'Katherine will soon appear and push a divorce note for signing.' Ivans thought.

He felt ill at ease.

'She might even invite us to her rumoured wedding with some Dutch designer.' Ivans remembered reading a headline in some magazine.

He grew impatient!

'Where is she?' Ivans asked Dr Samuels breaking a long and ugly spell of silence.

'Jo... I'm here!'

Ivans thought that he heard a soft murmur.

He turned around and looked at the bed.

Dr Samuels brightened up the light remotely operated through a dimmer.

'Jesus!' Ivans screamed and was almost thrown upwards with a shock.

What he saw was unbelievable and horrible. The spectacle would have scared even a devil.

Ivans could not take it. He sat on the sofa, beside Janet, broken and spent.

'My Lord, my God, Janet shouldn't wake up now. This sight would scare her to death.' Ivans prayed hiding his sweat soaked face in his palms. The air conditioner of the room could not comfort him.

'Jo...what happened to Janet?' the voice heard was like a whisper.

Ivans' celebrated guts forced him to raise his eyes and glance at the dreadful sight again.

He saw a distorted piece of flesh lying on the bed wrapped up in sheets. Only the face of the figure was visible. It was terribly grotesque and fully deshaped. The skin of the forehead was peeled off and the eyebrows were missing. The nose was scooped out of its place, and the nasal bone exposed. White cheekbones were out in the open. The lips were bee-stung and were almost torn off. They could not close the mouth. Those enviable teeth jutted out as if in a nightmare. The natural prominence of the chin was shrunk to the bone making the face frightful and maimed.

'A...r...e... you... Katherine?' Ivans stammered.

'Yes, Jo!' Katherine mumbled.

'But...h...o...w...?' Ivans panted.

Her eyeballs moved. Tears gushed out. Every single soul in the room wept, except for Ivans and Janet.

Ivans was in a shock while Janet was in a coma.

Clara sponged the tears of Katherine. Though her speech lacked clarity, she spoke slowly and firmly. Her unwavering narration told him that her brain was still alert and wholesome. It never lacked in legerity! It had never been at a loss for words!

'Jo... forgive me for being so arrogant and cruel to both of you. God has taught me that He is the Master: Creator, Preserver and Destroyer!' Katherine sobbed and Clara once again sponged the fuming tears away from those lidless eyes.

Ivans looked at her but said nothing and could not.

'When Christabel Marant invited me to Paris, after *Lakmé India Show*, I was in seventh heaven. I knew that my wish was fulfilling: to become the supermodel of the fashion gods.' Katherine paused and looked at Dr Samuels and Clara: a pathetic signal to them to leave the place.

Dr Samuels did not stop her from speaking for long, as he knew that Katherine had refused to undergo even sedation, to kill her pain, in anticipation of the arrival of Ivans and Janet to meet her.

She wished to be fully awake when they would come.

Dr Samuels and Clara left the room.

'I started enjoying life in the world of fashion.' Katherine's voice was very low and feeble. 'Ms Marant introduced me to all the top designers of the whole world. I soon became the hottest commodity, the most sought after model of the industry. I grew busier day by day. Shows after shows and parties after parties! I even stopped calling Papa and was lost in the world of glamour. However, the dreadful feel of imperfection in celebrities does not spare even the perfect.'

Ivans looked at the auto-drainage bags hanging from her bed and slowly filling with the yellowish fluid of pus and blood.

'I also felt that something or the other had to be shaped or done to my features whenever I met someone with a better property. Thus, I became a regular customer of renowned plastic surgeons. I had gone more than fifty times under knives to rectify and reconstruct my looks. The surgeons seemed to be happy cutting, stitching, puncturing, filling and bandaging my body. They wanted money, and I, perfection! Initially both were happy. I quickly went for a lift of my forehead, brows, nose and neck and altered my entire look.

All were wondering at my newly added features. I also received lip-collagen injections for augmenting my natural pout. The collagen was derived from pigs and I didn't know that I was allergic to it.'

Ivans sat on the sofa as if he were listening to a nasty fairy tale.

'How clearly she remembers all!' He wondered at her unfailing memory. 'Brain's not damaged. One can remember everything when the end is near!'

'In Brazil, I went for a liposuction on my abdomen to remove extra fat and stretch marks – a reminder of my little darling, Janet – as I had a longing for the hour-glass-figure of 38-22-38.

'My size zero was in fact enviable and admired by all the other models. But, I was not happy with that. I thought that it was not the ideal size. My friend in Brazil was Ms Bum Bum two years ago. I was taken by her to a doctor for the boob job. I wanted them to be lifted and pointed. The doctor also injected cosmetic gels into my butts, thighs and calves.'

Ivans looked at Janet. She was sleeping. He sighed with relief!

'In the beginning it worked wonders. I became the most wanted and richest model on the globe. The new dermal fillers made up of PMMA gave me a new aura of glamour. All praised me as the best in the business. I was rolling in money. The richest men in the world queued up outside my hotel room to have a turn to sleep with me, but I was picky. It was even rumoured that I had married designer Robinson Crusoe, the world's best.

'In fact, we were in a relationship and planning to get married. Both of us had to get divorce from our spouses.

Ivans gave her a vacant look!

'The world of fashion was reduced to Katherine Samuels. But, everything ended in eight months.' She cried like a child.

When she could control the emotional outpour she resumed, overcoming her troubled breathing.

Ivans wiped her tears with a piece of cotton and sadly looked at her.

'I slowly started feeling a pain in my breasts! They started to swell and looked like two inflated red balloons ready to burst. On the third day, I got admitted to the American Hospital of Paris and soon transferred to the ICU as the pain spread to my butts and legs. The next day, my face started burning with pain and armpits itched like hell. A white fluid, like pus, got slowly discharged through my already blistered nipples.

'*Her PMMA gets reacted as the hydrogel used in the fillers was contaminated.* Dr Paul Bayle, the Head of the Hospital spoke to the fashion world through a medical bulletin. *We are trying hard to remove the stuff and drain the gel. Katherine Samuels is very critical. Pray for her!*

'The whole fashion fraternity of the world prayed for me. Mr Crusoe came to the Hospital for a few days and then suddenly disappeared forever.' Katherine struggled for breath. Her tongue was parched and mouth was dry.

Ivans gave her a spoonful of the fresh apple juice kept beside her bed. She swallowed it like vinegar.

Ivans looked at the Crucifix at her head and said nothing.

There was an unpalatable silence between them as disgusting as the juice to Katherine. So was her story to Ivans.

Silence is sometimes a promoter of comfort, and at other times, it is like a hidden assassin whose presence is felt but still invisible: a harbinger of Doom!

At the end, Katherine broke the long spell of the frozen stillness.

'Infection laid his mighty hands on every inch of my body: my breasts, abs, thighs, calves, face, neck, armpits, and everywhere. Though my body was decomposed, my brain was made more alert and agile: the best form of the Divine Retaliation for my maternal transgressions!

'I know, Jo, God is terribly upset with me for what I've done to both of you.' Katherine cried like a darted quail.

'On the fourth day in the Hospital, I knew that I couldn't be alive much longer. My body started sort of peeling off in shreds, wherever the surgeons had put their knives for all those plasties. Even high dosages of sedation would not deliver me from gripping pain. On the fifth morning, my condition became very bad. While cleaning my breast for medicating, the nipple of my right breast got dissected and it got stuck in the fold of a cotton piece. It looked like a fresh coffee cherry: big round red and cracked! I was in a painful delirium. It had driven me mad. I grinned at the nurse. She stormed out of the room screaming. Soon, a host of doctors rushed in. Their hospitality and professionalism frightened me more than death. I was presently rolled away to the super-specialities. When I fought and came back to my senses, I realized that I was mastectomized. They had clinically and neatly removed my breasts.' Katherine got choked as she struggled for breath.

'My coveted and most admired limbs were also mercilessly hewn off. I remembered my Jan. I had slapped her quiet and even kicked her like a pup when she cried for a suck. I was always worried about the size and temper of my boobs. I wanted them to be tight and standing. My poor Jan would crawl away with a painful whine.'

Her voice started to break. Her speech became inaudible. She paused for a while and slowly raised her eyes and looked at Ivans.

'Now fate has kicked *me* very hard in the teeth. I'm deprived of everything. I'm a terrible mother and a cruel wife. I even refused to sleep with you for fear of my physical wear and tear.

'The silicon injections caused so many silent ruptures throughout my body which left me exposed to serial killers like Granulomas: localized tissue inflammations resulting in the formation of nodules and wandering pains!

'I used to wake up in the darkest hours of nights and my terrible cries made neighbouring patients weep and pray for my sudden death.

'One horrible night, I was somehow struck by the word Euthanasia – mercy killing – about which you were talking at a seminar as part of your Corporate Social Responsibility.

'It was early in the morning. I dreamed that the Chief Surgeon of the Hospital Dr Joshua Quindlen administering deadly poison into my veins while all the other docs and the entire world were watching it rubbernecked. Dr Quindlen had the face of Dr Solomon Samuels.

'I died happily by your side, Jo! But, unfortunately I woke up in the morning only to know that I was still alive writhing on the deathbed.

'I have no more tears to shed, Jo...! Can you please award me my death...please! I don't have hands to fold before you, nor have I legs to kneel down before you and beg... Jo!

'Kill me... Jo! Please...kill me... I can't take it anymore, my Jo...please...!'

Katherine's voice was getting louder with every breath. Her mangled trunk shivered under the pus-stained white sheets like a sacrificial lamb, just cut on the altar of some primitive deities.

Ivans sat there, beside Janet, not knowing what to do. He wanted to speak, and ask her so many questions which had punctually torn him apart every time when he lay on his unfortunate bed with a small child… mother-deprived. The same questions used to break the sorrowful bellows of his revolting lungs: why did she conspire against her own happiness? Why had she brutally turned a blind eye to her child's juvenile dues and a daughter's allowances? Why had he been awarded these spousal sorrows? Why did she go after the fleeting beauty leaving her spiritual feed? Why… why…why…?

A number of such irrefutable queries got stuck in his throat and started choking Ivans. But, he would not ask.

He raised his eyes to see Katherine beckoning him closer to her with her eyes. He moved to her and leaned over her.

The stink, the drain in the bags, the killer instinct of the dripping wounds, the battered and broken frame of Katherine and the Death himself sitting and yawning from a corner impatiently did not scare him at all.

He sat on his haunches beside her when she spoke again.

'Jo, in the West, everyone of the fashion fraternity prayed for my death. But, our good Lord will not hear them for my direful foul against you and Janet. Later, I was also resolved not to die. I withstood all those physical onslaughts and afflictions only with a sole intent: to meet both of you, ask your pardon and die. Though my pretty limbs were most cruelly severed, I would not die. I can see the ghastly face of Death and know that he hangs around in my room all the time. I had reasons not to surrender till I meet you and ask a final favour. That's why I forced Papa to send the mails to you.'

Katherine's voice was very weak. She could hardly speak.

'Don't strain, Kathy!' Ivans tried to speak.

'No, Jo. If I don't ask you that favour, never can I again…. I know!' She wept.

Ivans leaned towards her; now, almost on his knees. His eyes were full, sight blurred.

'Jo,' she said.

'Yes, Kathy.' Ivans replied.

'Can I be your beloved wife in the next birth; to love and to be loved; to be the loving mother of my Janet and many more?' She could not speak any more. Her voice was very low.

Ivans could not say anything.

How could he say that she was no one in his life anymore and Rose was enshrined in his heart till the end of the universe?

'I cannot be a cheat!' Ivans felt.

He relived the time when Rose stood beside him on the beach and looked at him with her inconsolable gaze begging him not to leave her alone.

Jose Ivans rose frantically to his feet blinking his eyes to clear his vision. A few crystal drops fell from his eyes crashing on to Katherine's face and the white sheets: the last rites?

Like a tigress biting her cub and leaping and bouncing to save it from a glaring danger, Ivans picked Janet in a frenzy and stormed out of the suite.

'Jo…..no…..don't go…. I didn't finish speaking…. I didn't see my Janet….. I didn't speak to my child…. Jo…..please….!' Katherine frantically cried!

Her voice was unheard and she was left totally devastated.

Dr Samuels and Clara ran out from their anti-chambers sensing something wrong. They rushed towards Katherine's bed. They stood there not knowing what to do.

Ivans and Janet were already gone!

Outside the suite, near the porch, they heard the roar of a Havana engine. Ivans' car desperately flew out of The Palace – the dreadful house of Death.

Back in the palace suite, there lay the crest of pride, broken down under the white sheets. The tattered trunk of the *Modelling Icon of India* – the legendary Katherine Samuels – waited there not for a deafening ovation, customary hug or kiss or a glamorous crown; but for a Priest and a Sexton, and to be laid to rest under a poor heap of earthly shelter among nettles and brambles.

Next evening, an ambulance drew closer and stationed at the rear gate of the old Queen Mary Church in the City outskirts. Four men in black alighted from the hearse and through its back-door they pulled out a poor box wrapped in black linen. They slow-marched with the black casket through unpruned bushes and creepers, deeper into the massive Churchyard, followed by the Parish Priest and the Sexton. In the far-east corner of the yard, in a crooked gravel pit they laid the poor remains of a once pretty woman which measured hardly three feet after Fate conspired with the surgeons. She had madly pursued her ambition jeopardizing life and losing all that was worthy being loved and enjoyed.

Jose Ivans stayed near the grave with Janet safe in his arms. He made Janet also throw a handful of earth into the grave as the casket was lowered into. They chanted:

Dust thou art,
And into dust thou shalt return!

There stood Shiela Khanna, Dr Mohan Prakash and Krishnan Potti near Ivans watching the obsequies. At the head of the grave sat Dr Solomon Samuels broken and paralyzed, in a wheel chair. His face was enshrouded in a veil of distress and detachment.

Ivans remembered how Dr Samuels took Katherine from *The Abode* that day.

When the soil was evened off, Clara rolled him away somewhere along the rock slabs of the pavement. The clatter of the wheels was soon heard no more.

The few mourners lingering there also slowly disappeared casting their bleak glances at Ivans and his child.

'None of them had a face!' Ivans thought. 'Pathetic!'

Soon, a mound was raised and a Cross was stuck at its head by the men in black. A wreath with a banner of Electronics India Pvt. Ltd. was offered on the crux of the red mound by Krishnan Potti.

The Priest had already left for the Church. The Church bell tore off the religious smugness of the faithful hypocrites urging them to come for the evening service.

Ivans remembered Macbeth mumbling after his Lady's death.

Life is a tale told by an idiot,
Full of sounds and fury
Signifying nothing!

Madam Shiela's Rolls Royce glided through the Churchyard gates with them, and its mighty gates grated behind them.

Ivans pinched on his arms to make sure that he was not dreaming. Janet lay on his lap in dreams already playing with Juan on the beach beside Jessica Rose.

28

April 23!

Saturday!

Evening!

8.30 pm!

Prem Khanna alighted from the podium of The Patriarch after outrageously enumerating his self-applauding accomplishments in Electronics India Pvt. Ltd.

The e-Indians were not a bit impressed hearing such incredible lies from their abhorred CMD's deliberations!

'Another Charles Darwin!' Krishnan Potti whispered in the ears of Jose Ivans.

Ivans could not help laughing. It infected Rose too. Like malaria it lingered in the air for some time.

Everyone clapped Prem Khanna out of the podium before he could even conclude his complimentary annual speech drafted by his crooked Headmaster – the COO, Mr Jayaprakash Sawant.

Prem Khanna had to leave the podium humiliated. His speech was adjudged as the boastful crowing of an upstart crook.

Jose Ivans discovered that the epicentre of the ovation was Krishnan Potti who was sitting beside him like a Buddhist Monk in deep meditation.

Then...!

There mounted the heart and soul of Electronics India – the most adored Madam Shiela Khanna. There erupted several rounds of thunderous applause.

Ivans realized that it broke out from his neighbour, precisely from the meditating Monk.

'Even the hawk-eyes of the CCTV would not have captured Krishnan Potti's heroics.' Ivans said to Rose.

'Yes, tremendous!' Rose agreed.

Sir Falstaff still sat there with his eyes closed as if he did not know anything.

Union Ministers, business magnates, foreign delegates, tycoons and icons of business fraternity, MDs, CEOs, country heads and administrative heads of different firms and the CMs of different states were also in the attendance to mark the Blue Ribbon Day of Electronics India.

Madam Shiela looked like Mother Mary in her white chudidhar: fair and immaculate; soothing and protective. The Guardian Angel of Electronics India!

She awarded Gold Medals to the best department, best e-Indians and the superannuating employees as per the annual practice of the Executive Dinner.

Madam Shiela's speech was full of maxims, aphorisms and quotable quotes. Every word from her was received by the executives with great appreciation and enthusiasm.

Krishnan Potti was very particular not to applaud untimely.

The untimely claps of Krishnan Potti to get Prem Khanna out of the podium had really gone viral in the hall.

Now, everyone's eyes were on the face of a sweet lady who sat in the front row of the VVIPs. She was so pretty that the entire crowd cheered at her whenever her face flashed on the big LED screens installed in the auditorium. She looked dashingly cute and highly royal, yet simple and gifted.

When the clapping and cheerful shouts died out, Shiela Khanna began.

'My dear brothers and sisters in this august gathering...'

Thunderous claps rumbled and rolled all over. Once again Potti was the unwavering epicentre of all these testimonials.

The Queen of Electronics India resumed.

'First of all, I wish all of you a marvellous Blue Ribbon evening on the eve of Easter, the Festival of Resurrection and Hope.'

A loud cheer broke in the hall as the crowd greeted Madam Shiela back.

'Thank you, Ma'am. Same to you!' They shouted.

She spoke again. Every word was delivered with great accuracy, calculation, wisdom and sincerity. Her speech instantaneously became the motivational anthem of every listener present.

'Electronics India Pvt. Ltd. continues scaling new heights every day. The past financial year witnessed our company retaining its supreme status among the e-manufacturers of the sub-continent. Thanks to you, dear ones. It's your hard work that made it possible. We're one!'

Cheers!

'We don't ever discriminate people in our company. We have all learned that *Temple, Masjid and Church* have been made up of an equal number of English alphabets, so are *Geeta, Quran and Bible.*'

Cheers!

'We are like the hands of a clock: no matter that one is fast and the other is slow. All that matters is to keep ticking and move together towards the goal. Or, we are like our feet.

The front one has no pride and the back one has no shame. Because both of them know pretty well, that the situation shall change soon.'

She had to pause as there broke a deafening applause.

Ivans looked at Prem Khanna and Jayaprakash Sawant. Both of them sat there like two kittens fallen into a duck pond and somehow escaped drowning.

When the cheers subsided, Madam Shiela continued.

'If you can't fly…..run, if you can't run….walk, if you can't walk….crawl, but, make sure that you keep moving towards your goal. If you think positively, sound becomes music, movement becomes dance, frown becomes smile, sleep becomes meditation and then life becomes….!'

'Celebration….!' Potti shouted from the rear of the auditorium which was chorused by the entire crowd. Everyone heard Potti shout, 'Therefore…, life is a feast…, celebrate it!'

Potti's face flashed on the big screen amidst a big cheer which made the condition of the kittens more pathetic.

Madam Shiela acknowledged Potti's effort with a sweet smile. It was reflected on the screen.

'Yes…., life is a feast, celebrate it!'

Cheers!

'But, it never seems to be the way we want it. We should learn how to live it the best way we want it. There is no perfect life....but we can fill it with perfect moments. Be happy in the moment. That's enough. Each moment is all what we need. Not more.....so.....celebrate it!'

Cheers!

'We all work for a better tomorrow and live with worries. But, when tomorrow comes, we postpone our celebrations and again start thinking of an even better tomorrow! Celebrate it today with a sweet smile on your face, now!'

Five thousand hands celebrated every word of Madam Shiela. The Patriarch had not heard, nor seen anything like that before.

'Smile and silence are two powerful tools of a successful person.' She resumed.

All fell back to silence with a smile on their face.

'Smile solves many problems while silence avoids many problems. Forget the past that makes you cry and focus on the present that can make you smile.'

This time they did not clap. Instead, they smiled at each other silently, which made her happier.

'How obedient our people are! Madam's charisma is amazing!' Rose said to Ivans.

'True!' Ivans said. 'She is like America's Martin Luther for India. She has a dream!'

With great admiration, Rose looked at Madam Shiela and smiled at Ivans.

'I have a dream.' Coincidently Shiela Khanna shouted from the podium.

Rose looked at Ivans with more appreciation and admiration.

'I have a dream that we shall all live with a heart free from sorrow, mind free from worry, body free from illness and a life full of spiritual wellness. We should all live in a state of perfect corporate harmony. Some people come into our life as a blessing, others as a lesson. We should learn how to receive both, silently with a smiling face. There lies the success of our corporate world.'

Shiela Khanna paused to look at Prem Khanna and Jayaprakash Sawant. They immediately withdrew their wrathful glance from her face and looked at each other muttering something. They neither smiled nor kept silence.

'In due course of time, I've learnt that an empty wallet can teach you a million lessons and a full one can spoil a million values.

'Compromises may gift you friends and happiness; ignorance may gift peacefulness and buoyancy whereas knowledge can alone gift you acceptance and existence. Do not base your life on the likes and dislikes of others. Fortunately, you are to live your own life. Seek only for the supreme knowledge and thus shape your life and live it.

'I've also learnt whatever you give others will definitely come back to you in multiples. You cannot stop what is coming back, but you can always decide what to give out. Creation is painful: be it anything!'

Silence!

'The enormous growth of our company didn't happen on a fine morning when we woke up on the right side of our bed. The journey was not easy. It inflicted physical and mental blisters on us. I've realized that there are mainly two types of pains in this world: pain that hurts you to ruin you and pain that hurts you to transform! When problems encompassed us I also realized that they were transient. They reminded me of the number locks. The solution is within the lock itself. We only need to show our mettle and patience to get them unlocked. In order to succeed, your desire for success should be greater than your fear of failure. A real winner shows his construction whereas an ideal loser exhibits his character. Both are courageous. Only the brave succeed! Cowards never rise after a fall to fight again to succeed.'

Silence!

'I've understood that courage is not the absence of fear. It is the ability to face fear, overcome it, finish the job and reach your destination. It took thirty odd winters for our company to occupy its current premier position in industry. Every struggle in our life has shaped me into what I am today. I am thankful to the mighty Heavens for the hard times we confronted in the past. They alone could make us stronger and perform better. Almighty God changed every mess that we confronted into a message; a test into testimony; a trial into triumph and a victim into victor.'

This time, Potti could not resist his impulse. He clapped and once again it went viral in The Patriarch.

'What a great speech!' Ivans said to Rose. 'Its spontaneity, clarity and phrasing show what a great leader she is!'

'The Harvard Effect!' Rose added.

'All these years, I've never prayed for my life to get easier. I just prayed to my God to make me stronger.' Shiela Khanna proceeded. 'Life has taught me that simplicity is the noblest stress-buster. The simpler you are, the nobler you become and you live the happier. Happiness in life solely depends on the quality of one's thoughts. Don't allow small things to depress you; you have very many great things to look up to God and rejoice!'

Cheers!

'We often think that others' lives are better than that of ours, but, we always forget that we are also *others* for others.

'No man in this world is rich enough to buy his past. That's the only time God has also admitted His helplessness. He will also wear a helpless countenance and smile at us silently when we pray to Him for our past. If you live the present sensibly, we needn't buy our past!

'Life is not qualified by our fluent tongues, branded belongings or flashy costumes that we are clad in, but the number of faces that bloom when they see ours.'

A sensational cheer broke out in the hall which took a few minutes to settle.

When she raised her hand, silence prevailed.

'Now the time has arrived to unveil the number we target for the current Financial Year. The turnover of the previous FY was 1,66,000 crore.'

Cheers!

'We have reached the magical number for the current FY after great mathematical deliberations held among all our departments. Finally, the HR department has arrived at a figure with the strong conviction and support of the BD. And the number is...3,50,000 crore...!'

As the figure flashed on the big screen, the entire crowd went berserk with excitement.

'We have so many reasons to rejoice about tonight.' As Shiela Khanna resumed, the acclamation subsided.

'I proudly announce that, Rahul is coming into the Board of Directors. He will be designated CEO of Electronics India Pvt. Ltd.'

Applause cloudburst in The Patriarch. Rahul Khanna's face flashed on the giant screen. The CMD and the COO went into their shells. This was beyond anything that they could imagine.

'How could it be possible?' the COO frowned at the CMD. 'It was not agreed upon in the board meeting. We had decided to bring him into only as a Director.'

'I don't know anything!' Prem Khanna expressed his ignorance through restless gestures.

Shiela Khanna and Rahul Khanna were the stars of the evening: all admired the absolute makeover of their Crown Prince!

'But, the most important event is yet to come.' Shiela Khanna declared.

The audience pricked up their ears as earnestly as warhorses did on ancient terrains.

'I call upon Prem Khanna to come to the podium. *Prem, please...!*'

Prem Khanna could not stop going as he could read her body language. It was almost a command. Disobedience would invite afflictions.

He rose from his seat and rolled like a defeated Sumo wrestler towards the podium. The astonished and crestfallen JPS sat there alone wondering what the surprise would be!

'Is the bitch going to terminate me?' He asked himself and started sweating.

'I thank all of you for having come to witness this moment.' Shiela Khanna said.

JPS kept his hand right on his heart lest it would burst.

'The most important and most crucial in our life.' She resumed.

'Finish your damned speech fast, you bitch or else you will be carrying my body out of this hall on a stretcher.' JPS mumbled.

Prem Khanna was now on the stage.

'What is going to happen there?' Potti could not hold the anxiety anymore.

'Wait and see.' Ivans smiled at Potti.

'The termination of the COO?' Potti queried.

Rose smiled at Potti and looked at the podium.

'You might have been guessing all this evening who this pretty lady is.' Shiela Khanna said pointing at the most beautiful face around, which was now on the screen.

The COO took a deep breath and sank into his chair relieved from his tenterhooks.

The entire crowd cheered at the pretty face as it smiled like the freshness of Indian dawns.

'We, the proud parents of Rahul are delighted to announce that she is Rahul's Valentine, Dr Julia Michael George. She is the only daughter of Padma Vibhushan Dr Michael George, Founder Patron of *Good Hope* – Global Centre for Detoxification and Rehabilitation Programmes.'

The crowd did not allow Madam Shiela to complete the announcement. They had already started celebrating the good news. Potti was the epicentre as usual!

'Therefore, life is a feast..., celebrate it!' Potti shouted at the top of his voice which was echoed against the roof of The Patriarch. The crowd was simply unstoppable.

JPS glared at Prem Khanna. Prem Khanna avoided his look!

Madam Shiela invited Julia, Dr George, Dr Prakash and Rahul to the stage. Julia, in a moonlight suit stole the thunder of the evening with a sparkle in her eyes and an exquisite smile on her pretty face.

As Madam Shiela hugged Julia, Prem Khanna stood there clueless. Dr George came and shook hands with him. So did Dr Prakash and all the other dignitaries. While his hands were aching, Prem Khanna's eyes were searching for the wily COO. JPS was traceless.

But, Ivans, Rose and Potti were watching Jayaprakash Sawant stealing his way out of the hall rubbing his plate and muttering to himself like a lunatic.

Haughty Rekha Sawant and her obedient mother closely followed him and quickly vanished into the murky night of the fluorescent City.

As celebration peaked in the patriarchal guildhall, the band was playing the most popular number of the evening, Andy Williams': '*Where do I begin...*'

The song peaked and died out...!

All had gone!

Prem Khanna still stood on the podium, single in an alien field, blinking and grinning at everyone off the stage.

He had *really* understood *nothing*!

29

Jose Ivans was woken up by his cell phone.

Switching on the bed lamp, he looked at the clock. It was 3.30 in the morning.

When he went to sleep, it had been 2 am.

After the Executive Dinner, Rose and Ivans picked up Janet and Juan from *The Abode* and went to Church for midnight mass at the Church of Mary the Immaculate on the hilltop.

After Easter Mass, Ivans dropped off Rose and Juan at home and reached *The Abode* only after 1.45 am.

Ivans' cell phone vibrated again.

Rose!

He sat up!

'Martin must have surely come home for *celebrating* his Easter!' Ivans became restless. 'I shouldn't have let her stay there tonight.' He felt guilty.

'But, how could I have asked her to stay here...?'

The cell phone was still blinking and shivering.

He soon received the call!

'Yes, my Rose?'

'Jo...!' Rose panicked.

'Tell me, Rose, what happened?' Ivans urged.

'Jo..., switch on the TV...soon...and see the news breaking now! I am afraid! I don't know what to do?' Rose almost broke down.

Ivans sprang out of his bed and ran into the library.

Switching on the TV, he grabbed the remote from the drawer and flipped the screen to CNN-IBN. What he saw made him almost senseless. It totally rattled his secure composure.

BREAKING NEWS

Doctors killed in ambush. Renowned addictionologist and philanthropist Padma Vibhushan Dr Michael George (60) of Good Hope and his Personnel Head Dr Mohan Prakash (35) die in a suspected terror attack near their hospital. Dr Michael's daughter Dr Julia Michael George has been seriously injured in the incident and admitted to St Lucia Medical College where the bodies of the deceased are kept in the morgue. Their car was ambushed on their

way back to Good Hope after attending the Blue Ribbon Day celebrations of Electronics India Pvt. Ltd. at The Patriarch in the City.

Ivans blacked out. He sat on the floor holding the phone in one hand and the remote in the other.

Rose screamed out to get the response from Ivans over the phone, but, he did not hear anything; he did not see anything and did not feel anything. What he could hear was sobs. He could see only blood and feel only was death.

He even got the smell of blood! 'Had not Mohan visited me at *The Abode* before going to The Eternal Abode?'

As Rose dropped the line, his cell phone shivered again. It called him back to his senses.

'Ma'am...!' Ivans raved.

His hands were numb. Somehow he pressed the key to receive it.

'Ma'am...!' he cried.

'Ivans, please come soon to St Lucia. I don't know what to do. We're destroyed!' Madam Shiela snapped the line.

Ivans dialled up Rose.

'Rose, drop Juan here. Come to St Lucia immediately. I'm starting now!'

Dropping the line, he shot through the porch to his car.

The next moment, his Havana flew out like a Peregrine Falcon on hunt.

Sparing a few drunken peddlers and occasional motorists, the road was almost free during those wee hours. Ivans even overtook a speeding ambulance with Death howling through its red beacon lights.

Madam Shiela was standing at level 3 ICU on the first floor. Two armed black cats of the RAF were guarding the ICU. She looked shattered. Her eyes were full. She was on the verge of breakdown.

'Ivans...!' Madam Shiela sobbed.

Jose Ivans held her tightly lest she should fall.

Rahul was sitting on a bench; with eyes cast down, shaking his head and outrageously muttering.

Retaining his reputed presence of mind, Ivans helped Madam Shiela to stretch on a sofa. She lay there with her eyes tightly closed. Tears flowed out through her eyes and fell on the granite slabs drawing a few quaint patterns on them.

Ivans touched Rahul's shoulder.

He raised his eyes.

Ivans had another shock seeing Rahul's face. It was bleeding as he had dug his nails into his temples and cheeks.

Seeing Ivans, he cried bitterly like a child.

'Uncle...! Julia...! I want to see my Julia...what has happened to her...? Uncle..., please...u...n...c...l...e...! They don't let me in... I must see her...!'

Rahul's pitiful cries could be heard throughout the floor. He held Ivans with both his hands and shook him violently.

Ivans knew that Rahul's sight was slowly dimming...! He could not cry any more.

Blood oozed from the nail ruts on Rahul's face. His left eye was also bleeding from a deep dig. It was clear that he would hurt him again.

At that very moment the Head of the Medical Staff, Dr Jouhra Begum came out accompanied by a few of her colleagues. Seeing Madam Shiela lying, she gave orders to shift her to one of the deluxe VVIP rooms on the wings.

As Rahul was growing more violent, he had to be put on sedation in another room.

Rose too arrived at that moment.

Ivans let out a sigh of great relief upon seeing her. It revived the *Jose Ivans* in him: the undisputed champion of emergencies.

Madam Shiela and Rahul were soon shifted to their rooms on the wings. Ivans asked Rose to be with Madam Shiela. Rahul had to be manoeuvred to rest until the sedation started working.

As Rahul slept, Ivans looked at his disfigured face. Blood was leaving red spots on the medicated cotton of the bandage.

Soon, the City Police Commissioner Dr Dona Sandra, IPS arrived there with a few officers and assessed the security blanket of the hospital.

Both Dr Begum and Dr Sandra met Ivans in the former's office and discussed the aftermath.

'The reasons of the assassination will be known in an hour.' Dr Dona Sandra said. 'Before that their autopsy has to be done. We need the medical report.'

'All arrangements have been made for the autopsy.'

'It will be done under tight security as we expect another attack on the young doctor as the RAW has issued a red alert.' The Commissioner said.

'How is Julia now, Doctor?' Ivans asked.

'Very critical.' Dr Begum said. 'We are trying our best to save her life. I've left everything to God.'

'We have already cordoned off the hospital and it is under the surveillance of our radar.' The officer asserted. 'Our team has already visited the spot and the FIR...'

The Commissioner's wireless alerted.

'Excuse me!' Dr Sandra received the call.

'My God...! What...?' She reacted with a shock. 'Okay, don't let it out now! Do what I told you in the meeting.'

She cut the line.

'It's a missile attack.' The Commissioner said. 'They are making the FIR. We have already laid siege to all strategically important places and blocked all the outlets to prevent the escape of the militants. Security has been beefed up as best as possible!'

A staff nurse came rushing and wanted Dr Jouhra Begum in the ICU immediately.

'Sorry, I'll meet you later.' Dr Begum rushed out.

The Commissioner also left Ivans to give fresh instructions to her team.

Left alone in the room, Jose Ivans wept for his dearest friend, Dr Mohan Prakash.

He was Ivans' greatest fan, friend and helper in all his difficulties.

'You ran to me when Katherine died and stood by me and comforted me.' Ivans mumbled. 'How will I console your Mummy, Alice and kids?' He knew that depression was gripping him fast.

He grew restless.

'Depression grips the weak like a malady!' Ivans thought. 'But, he cannot ruse me to conquer my will anyway. Depression is my rival captain. Both of us play to win. He will be always under pressure as he is playing against *Jose Ivans*: the man born to win.'

Ivans got up and hurried to Rahul. A staff nurse was attending to him.

'Poor boy!' Ivans thought. 'Though being a millionaire and Crown Prince of an MNC, he is peace-deprived.'

Rose came to Ivans and called him to Madam Shiela's room.

He went with her.

'Any information, Ivans?' Madam Shiela asked.

She looked steady despite her voice being low.

'We are defeated, Ivans; we are ruined.' Madam Shiela said.

'Ma'am....!' Ivans did not know what to say.

He looked at Rose and then at Madam Shiela.

'These are moments when silence plays a double role: friend and foe, hero and villain or saviour and tormentor.' Ivans thought.

'Ma'am', said Ivans after an tedious pause, 'it's a terror attack. They've used a very powerful missile in the operation. Security has been tightened and search being launched everywhere.

'This damage can never be repaired!' Shiela Khanna could not control herself.

She wept silently, but bitterly.

Ivans and Rose grew more helpless.

'I know we shouldn't be shaken at this time.' Madam Shiela said reviving her mettle. 'We have to put our heads together to proceed. We will not concede defeat.'

Once again, the SIR was operational.

'Ask Mr Potti to come here.' Madam Shiela said. 'Also tell him to pick up Venkat along with him. Let James drive my Phantom.'

Ivans' cell phone shook in his pocket.

'Krishnan Potti.' Ivans said while receiving the call.

'Yes, Potti?'

'Sir, I am at the gate. The RAF don't let me in!' Potti showed his helplessness.

'Okay, wait.' Ivans snapped the line and called the Commissioner.

Potti came into Madam Shiela's room in two minutes.

Ivans took him to Rahul's room and briefed him.

Potti understood the gravity of the situation and voluntarily chose to stay with Rahul.

'Easter is celebrated throughout the world.' Ivans thought. 'But, here it is still Good Friday!'

Dr Jouhra Begum rushed out of the ICU and beckoned Ivans to her. He went out to meet her.

She whispered something in Ivans' ears and hurried away.

'What happened?' Rose gestured to ask him.

He called her out of the room to speak to her lest Madam Shiela should hear.

'Julia is on ventilator.' He said. 'Very critical.'

'Jesus….!' Rose gasped.

Presently the Church bells rang for the Angelus waking the doves in the belfry of the Old Portuguese Church.

Rose and Ivans crossed their forehead closing their eyes in holy fear!

30

Easter Sunday!

Print media – both national and global – dedicated their frontlines with mournful eulogies to the two deceased Good Samaritans of *Good Hope* for their nearly impossible philanthropic efforts in just filling hopes in the hopeless and life in the lifeless.

Visual media encapsulated the sad demise of the two docs as a loss to the entire mankind.

National flags across the world would fly half-mast.

President, Vice-President and Prime Minister of India termed it, a national tragedy.

The President of USA and the Prime Minister of UK condoled the demise of Dr Michael George and his colleague. UNO expressed its shock over the incident.

The whole world condemned the attack and hoped for the immediate arrest of the culprits.

In an emergency meeting, the Union Cabinet unanimously handed over the probe to CBI – Central Bureau of

Investigation. The CBI could already trace out the militant movements. They had already received some vital information about the assassination.

Condolences flooded at *Good Hope*: a marooned mausoleum on *Haunting Meadows* among those possessed pine trees. Ms Pooja and Mr Shabbir had already reached St Lucia to be with Dr Julia!

The nation would see off the brave hearts at a full state funeral on Easter Monday.

The bodies would lie in state at the Civil Station for the public to pay their homage.

The District Authorities received the bodies from St Lucia Medical College by 4 pm and took them to the District Headquarters.

The doctors lay at the headquarters in state covered by the Tricolour, the National flag of India.

Mourners thronged highways, byways and subways near the Civil Station in salutation.

Madam Shiela decided that Jose Ivans would escort his dearest friend Dr Mohan Prakash to his birthplace for his funeral.

Jessica Rose and she herself would accompany Dr George to *Good Hope* in his last journey.

Potti would stay back with Rahul and Julia at St Lucia.

Rahul would not be released from the hospital and would be kept under sedation as he tried to break open the door of the ICU earlier in the morning to see Julia. He was uncontrollably violent.

'No….she won't sleep without talking to me, so long….she can't sleep like that! I want to see her, you are lying…..! She is mine…only mine...please, I beg you, please! I want to see my Julia…!'

Rahul screamed out and hit the huge doors of the ICU with his head and fists.

The security personnel had to finally handcuff him for fear of getting himself hurt and attacked.

They brought him to his room. Dr Begum immediately ordered to administer strong sedatives to him.

At the Civil Station things did not turn out as scheduled. Long queues of mourners still stood patiently outside to see the departed.

By 11 pm, Alice and her daughters arrived from the US. It was a heart breaking spectacle. Alice swooned on the coffin by seeing Mohan's body. The children did not know how to react. They were already under the strong grip of a cosy numbness. They would not know the foul game of the cruel Fate.

Seeing Ivans, both of them cried in his arms. Slowly, they realized what had happened to their life. Their beloved Daddy was gone….gone forever! No one in flesh and blood could console the puerile sobs of their tender hearts.

The able Commissioner of Police, Dr Dona Sandra IPS and her efficient officers had to struggle a lot to take the coffins out of the Civil Station premises through the crowd. They placed them on Wagon Hearses wrapped in wreaths and garlands.

Jose Ivans sat near the coffin of his good comrade at Stanford.

'What an amazing pal he was!' Ivans wept.

He agonised over the good old days at their Alma Mater. How they held on to each other at hard times and how they together celebrated each of the winning moments in their great academic and literary pursuits. Ivans recalled *Twelfth Night* on the stage! What a great performer Mohan was!

Somehow, Ivans managed in persuading Alice and the daughters to escort the body in his Havana driven by Rashid, the best driver of Electronics India.

Dr Mohan's funeral cortege began at 11.30 pm.

The procession to *Good Hope* would only start at 1 am, the following day.

The crowd at the Headquarters was still uncontrollable.

No one knew what Dr George and his *Good Hope* gave to the world of addiction: fumes, sniffs and pricks, and how much he meant to the liberation and redemption of an otherwise lost generation!

Though the freezer was on, Ivans knew that his brows were sweating.

He started reading the e-Bible on his cell phone.

Psalm 18:

> *Yahweh is my rock and my fortress,*
> *My deliverer is my God.*
> *I take refuge in Him, my rock,*
> *My shield, my saving strength,*
> *My stronghold, my place of refuge.*
> *I call to Yahweh who is worthy of praise,*
> *And I am saved from my foes…*

No weeping of the hearts, no howling of the sirens and no shouting of the slogans did Ivans hear! Instead, he heard the voice of the Angels, singing a welcome song stationed at the mighty Gateways of the Paradise.

He also saw his Lord and two glorious flames ascending to the Garden of Eden beyond the Gulf of Fire and Brimstone: the Inferno!

Before the Angelus they reached Dr Mohan's ancestral home. The mourners, bursting with sorrows, stood there to see their beloved doctor. Mohan was the first one to study at Stanford from the district and was their pride.

As the coffin was laid on the stands, Mohan's mother fainted. Ivans held her close to his heart.

He recounted the delicious meals cooked by her for both of them whenever they visited her in the village.

'Now, she is totally broken down and benumbed!' Ivans thought. 'She senselessly lies on my shoulders.'

He remembered **Mathew 11:17:**

> *We played the pipes for you,*
> *And you wouldn't dance;*
> *We sang dirges and you wouldn't be mourners!*

His cell phone alerted an SMS from Rose. She told him that the authorities had decided to fly the body to *Good Hope* as they had to cross the tragic spot.

The RAW had warned them of more similar militant operations.

Easter Monday!

The body of Dr George was flown home to *Good Hope* early in the morning. Five army choppers landed on the bereaving air strip beyond *Primrose Garden* at 6.30 am.

The weather soon turned inclement.

The pine forest to the west of the *Canyon of Hellhounds* started agitating unusually. They heard the groan of the wounded and the yelp of the hellhounds as if some souls were being hunted down. A storm was gathering in the forest.

The coffin was placed in the vestibule for all to pay respects.

Madam Sarah Michael George looked at her beloved's mortal remains from her portrait beneath the Sacred Heart of The Lord.

Her fresh smile was dimming out on her face!

31

A storm howled in the pines of *Good Hope*.

The addicted patients in the cells stared at the horrible sight. They understood very little.

Madam Shiela and Jessica Rose once again became the champions of the situation rising to the occasion.

The leaders and the organizers in them were magical.

Soon, drinking water was available; breakfast was ready for inmates and escorting crew; floral display was hung everywhere, mournful banners were printed and hung, tomb was almost ready and a convoy was sent from the City to escort the Archbishop and the other clergy.

A canopy was raised on *Tom Quad*, near *Mercury*. Stands were prepared for the body to be laid. The entire area was spick and span in an hour. All was in place.

Presently, a number of armed troopers entered surprising everybody. They occupied all the strategic points and took control of everything.

The bomb squad became active with screeners, scanners and sniffers.

At 9 am, a police wagon and a few more vehicles stopped at the South Gate.

Dr Dona Sandra IPS, Dr Jouhra Begum and her father Dr Ali Masood came in and were soon with Madam Shiela and Jessica Rose.

The Police Commissioner confided in Madam Shiela and Rose that Prime Minister of India and High Commissioners of the UK, Canada and Ambassador of the US would attend the funeral.

Dr Ali cried like a child at the coffin of his bosom friend. He thought about Julia fighting for life at St Lucia. Only Dr Ali knew how Julia came into Dr Michael's life.

He was now revisiting the entire episode of that fateful night, five and twenty years ago. He remembered the pallid face of the hapless mother and her twin daughters. The mother and the other daughter were interred in *Primrose Garden*. He recalled how his friend was forewarned by the yelling spirits for being driven into the pine trees by Fr Henry Narimann. He also remembered the two letters on the pendent held by the unfortunate mother in her hands when she died divine and smiling.

Dr Ali refused to go anywhere leaving Michael cold in the coffin. He insisted sitting beside him as he wanted to see his friend.

Jessica Rose was entrusted with the Herculean task of preparing a makeshift altar for the funeral mass in *Tom Quad* as the *Good Hope* cathedral was too small to house an expected crowd of 25,000 mourners.

Rose prepared a beautiful altar for the offering near the East Gate apartment where Dr George lived. She arranged the flowers tastefully in Japanese Ikebana style!

A team of 30 youngsters of the *Good Hope* staff soon joined Rose to shift most of the mass-tools from the cathedral to *Tom Quad* altar. All of them joined Rose and whole-heartedly carried out her instructions as most of them were known to her when they celebrated Juan's birthday at *Good Hope* the previous year.

They removed the pews and the chairs from the cathedral and placed them in order which created innumerable aisles under the shamiyana. Hundreds of chairs were laid in anticipation of holding a large number of mourners in *Tom Quad*.

The Tabernacle was placed above the altar, under the big Crucifix. Stoups were fixed in every corner with holy water. Ciboria were carefully arranged. The lectern was ready with the Gospel and the Ambo and the Missal on the altar.

The Chalice, Paten, Corporals, Purificators, Host and Cruets were piously set on the Pall, waiting for the Celebrants.

The Presidential chair and the Celebrants' chairs were put on the sanctuary.

The processional cross and candles were neatly arranged at the entrance.

Bells and censors were given to the boys for the procession to the altar.

Hymnals and ordines were placed on the pews and the chairs.

Sanctuary lamps started burning.

Mikes were set on the lectern, the ambo and the altar. All the sound engineers were well informed of the frequency response of the speakers.

The *Good Hope* Grand Choir was ready and well set for the liturgical chant with the grand piano, violins, organs, guitars, drums, flutes, trombones, tubas and trumpets.

5 specially raised podiums stood and waited for the bass, tenor, alto, soprano and treble singers.

Madam Shiela knew very well that Jose Ivans was with Rose every time over the phone while setting up *Tom Quad* for its Patriarch's last rites!

Rose neatly set the vestment for 25 celebrants.

The main celebrant would be Cardinal Giovanni Domenico, the President of the Pontifical Commission of Vatican City State.

Jessica Rose gratefully remembered Sr Anita of Adoration Convent for teaching her how to prepare a church for the Holy Mass.

Vestments neatly lay spread out in their proper vesting order: Amices, Albs, Cinctures, Maniples, Stoles and finally Chasubles.

Jessica Rose could create there the aura of a new world of divine habitation.

In less than two hours, *Good Hope Tom Quad* looked like a worthy High Altar! The best farewell that can be given to its dear *Michael Sir.*

The storm was swooping down the pine woods!

32

At 12.30 pm all security personnel took their strategic positions which alerted the entire crowd of more than 25,000 people from all walks of life.

Jessica Rose announced that the Prime Minister of India and the other dignitaries would arrive shortly.

The runway beyond *Primrose Garden* was under a police cordon which was equipped with all the modern defensive and offensive equipment.

Police Commissioner Dr Dona Sandra was at the helm of the squad.

Haunting Meadows accommodated more than 10,000 cars, with a very clear parking strategy.

Tom Quad patiently waited for the bigwigs.

The Holy Congregation of the Clergy prayerfully awaited the arrival of Cardinal Giovanni Domenico.

The hearse carrying Dr Michael's body slowly and ceremoniously moved towards *Tom Quad* from the Vestibule of *Good Hope*. He lay in state on a flowery bier in front of the altar.

Dr Ali sat before the bier always looking at his friend.

At 12.45 pm, the thunderous drones of the choppers made all quiet.

The howling of the storm and the droning of the copters made everyone tense.

Commands of the inspectors were heard beyond *Primrose Garden*.

'How is Rahul, Mr Potti?' Madam Shiela asked over the phone.

'Sleeping, under sedation Ma'am.' Potti said. 'They gave him a double dose!'

'Julia?'

'Still in coma, Pooja and Shabbir are with me!'

'Be there, please.'

'Sure, Ma'am.'

Madam Shiela snapped the line with a sigh.

'You can't change anything. Everything is predestined. You can only watch them occur and wonder how they are going to change you!' She remembered reading somewhere.

Soon, five Sikorskys appeared above the pines.

The trees diabolically threw up their branches in the storm and yelled at the flying machines. The pilots could not locate the airstrip. It seemed that they would crash as they were caught in whirlwind.

Dr Ali, realising the danger, told Dr Sandra to inform all the pilots through the wireless to retreat and get out of the sky above the forest and approach the airstrip from the opposite end.

The pilots meticulously followed the instruction and landed safely!

Dr Ali alone knew why there was such a big tumult in the air, and he also knew that all the flying copters would land safely as there was the saintly Cardinal Giovanni Domenico on board in one of them. The Cardinal was hailed as the holiest clergyman of the present Catholic Fraternity! Nothing untoward would befall in presence of the Cardinal.

The Prime Minister of India and the other dignitaries offered floral tributes to the deceased who was draped with the Tricolour with the Saffron over the head.

The placing of the pall and the Christian symbols was already done.

Leading the procession of the Ministers, Cardinal Domenico entered the aisle of *Tom Quad*.

Great Tom, the massive brass bell, chimed breaking through the satanic howling of the pine woods swaying in the storm like a host of frenzied Maenads. It echoed everywhere: in and around *Haunting Meadows.*

Along with *Great Tom's* toll, the *Good Hope* Harmony of Minstrels exulted the divine glory of Supreme God through a heavenly entrance-antiphon.

The Cardinal mounted the altar steps for its veneration!

Just then…., a bleaching flash of lightning followed by a horrendous clap of thunder hit *Tom Quad*!

Julia's beloved *Champaka* was burned down in the lightning. It panted and smoked in the shock as if alive.

A few mourners also received burns. They were rushed to *Good Hope* Hospital and nursed as instructed by Dr Jouhra Begum.

After the Veneration, Cardinal Domenico stood at the Eucharistic Altar and raised his right hand, flanked by two Major Archbishops.

He smiled at the Heavenly Father and chanted, laying his right palm on his forehead:

> *In the name of the Father,*
> *The Son,*
> *And the Holy Spirit….!*

The Congregation with the *Good Hope* Grand Choir chanted:

Amen!

The chanting echoed everywhere in the *Meadows*. At that moment a soft divine sunshine filled the entire arena. Calm returned and prevailed in *Good Hope*.

Only the Cardinal and Dr Ali could hear the occasional wailing of tormented spirits, thirsting for release, from the morbid interiors of the pines.

After the Holy Communion, Dr Ali stood up for the funeral speech. Each word he spoke was with great conviction, and thus was from his heart.

He tearfully remembered how Dr Michael George came to *Haunting Meadows* after their studies at Christ Church, Oxford and built *Good Hope*: brick upon brick and heart upon heart.

His speech made the mournful congregation weep every time and shout the name of Dr Michael George and his beloved daughter Dr Julia who lay senseless at St Lucia.

He hailed Dr Michael's tireless struggle towards emancipating the unsettled and jinxed victims of drugs who were hit by dismal mental agitations.

When Dr Ali spoke about the colourful life of Dr George and Dr Prakash, even the Iron Lady and the President of the Global e-League, Madam Shiela Khanna, could not hold back her emotions. She sat beside Rose and cried like a mother whose child had been ripped off from her breast. She was totally disheartened and inconsolable.

At the end of his mournful chronicle, Dr Ali unexpectedly swooned at the coffin of his friend!

The security personnel, quickly responding, transferred him to the STICU of *Good Hope* Hospital.

Cardinal Giovanni Domenico described Dr Michael George as a true disciple of the Lord.

The British High Commissioner proudly remembered Dr George as one of the greatest Alumni of Christ Church who had always devoted himself to the cause of the poor and the needy with Dr Ali. He also maintained that the young Dr Julia was hailed as the Hope of tomorrow during her stay at Oxford! He wished her a speedy recovery!

The US Ambassador hailed the doctors as true champions of Medical Science, especially detoxification and de-addiction: the best in the world.

The Prime Minister's announcement was the greatest tribute to the Dr George and his colleague Dr Prakash. He announced that *Good Hope* would be fully taken over by the Union Ministry of Health and Public Welfare and upgraded as a Medical College and a Centre for Global Research in Toxicology and Applied Medical Sciences.

The declaration that followed took everyone by surprise. The PM declared *Bharat Ratna* for Dr Michael George, the highest Civilian Award in India.

Mourners could not control their tears anymore. Nor did they know how to name the emotions filling in them; what to call them; how to show; how much to show; how long and how often!

Some hailed, some wailed; some stared, some shared; some clapped, some tapped; some wept and some left!

When the Grand Choir chanted the hymn to mark the farewell, all broke down, especially when the British High Commissioner joined with the choir:

> *We'll meet again,*
> *Don't know where, don't know when,*
> *But I know we'll meet again, some sunny day…*

After the hymn the bier was lifted for the procession to the place of Committal for interment. Just then, it drizzled through the sunshine!

'There is a great celebration going on in Heavens!' Rose said.

'Yes, Rose! There is….! The Angels must be happy…. to receive them back!' Madam Shiela said looking at the Heavens through tears.

All the mourners slow-marched to the uniquely cut-up grave near *Mercury*. Near the new stone of their beloved there lay the stone of Madam Sarah Michael George.

The fresh heap of soil let out an enticing whiff in the drizzle inviting and reminding everyone present there of their own resting places....somewhere, one day, anyway. A strong reminder!

The soldiers lowered the bier and placed it near the tomb.

The mortal remains of the deceased were then submitted to the clergy for the rite of Committal. Cardinal Domenico prayed.

> *We have gathered here*
> *To commend our brother, George,*
> *To our Father in Heaven,*
> *And commit his mortal remains to the elements of the*
> *Earth.*
> *Let's raise our voices in song and offer our prayers for*
> *the departed,*
> *In the Spirit of Faith, in the resurrection of our Good*
> *Lord,*
> *Jesus Christ, from the dead!*

Archbishop Mar Abraham Luka read from the New Testament!

'A reading from the Holy Gospel according to **John, 12:23-25**

Jesus replied to his disciples:
Now the hour has come
For the son of man to be glorified.
In all truth I tell you,
Unless a grain of wheat falls into the earth and dies
It remains only a single grain;
But if it dies
It yields rich harvest.
Anyone who loves his life loses it;
Anyone who hates his life in this world
Will keep it for eternal life.

The Cardinal prayed over the place of the Committal and blessed the tomb! Then he said the invitation to prayer before the final commendation.

The entire ambience was under the grip of a terrible lull as all prayed in silence for the departed.

The *Good Hope* Grand Choir Minstrels chanted the song of farewell as the tomb was being sprinkled and incensed.

I know that my Redeemer lives!

Cardinal Domenico led the Prayer of Commendation.

The brigade closed in for the removal of the Tricolour. It was decorously removed from the coffin.

The glass lid of the coffin was now removed for sprinkling holy water and incensing. The farewell kisses were offered to the great man of *Good Hope*.

The pall bearers closed the coffin after covering his face.

After locking it, they lowered the box of Dr George– the Alpha and the Omega of *Good Hope.*

The rifle brigade took position for the guard of honour, and the ceremonial gun salute of 21 shots was offered to the departed.

The doleful knell of *Great Tom* ripped through the frozen confinements of *Haunting Meadows.* He never knew that his loud salutations would not be accepted by his creator anymore!

The brass band played the funeral hymn: *Abide with me; fast falls the eventide...*

Madam Shiela could not hold her tears back though she tried to hide them. The heart of the mother throbbed and wept thinking of Julia and her son lying in the hospital brutally battered by a faithful Fate.

Rose and Madam Shiela held on to each other lest they should fall.

Rose remembered her cell phone had once vibrated in her bag while the Gospel being read.

She opened her bag and looked at the screen of her phone.

'Interment over! Starting at 6 pm.'

'Drive slow...be safe, missing!' Rose quickly texted back and dropped the phone into the bag.

Her heart started beating unusually faster! She did not know, why.

As they walked back, the Minstrels of *Good Hope* Grand Choir were still chanting:

I know that my redeemer lives!

33

It was 6 pm when Jose Ivans left the ancestral home of Dr Mohan Prakash.

Alice and children were disconsolate and in a state of loud depression! Their tears could not drown their distress and fears!

Dr Mohan's mother was in a trance. She did not know that Ivans had left.

Reclining on his seat, Ivans texted to Rose:

'Started! Don't go home, my Rose. Stay at *The Abode*!'

Ivans dialled Madam Shiela's number and briefed her everything.

'Come safe, Ivans.' She said.

'Yes, Ma'am. Thank you!'

Madam Shiela dropped.

Ivans received a smiley back from Rose.

He smiled at the smiley.

The evening glow of the sunset made everything in nature seem natural once again!

The Havana of Ivans glided gently along the never ending stretch of the paddy fields flanking the country road of Mohan's native soil.

'Time is a funny thing', Ivans thought. 'It beautifully but cleverly wraps up the misfortunes of our pitiable Past with the hustle and bustle of a fleeting Present and pushes us to go in search of a fabled Future!

'There is surely an antidote to one's family sorrows in the boastful Glossary of Forgetfulness, but to a friendly anguish, no redress.' Ivans sat on the back seat of his car and stretched his legs.

Rashid slowly but steadily picked up the momentum….!

Both seemed enjoying the ambience of rural India.

'Indian villages still abound in some of the unique charms of life vanishing fast from the urban metabolism!'

Ivans tried to list a few: fate, honesty, help, self-respect, gratitude, fortitude, charity, parents, siblings, teachers, students, virgins, God, faith, devoted devotees and so on.

'Peace has been exchanged with speed; chastity with fun; smile with smileys; pride with arrogance; simplicity with hypocrisy; education with business; purity with guile; love with vanity; truth with money; God with man-gods and life with death!' Ivans smiled to himself.

'Death is the only known truth in this world! Nothing else…..! Motherhood was his counterpart but unfortunately real mothers are almost extinct', Ivans thought.

'A variety of mothers are now available in Family Supermarkets: stepmother, housemother, super-mother, foremother, godmother, namesake-mother, single-mother, neutral-mother, rebel-mother, hired-mother, caged-mother, ex-mother, e-mother, online-mother, instant-mother, future-mother, one-day-mother, weekly-mother, monthly-mother, weekend-mother, weakened-mother, hardened-mother, off-day-mother, day-mother, night-mother, day-care-mother, hands-off-mother, hands-on-mother, flash-mother, biological-mother, surrogate-mother…..so many mothers!' Ivans lost count.

'My mother, Liz Ivans….! The most ideal mother!' he thought.

'She always let herself suffer from her own worries: the worries and the anxieties of the future of her son. She regretted that single vital mistake in her life: her son's marriage! But, there were blessed moments too, in his life.'

Ivans thought about his Jan….a blessed daughter indeed…..!

Rose and Juan are his prized possessions….!

Joseph Ivans and Cecily Ivans were gifted grandparents!

His Dada and Mama were divine.

He felt that he was now moving along the country road of Udayagiri.

While passing through Shanthipuram, he peeped out of his Havana.

Driver Philip was standing in the front yard of *The Arcadia* as if waiting for someone!

Kunjappan Chettan was sitting at the nostalgic *CHE* writing something in the Book of Credit and waiting for the *Twilight Audience*! Barber Neelandan was spreading his shaving paraphernalia at the corner in anticipation of some five o' clock shadows! Kadachirakkunnel Iyppachan was returning home after recovering from the shock of another crotch shot from Annamma. His *undas* were in place!

His grandma Cicely Ivans was making his favourite mango milkshake in kitchen.

Broker Thommy came chasing Kozhi Andrews! Crossing the road, they disappeared through the thicket! His eyes followed their route for some time and then they were soon traceless!

His inspirational country brook still rushed down the hill with its crystal gush!

His beloved *Gulmohar* was in full bloom and the stretch was red-carpeted.

The little Ivans passionately rolled on the road.

'Jo...don't soil your trousers.....get up my darling, please...!' Liz Ivans said.

'No, Mama.....please.... I love my *Gulmohar*....! She sheds those blooms knowing that I am coming. See Mama.... see.....she loves you too Mama!' Jose Ivans pleaded.

Seeing his grandfather at *CHE*, Jose Ivans went to him climbing the slope from the road.

Driver Philip drove the Army Willys down the country road to drop Liz Ivans at *The Arcadia*.....! The little Ivans soon joined the *Twilight Audience*!

'*San Ernesto de la Higuera*! Saint Ernesto of la Higuera.....' Major General Joseph Ivans paused and smiled at the little one! He sat near his grandpa and looked into his eyes. They were blue and deep!

'Crowds of pilgrims progress along the country road of la Higuera to the village school and the manger-like rock slab in the laundry house on the hilltop where Che's body was laid for embalming.

'Millions across the world believe that Che's was martyrdom, and he is a martyr of the Christ to the cause of Socialism.

'Che is hailed as a saint by the locals. They light candles at his huge idol, erected on a rock, and pray to him for fresh showers and good crops which are immediately granted.

He is the guardian spirit of the village, who paces up and down and day and night, safeguarding their children, cattle, property and health. When they pray to Che, maladies flee, children pass tests, marriages happen, babies are born and their barns overflow.

'Che's legendary visage, a photograph captured by the Cuban photographer Alberto Korda, has been emblazoned on posters, t-shirts, walls and almost everything and everywhere possible! His portrait is worshipfully hung on hut walls alongside Virgin Mary and Jesus by the poor locals!'

'We'll also hang it at our homes!' Karankal Thankan declared.

'Yes.' The rest replied in consent.

'The newborns are named after Che in the village', the Major General picked up the thread, 'and they proudly hold his face in pendants, lockets, rings and studs.

'In Argentina, Che museums and schools are sprouting everywhere. In Cuba, the schoolchildren's everyday pledge is: *We will be like Che*!

'The seven gunshots of Mario Terran could not kill Che! Nor could they extinguish the ever burning fire of revolution in his heart! His blood was showered on the oppressed and the exploited like the blooms of my grandson's *Gulmohar* on the road! They brightened up and crimsoned the coral hearts of the unwavering revolutionaries already bleeding for the downtrodden across the world.

'No, Che was not dead....!' The Major General declared. 'Guns and grenades cannot quell the eruptions of the emotional fujiyamas burning in the hearts of the unprivileged. In that case.....a few bullets won't be enough...!'

A gun shot!

Ivans jumped out of his seat with a jerk.

He knew that he was no more at *CHE*! The kaleidoscopic twilight scenes of Udayagiri had already vanished.

His Havana was no more riding like an unruffled swan in the placid waters of a friendly lake. The drive was not smoother. The engine of the vehicle was roaring like a charging brigade!

Rashid was struggling hard to steer the vehicle steady.

'What's happening?' Ivans asked anxiously.

'Sir...., firing.....! A car is following us!' Rashid gasped. 'A gun shot...!'

Just then a volley of shots punched a few holes in the rear windscreen which riddled the dashboard.

Ivans saved his life by a whisker as he crouched, but a bullet hit Rashid's left elbow!

'Oh, Sir..., I'm hit.' He cried.

'Steady the wheels and jump onto the other seat.' Ivans shouted.

Rashid steadied the vehicle and threw himself to the co-driver's seat in a wink.

Ivans leapt from the rear seat, double bent, like a leopard and landed right on the driver's seat!

Rashid was lying down on the seat and tying a hanky to stop bleeding!

'Don't get up…..! Keep your head down.' Ivans commanded. 'It's AK47…..terror attack…..! Targeting me!'

Another volley was showered by the hunters! The deafening noise said that bullets rattled the rear bumper.

His Havana was now tearing through an unknown landscape. She seemed whizzing through the air like a Hawk200.

It was 8.15.

'Do or die!' Ivans said to himself.

'My Lord…..my Jesus….take charge….! I give the wheel in your hands!' Ivans screamed.

He just glanced in the rear-view mirror and quickly realized that the chasers were very close.

'Man can be destroyed; not defeated!' He remembered Hemingway's Santiago!

It revived his already sinking gusto and propelled his guts!

He stamped the pedal, the engine roared louder.

They were now 300 meters away.

'Before, it was only 50 meters!'

'It looked like an urban assault vehicle!' Ivans assumed.

He pressed on and on, and his Havana dashed along the long stretch of the highway which had already dropped some of its traffic.

Shelling from rear was getting thicker.

Rashid was crouching under the seat. He looked at his master with awe and wonder!

'What a man....! Lion-hearted!' Rashid could not help admiring his boss.

Another dashing car on the highway was accidently hit by a few random shots from the assailants; it overturned and there rose a trail of sparks and flames on the road.

Ivans heard many vehicles crashing behind bumping into each other.

'Many must have ramm'd!' Ivans thought.

After the collision, everything seemed to be peaceful.

'The terrorists must have also been caught into the trap!' Ivans thought.

Once more Ivans' Havana started breathing steadily.

The vehicle forged ahead after overtaking a fast truck and entered a bridge.

Ivans looked at the needle quivering at 150 km/h.

'It had once clocked 190,' he quickly thought.

'They are either militants or hired goons', Ivans said to himself. 'But, their modus operandi is that of militants. Their weapons are highly sophisticated and thus lethal too.

'I've no weapons, my Lord! You're my shield and my fortress in whom I'm sheltered!'

Jose Ivans sang **Psalm62:5-7**

> *Rest in God alone, my soul!*
> *He is the source of my hope.*
> *He alone is my rock, my safety,*
> *My stronghold, and I stand unwavering.*

In God is my safety and my glory,
The Rock of my Strength!

Just then, he saw a fearsome spectacle on the reflector right behind his Havana! The scary darkness of the night was menacingly lit up by a sky-high sea of flames!

The truck behind was mishit and flared up by a rocket launched from the assault vehicle! Ivans watched the flaming debris of the blown-up truck fall off the bridge into the floods after blazing the entire sky-scape!

He had seen such an episode only on silver screens. It was phenomenal and hair-raising too!

His Havana once again picked up momentum! She was not only flying like an arrow but also oscillating on its course dodging further attacks.

It needed concentration, competence, courage and class; above all the clemency of the Creator!

'Your Grace is sufficient for me, my Lord!' Ivans shouted.

Rashid still sat under his seat holding his bleeding elbow and gazing at his master, jaw-dropped!

In a Himalayan effort, Ivans dodged two more mighty buck-shots in a quick succession!

Shelling was getting thicker every second!

Suddenly, his Havana started wobbling!

'We're hit!' He screamed. 'The right rear wheel is unsteady. We're gone!'

Ivans saw Rashid closing his eyes in panic and saying his last prayers!

His car was slow and unsteady! It was not picking!

Steering the car diagonally and keeping the speed was now nearly impossible for Ivans.

His cell phone moved once in his pocket!

It was 8.26 pm on his Havana clock.

'Good bye, Rose! Take care of our children! We'll meet in Heaven some day!' Ivans whispered.

He started singing **Psalm 3** frantically!

> *Yahweh, how countless are my enemies,*
> *How countless those rise up against me,*
> *How countless those who say of me,*
> *'No salvation for him from his God!'*
>
> *But you, Yahweh, the shield at my side,*
> *My glory, you hold my head high,*
> *I cry out to Yahweh;*
> *He answers from His holy mountain!*

At that moment, another bullet punctured his Havana's rear left wheel too!

He cried out of joy…..for he knew that steering his vehicle would be much easier as both the rear wheels are evenly crippled!

'A boon in disguise!' Ivans shouted, and sang the rest of the **Psalm** in delirium:

> *As for me, if I lie down any sleep,*
> *I shall awake, for Yahweh sustains me.*
> *I don't fear my foes in multitudes*
> *Who range themselves against me on my way!*
>
> *Arise, Yahweh, rescue me, my God!*
> *You strike all my foes across the face,*
> *You break the teeth of the wicked.*
> *In Yahweh is the salvation and life!*

8.29 pm….!

Ivans saw a cross junction ahead with a traffic island and bright signal lamps!

'Jesus…!' Ivans called out.

He saw the high beams of the assault vehicle on his reflector fast approaching his Havana.

His hope started sinking!

Red light!

Ivans looked at the digital clock blinking on the signal board!

'58!'

'Gone for ever…!' He muttered.

'First be practical to live, and then be ideological to validate and sustain it!' Ivans murmured and closed his eyes!

In a fraction of seconds, his Havana went great guns! She swished like a flash of lightning in an attempt to jump the signals!

In that desperate attempt Ivans had not seen a speeding Volvo B8R dashing from the left…..!

It was all over in fraction of a second!

The trace, the shells, the frenzy, the fear…..all over!

Everything was reduced to mere fumes and flames!

A head on collision caused a powerful explosion!

The vehicle banged the bus and both were blown up blazing the entire landscape.

The explosion was heard across the cheerless horizons of the obscure night.

The spot was soon cordoned off by the force.

Security personnel took possession of the entire area!

They were busy gathering the mortal remains of the victims and shifting the mangled bodies to their ambulances!

34

Shiela Khanna and Jessica Rose reached St Lucia Medical College with Dr Jouhra Begum by 4 pm.

Dr Ali Masood preferred to stay back at *Good Hope* to regularize everything. He would return only after a few days.

Rahul was still under sedation. His head was bandaged and the ruts on face were well dressed with fresh medicated cotton.

The head got injured when he went wild while trying to open the ICU by hitting the heavy doors with his head.

His limbs were chained!

'Sorry, Ma'am!' Potti wailed. 'There was no other way to tackle the situation.'

Madam Shiela looked at Potti empathetically and observed the swelling on his cheekbone.

Potti looked out of the broken window, with a broken heart, to see a broken cloud floating aimlessly in the western horizon!

She saw damaged LCD screens and rends in the glass panels of the partitions of the room.

Madam Shiela could make out and fathom the intensity of the situation.

She looked at her son!

'The Iron Lady of Electronics India shouldn't become lily-livered!' She said to herself controlling the compassion filling in her eyes.

She looked at Dr Jouhra Begum sadly.

Dr Begum was busy studying the medical report.

'Everything's normal!' The doctor said. 'You can take him home! He will sleep for another six hours!'

Madam Shiela looked at Rose.

'In case he behaves strangely....?' Rose said notwithstanding her deference she carried for Madam Shiela!

'Normally, he shouldn't!' Dr Begum said. 'The tranquilizers are capable of keeping him calm unless something very unusual strikes him which can disturb him more than Julia's condition! It's impossible at the moment!'

What about Julia? Shiela Khanna Said. 'I won't go leaving her alone.'

Don't worry about her. Dr Begum said. 'I'm reported that she shows improvement. I'll always be in touch with you. Go peacefully. I'm here....not going home!

A much relieved Shiela Khanna drove Rahul back home to Dream Mansions.

The gnawing stillness of the house was suffocating and thus intimidating.

'Take him for a pleasure trip to one of his favourite destinations when everything's settled!' Rose said to Madam Shiela.

'Done!' Madam Shiela said. 'Let Ivans come back. We'll go together. The kids are already on their summer break, aren't they?'

'Yes, Ma'am.' Rose smiled.

'But..., Julia?'

'She'll also be alright by that time!' Rose said.

Madam Shiela took Rahul to his *Glass Case* of the *Crystal Mansion*, with a staff nurse of St Lucia whom Dr Jouhra Begum had sent with them to meet any emergency.

When Rose reached *The Abode*, both Janet and Juan were sitting in the parlour. They looked broken down and smouldering from within.

They were watching the entire ceremony on TV. All the channels had covered the rituals globally.

'Auntie....!' Janet came running and hugged Rose!

She was crying. Juan tried to console Janet by petting her, with tears in his eyes!

Though Rose felt proud of Juan, she did not know how to console both of them.

'Poor things!' She thought. 'Both are broken: one vents and the other hides!'

Roshini brought hot coffee, milk and Finnish doughnuts for them.

They did not feel taking them as they were fully drunk from the mournful gush of a steady fountain springing from the depth of their woebegone hearts!

It was 6 pm!

The evening twilight filled every nook and cranny of *The Abode* with an unusual outlandish glow for a moment!

The cell phone vibrated.

'Jo!' Her heart leapt.

She read the text: 'Started....! Don't go home, my Rose! Stay at *The Abode*!'

She sent a smiley to her Jo and took the children to the guest room for a nap!

'Auntie….! Come, let's sleep in our bedroom!' Janet pulled Rose to the master bedroom where Ivans and Janet used to sleep.

But, she would not…..she should not!

'Time hasn't arrived yet.' She said to herself.

'No, Jan! We'll sleep here now!' She carried Janet to the guestroom.

It was a palatial suite!

Rose lay down on the cosy bed with Janet in the middle.

All the three soon dived headlong into the unfathomable depth of the merciful sleep!

Jessica Rose was presently sitting with Janet, Juan, Madam Shiela, Julia and Rahul in the grandstands of *Autódromo José Carlos Pace – Interlagos – Circuit, Sao Paulo!*

The Brazilian Grand Prix last lap was being raced….!

Jose Ivans entered the fast lane after the last and final mandatory pit-stop. During the stop the pit-crew had really offloaded the fuel to make the car lighter and got all the four wheels replaced with newer ones.

Only three more laps to go!

Ivans was now leading the race by 1 sec less than the closest contender. He was flying through the DRS zone.

He maintained the lead till the last lap!

The last lap was raced.....!

Jose Ivans just entered the final straight for the race in front of the grandstands for the finish.

Janet and Juan shouted and cheered at him! He gave them a fleeting glance and flashed a thumbs-up. His rivals were trying hard to catch up with Ivans, but he would not let anyone!

All in the gallery were on their toes, biting their nails!

Ivans was now flying through the final straight at 325 km/h!

He was only a few yards away from the finishing point! He gave Rose a passing look and smiled.

The gallery was bursting with shouts and screams!

1,25,000 spectators chanted only one name!

'I..v..a..n..s….! I..v..a..n..s….!'

Rose saw that Jose Ivans crossing the finishing line in his *Havana*!

But, at that fatal moment the third racer made an unforced error, lost his control and hit the car in front! Both the cars lifted in the air and somersaulted high up in the sky!

They witnessed the inevitable!

The cars nosedived, hit the track and landed upside down!

They presently exploded like two potential bombshells!

What they saw there was frightening and caused goose-bumps on them.

As it was the final straight, all the cars were above 300 km/h.

The drivers lost their ground grip and ran into each other.

The collision literally halted the *Interlagos* to a standstill!

'Jo…!'

Rose screamed and woke up.

She sat on the bed soaked in sweat and anguish and wept kneeling at the Crucifix….!

Fear gripped her like an octopus! He clasped her with his mighty arms not to leave her easily! She struggled hard…. but no escape.

Rose saw the huge clock blinking at 8.26 pm.

She had gone to sleep at 6.30.

'2 hours have passed!' She thought. 'No news from Jo!'

She tried to muster the incidents on the speedway of the *Interlagos*, wiping the precipitation of agony from her brows. The big drops fell on the bed and were soon absorbed! But, she could not absorb them!

'My Jo….!' Her heart sobbed. Tears rolled down her cheeks!

She soon texted to Jose Ivans **Psalm 65:6-7**

> *By your strength you hold the mountains steady,*
> *Being clothed in power,*
> *You calm the turmoil of the seas,*
> *The turmoil of their waves!*

8.29 pm!

'Ma'am…!' Rose heard someone knocking on the door!

She hearkened!

'Ma'am…!'

'Yes!' Rose replied.

'Ma'am, please open the door.'

It was Ashok, the Durwan!

Rose opened the door. Ashok and Roshini were standing at the door!

'What happened Ashok?'

'Ma'am….!' Roshini said. 'Switch on the TV and see the news breaking now!'

Rose turned around and looked at the kids….! They were still sleeping.

Ashok soon went back to the gate but Roshini stayed with Rose.

With a pounding heart, Rose switched on the TV and looked at Roshini.

She took the remote and flipped the screen.

'Ma'am, NDTV!' Roshini insisted.

Rose turned towards the TV, and stood aghast and alarmed with shock and disbelief!

Roshini sat on the doorstep, confounded!

Major BREAKTHROUGH in Good Hope Doctors' Assassination Case! In a dramatic twist the CBI has arrested Mr Jayaprakash Sawant, alias JPS, the COO of Electronics India Pvt. Ltd. from the City Billiard Club, in connection with the brutal assassination of Dr Michael George and Dr Mohan Prakash. He has been arrested from the CBC while engaged in the sport by 8.30 pm today. It is believed that Mr Sawant also has strong business connections with the big names of the underworld. The City Police Commissioner Dr Dona Sandra IPS said at a press conference that the Police would be able to register more arrests after questioning Mr Sawant who is suspected to be involved in drug dealing, money laundering, organ trafficking and flesh trade in the sub-continent.

Rose remembered watching Mr Sawant sneaking out of The Patriarch soon after Madam Shiela had announced the engagement of Rahul with Dr Julia.

She sat on the bed looking at the kids listlessly.

Jessica Rose pulled out her cell phone from her bag and dialled Jose Ivans.

It rang but he did not respond!

She tried again and again! He did not receive her calls! She panicked.

At that moment, her phone trembled in her hands!

'Madam Shiela!'

'Yes, Ma'am!' Rose sounded miserable.

'Rose', Madam Shiela said grievously. 'It seems that the Heavens are against us! It's shocking and unbelievable that the crook has been arrested. I tried Ivans. He is not receiving my calls.'

'Yes, Ma'am!' Rose said wistfully. 'I also tried….but….!'

She wanted to sit alone and cry.

'Venkat has just spoken to me that a big group of e-Indians has already ransacked the house of JPS and set fire to it.'

'My goodness!' Rose could not take it.

'The police has fired rubber bullets and tear gas but they are still stationed there shouting slogans against him. I wish Ivans were here with me now!' Madam Shiela said sadly.

Rose did not respond….she did not know how to….!

Both held the phones quietly for some time!

Finally, Rose spoke abruptly.

'Ma'am, I'm going to Lake Street! It seems that condition is very critical! The NDTV is giving us a live coverage of all!' Rose said glancing at the screen.

It showed the people, mainly e-Indians, in their blue uniform pelting stones and hurtling burning torches at the residence of JPS. The house was on fire!

The police could not reach the house as the people had built a strong human wall in front of them.

Guns and grenades could not stop the volcanic eruptions in their wrath-ridden hearts!

'No Rose,' Madam Shiela reacted quickly and seriously. 'Don't go alone. I'm also coming. I'll pick you up….wait!'

Situation was unimaginably grim at Lake Street!

The mob was trying to break open the mighty gates of *Shanti Nilayam* – the house of peace!

Some had already clambered over the gates and damaged the Porsche in the porch. They were engaged in an act of wrecking and blazing!

Havoc was the byword of the situation!

Shiela Khanna and Jessica Rose sat on the car.

The Commissioner of Police quickly approached Madam Shiela and Jessica Rose and gestured the glasses of the windows down.

'It's out of our control. Baton and shield charge didn't work. They don't care tear gas, water cannons and rubber bullets! Only firearms are left now!' the Commissioner howled over the crowd-rage.

'Give us the mike!' Rose cried out!

Mike was soon handed out to Rose!

'Ma'am!' Said Rose. 'Please tell them to stop. Hearing your voice they will stop it! If anyone can, it's you!'

Madam Shiela took the mike sceptically. The situation was beyond anybody's control.

Rose sat beside Madam Shiela prayerfully closing her eyes!

Both longed for Ivans' presence there.

The noise of the angry mob was uproarious! The entire hell was present at the Lake Street.

'My dear Brothers!'

Everything came to a standstill!

They turned their heads like an owl and looked at the source!

'I pray to all of you to kindly lay down the arms!' Madam Shiela was literally crying!

Her sobs shot through their hearts puncturing holes in them!

Rose heard the clatter of clubs, stones, spears and blades falling on the ground! She opened her eyes.

The angry mob had already become a pacified crowd!

'Please think about your families! Your mothers are tearfully praying to the heavens for your health and success like me;

your fathers are waiting for you at homes. Think about your dear wives and your little children longing for your presence at home. They won't sleep until you reach home! Your beloved siblings will be dreaming to spend some time with you at home!'

The crowd became an assembly!

'That crook has been arrested and locked up! I will make sure that he will not walk a free man if found guilty. His wife and child are innocent, to my knowledge. They are unaware of all his treacherous schemes!'

Rose knew that the assembly was now listening to Madam Shiela's oration as if it were a homily from their High Priestess!

The assembly became a congregation!

'It's a testing time for us. Show our personal integrity, brotherly compassion and profound love towards his family. Therefore, leave them alone, go back to your homes and come to the firm tomorrow to resume your work. We need all of you and I, being your Ma'am, solicit all of your unconditional love and support to take our company to the new pastures awaiting us ahead. Ours is not a life that can be wasted on silly matters! If we sacrifice our life for anything that should be for much nobler things than this.

'We love you all! Kindly disperse! Please….!'

The congregation became pure devotees!

They all dispersed like little lambs with their eyes downcast, shoulders stooped and heads hung!

Immediately the fire brigade closed in and took over.

Dr Sandra smiled with great gratitude and gave Madam Shiela a passionate hug and stepped back and saluted her.

Rose leaned on Madam Shiela's shoulders and smiled at her through tears.

The Commissioner's wireless beeped. She walked away speaking over the system.

'Thank you, Ma'am! You did it.' Rose said.

'We did it, Rose!' Madam Shiela said holding Rose close to her. 'It was you who nudged me when I was down! But for you, I'd not have ventured out leaving Rahul alone!

'James!' Madam Shiela called.

'Yes, Ma'am!'

'Let's go home! Drop Rose at *The Abode* on the way. Ivans must have reached home. It's 10.30!'

The Commissioner approached them quickly.

Her expression showed great urgency.

'We have to reach St Lucia in a jiffy!' The officer said! 'Follow me!'

Dr Sandra's Black Panther flew along the express highway howling through the beacon light!

'James!' Madam Shiela commanded.

'Yes, Ma'am!'

Madam Shiela's Phantom soon started racing on the highway tracing the Commissioner's Black Panther!

35

On the other side, beyond the signal lights, in the interior of the dark night there lay a worn-down, ripped and riddled 7 series Havana: in total ruins.

Rashid slowly clambered out from under the seat!

The biting pain on his elbow had already negotiated itself with an unschooled numbness!

The car was lying tilted towards the driver-end!

He tried to push the door open in an unprofitable attempt!

The door was clogged in the frame. Its handle was stiff like his hand.

Lying supine on the seat he broke the window open by kicking it with his hard shoe-soles.

His head, in the effort, touched his master's leg which brought him back to his real senses.

Though he could not discern anything in the pitch dark, he clearly remembered everything in a quick flashback… the freakish experience of the mad-chase.

He rewound the entire episode quickly: right from the first gunshot!

He recounted the mad pursuit: heavy shelling; elbow strike; crouching; rocket attack; unsteady wheels; scripture incantation; signal jumping and the subsequent blast!

When the assault vehicle ran head on into the Volvo B8R, Ivans' Havana had just managed to jump the signal!

Ivans held on to the steering wheel closing his eyes!

Their car, jumping the red signal, rammed into a track divider; slid out of the track and hitting the other end of a bulwark, somersaulted and fell on the gravel dune, on the left, unloaded for laying roads!

Crawling out of the window, Rashid knew the jagged glass-edges cutting through his raw flesh and ruddy drops trickling throughout his body.

His elbow started to let out a fresh gush of blood, being terribly disturbed in the effort.

His tattered clothes got stuck to his furrowed sinews.

The sharp glass-edges were heartless!

An excruciating pain seethed through the innumerable gashes making him howl like a laid-up tusker!

His legs would not hold him up anymore!

Rashid fell on the gravel dune. His vision dimmed out and trauma gripped him like a monster.

He looked around!

He tried to summon up his mindfulness by awakening his senses!

He knew that he was lying down, bandaged all over, in the middle of the sterilized tang of antibiotics and disinfectants.

Slowly his vision regained its clarity.

Rashid realized that he was in a hospital bed, in ICU, with red and white tubes and syringes biting him.

His rolling eyes searched for his master in vain.

He could see only a sea of whiteness: white clothes, white bandage, white walls and ceiling and white uniforms!

He wanted to shout his master's name, but ineffectually tried to open his mouth.

At the end Rashid surrendered himself to the mellifluous gurgling of the drips of a snooze-inducing fluid.

The clock struck 11 at City Clock Tower!

The Black Panther and the Phantom screeched in the porch of St Lucia and winked their eyes!

Three fair ladies emerged out of those Plutonic cabins! They were smart and brave too!

Madam Shiela Khanna, Ms Jessica Rose and Dr Dona Sandra IPS! They hurried through the parlour and climbed stairs to reach the CCU on the 1st floor!

'Come fast, we need blood!' Dr Jouhra Begum shouted. She was waiting for them impatiently at the door of the CCU.

Rose was soon pushed through the mighty fibre doors of the chamber adjacent to the CCU and made to lie down.

She sensed the prick on her vein and watched the thick red verdurous flow into the hi-tech Terumo blood bags. It was quick!

'But, why?' Rose asked herself.

She looked at the smiling angel standing by her bedside. She was unusually white and bright!

Her eyes soon captured something more striking beyond the angel in the sterilized glass chamber of the CCU: something whither, brighter and more enlivening.

The very sight of the same gave a lift to her already sinking hopes!

'No news from my Jo...! 5 hours have passed! It's like 5 years of the bothersome sublunary rotations!

'Ah, Jo….! Where are you? At least one text to your Rose! She's so anxious and careworn!' Rose wept on the bed.

However, the inquisitiveness grew beyond her coveted tolerance which drove her glances beyond the smiling face of the dovish figure in front of her!

No sooner did she see it clearly than she sprang up and sat on the bed upright!

Rubbing her eyes with her palms, she looked at the CCU bed!

'Jo…..! My Jo…!' She gasped.

More uniforms….! More force…..! More noise….! More struggle….!

There was a big agitation in the chamber!

Finally, Rose was thumbed down to the bed by a dozen smiling angels as the needle was still in the vein.

She longed for her Jo! She wanted to know how and why he was there in the CCU.

Her heart had throbbed when Dr Begum said that she wanted blood.

Jose Ivans and Jessica Rose were two of the very few AB –ves in the City!

Their names were in the records of the Medical College.

Rose held her breath and threw her arms and legs up in an aborted attempt to release herself and reach her *Jo*. But 24 hands were pressing her down!

Jessica Rose suspended her effort for a while and lay there as if dead.

She surrendered!

'I had the other negatives, but as Rose has it, why another type!' Rose heard Dr Begum's voice.

The white doves immediately released Rose and marched out of the chamber when they heard Dr Begum's voice.

Though released from her captors, Rose did not want to move! She did not need to struggle now, but now she wanted captivity. She could at least struggle for freedom if she were a captive.

Rose felt like an average citizen of any independent nation. Having got freedom and nothing to do, one shall necessarily slip and fall into the sunless sea of passivity and immunity!

'Independence is a curse if we don't know how to use it! We will start to misuse, overuse and abuse it. One should learn how to use it before winning it!' She thought.

'But, when were they brought here?' Madam Shiela asked.

'Twenty minutes ago.' Dr Begum said.

'Okay! How's he? May I see him?'

'Yes, Ma'am. He is out of danger, but under observation for another 24 hours!' Dr Begum said. 'His head got injured and he suffered a minor chest compression too. Thanks to his great build! Or else, it'd have caused myocardial contusion. It seems that he fell on the steering wheel. The air bag also helped him to withstand the effect!'

'O, God!' Madam Shiela let out a big sigh of relief.

'It's also most probably a terror attack by the same group!' Dr Sandra approximated coming into the CCU. 'Very similar to the *Good Hope* attack!'

It sent chills down the spine of Madam Shiela and Jessica Rose!

They closed their eyes in fear and prayer folding their hands and thanking the Almighty!

'Our traffic officers are decoding the videos and the signals. We will soon get to know what exactly happened.' The commissioner said seriously. 'My colleague, Adarsh, reached the spot immediately after the accident and brought them here.'

'Mr Adarsh, IPS?' Madam Shiela said.

'Yes.'

'I know him. An able officer!'

'A real daredevil!'

'How's Rahul now, Ma'am?' Dr Begum inquired.

'He was sleeping when I left.' Madam Shiela said.

'Okay.'

'How's Julia? May I see her?'

'Fighting back. Don't worry! She'll be alright. Come. Let's go to her.' The doctor sounded confident.

'Thank you, Doctor.' Madam Shiela acknowledged and rose.

'Excuse me!' The Commissioner exited.

'Rose can go home now.' Dr Begum said.

'That's right.' Madam Shiela sounded relieved. 'I'll drop her back at *The Abode*. The kids are there. We'll come back tomorrow morning.'

As Rose hesitated, Madam Shiela's cell phone rang!

'Anarkali!' Madam Shiela Khanna exclaimed. 'Something's wrong!'

'Yes, Anu?' She said.

Jessica Rose sat up on her bed, stiff and anxious.

'My God!' Madam Shiela was breathless.

'What happened, Ma'am?' both asked together.

'Rahul woke up!' Madam Shiela panicked! 'Freddy, the peddler, was in Rahul's room. He has brought shots and stuff!'

'Jesus!' Rose exclaimed. 'He was the one who used to supply narcotics to Rahul as his room-boy, wasn't he?'

'Yes, the same!' Madam Shiela confirmed!

In the meanwhile, Dr Sandra IPS rushed into the room.

'Ma'am, our officers have just arrested one Mr Freddy from the vicinity of *Dream Mansions*! He was trying to escape from your house by jumping over the parapet at the back. Fortunately for us, he fell into the moat and the night watchmen caught him red-handed with brown sugar worth crores!'

'Thank you very much!' Madam Shiela bowed down to the Commissioner with great gratitude!

'But, he must have supplied some of it to someone in your house.' The Commissioner said.

Madam Shiela's cell phone rang again.

'Excuse me.' She said. 'Yes, Anu?'

'Ma'am, come fast.' Anarkali said. 'Rahul is really wild. He is breaking the curios in his room. Ma'am….please come fast! I'm scared! He is hitting his head against the glass. It's blood everywhere! Only blood!'

Madam Shiela sat on the bed near Rose sweating profusely! Her legs had already grown heavier than she could carry.

The Commissioner's wireless beeped again.

'Excuse me.' She rushed out.

'Ivans, why do you sleep? Wake up and save us! Don't sleep any more, Ivans…rise….please…!' Madam Shiela cried like an orphan!

As if endowed with telepathy, Ivans opened his eyes!

'Ma'am….!' He beckoned to call her.

Madam Shiela rose and moved towards the glass-room as if in a dream.

Rose also followed Madam Shiela. Her heart tasted the bitter-sweet fruit of a life which is full of situational ironies!

Dr Jouhra Begum let them enter the CCU.

Ivans laboriously opened his eyes.

'Ma'am! Don't….waste….time….!' Ivans stammered! 'Go…. home…..and….save…. Rahul….! I….heard….what ….you were….speaking…! If…you're late….it will….be….'

Jose Ivans closed his eyes and fell back into a deep sleep.

'Done, Ivans! Done! I'm going home.' Madam Shiela shouted. 'Rose, you will stay here.'

'Yes, Ma'am!' Rose agreed.

'Where's Rashid, Doctor?' Madam Shiela asked.

'In the ICU! He's okay.' The Doctor asserted.

'Thank you, Doctor.' Madam Shiela said. 'Take care of Julia too, please!'

'Done!'

She suddenly turned about and rushed out of the CCU.

Dr Jouhra Begum quickly accompanied her.

A frightening quietude prevailed in the CCU. Rose looked at *her Jo* kneeling beside his bed.

'Jo….!' Rose grabbed his hand and wept. 'My Jo….my life….my everything….! I love you so much….!'

She kissed his hand!

Ivans opened his eyes.

The warmth of her tears relieved him of the dreadful memories of that scary encounter!

He looked at the red tubes through which Rose was entering him and revitalizing his life!

'My Rose….!' Ivans mumbled.

'Hmmm….!'

'Where are the kids?'

'At *The Abode*!' Rose replied without lifting her eyes!

'*Then*, they are safe!'

Ivans slowly raised his hand and laid it on her head!

His fingers told her locks the fabled truth of his incredible getaways and the Providential Arbitrations when Misfortune conspired with Death and both stood on his way, point blank! The clock on the City Tower clanked 12 as if calling the spirits, out of their lowly beds, from down-under! At that moment a Phantom shot through the city-bosom, unravelling the blanketed urban mysteries with its high-beams, towards the star-crossed *Dream Mansions*!

36

'A mother's sacrifice is the most sublime and sensible of all.' Shiela Khanna thought peering through the dark curtains of the midnight gloom.

'The entire universe has been bound together by the unseen force of motherhood.

'Her heart is a farm!

'The farmer ploughs it, waters, manures, fortifies and patiently waits for the harvest. When Autumn sets in, the reapers come and cut the stalks away from it leaving a few uncut. They fall and die in the farm itself. It will accept all the unwanted and the discarded without any protest, nor reproach! It belongs to all and all to it!' She thought.

'I'm heavily weighed down by the filial distress. My son must have already re-trodden many a steady mile on the narcotic corridor of irrevocable dejection and rejection. No more *Good Hope*!

'Pulling Rahul out of those smoking byways will be nearly impossible!' Madam Shiela could not control the mother in her. She wept for her son who was pushed forward by the cruel Fate, exposed to be on the frontline of an unfair battle and cruelly crushed by the mighty lords of opium and cocaine.

Her Phantom's heightened roar was loud enough to frighten even the devil himself.

'James is as skilled a driver as Rashid is. They won't fail under any circumstances!' Madam Shiela thought.

The lampposts on their way quivered, neared, reeled and were thrown backward into oblivion!

'They are like unsung heroes. They perform their duties silently but steadily.' She thought.

'*Dream Mansions* was constructed with a great dream and we chased the dream running along the synthetic tracks of life leaving the green aside. Thus, we lost out the real life and the real dream of a beautiful life became as synthetic as the track.

'It's a mansion, not a home!

'Everybody knows how to build a beautiful house, but very few know how to live there beautifully! A beautiful life can make a house beautiful; however a beautiful house shouldn't necessarily make a life beautiful!'

Phantom was relentlessly pressing itself forward on the speed track!

Madam Shiela's cell phone startled her back to the world of gloomy disquiet and yawning pessimism.

Every time the phone rang her heart pounded like a big fish thrown ashore by the tidal fury!

'The harbinger of disaster!' She received the call.

'Yes, Anu!'

'Ma'am….!' Anarkali sounded very nervous. 'Khannaji has just arrived. He has just rushed into the house with some people. All of them have guns in their hands!'

'Closely watch them and quickly report.' Madam Shiela spoke with telegraphic precision.

'Yes, Ma'am. He seemed drunk and was swinging!'

'Watch him….have you ever seen those men before?'

'No, Ma'am.'

Shiela Khanna heard the howling of a police wagon over the phone!

'What's that, Anu?' Madam Shiela asked.

'Ma'am….armed force! They are pouring into the garden!'

'But, why?' Madam Shiela asked herself.

'I don't know, Ma'am.' Anarkali reacted as if the question was to her. 'We are all on the ground floor, Ma'am! The house is under siege! Police is all around. They're with guns, shields and batons!'

Madam Shiela sweated bullets!

'Ma'am.' Anarkali started crying.

'Position....!' Madam Shiela heard a familiar voice commanding!

'Yes, Anu?' She mumbled.

'The gunners are ready! We're scared....!'

'Cool...., Anu....nothing will happen, my child! I'm there in 10 minutes.'

'Search....!' Another command.

Anarkali's line was snapped.

Shiela Khanna's cell phone cried again in her hand.

'Yes, Rose....?' Madam Shiela was breaking down.

'Ma'am, Potti has just informed that JPS has named a few VVIPs along with a few more underworld dons like MG, on being interrogated in the *Good Hope* case!'

'Really….?' Madam Shiela sat up wiping her face. 'Who's MG?'

'A very powerful Don of the global syndicate of the underworld.' Rose said. 'Excuse me Ma'am, Potti is calling me again. May I?'

'Yes.'

Madam Shiela dialled Anarkali.

She heard a big commotion from the other end.

Rose's number flashed on the screen.

Madam Shiela received the call.

'Yes, Rose?'

'Ma'am, Potti says that our CMD has also been named by JPS. The police have tried nailing him in the Golf Club, but he cleverly broke their cordon! Then they started chasing him. Now, Mr Khanna is in *Dream Mansions*. The police have laid siege to the house. The Commissioner is commanding the entire operations! Live telecast is there on TV!'

Madam Shiela remembered the Commissioner rushing out of the ICU in a hurry.

She sat on the car staring at the eternity; where all shapes blend to become a shapeless oneness and dissipate to force one into the servile infirmity of one's heart, head and hand!

A numbness had already started to creep up on her; right from the toes!

Rose was screaming over the phone!

She neither heard her fretful clamour nor saw Anarkali's crucial attempts on her cell phone!

'Jo....!' Rose shouted. 'Ma'am doesn't respond. Something's seriously wrong!'

She started to cry.

'Rose....! I cannot be impassive like this anymore!'

Ivans got up and sat on the bed, upright!

'No, Jo....!' Rose said wiping her tears. 'You shouldn't move now!'

'Nothing doing!' Ivans said plucking the tubes and needles from his limbs.

Dr Jouhra Begum came running and tried to stop Ivans.

'Ivans, you *cannot* go! You're very critical!' The Doctor screamed.

She looked at Ivans. His tall and glorious frame was abiding and authoritative.

He stretched out his right hand to Dr Begum.

She looked at him. His eyes were blazing like two strong hurricane lamps, she felt!

Dr Jouhra Begum felt ill at ease and stared at him.

'Yes, Ivans?' She asked.

'Car key!' He commanded.

Dr Begum's hand went down to her pocket.

She did not look into his eyes again, lest they should burn her down!

'Follow me!' Ivans directed Rose while receiving the key from Dr Begum.

In a few secs, a Jaguar shot out of the Doctor's Porch of St Lucia!

The name of its driver was Jose Ivans and his co-driver was Jessica Rose!

After quickly regaining her poise, Dr Jouhra Begum followed the Jaguar in a medical ambulance within earshot!

37

The mayhem at *Dream Mansions* was unimaginable!

It had already drawn the neighbours out of their doors on to the main road.

The Commissioner announced to the public to keep away from the scene.

Press reporters pressed hard their way to Dream Mansions. They were swarming like bees around the house.

The force was in position and waiting with loaded guns for fresh orders from the Commissioner.

ACP Roy Francis had already reached the 5th floor of the 10 storeyed *Dream Mansions*.

Prem Khanna stayed on the 6th floor, Rahul 7th and Madam Shiela on the 8th.

The Phantom roared, letting out terrible growls, at the gates of Dream Mansions.

There sat Shiela Khanna in the vehicle like a statue!

'Ma'am!' James tried to wake her up.

She did not move, nor did she wink!

Her eyes were staring at her *Dream Mansions*!

The Commissioner cut her way through the crowd and reached Madam Shiela.

'Ma'am.' Dr Sandra spoke. 'Don't go inside now. Stay here. We've already started the in-house operations!'

Madam Shiela nodded to the Commissioner without knowing what she was doing.

'Ma'am!' ACP Roy spoke to the Commissioner through the wireless.

'Yes, Roy?' The Commissioner asked.

'Ma'am, the 5th-floor-operation is over. There isn't anybody. We are moving up to the 6th floor. Over.'

'Okay.' Dr Sandra said. 'Mr Khanna's floor! Be careful. Over.'

'Okay, Ma'am. Over.' ACP Roy cut the line.

At this moment the Jaguar braked to a halt at Dream Mansions. Its wheels burned and engine smoked!

'Ivans', Dr Sandra shouted. 'Sit in the car itself. Situation is not under control. The search party commandos are on the 6th floor where Mr Khanna is hiding, we think!'

Soon, they heard a series of gun shots....!

'Ma'am!' Ivans said to the Commissioner. 'Situation is more serious than what we know. Act immediately before it's late.'

The Commissioner's wireless beeped.

'Yes, Roy?'

'Ma'am, the bodyguards of Mr Khanna opened fire. CI Ben is injured in the shoulder. But, two of them are gunned down. Over.'

'Okay!' Dr Sandra said. 'Bring Ben soon down. Over.'

'Ma'am, Mr Khanna has escaped to the 7th floor.' The ACP said. 'He is well covered by trained bodyguards. Over.'

'Okay.' The Commissioner said. 'The 7th floor is Rahul's. You've to act immediately. Over.'

'Yes, Ma'am. Over.' The ACP said.

'Ma'am.' Ivans said. 'I'm going in.'

Jose Ivans left the car in a flash and was presently joined by the Commissioner in the flight!

'Roy, wait there. We're coming there in a wink. Over.' Dr Sandra dashed into the house with Ivans. 'You take charge!' She turned around and instructed DCP Vikram.'

'Yes, Ma'am.' Vikram shouted proudly.

They heard an ambulance drawing nearer and halting outside the gate.

'Ma'am.' Ivans called the Commissioner. 'Let's go by the high speed elevator. I know everything about the house. The interior was done by my people from Madrid.'

'Okay, but….are you alright? You're in bandage.'

'I'm perfectly alright.' Ivans tried to be collected.

'You were on drips!'

'Don't worry, Ma'am.' Ivans said. 'I can deal with the entire gang.'

The elevator shot up to the 6th floor.

Outside Dream Mansions, Jessica Rose and Dr Jouhra Begum shifted Madam Shiela to the ambulance and gave her the first aid.

She lay in the carriage fully drained: a total wreck!

'Roy.' The Commissioner called the ACP. 'We're in the high speed elevator. Is it safe to come out? Over.'

'Yes, Ma'am.' The ACP replied. 'You can. This floor is safe. Over.'

Ivans and the Commissioner came out of the elevator cautiously.

On the corridor two mangled bodies lay bullet-riddled holding machine guns with their pointers on the triggers!

The Commissioner looked for the ACP.

'M..a..'a..m..!' Ivans pounced on her and both of them fell down and rolled a few rounds with Dr Sandra in the curl of Ivans!

They heard the rattling of bullets around them.

From the staircase above, a body fell on head with a thud near them. Hot blood splashed and streamed all about from the body!

ACP Roy Francis stood near the body of the thug proudly with his fuming weapon.

Ivans got up releasing the Commissioner from his hands!

She looked at both her saviours with eyes full of gratitude!

'Be not late....quick!' The Commissioner said recovering from the shock!

Ivans quickly grabbed the firearm from the senseless thug and moved up!

The Commissioner cautiously followed Ivans, climbing the stairs with the ACP and the other commandos.

Their arms were ready to face any more assault as they expected more Khanna-aides on the next floor.

Lights were off on the 7th floor!

They could hear a big brawl boiling in Rahul's room!

Ivans struggled on the granite floor while crawling on his elbows. He quickly remembered the NCC summer camps where he was trained in all military drills and stunts!

'Thanks to Dadda.' He whispered.

The floor was slippery as blood dripped from his head through the bandage.

Ivans reached the door of the *Glass Case*.

A CFL of low intensity forced him to peer into the hall.

'S..o..f..t..!' He cautioned.

The commandos quickly took position to cover Ivans and the officers!

'Why did you do that to Julia and me, Dad?' Rahul was very loud.

It seemed he was crying.

'Because you and your mom, that bitch, cheated me.' Prem Khanna shouted. 'I'd given my word to Mr Sawant! Both of you insulted me!'

'But, how could I marry Rekha? Her father is an underworld don!' Rahul asked still crying. 'Rekha is equally bad and a patient too!'

'To hell with your ethics!' Prem Khanna roared through his alcoholic breath. 'Your mother destroyed my dreams. You are not less….just like your mother: wilful and wayward!'

'Don't blame my mom. She's my God! She's not like you. You're a brute….you destroyed my life! You destroyed our family. You're not a human…you're a devil…!' Rahul was very furious.

They heard a slap….!

'You hit me…? You devil…!' Rahul shouted.

Ivans signalled the Commissioner that he was going in…. and darted into the *Glass Case*.

Before they could do anything, it happened!

The entire *Dream Mansions* shook again with a gunshot!

Ivans, with officers behind, watched Prem Khanna reel and fall on the floor with a thump!

A bullet had already gone out of the chamber punching a hole in the glass wall after tunnelling through Prem Khanna's cranium.

'No....!' Ivans shouted and his gun simultaneously spat fire!

To the utter shock of the officers, they saw Rahul fall near Prem Khanna, after hitting his head on the arm of a huge Chesterfield!

Prem Khanna's Smith & Wesson had already fallen from Rahul's hand to the ground with a loud clank before he could blast his own skull.

Outside the premises Madam Shiela lay in the ambulance unaware of all these catastrophic tumults inside her *Dream Mansions*!

Rose sat beside her and heard the gunshots which almost tore her apart into several shreds. She closed her eyes and prayed for her Jo and the other commandos.

Those beautiful eyes of Rose rained molten rubies: the most precious offering at the feet of her good Lord for her beloved!

Through the windows she saw the bodies of the dead being shifted to the police ambulance.

With every single body coming out, her heart pounded more turbulently and loudly!

She counted five….!

'But whose are they?' Fear gripped her and started clawing into her already damaged heart.

'The corpses are twice blanketed!' Rose desperately thought. 'The resolve of the thick fabric of the shrouds over them is well served by the midnight gloom. Nothing is exposed!'

Soon she saw her Jo emerging out of the darkness!

He was held by two commandos as he was too weak to hold himself up.

His head bandage was soaked in blood like a red crown!

'*Uneasy lies the head that wears a crown!*' Rose remembered King Henry IV.

'My Jo is safe. That's enough my Lord! Thank you my Christ!' Rose raised her eyes up to Heavens thankfully and crossed her forehead!

Presently, the doors of the ambulance were opened.

Dr Begum and Dr Sandra helped Ivans climb the steps.

Rose saw the staff nurse of St Lucia, who came with them earlier to Dream Mansions, standing behind Dr Begum like a frightened kitten.

Ivans slowly climbed the steps and lay on the bed, smiling at his Rose.

Dr Begum closed the door of the ambulance from outside.

Rose wept near Ivans.

Her love for her *Jo* gushed out, flowing through her pale rosy cheeks, it washed out the blood and sweat from his face.

While Shiela Khanna dived into a dreamless doze on the other bed, Jose Ivans was revisiting the 7th floor of Dream Mansions!

As the ambulance howled and rushed through the high speed highway, the streetlights peeped into the carriage and quickly withdrew their glance.

They did not want to disturb the two angels of God comforting each other in a divine hug!

God had selected their nomenclature with a lot of care and love: Jose Ivans and Jessica Rose!

Two real *Tedium Troopers*!

38

Easter Monday was long and action-packed!

Tuesday dawned with many surprises for the public.

They watched the morning news with bated breath.

Print and the visual media had employed their best reporting brains to cover the midnight horror in Dream Mansions.

Most dailies dedicated their front pages to the *Good Hope* case, in red letters!

They had their own peculiar nuances to report such cases which shook the conscience of the entire nation.

Some of them captured the incident with photos of Rahul Khanna and Prem Khanna.

Good Hope Case: *The Crown Prince of EIPL Kills His Father to Save His Own Life*

Mr Khanna of Electronics India Shot Down by Son

Electronics Baron Pays His Debt as His Son Accidently Shoots Him Down

TV and internet gave full coverage to the entire story.

The press conference of Dr Dona Sandra IPS went viral on the media.

It told the inside story of the previous night's operations at Dream Mansions! All attempts to capture Prem Khanna alive were stalemated by his resolve to destroy his own family.

She narrated how the police tried to nab Mr Khanna at the Golf Club; how he took shelter in his house; and how the police wanted to take him alive for interrogation.

If Rahul had not shot Mr Khanna down, it would have been the other way round!

She also praised the heroics of Jose Ivans, son of former ADGP Francis Ivans and grandson of Major General Joseph Ivans AVSM, in saving Mr Rahul Khanna from a desperate suicidal attempt!

She told the world how her own life was saved by Mr Ivans and ACP Roy Francis from an ambush in a darkly lit staircase of *Dream Mansions* where Death was hiding behind every pillar and every curtain.

At St Lucia all watched the news with ardent anguish and utmost anxiety! Madam Shiela collapsed on bed. God alone knew what was going through her heart: even she did not!

Jose Ivans, Jessica Rose, Krishnan Potti and Dr Jouhra Begum watched the news with a feel of personal affliction and private sorrow!

Rahul lay unconscious in a level 3 ICU totally unaware of the aftermath of the domestic terror!

By afternoon, an unwanted body was thrown into the morgue of St Lucia after autopsy. It must have been waiting for a decent funeral, but no one was there to give it the final rest.

In the evening, Dr Begum and the Commissioner came and held a short conference with Jose Ivans and Jessica Rose in the CCU.

After half an hour the SIR met in Madam Shiela's room at St Lucia. The Trinity was once again at work.

At 5 pm a police wagon carried the body to the crematorium in the City suburbs.

A fair lady in big thick sunglasses sat in the Phantom with Jose Ivans and Jessica Rose.

Krishnan Potti's hatchback moved in front of the car, right behind the hearse.

In the crematorium, the lady with the sunglasses lit the pyre of the most hateful creature in the world.

The evening sun augmented the glow of the funeral flames with the usual glare on his face.

Jessica Rose assisted the noble lady back to her car. As the funeral fire burned on her sunglasses, a bonfire was flaming in her heart!

Back in St Lucia, they were awaited by the most shocking news of all:

MG, the most wanted underworld don had been arrested by the Commissioner and the ACP in a cracking joint operation with the CBI.

Jessica Rose held Ivans with a tight grip and fainted in his hands!

For, MG was none other than Juan's father, Martin Gomez!

39

Ivans' BMW glowed like a new bride in the amber rays of the setting sun.

She looked happier, prettier and dearer!

Jessica Rose emerged out of the car like the loveliest of all brides with Janet and Juan.

Leaving their footwear in the car, they sprang on the shingled shore like 3 deer on a lush green meadow in a fearless forest.

Ivans watched them playing with the approaching and the receding even tides.

The Venetian Gondolas were sailing like wild geese beyond the oilrig.

'They looked like real geese.' Ivans thought. 'Life is a *Phantasmagoria*! It's an exhibition of constantly shifting complex succession of illusory spectacles as if in a dream! Now seen; and then not!'

The beacon light of the rig complimented Ivans' thought by flickering brighter and then not seen momentarily.

The breeze gathered momentum to blow cooler....!

Tides dashed to crash into the creek, fuller....!

The crimson disc began the last journey to dip deeper....!

Wanderers flocked on the beach to grow denser....!

Stars in the sky showed up to shine smarter....!

'After sometime they also won't be seen anymore.' Ivans thought. 'They will either die out or will lie wrapped up in the murkiest entrails of the cloudy night.'

Ivans slowly came out of his Havana!

'The car looks really beautiful!' He thought.

He petted the vehicle and looked at her with a grateful glance.

'Thank you for saving my life, my fair lady!' He said to her.

'Daddy....!' Janet called out. 'Come fast....!'

'Jo, come fast for a selfie with the sun.' Rose could not hold back her joy. She sounded confident and fearless.

'Yes, Uncle....!' Juan insisted. 'Come fast....!'

Ivans ran and joined them in the sea.

Rose clicked her cell phone.

The selfie was a unique snap in which Rose and Ivans had no wedding rings on their fingers.

In a few seconds the sun sank fully and the eastern sky started crawling under the melancholy carpet of night.

'Daddy....!' Janet ran to Ivans.

Ivans led all three to a nearby sand dune and sat on it facing the sunset zone.

'If you are smart enough, you can see two new stars in the horizon of the Happy Isles.' Ivans said.

'Yes, I wanted to tell you that Daddy....!' Janet said.

Rose sat close to Ivans and smiled at her Jo.

Their eyes started to look for new stars shining brighter beyond the oilrig, just risen after the sundown!

Soon there appeared two new stars which began to wink at them!

They named them George and Prakash!

All the four waved and cheered at them calling out their names.

In response, the stars smiled brightlier at them.

The Church bell from the hilltop chimed for the Vespers!

They watched the fisher huts getting decked with the golden flames as innumerable and beautiful as the stars in the sky.

The valley was full of golden spots in a minute.

Old Joppe lighted the huge candle at the idol of Mary the Immaculate!

Tourists gathered at the grotto for the prayers.

Janet led the rosary and the entire Vespers! All those devotees kept their eyes cast on the little prodigy's face.

At the close of the prayer the Church bell chimed again and the choir sang the recessional hymn which overflowed the valley.

As the quartet entered the highway, Ivans joined the Church choir: *Precious memories, I've seen angels...!*

All of them were soon singing the hymn.

The stars in The Milky Way peeped down to see those unseen angels singing so well.

Ivan's Havana picked up...!

40

Eos had just risen to forerun Apollo, the mighty Sun-God!

The 7 series started to move….!

Jessica Rose proudly sat beside Jose Ivans.

Janet and Juan reclined quietly on the back seat looking out.

They had promised their Potti Uncle that they would bring him two surprises when they met him next.

Ivans saw Potti waving at them standing in the porch.

There were tears in his eyes.

Both great friends found it difficult to look at each other.

'A friend is the one who walks in when the whole world walks out!' Ivans recalled.

Roshini followed the car, crying.

At the gate, Ashok gave his beloved master a solemn salute.

Ivans waved and smiled.

Jose Ivans' BMW slowly glided out of the pristine precincts of *The Abode.*

It was hardly 5 am!

Ivans drove slowly, reluctant to leave the City limits.

They passed by the ill-fated *Dream Mansions*! Light was burning on the 8th floor….!

They did not speak anything to each other, but knew what the other was thinking!

Emotions overflowed and images flashed back!

Janet and Juan were busy counting the pebbles they had picked from the beach the previous day!

The car slowly picked up!

Electronics India Pvt. Ltd. stood sky-high by the road!

Further on, Rose and Ivans saw the kids' school lying idle and bored without its students. The school blocks were being painted to receive the children back after the summer break.

Rose saw the picket fence gate of her house….! Her hands spontaneously went into her bag for the keys!

'It's with Potti!' Ivans thought.

She looked at him with a blush on her rosy cheeks. They could read each other's hearts.

Soon, they crossed St Lucia Circle!

'The hospital buildings await a fresh lot of victims!' Ivans tried hard to swallow the bitterness of a life full of ironies!

'Life has become more tedious trooping tedium.' He thought.

His Havana was now on the speed track. It seemed that even the car knew what the master wanted.

Presently, they saw *The Abode* to the right hand looking forlorn.

Till then they did not realize that the car had taken a full circle round the City on its own.

The car slowed down....!

Rose and Ivans anxiously looked into the garden. Rosebuds were busy preparing themselves to receive the Sun.

The garden lights were on.

Ashok and his wife Ashwini were watering plants....!

Krishnan Potti was giving various instructions to them!

Their heart throbbed fast....!

They wanted to break journey...., but, the car did not stop. Instead, she picked up once again by herself...!

She started flying on the high speed highway.

In a few minutes, they could hear the praise song from a distance....flowing through the morning freshness of the east like the roll of a thousand drums.

Soon they watched a host of golden spots of light flickering in *Fisher's Valley*. The creek lay by its side like a tapering glass-piece!

The beacon on the oilrig still flickered brightly as it did the previous night.

Old Joppe was blowing out the candles at the grotto of Mary the Immaculate.

The Church on the hilltop stood majestically bright, in nostalgia.

When the white light of the CFL interacted with the daybreak, the Church made one think of the pearly domicile of the Heavenly Father.

Ivans drove his Havana up the road which half-wound from the foothill and disappeared midway into the matted canopy of old chestnuts and almonds.

The morning mist made the driver's visibility hazy though both the low beam and the fog lamps of the Havana were helping herself moving up the hill.

The day was slowly breaking brighter….

Ivans took a diversion to enter the bridge connecting *Fisher's Valley* and *Valley of Flowers*. It lay at a never-ending stretch before them.

The journey seemed like the Exodus in search of a lost Paradise.

The clear stream of River Immaculate was not in a hurry under the bridge and looked as though gallons on molten gold were just poured into its depth by the rising sun.

Now, the car gave herself to the hands of her master.

'Men are like moving carts.' Ivans thought. 'They give themselves into the hands of the Absolute Being during their journey on this temporal valley. He will drive them into the Eternal Valley of Peace! Beyond that lies the Paradise!'

Crossing River Immaculate, they entered the State Highway. The hill had already been left behind just before the bridge. The Hill Highway wound up the hill to explore the mountain mysteries at dawn.

Rose and Juan had never gone beyond the bridge before!

Ivans watched her big eyes bloom and shine in the morning glow as they entered *Valley of Flowers*!

The country road looked as if it were calling them home.

Ivans sang…, and all joined…

   Country Roads, take me home,

As the City woke up behind them into its hectic routine subtleties, it did not see its own Jose Ivans; nor Jessica Rose.

41

Udayagiri!

Jose Ivans drove past Prathyasha UP School where years ago he had started his schooling!

Udayagiri looked like a new bride: beautifully adorned with new shops and enterprises. However, the purity of the township bubbled everywhere!

Rose was thrilled to see the place where her *Jo* was born. Her heart was getting filled with a heavenly bliss. Her past dissolved into an irrevocable nothingness.

The awe and wonder of the children reflected on their guileless eyes!

There was a big crowd awaiting them at *The Arcadia*, Ivans' ancestral home.

Phillip had kept the house clean and his wife, Mercy had prepared all their favourite dishes.

Ivans had already informed them of their dining habits.

While the crowd engaged in unloading his Havana, Ivans took out his vintage Jerusalem Bible and placed it on a raised platform before the huge Sacred Heart in the vestibule.

The lively portraits of his royal grandparents and parents evoked awe and pride in Rose and the children.

The entire Shanthipuram was assembled at *The Arcadia*.

Kunjappan Chettan, Iyppachan, Annamma, Barber Neelandan, Broker Thommy and even Kozhi Andrew were there to receive their squire-like Jose Ivans.

They left after lunch with the Che Guevara t-shirts from the City.

Mercy took Rose and the children to show the rural goodness and privileges.

In the meantime, Ivans discussed the pros and cons of coffee and rubber plantation with Phillip and decided to buy a few more acres in Karthikapuram where his Dadda did his High School.

He also decided to get the High School buildings renovated before monsoon set in.

After tea, all of them went for an evening walk.

The villagers bowed their heads before Ivans as a mark of honour and love.

On reaching the *Gulmohar* tree, Ivans remembered his mama, Liz Ivans!

The country road lay with full of red blooms on her bosom, newly showered for Ivans. He wanted to roll on the flower carpet.

Soon, to his utter wonderment and surprise, Juan lay on the road and started rolling on the *Gulmohar* blooms!

Janet encouraged Juan by clapping her hands and laughing loudly.

Ivans fondly scolded Juan for rolling on the road filled with the crimson petals.

'Juan....don't soil your clothes....get up my darling.... please....!'

'History repeats!' Ivans thought. 'Life is the Phantasmagoria of recurring spectacles!'

The Sun had gone behind the hillock.

They reached *CHE*!

The *Twilight Audience* was waiting for Ivans!

He entered the veranda of the shop.

The iconic Kunjappan Chettan was sitting on a stool with his Book open. He was now running the shop in a partnership with Iyppachan's sons - Denis and Toms.

Though all of them were aged and decrepit, they looked very energetic and enthusiastic.

Phillip's Willys went to drop Rose and the children at *The Arcadia*.

Seeing Ivans, everybody got up from their seats. They would not sit until he did.

'These people are still the same.' Ivans thought. 'Goodness overflows in their heart!'

The crowd was comparatively larger than before as some members of the younger generation had also joined them!

All sat down passionately encompassing Ivans!

'Tell us a story of Che!' Barber Neelandan insisted.

'Yes....!' All chorused.

Ivans rose from his seat and stood in the middle.

'His glorious form resembles Major General Joseph Ivans.' All of them thought.

Ivans looked around.

He saw two small eyes staring at him from behind Thadathippara Avaran!

'Juan….!' Ivans called.

'Yes…. *Daddy*….!' Juan replied.

Ivans picked him up and kissed him. Their eyes were glossy.

Ivans placed Juan on his own seat and started as his grandfather used to.

'In 1960, Fidel Castro, Ernest Hemingway and Ernesto Che Guevara went to the Great Blue River to catch a massive Blue Marlin….!'

The *Twilight Audience* at *CHE* fell back to silence….!

About the Author

Sunny Francis, a teacher by profession, is highly successful in coaching and mentoring the young and the curious when they meandered having been caught in the evil eye of a whirlpool of indecision.

He could cut out his own image in marble as an inspiring public speaker, a much sought after motivator and a gifted corporate trainer.

His classroom experiences with students, over a score and five years, shaped up the cutting edge of his language and helped him perfect the flawless predisposition of the writer in him.

His profound understanding and ability to perfectly interpret and interface the occident and orient cultures and myths make his school classical as well as postmodern. His self-invented histrionic nuances in story-telling quickly restructure the well laid foundation of the edifice of fictional ethics, over a few centuries, which enable the curious greenhorns as well as veteran pundits of the expository guildhalls, sponsored by the hair-splitting nutty columnists, devour everything served on the High Table of his Franciscan Refectory.

Tedium Troopers is a clear mirror held out into the society which reflects a clean cloned image of one's life. This even-simulation enables the readers view a microscopic cross section of the global life standards of the day.

The Gospel, in my knowledge and judgement, was never proclaimed ever before as spiritedly and heartily by the laity as done in Tedium Troopers. This is a must-read for all who find it hard to keep the flames of their faith lit as I experienced among the fisher-folk in the Fisher's Valley.

I felt Gabo revisiting me every time when I opened Tedium Troopers.

It will be a decent tribute to the Herculean effort of the author if all our schools and colleges proudly initiate Phantasmagoria Clubs for providing the young catalysts' superlatives a platform to showcase their exploits.

This author is going to stick around longer than all his contemporary writers.

Let us kindly allow him walk fearlessly along the thoroughfares of life, and join him in trooping the tedium of reading the present day fiction which is like eating the junk food ignoring our Mama's traditional dishes. We will soon fall sick and feel tired of the junk if we ignore our home delicacies!

This book is like a tropical shower after the long spell of a bothersome drought!

Rev Dr Fr Jose Aikara CM